Children of the Night

of Vampires and Vampirism

Tony Thorne

'Tis now the very witching time of night
When churchyards yawn and hell itself breathes out
Contagion to this world.
Now could I drink hot blood.

William Shakespeare, *Hamlet*

VICTOR GOLLANCZ
LONDON

To the suckers and the sucked

Copyright © Tony Thorne, 1999

First published in Great Britain in 1999 by Victor Gollancz
An imprint of Orion Books Ltd,
Orion House, 5 Upper St Martin's Lane
London WC2H 9EA

A CIP catalogue record for this book is
available from the British Library.

ISBN 0 575 06646 6

Typeset by Selwood Systems, Midsomer Norton

Printed and bound by
Butler & Tanner Ltd, Frome and London

Contents

Illustrations

To the Reader

Vampires exist and have coexisted with humanity for most of its history. The Vampire is ancient and modern and prodigious and universal, and for those reasons and because it is the most interesting of our *bêtes noires*, (though its most familiar face is its least interesting) we should study it carefully.

To learn about the Vampire of history, you must visit its terrain; to come to know the Vampires of today you must listen to them and talk to them.

Most respectable scholars in the English-speaking world have shunned the Vampire for fear, presumably, of the professional taint which attaches to it, a stigma which apparently does not attach to the Witch or Serial Killer, for instance. The pariah status of Vampires and Vampire studies are in themselves a good reason for pursuing the theme.

The Vampire has never been a respecter of boundaries – even those separating life and death – and to grasp the meaning of the Vampire we must set aside the boundaries and conventions that limit intellectual exploration. Divisions into high or low culture, into tragic, comic or serious, into fiction, travelogue, essay, anthology, between critique and celebration, all are rendered irrelevant by the Vampire's presence. And we must banish 'respectable' or 'disreputable' from our repertoire of judgements.

For the purposes of this investigation, squeamishness is not an option. If you are repelled by the thought of blood, go no further.

T.T., London, May 1999

Introduction

'... living on a mere pittance ... he devoted himself to the minute and laborious investigation of the marvellously authenticated tradition of vampirism'.

J. Sheridan Le Fanu, *Carmilla*, 1872

Even in early summer the easterlies off the North Sea ('snot-green and scrotum-tightening' were W. B. Yeats's pitiless words) gusted around the town and angry waves lashed at the harbour walls, the jetty and the cliffs. On one side of the river that splits the community in two a steep green incline topped by rows of grey-tinged tombstones, St Mary's Church, and higher still the remains of a thirteenth-century abbey, 'a most noble ruin, of immense size, and full of beautiful and romantic bits...'[1] looked much as they must have looked a hundred years before, when a descendant of ancient Magyars, the Székely nobleman, Count Dracula, had arrived here on the coast of England for the very first time.

During the June afternoon the wind dropped to a breeze and the heat of the sun could be felt, warming up the cobbles, flagstones and slates so that they radiated the heat back into the streets. A bizarre promenade was taking place in the little lanes and across the narrow bridge that joined the two halves of the town. Among the weekending families, in their pale pink and mauve shell-suits, pastel T-shirts stretched across white paunches, cotton sleeves pulled up over mottled, puffy arms, came a sudden rustling of black taffeta, glimpses of black silk veils swishing over velvet and lace bodices, the hems of black frock-coats flicking impatiently at the tops of polished, laced and buckled knee- and thigh-boots as they clicked along the quayside past the fishing-boats and the drying nets. Here and there top hats and black ribbons bobbed above the heads of the jostling crowds.

The ungainly tourists in their garish colours stared, bemused, as the exquisitely dressed and beautifully pallid strangers paused at stands selling fish and chips, whelks and mussels, or strode in and out of the Dracula Experience and peered into the craft stores where locally hand-made Vampire fudge was set out on display.

The tradition of the Whitby Gothic Weekend was then only three years old, but this year was special: this was the centenary of the 1897 publication of the novel that defined the late-Victorian Gothic and implanted a bundle of dark fantasies once and for all in the popular imagination.

To a novice, the celebration that took place over three days in a vast, half-abandoned 1930s mock-Tudor-Gothic hotel on the wind and spray-swept clifftop at Whitby was a revelation of the intricacies and the charms of British Vampire culture. The crowd in attendance well represented the Vampire phenomenon in its main aspects. A thousand Goths, a handful of youngsters in heavy-metal, biker or punk regalia, a few middle-aged men in the dun-coloured safari suits and Cornish-pasty shoes favoured by provincial schoolteachers or unfrocked priests, some children, the Hammer Horror star Ingrid Pitt, one or two journalists with a real curiosity and a dozen more hoping for evidence of scandal. Entertainments included Transylvanian folk-songs, Gothic opera and a series of balls accompanied by hypnotic ethereal-funerary rock music, with its sepulchral voices alternately yearning then menacing. As the bands played, the Goths, in their most ornate finery, undulated impassively in their 'tree-dance'. In the hotel bar between acts the same lanky, gaunt-faced fops and statuesque ladies (this self-selected species seem all to be taller and thinner than the average human) held cheerful conversations, plan-ning expeditions to Transylvania, debating the price of second-hand hearses; there were also erudite exchanges on the subject of Bram Stoker's sources, Sumerian hieroglyphs.

On the last day, a Sunday, a debate had been scheduled, in fact a sort of vampiric symposium with lectures to the grave, attentive audience from a series of experts on such topics as the role of the fang in piercing and sucking, and the ultimate origins of Vampire fashions in clothing (I gave a short talk on Elisabeth Báthory, the historical 'Countess Dracula'). Early that morning the doors of the little boarding-houses had opened simultaneously all along the Victorian terraces and around the crescents, and the Children of the Night lurched one by one into the bright chilly light and stalked silently, robes and ribbons flapping, up the deserted clifftop road towards the great silhouette of the hotel.

After the event the tabloid press duly wrote as they did each year of the potential corruption of children (the few infants there, some in costume, had been as personable as the adult participants), finding an Anglican vicar to condemn the ungodliness of it all.

✝

'We are as ignorant of the meaning of the dragon,' wrote Jorge Luis Borges in 1970, 'as we are of the meaning of the universe, but there is something in the dragon's image that appeals to the human imagination, and so we find the dragon in quite distinct places and times. It is, so to speak, a necessary monster, not an ephemeral and accidental one, such as the three-headed chimaera or the catoblepas.'[2] Had Borges been opining thirty years later, he might have replaced the dragon with a different and more topical being. His comments would have remained quite remarkably apt.

Today at the millennium a supernatural predator, neither alive nor dead, human nor alien, a product of antique imagination, is still thriving, still evolving. The begetter of the Whitby weekend, and of the fiction that inspired it, and of the older fables that influenced that fiction, is a squalid aberration, a probable hallucination, which has been reduplicated, trivialized, debased, done to death and yet remains full of ... no, not 'life', this would be entirely the wrong word ... but some strange vitality. Not the dragon, but '... the Vampire, a pariah even among demons. Foul are his ravages; gruesome and seemingly barbaric are the ancient and approved methods by which folk must rid themselves of this hideous pest.'[3]

Vampires are endemic in popular culture, to an extent that is actually astonishing at first sight. Surely they belong to a quite outdated belief system; surely they should have faded with the fading of Victorian ideas of propriety and all the repressions that went with them. In 1994 the venerable poet and critic D. J. Enright wondered, 'Does one have to be a certain age to flinch at the casualness with which extreme displays of squalor and depravity – an advance on what was chummily known as sex 'n' violence – figure in today's world of entertainment? ... The current fascination with the supernatural extends to its more extravagantly horrible forms, in particular vampirism.'[4]

The creature is a bundle of paradoxes: it is, or has been at one time or another, a warning (to children), a denial (of death and decay), an apology (to the dead), a recrimination (to the living), a triumph (over pestilence and contagion), a nuisance. Grand themes – immortality, damnation, redemption – are caught up in the vampire net, but so are the seedy, the abject, the vulgarized. It has become a stereotype and a cliché. But as the French proto-absurdist Alfred Jarry declared gnomically, 'Cliché is the armature of the absolute.'

The Vampire we know best, the opera-caped, fanged and bat-like coxcomb, may be a tired and tacky beast, sidling from its grave and shuffling through the shadows, almost embarrassed at its kitsch persona. But despite the enduring Cult of the Count, there is much more to the Vampire than that dusty Victorian rogue, Dracula. A closer look at any period in human history – from Sumer and Babylon, by way of the East European panics of the seventeenth and eighteenth centuries, through to the excesses of Gothic literature – reveals the constant presence of a Vampire or vampire-like monster in our narratives – both grand and humble – and our popular culture. But constancy is not the Vampire's virtue: the creature has survived by repeatedly mutating into whatever our society shuns, but secretly demands; its uncanny power is that it is always familiar but almost impossible to define, never one thing, but always many.

Although the Vampire that has come down to us via novels and film is a distinctly European creature, new research shows that this protean blood-fiend is almost universal in human societies and has its counterparts in belief systems as far apart as Central America, West Africa and the East Indies. The striking similarities between vampire-related beliefs worldwide argues for the great age of the being and its profound cultural importance – a significance that we can now see did not end with 'primitive' rural peoples of the past but that still resonates through our own post-modern era.

꙳

Damp city pavements glittering under neon strips and sodium-yellow streetlights; the all-pervading petrol smell, shot through with kebab, curry, charcoal pungencies and momentary wafts of incenses and perfumes. Camden Town is metropolitan, cosmopolitan, louche, shabby; quintessentially part of what London (the 'city where the devil lives', wrote Bram Stoker) has become. The dark interior of the much too small, much too tall and narrow Electric Ballroom, once a variety theatre, was a futile parody of operatic opulence: all balustrades and boxes, with the blue-tinged ornamentation chipped and cracked or faded to invisibility. Somehow, and quite appropriately, it was simultaneously cavernous and claustrophobic, grandiose and profoundly tawdry – words that seem appropriate to the late twentieth-century experience of the Vampire.

First came the slow, ritual bleeding of a naked 'virgin' by an Egyptian priest-figure (during which middle-aged agency photographers, the only people present in civilian dress, grimly jostled for flesh-shots), actually His Vampiric Eminence Louis Ravensfield, member of the London Vampyre Group, impresario and publisher of the magazine *Bloodstone*, the first glossy in the UK catering solely to a Vampire market. 'The Vampire is about three things: Death. Sex. Power,' he vouchsafed to the interviewer from the *Sunday Times*.[5]

This was *Vampyria II*, lavishly advertised and billed as the largest gathering of its kind in the UK. Although there were a few stately Goths and a sprinkling of rubber fetishists here and there among the clothing, poster and prosthetic fang stalls, the majority of the revellers seemed to be tattooed and pierced aficionados of Death- and Dark-metal music, there to mosh and crowd-surf to the sustained screaming grind of their figurehead band, Cradle of Filth, whose slogan, 'Jesus is a c**t' could be seen on dozens of T-shirts. The regulation appearance by Ingrid Pitt, the charming, still voluptuous doyenne of Hammer movies of the 1970s, barely distracted the increasingly volatile mass of writhing and pulsating groundlings. A scheduled lecture by this author was abandoned when it became clear that the organizers had forgotten about it and that the audience was in no mood for anything but a total and immediate derangement of the senses. As the main house-lights dimmed to a reddish glow there was a momentary vision of a medieval hell, the doomed souls contorting and rearing up out of the pit as lesser demons in the form of bouncers hurled them back into the maelstrom. The ecstatic baying of the crowd segued into a grinding metal wall of amplified sound, and then there was the death-roar: a deep-voiced ululating guttural prolonged monotone. Flanked by half-naked Vampire go-go dancers in suspended cages and stamping a stage strewn with skulls and bones, Cradle of Filth's singer bared his teeth, which had been filed to gleaming points, the band began their set and I slipped into the night.

ᚠ

The title of this book is taken from the best-known fictional presentation of the Vampire, the excuse for celebrations at Whitby, an inspiration for Vampyria's legions, the novel *Dracula:* 'There seemed a strange stillness over everything, but as I listened I heard, as if from down below in the valley, the howling of many wolves. The Count's eyes gleamed, and he said: "Listen to them – the children of the night. What music they make!" '

For their full effect the crucial last lines should probably be declaimed in a theatrical East European accent, each syllable elongated and exaggerated. It is thus that they were rolled around the mouth of Bela Lugosi, the cinematic Dracula for whom the words became an inseparable catchphrase. Once replaced in their original text it is clear that the children are wolves, not Vampires as is often assumed: the common insertion of the word 'sweet' before the word 'music' is seen to be a misquotation. But for the great confederacy of Vampire enthusiasts and for the purposes of this book, accuracy is not the issue: the words have filled with associative meaning far beyond their author's intentions. In Lugosi's mouth they epitomize the melo-dramatic self-parody with which Vampire entertainments have been stamped, while at a more serious level, the word 'children' summons up ideas of feral innocence, connects us with the reality of adolescents who long to play in the dark and flirt with the dangers concealed there. 'Music' reminds us that as well as a personification of implac-able cruelty, the Vampire is a thing of 'sad, spectral beauty'. And even the difference between wolf and Vampire begins to blur once we have unfastened the locks of the archives and libraries wherein the histories of the creature are preserved.

🜦

How do the eruptions of the Vampire into modern popular culture link to the literary and historical tradition from which its persona sprung? Where in the world *did* it come from? Exactly how old is it? What does it mean? Should we fear it? Is the congregation whose members gathered at Whitby and Camden a harmless hobbyist ghetto, or a dangerous underground cult? Should we fear *them*? In the following pages these questions will be answered, still others will be raised, and one more author will try and fail to have the final word, to lay to rest a protean monster who, as we all well know from the start, will not lie down for long...

✝V✝¹ Children of the Night

'... *Demons, which are but Idols or Phantasms of the braine, without any reall nature of their owne, distinct from humane fancy; such as are dead mens' Ghosts, and Fairies, and other matters of old Wives' tales.'*

Thomas Hobbes, *Leviathan*, 1651

It is interesting that there is little evidence of the Vampire legend as such in England after the medieval period. In a countryside comprehensively infested with witches, white ladies, headless horsemen, wild hunts, poltergeists and sightings of the devil, there were few signs of the bloodsucker. Could it be that in an aristocratic society (many of those said to have returned from the dead were either members of the gentry or their wronged servants) and a tamed and cultivated landscape, folk superstitions were focused differently? In contrast most of Eastern Europe, where the nexus of Vampire superstitions was most deeply embedded, remained essentially a colonized, undifferentiated rural environment up to the arrival of Communism.

Years before, however, the same legends had been rooted in the island of Britain, too. The eleventh-century ecclesiast, Walter Map, recounted in his collection of gossip, rumour and anecdote *De Nugis Curialium* ('Of Courtiers' Trifles') how troops of demons, including *larvas* – spectral child-devouring female Vampires – haunted the English night. He also told the story of a monstrous stranger, again female, who preyed upon a nobleman's newborn children in the night, biting out their throats one by one and filling their bedchamber with blood.[1] At almost the same time William of Newburgh was describing three 'true' cases of Vampire infestation, in Buckinghamshire, Melrose and Berwick, where it was said that recently deceased men had come back to life to ravage their surroundings in search of flesh and blood nourishment, tormenting the living by assaulting them in the fields and in their beds.[2]

Gervaise of Tilbury, writing around 1214 in his *Otia Imperialia*, told of male and female sorcerers who travelled abroad by night, flying above the countryside and into the rooms of sleeping victims. These intruders sat on a sleeper's chest, giving rise to nightmares of falling and suffocating. The female witches were the more voracious: they had sex with male sleepers, sucked blood, abducted children and stole food.

Earlier still, and neglected by nearly all previous historians of the undead are the pre-Christian Norse cultures of Scandinavia and Northern Europe whose surviving saga manuscripts tell of vampire-like beings, the corpse-pale *draugr* or the *aptrganger* – blue as death – who were said to leave the chambers beneath their burial mounds to roam the cold earth, molesting living humans and animals. In Iceland, Norway, Sweden and Denmark the bodies of the dead, often buried on the boundaries of the homesteads in which they had lived (the spectacular Viking boat-cremation was reserved for certain heroes and seafarers) were thought to remain animated in their tombs, consumed by malevolence towards those who lived and suffering from a terrible, preternatural hunger. These restless cadavers could take on the hues of death, but remain uncorrupted and become possessed of enormous physical strength, swelling to the size and weight of an ox. In death the *draugrs* and *aptrgangers* had also acquired magical attributes: the ability to shape-shift into animal forms – seals and cats or more terrifying apparitions such as a flayed bull or a mutilated horse – and the power to foretell the future and control the weather. Although corporeal they could pass magically through earth and rock.[3]

Attacks by the dead intensified as the nights lengthened, reaching a peak at Yuletide: among the shadows, the pools of moonlight, and in the mists raised by these roaming predators domestic animals and shepherds were crushed to death or driven to fatal exhaustion or madness and sometimes eaten, while in the sagas mortal heroes might take on the monsters and do battle with them. To destroy the revenant it was necessary to overpower it by wrestling or beating it into submission, then decapitate it, stake it, burn it and scatter the ashes.[4]

Whole animals and abundant stores of food were often buried with the dead but were not enough to assuage the insatiable post-mortem hunger of the corpse-demons for blood along with flesh and any other form of sustenance. Grendel, the *draugr*-like monster in the story of Beowulf, was described as *maere* – a word cognate with the *mara* of later legend and the word nightmare itself – and drank the blood of his victims...

> ... but he quickly caught
> firstly a sleeping man,
> rent him greedily,
> bit the joint,
> drank down the streams of blood...[5]

In England, unlike Scandinavia, the early reports did not find a name for the creature, only a Latin designation for the phenomenon: *cadaver sanguisugus*, bloodsucking corpse. If there was a folk-name in use among the Saxon peasantry, and there probably was, it is lost to us, together with all references to it in the fireside tales and oral traditions that went unnoticed by the Church and those in authority.

Judging by the scant records we do possess, it seems that in medieval times and the early modern period in the British Isles the bloodsucker did not retain a separate identity, but its features merged with those of the two main creatures that straddled the human/supernatural boundary: the witch and the ghost. In fact, to simplify the two traditions it could be said that while in central, east and south-eastern Europe the Vampire persona absorbed the characteristics of the ghost and the witch, in Britain the reverse happened and the Vampire's main attribute, bloodsucking, was appropriated by those more popular magical beings.

The witch-craze dominated the imaginative and religious landscape of the British Isles from around 1300 to well into the eighteenth century; once the hangings and torturings subsided, the ghost came into its own in the nineteenth and early twentieth centuries. One of the accusations commonly made against female witches was that they allowed the devil to suckle from their bodies – blood rather than milk, and from supernumerary teats or magical orifices in their torsos. Like nearly all apparently exotic superstitions the idea was probably a transference of a commonly felt terror or set of anxieties. Among other things, it was a reflection of the fear that the wet-nurse could interfere with the process whereby, it was then believed, blood was transformed in the body into mother's milk by the effect of maternal love.

Although the Vampire was not an important presence in the British tradition, a number of local legends from around Britain closely resemble the Continental stories of afflictions by revenants, with or without the accompaniment of blood-drinking.

Near the English city of Leicester at Dane Hills is a cave which is associated with an ancient vampire-like presence with Celtic connections. The cave, which has been blocked off since some time in the nineteenth century, ostensibly because of its sinister reputation but perhaps simply because it was unsafe, was known locally as Anne's Bower. The Anne in question, a blood-sucking bogey-woman whose name was invoked to terrify unruly children, has been identified by some folklorists as a late incarnation of the medieval figure of the supernatural crone 'Black Annis', who is herself a descendant of the much older Celtic goddess Anu, the earth-mother personified as an old woman.[6]

The survival of a prehistoric deity or monster, even in a debased form, indicates, if it is true, a remarkable continuity in the popular imagination and this is the key to the eastern European Vampire. In the case of Britain we cannot know how many colourful hobgoblins or ghouls have been forgotten over the centuries, but a surprising number persisted in place-names, songs and nursery rhymes into the 1950s. The complexity of Celtic paganism is lost: only fragments of it – headhunting, sacred cauldrons, water-sacrifices – were noted down by the Celts' literate neighbours and later embellished for modern consumption. It does seem likely, though, that their mythology contained versions of the same blood-related myths and superstitions that appeared in other Indo-European cultures. We know also from the dismembered and rearranged skeletons and protective charms found in Celtic Iron Age burials that they feared the return of their dead.[7]

The realm of Celtic faery is immensely attractive to New Age pagans and Vampire fans alike, and modern compendia often include the names of lesser Celtic deities such as the Irish *dearg-dhu*, the *bean-sidhe* and the Scottish *baobhan-sith*, popularly known as the banshee, as if these were proto-vampires. In this book, too, a Vampire connection is suggested for a wide range of mythical beings who at first sight are only distantly related. But a line can be drawn; the dearg-dhu is described as something more like a nymph or 'place-haunter' than a Vampire, but in any case seems to be an invention on the part of Montague Summers. The banshee, who preys on young men in the form of a cloven-footed maiden and wails to portend a death in the family, forms part of an international family of evil fairies, including the Hungarian *kis-asszony* ('little-ladies') who dance unwary suitors to death.[8]

࿎

In the early nineteenth century, villagers at Tarrant Gunville in the deeply rustic English county of Dorset were subject to the depredations of a Vampire whom they identified as William Doggett, the late steward of the nearby great house of Eastbury. In the previous century Doggett had been the servant of Lord Temple and had defrauded his master before committing suicide, either by hanging or shooting himself. He is still said to haunt the inside of the house, where an indelible stain marks the spot where he died, and the long drive outside, where a headless coachman in a coach and four (the horses are also headless) pauses to collect the steward's spirit before galloping past the yew trees to the door. The focus of this legend was the rebuilding of Tarrant Gunville church in 1845, which involved the removal of the old graves: Doggett's corpse was discovered intact and undecayed with a rosy-red complexion, his legs bound by yellow ribbon (a detail that might suggest he had been 'hobbled' to prevent him wandering). The story of Doggett forms part of a set of fables based on the figure of the 'bad servant', the counterpart to the 'wicked lord': both derived from a series of real cases in which the symbiotic, sometimes fragile and fraught master–servant relationship ended in tragedy (a surprising number of butlers and manservants killed themselves, more than one or two killed their masters or were murdered by them).

Suicides, as in other parts of Europe, have offended the laws of the Church and compromised the values of the community, were among the outcasts whose souls could not find rest and were commonly suspected of returning to harry the living. Between Redenhall and Harleston in Suffolk is the reputed grave of a woman named Lush who was ostracized by people thereabouts who suspected her of murdering her own child. As a result Mistress Lush poisoned herself. The stake that was driven through her body in 1813 to prevent her leaving the grave prematurely grew into a tree at the site of her otherwise unmarked burial, providing an unofficial monument to commemorate a simultaneous sinner and object of pity, inscribing an obscure and poignant death into the collective memory.[9]

In north-east Scotland, between the Forest of Atholl and the Braemar Hills at a place called Fealaar, two poachers were attacked by a Vampire who haunted a bothy, an isolated hut providing shelter for hill-walkers. Details are fragmentary, but according to recollections recorded in the 1970s the incident took place about fifty years earlier and one of the poachers exhibited the marks left by the Vampire for the rest of his life. Also part of Scottish folklore, and far better-known, is the story of the monster of Glamis, the castle seat of the earls of Strathmore (the sixteenth earl was the maternal grandfather of Queen Elizabeth II). There are several different legends attaching to the castle itself, which lies in Forfarshire, north-west of Dundee, all based on the existence of a secret room in which shameful things have been concealed for generations. Tales that seem to have been circulating among local people at least since the nineteenth century relate how workmen who have stumbled upon the bricked-up entrance to the room have been bribed into silence and paid to emigrate; iron floor-rings, to which manacles might be fastened, have been seen by visitors in spite of servants' attempts to cover them up; guests in the castle have been plagued by dream-visions of deformed figures cowering in dark cells or passing through locked oaken doors. Just as every seven years Dean Water, the lake beyond the castle, claims a victim from the local people, so, they say, every seventy years a monster-child is born to the Strathmore family: a Vampire whose existence is known only to the heir and his factor and who is condemned to live out its miserable life in the hidden, permanently locked room.

Before being thrown into a pond and drowned at Sandhill Farm, east of Withypool in Somerset, Madam Joan Carn, both witch and Vampire, was said to have murdered four husbands and practised black magic with the aid of the blood of innocents. After her death in 1612 she was buried none the less within the precincts of Withypool churchyard, but mourners at her funeral returned to the farm to find her cooking bacon and eggs in the kitchen. An exorcism was hurriedly arranged, which resulted in Madam Carn's bloodlusting ghost returning to its resting-place at the rate of one cock's stride a year.

The worldwide superstition whereby the wandering undead can be thwarted by forcing them to count innumerable objects – such as grains of sand or seeds – is also represented in British folklore: for instance, in the Quaker burial ground in St Buryan in Celtic West Cornwall is the reputed grave of a mischievous apparition or ghoul named Kenegie (the same creature appears in Northern British legend as Kenickie) whose spirit was harnessed by a parson who condemned him to count the blades of grass in an enclosure at Castle-an-Dinas, a site also associated with King Arthur several miles further east.[10]

Despite these similarities with vampire legends as recorded elsewhere, the clearly delineated figure of the Vampire itself is missing from British folklore; the use of the name to describe local apparitions, as in the stories cited, seems to date from the early nineteenth century – precisely when the Vampire, in its ethnographic and literary incarnations, was reimported into Britain from the Continent. The various native stories in which blood-suckers occur all belong to other stock components of island folklore: the bogey-woman, the feared widow, the haunter of wild places, the unquiet soul of the poor outcast or the faithless servant; the castle myth of the 'family taint'.

✢

Today the attributes of Vampires are well established: they are blood-drinkers, they are dead, they are malignant and dangerous, and they assume, for at least some of the time, a roughly human appearance.

There are secondary characteristics, too, which have come to be seen as defining features: the Vampire is contagious; it is somehow potentially immortal while not actually invulnerable; and it is fanged. Although it is not always recognized, it has generally been a feature of the Vampire that it is both multifaceted and multinational. The cowboy is American, the Gangsters, too, although they can become French, Italian or Hong Kong Chinese at a pinch; the knights and the ladys are European; the Serial Killer seems to belong particularly to the USA, Germany and Russia, but the Vampire? One of the keys to its survival is the fact that it has been reinvented for every culture that required or desired it. In Dr van Helsing's comical English; '... he is known everywhere that men have been ... he have follow the wake of the berserker Icelander, the devil-begotten Hun, the Slav, the Saxon, the Magyar...'[11]

Since the early nineteenth century it has been possible to discern the 'flavours' of the various traditions: there is, for example, a peculiarly French strain of exquisite, euphoric delight in the macabre as indulged by such masters as Gautier, Nodier and de Maupassant. A startling modern invocation of the Vampire-as-outsider came in the writings of the young prodigy Isidore Ducasse, who styled himself 'Le Comte de Lautréamont':

... You, young man, do not despair, for whatever you may believe to the contrary, you have a friend in the Vampire ... He goes from land to land, and everywhere he is abhorred. Some say he had been afflicted since childhood with some sort of innate madness. Others maintain that he is extremely and instinctively cruel, is himself ashamed of this, and that his parents died of sorrow. There are some who claim that he was branded with a nickname in youth and that he has been inconsolable ever since, because his injured pride saw in it glaring evidence of the wickedness of man, which becomes apparent in his earliest years and only increases with age. That name was the *Vampire!*[12]

Ducasse's unclassifiable fiction – neither novel nor poem – was a prolonged cry of adolescent revulsion, mingled with savage delight, at the folly of the world. As part of the self-induced delirium that the writer conjures into being, he fantasizes the defiling of a youth: '... thrust your long fingernails into his tender breast ... drink his blood, sucking the wounds ... nothing is as good as his blood ... unless it be his tears, bitter as salt ... have you ever tasted your blood, when you have accidentally cut a finger? Good, is it not, for it has no taste? ... the tears that fall from your eyes ... how good they are: they taste of vinegar.'

In a more controlled version of de Lautreamont's unbridled horror-feast of 1868, the decadent novelist Joris Karl Huysmans used the real-life Bluebeard, the French aristocrat Gilles de Retz – condemned in the fifteenth century for witchcraft and sodomy, he was also accused of the mass murder of young boys and of necrophilia – as the protagonist in *Là-Bas*, his revel in bloody and blasphemous excess: 'Gilles conserves the blood of this child in order to inscribe the formulae of invocation and conjurings. It fertilizes a horrible harvest ... Vampirism satisfies him for some months. He pollutes dead infants, assuaging his fevered desires in the blood-smeared chill of the tomb.'[13]

The *fin de siècle* did not mark the end of this febrile sensibility. It can be found again as part of a modern fascination with the extreme, for instance in Georges Bataille's poem '*Archangélique*', verses that might have been dedicated to a female succubus...

> Cover up my eyes
> I love the night
> my heart is black
>
> Push me into the night
> All is black
> I am suffering
>
> The world smells like a corpse
> birds fly, their eyes put out
> you are dark like a black sky
>
> You are beautiful, like fear
> You are mad, like one dead'[14]

A specifically German interpretation of vampirism, composed of matter-of-fact resignation to tragedy, frank eroticism and a dash of *Schadenfreude*, is represented in the writings of Kleist, Tieck and Bürger, but before them by a little-known landmark, the first literary work to connect the folk Vampire with *eros* and *thanatos*, sex and death, the poem published in 1748 by Heinrich Ossenfelder.

> And when in peace you slumber,
> from thy beauteous cheek
> The fresh purple suck
> Then when you start with terror
> I would kiss you
> And as a vampire kisses:
> Then when you straightway tremble
> And sink exhausted into my arms
> Like one dead
> Then I will ask you
> Is *my* teaching better
> Than that of your good lady mother?[15]

ⱽ

Another assumption now routinely made about the Vampire is that it is Transylvanian, not because that mysterious territory was a source of innumerable Vampire legends, which it was, but because it was the supposed homeland of the premier Vampire, Count Dracula. Transylvania, the vassal state that had long been contested between Hungary and the Turks, held a special place in the Magyar imagination. For patriots it was the 'fairy-garden' in which they hoped their nationhood would be reborn, and it was indeed a hotbed of magic and superstition, as foreign visitors testified over the centuries. The Scotswoman Emily de Laszowska Gérard, wife of a Polish officer in the service of the Habsburgs, wrote in English on the country and a copy of her book, *The Land Beyond the Forest*, was used for reference by Bram Stoker. 'It would almost seem,' she observed, 'as though the whole species of demons, pixies, witches and hobgoblins, driven from the rest of Europe by the hand of science, had taken refuge within the mountain rampart, well aware that here they would find secure lurking-places, whence they might defy their pursuers yet awhile.'[16]

The image conjured up of Transylvania as a dank and gloomy place of benighted villages crouching beneath black peaks is not quite accurate. True, the villages were poor and the roads often impassable, blocked by snow in winter and floods in spring, but in hot summer the rolling pastureland is covered with wild flowers and the mountains and forests stand benign. What had tainted Transylvania was its terrible history, an unending bloody instability in which the Magyar, Romanian and German inhabitants fought among themselves as Turks, Austrians and their local satraps mounted invasion after invasion. Impoverishment, betrayal and atrocity became a way of life and the troubles that beset neighbouring regions took on exaggerated forms behind the Carpathian barriers.

The true flavour of Magyar romance – rather too melodramatic for the English palate – can be found in one of the very few novels of the nineteenth century to be translated from Hungarian into English, Maurus Jókai's *'Midst the Wild Carpathians*, published in 1894, and also quite possibly read by Stoker during the long gestation of *Dracula*.

As its translator, R. N. Bain, wrote, 'We are transported into a semi-heroic, semi-barbarous borderland between the Past and the Present, where Mediaevalism has found a last retreat, and the civilizations of the East and West contend or coalesce.'

Among the ingredients in this rich mixture are visions of reliquefying blood and the return of the heroic dead ...' The body of that dominating form reposes in the crypt of the church at Bethlen, and no-one has inherited his spirit ... But the chronicles say that wherever danger threatens Transylvania, the blood of the buried patriot flows from his simple tomb, a terror to the people and a wonder to the world.'

The land's inhabitants are under constant siege by evil spirits, 'Dost thou hear how they howl, those invisible beings, and rattle at the barred and bolted windows with a mighty hand?', obliging them to turn to necromancy: 'Oh, seek me out some such dead man who will change names with me. Thou dost know the incantations. Go! call up one from the grave! Promise him anything, everything, whoever he may be ... hurl the magic wand into the nearest grave, and so compel the dwellers therein to appear before thee.'

Although Communism put a stop – for the first time in Romanian history – to the staking of corpses and the killing of witches, the ancient savageries festered in, were nurtured by, Ceauşescu's regime, which banned all references to the Victorian *Dracula* as an insult to the real individual whose name the novelist had borrowed, and which became another of the key words henceforth inseparable from the image of the blood-sucker.

Vlad III Ţepeş, 'The Impaler', indeed figured in Transylvanian history; he was actually a Wallachian warlord who was and is venerated by the Romanian people as a heroic defender of their country against the Ottoman Turks who oppressed them for more than four centuries. He was born in Sighişoara in 1431 to Vlad II, *voivode* of Wallachia, and Princess Cneajna of neighbouring Moldavia. For Bram Stoker this ancient tyrant was an exotic name and a ferocious countenance rendered in the woodcut produced by his German enemies with glittering eyes, a hook-nose and a giant moustache. Although his name appears in every anthology, at nearly every website, and despite a minor literary industry devoted to his life and times, Vlad Ţepeş, Lord Dracula, was not – was never even considered to be – a Vampire. He was notorious as a genocidal warrior at a time when leaders were accorded respect in proportion to the scale of the atrocities for which they were responsible. His trademark impaling was a spectacular form of public execution, used by all factions in the Turkish wars, whereby victims were skewered 'from fundament to throat' on upright stakes, their corpses left in massed ranks as a terrible warning. Vlad's reputation was also based on his improvising other ingenious punishments to suit the occasion: nailing of turbans to heads, burning and baking alive, for instance. Like most of his predecessors and successors, he was eventually betrayed and assassinated, but the propaganda put out by the Saxons, who hated him, ensured that his name and portrait survived.

ᵛᵛ

The elements that eventually went to compose the Vampire's image were present for some centuries, but at first were applied to demons. There is almost no representation of the Vampire revenants in popular iconography anywhere until the nineteenth century, but cradle-snatching witches and the devils of the underworld were portrayed again and again, often with prominent fangs and sometimes with bat-wings.

The pre-eminence of the bat in Vampire iconography, though, is a late addition, dating only from the end of the eighteenth century. When Napoleon's soldiers were exploring South America and came across a small bat that sucked the warm blood of larger animals and birds, it was quite natural to name it after the European blood-suckers who had fascinated the *ancien régime* of Louis XVI. The discovery continued to cause excitement since it seemed that nature was corroborating myth. If a furry mammalian blood-sucker with sharp teeth really did exist, might not other legendary monsters come to light? The little *desmodus* or *diphylla* can live for up to thirty years and just like the human(oid) Vampires of Slavonic folklore returns to roost with its fellows and regurgitates blood for them to share.[17]

Physically, the most famous Vampire, Count Dracula, was only part-bat: the rest was a composite made up of the woodcut portrait of Vlad the Impaler in the British Museum Library, a hint of Polidori's Byron, perhaps, Bram Stoker's tyrannical employer the actor-impresario Henry Irving, Walt Whitman and Franz Liszt, whom Stoker had met and admired, and, notably, the gimlet-eyed, moustachioed African explorer and translator of eastern legends, Sir Richard Burton. So the two most charismatic and devilish nineteenth-century English gentlemen, Byron and Burton, were brought together in one archetype.

In Victorian England, thoughts of those who had passed away might result in a more delicate morbidity of mind, as in Oscar Wilde's verse:

Tread lightly, she is near
Under the snow,
Speak gently, she can hear
The daisies grow.[18]

And it was, of course, in England that the most famous Vampire fiction of all appeared, a work that quite dispensed with Oscar Wilde's nostalgia, although its author, Bram Stoker, was a friend of Wilde's and, like him, Irish by birth.

Among the non-fictional works to treat the subject two volumes, above all others, deserve attention. They, too, were written by an eccentric and intriguing Englishman. Montague Summers was born on 10 April 1880 and died on 8 August 1948. Much of his life was mysterious – the period between his ordination as an Anglican deacon after graduating from Trinity College, Oxford, and his reappearance in Oxford and London in the early 1920s (he seems to have renounced the Church of England before the First World War) is a blank. Summers himself suggested vaguely that he had been refining his new-found Catholic faith and ministering to believers in Britain and abroad; others suspected that he had been a member of one of the many occult or theosophical groups active at the turn of the century and had been studying, if not practising, more sinister rites.

The word pederasty was whispered in connection with Summers, and his admiration for the Great Beast Aleister Crowley (the bibliophile and the black magician met only once, exchanging gifts, each enjoying the other's company) did his reputation no good. Dennis Wheatley, the author of best-selling stories of Satanism, was unnerved by Summers, who invited him and his wife to stay and offered him a rare and expensive book from his library. When Wheatley reluctantly refused to buy it, Summers became enraged. The couple fled: they had already been terrified by the unnaturally large spiders and toads that seemed about to overrun the property.[19]

What is certain is that during the 1920s Summers, flamboyantly dressed in the robes of a Roman Catholic priest although there is no unequivocal evidence that he was ever ordained, gained a minor reputation by editing and helping to stage the works of the racier English Elizabethan and Restoration playwrights, subsequently publishing a series of books including *The History of Witchcraft and Demonology*, *The Geography of Witchcraft*, *The Vampire, His Kith and Kin* and its sequel, *The Vampire in Europe*, published in 1928 and 1929 respectively. He feuded with Margaret Murray, the proponent of the survival of a pagan witch-cult, and with the Jesuit Father Herbert Thurston, whose Catholic interpretation of witchcraft was more cautiously orthodox than his own.

Summers's works on the Vampire display great erudition based on long months, perhaps years, of poring over texts from his own collection, in the Bodleian Library at Oxford and in the British Museum Reading Room (where he would brandish his folder, conspicuously marked 'Vampires', at speechless fellow scholars) and a good command of several languages including Greek and Latin. His style was that of a gifted gentleman-amateur, mixing personal digressions and subjective observations among citations from the widest range of written sources. At all times presenting himself as a devout Catholic, he emphasizes again and again his belief in the reality of the supernatural evil that he is describing, in the existence of Real Vampires as well as witchcraft and other manifestations of the occult. It would be churlish of any Vampire scholar to dismiss Summers. There are those who have sniped at his use of archaic phraseology, his habit of amassing quantities of texts at the expense of subjecting all of them to rigorous analysis, and his apparent credulity. Nevertheless, all the serious attempts at writing on the same subject have referred to Summers and several have shamelessly plundered his pages without acknowledgement. Any new non-fiction treatment of the Vampire must pay its respects to his two volumes and any new writer on the subject risks the occasional sense that the larger-than-life, slightly doubtful figure of Summers himself is hovering some-where just out of vision . . .

✝

Another very English approach to the Vampire emerged from the sort of parlour-room mysticism that used to fascinate the leisured classes and their emulators, too. Summers, like Aleister Crowley, was part of this milieu, as were Theosophists, Rosicrucians and Spiritualists, and a host of lesser cranks and table-tappers. A frequenter of these circles, Albert Osborne Eaves, came to the rescue of Edwardian England with his fifty-four page tract, *Modern Vampirism: Its Dangers and How to Avoid Them*. In his preface Eaves wrote: 'If an apology be needed for the appearance of this little book it is the increasing neurotic tendency of the age, when to be healthy is to be abnormal, and the dangers in which the wholesale dabbling in the unknown will enmesh the feet of the unwary.' He is convinced that there is no such thing as 'dead matter'; after physical death or in sleep the body, which is merely a 'vehicle', moves on to the astral plane with its concomitant 'vibra-tions'.[20]

In keeping with Victorian and Edwardian ideas of 'station', the afterlife was seen as hierarchical in a reworking of the spheres and circles of medieval cosmogony: 'Among the "dead" is the ordinary person, but he does not stay here long, the atmosphere not being conducive to tranquillity or happiness. Generally speaking, the lowest class of man preponderates, the length of time they remain depending on many circumstances, and varying in duration.' Using the same logic as ancient folklore, the author singles out those who have taken their own lives as potential Vampire:

> In the case of the suicides, seeing they have not accomplished their end, viz., to put an end to existence, the return for earth-life grows upon them with terrible zest ... It is here that the danger of Vampirism occurs. If the experience they seek cannot be obtained without a physical body, only two courses are open for them. One is to do so vicariously. To do this they must feed on the emanations arising from blood and alcohol; public houses and slaughter-houses are thronged with these unhappy creatures, which hang about and feed thus.

Elsewhere he declares, 'It is only possible for a man to become a Vampire by leading a really wicked and utterly selfish life,' and prescribes a spiritual remedy: 'thinking pure thoughts only, sympathetic, helpful thoughts ... a good conscience is an invincible coat of armour, and it can be created atom by atom, by right thought and right living.'

But, again, earthbound common sense dictates that tangible means should also be used against the pest, rather as with ants or wasps:

> garlic ... or placing small saucers of nitric acid on the tables (out of the way of children and animals) for a short time daily, but not in the bedroom, unless the window is left open each night, will be found to counteract any Vampire influence. The use of incense in places of worship is not 'superstition', or to have a theatrical effect, but to keep undesirable entities away, just as the origin of church bells was to free the sacred edifice of their presence. The gargoyles seen on cathedrals &c. are the 'demons' escaping.

✝✝

The spiritualist Osborne Eaves and the vampirologist Montague Summers firmly believed that inhabitants of the modern world could become Real Vampires, a conviction that is nowadays more widespread in North American than in England. Proof that the notion is entirely justified began to come to light in 1996.

As the Vampire 'Vlad' put it, in a slew of press interviews, 'Why would a bunch of East Village Vampires have to go all the way to Jersey when there are eight million people to feed off here?'[21]

Vlad was being a little glib. Nutley, New Jersey, a shabby community strung together around depots, truckstops, freightyards and road-houses, is precisely the kind of place where American vampirism can suddenly burst horribly through the bleak, suburban calm. It was in Nutley on a hot, quiet day in July 1996 that thirty-six-year-old Susan Walsh abandoned her cramped apartment, her keys and her eleven-year-old son and disappeared without trace.

She was suffering from a stomach ulcer, weight-loss, anxiety and the hallucinatory side-effects of the tranquillizing medication Xanax. She had also been taking lithium, the standard prescription for manic depression, and quantities of alcohol, on which she had been depend-ent in the past. Two years earlier Susan Walsh had begun a masters degree in literature to complement her college degree in English and communications; she had also begun in earnest to pursue her ambition of a career in journalism while earning money on the side as an 'exotic dancer' – a stripper and sometime star of private stag-nights and public live sex shoes – as she had for nearly a decade. The disappearance of a blonde single mother and would-be writer from a small town in the shadow of New York City would mean nothing in the greater scheme of things, were it not that those suspected of abducting her, at least during the first stages of the fruitless police investigation, were vampires.

The aspirant reporter had been doing research jobs for the *Village Voice* newspaper among others, and it was while on assignment from them, detailed to look into the disappearance of supplies from New York blood banks, that she had stumbled across the networks of recreational blood-drinkers, most of them claiming to be part of a Vampire cult or Vampire sub-species, which had been operating in the city since the 1970s.[22]

The notion of enchanted underworlds existing somewhere beneath the streets of the metropolis had become a potent pop-cultural myth, refracted through movies, TV series and comic-books, and Walsh had been fascinated to the point of obsession with the Real-Vampire underground that she alone had uncovered, with its secret rites and its surprisingly compelling philosophies: redemption through transgression, tapping into the life-essence; even the emergence of a new genetic strain.

She haunted the Vampires' clubs and bars in her search for stories, and she probably penetrated the covert gatherings in restaurant annexes, cinema back rooms and private apartments where outwardly respectable professionals joined full-time Bohemians in ritualized feeding sessions. Although these coven-meetings were supposedly consensual, they depended on a hierarchy of dominance and sub-mission: so-called 'minions' were delegated to organize the feast and serve the all-powerful Vampires who took from members of the 'herd' who submitted to being bled. Usually one Vampire would have four or five herd members at his or her disposal, but during a 'sanctuary feed' a large group would converge on one single, presumably willing donor.[23] Just as in the commercial 'dungeons' where similar power games were enacted, the atmosphere in these congregations is heavy with half suppressed and channelled anger and fear, the role-playing hovering always on the edge of uncontrollable abuse.

Although she did not resemble one, with her loose long blonde hair, leather jacket and blue jeans, Susan Walsh had much in common with many American Vampires: she was a second generation baby-boomer whose mother was young enough herself to have been a sixties rebel; Susan had tried to exorcize her own self-doubts in creativity, composing autobiographical poems and short stories, and she had been tempted by the seamy glamour of the Dark Side. She was OK, nice, but maybe rash and naïve, said people who had come into contact with her in the Vampyre clubs on the Lower East Side.[24] These club-goers' unconcern at the thought of her fate recalled a review of the latest vampire movie to be made in the city: 'Let's face it: in New York City, everyone is a Vampire in one way or another. So it should come as no surprise that . . . one of the undead roams around the Village sucking the life out of yet another struggling, scraggly artist-type.'[25] For her part Susan Walsh found the Vampires, she said, mostly harmless and interesting.

As police and journalists looked more closely into the preceding three years during which Walsh had been researching the *demi-monde*, they found other lines of enquiry to follow. Perhaps she did stage an encounter with a Vampire, who just went too far, or perhaps one of the cloaked, top-hatted Manhattan blood-suckers (or his stilettoed, corseted female counterpart) doubled as an old-fashioned stalker, but in her other life Walsh had been antagonizing more obvious preda-tors: the 'agents' and minders, said to be members of the Russian and US Mafias, who controlled the working girls she mixed with, bikers, habitués of the louche bars and strip-joints where she performed, sex addicts and sex pests, would-be lovers . . .

Only an obscure bit-part player in a three-thousand-year melo-drama, Susan Walsh was – we must hope *is* – significant nevertheless. Her disappearance drew the attention of the world's media for the first time to the fact that the incubi and succubi of fiction had crossed over and were operating in our 'real' world. Her sad story also symbolizes the tension that has always been central to the Vampire myth, the contrast between dreams and bathos, pornography and poetry.

⚥

As far as this book is concerned, this would be the end of the Susan Walsh story, were it not for a press cutting discovered much later. In 1980, an unnamed young mother, described as a pale, thin recluse, was confined for life in a psychiatric hospital after murdering her four-year-old daughter and draining her of blood. The tragedy took place in the 'quiet' suburb of Nutley, New Jersey.[26]

2
Femmes Fatales

The female [mosquito] does the biting, gulping down her own weight in blood every three or four days, whereas the male of the species displays a preference for flower nectar.

Independent, London, 6 July 1998

Oh what a world of witchery was in that mouth, slightly parted, and exhibiting within the pearly teeth that glistened in the faint light that came from that bay window. How sweetly the long silken eyelashes lay upon the cheek. Now she moves and one shoulder is entirely visible – whiter, fairer than the spotless clothing of the bed on which she lies, is the smooth skin of that fair creature, just budding into womanhood, and in that transition state which presents to us all the charms of the girl – almost of the child, with the more matured beauty and gentleness of advancing years.[1]

The delicious – to many men, at least – picture of recumbent Woman as potential victim, her accustomed role in the modern Vampire mythos, has become wearyingly familiar. But it was not ever thus. Among the earliest artefacts and inscriptions from the old near-eastern civilizations, Assyria, Akkadia, Sumer, Babylon, there are a number of references to evil entities who suck the blood of mortals. Most are in the form of terrified prayers designed to chase away some eldritch force:

They rage against humankind
Spill mortals' blood as if it were rain
Devour their flesh

Suck dry their veins
They are demons filled with cruelty
Imbibing blood without cease
Call down upon them the curse
That they never more return to this place
By heaven be thou exorcized!
By earth be thou exorcized![2]

Of these most ancient demonic creatures, many of whom were unmistakably female, there is only one whose name still resonates today and whose cult has, like that of the Vampire himself, been resurrected in new forms for a post-modern age. This is Lilith, *Meyalleleth*, 'The Howling One'; 'The First Eve'.

Carved on a three-thousand-year-old tablet in what is now northern Syria was another protective incantation:

O, Flying demoness in the dark chamber
Be on your way at once, O Lili!
O, Robber-murderess,
Be gone![3]

A goddess, or just possibly a female shaman, wearing a conical cap, her hair pulled back and up, stares expressionless from the clay relief across three thousand years. She stands naked upon two crouching lions, arms raised and palms forward, holding what might be wands or scourges. She is flanked by a pair of owls whose claws are identical to her own feet and whose wings are smaller versions of those growing from – or laced around – her shoulders.

And from the prologue to the *Epic of Gilgamesh*, a Sumerian creation myth of the second millennium BC, comes a passage that has sent its echoes along the centuries, spawning or reinforcing successive reimaginings of a dark presence in Eden:

. . . on this day a Huluppu [willow] tree,
Which had been planted on the banks of the Euphrates,

And nourished by its waters,
Was uprooted by the south wind,
And carried away by the Euphrates.
A goddess who was wandering among the banks,
Seized the swaying tree,
And, at the behest of Anu and Enlil,
Brought it to Inanna's garden in Uruk.
Inanna tended the tree carefully and lovingly;
She hoped to have a throne and a bed,
made for herself from its wood.
After ten years the tree had matured,
But in the meantime, she found to her dismay,
That her hopes could not be fulfilled,
Because during that time,
A dragon had built its nest at the foot of the tree,
The Zu-bird was raising its young in the crown,
And the demon Lilith had built her house in the middle.

Then the hero, Gilgamesh, comes to Inanna's rescue, killing the dragon, driving off the Zu-bird and its offspring and ... 'Lilith, petrified with fear, tore down her house and fled into the wilderness.'[4]

Some argue that the reference here is not specifically to a being called Lilith at all, but simply to an unnamed earth-spirit. The word in question is *kisikillillake*, which contains the elements *lil* 'air' and *ki*, 'earth', but not necessarily *lilla*, which might be related to the Sumerian words for wantonness and luxuriousness, *lulu* and *lalu*, respectively. In trying to trace the etymology of the name, most scholars have referred to the term *ardat-lili*, used in Sumer and Babylon to mean a young and beautiful female succubus. *Ardat* here means 'nubile girl' and *lili* seems to mean 'spirit'. Later in Lilith's history commentators tried to connect the name to the Hebrew terms for screech or howl, and with *layil*, the word for night, but these links are spurious.

Sphinx-like creatures, women with wings and the talons of hawks or owls from other early tablets, and a winged predatory female looming over a tiny recumbent male victim on a Hellenic frieze have all been identified with Lilith. The Old Testament seems to invoke the same awful presence in a sequence describing dwellers among ruins in the Edomite desert...

> Wildcats shall meet with hyenas,
> Goat-demons shall call to each other;
> There too Lilith shall repose,
> And find a place to rest.
> There shall the owl nest,
> And lay and hatch and brood in its shadow.[5]

Again the translation is problematical. The closer one looks, the more the names of all the creatures infesting this place are disputable: is it a centaur, a satyr or a *djinn* in the form of a goat? Is it a jackal or a hyena? And the word translated as 'Lilith' can also be rendered as 'screech-owl' and 'night-monster'. As with the many other names bestowed on the many forms of the Vampire, we are projecting back on to a group of letters and sounds from another time the images and associated ideas from our own imaginations, formed as they are by a quite different context. We use comparisons that seem to suit – a 'centaur', a 'gorgon' – but we must remember that these well-defined terms, like 'Vampire' are anachronisms, approximations.

From the late Roman and early medieval eras onward, Lilith acquired a new history that cast her as the First Wife of Adam, who was then banished from Eden and became a demoness and mother of demons and, in the mortal sphere, a scourge of helpless children and sleeping men. This legend, which in one form or another had great influence on Jewish folklore and Hebrew mysticism, originated in a curious text whose real provenance and dates are unknown. This was the *Sepher Ben Sira* (the *Alphabetum Siracidis* or 'Alphabet of Ben-Sirah'), which was composed some time between the eighth and tenth centuries AD. There is no written evidence that this detailed Lilith-legend predated the Alphabet, which is not a *midrash* – a rabbinical commentary on the Scriptures – as some people have assumed, but what seems to be a satirical reworking of various Hebrew stories from the Scriptures. It may even have originated as a subtle piece of anti-Jewish propaganda in that its parables are nearly all perverse or amoral, but it certainly became a key source of later beliefs among the Jews themselves.[6] According to this account, God first created Adam from the earth, whereupon Adam complained that the myriad creatures each had a mate, but he had none, and God then realized that it was not good for His creation, man, to remain alone. He therefore created a woman from the same earth (although some versions of the legend have it that He created her from sediment and filth), and gave her the name Lilith.

Adam enjoyed sexual congress with his new consort or, rather, he tried to and failed, as Lilith refused to adopt the inferior position and demanded to lie not beneath him but on top. When he tried to command her, she riposted that they were equal to one another for they had both been created from the same dust. Some stories hold that Adam did mate with Lilith and also with another female creature, Naamah, and that the devil Asmodeus and hordes of lesser demons known as *shedim*, tormentors of mankind and bearers of pestilence ever after, were their issue. (On the other hand Talmudic sources tell that the demons were spawned by Adam's nocturnal emissions.)

Adam and his wife could not agree, and when he attempted to have his way by force Lilith became enraged: in her fury she uttered the Ineffable Name of God and, using the magic powers that she possessed, flew away into the air. When Adam complained to his Creator that his partner had abandoned him, God despatched three angels, Snvi, Snsvi and Smnglf (the lost vowels were spoken but not written in Hebrew), to bring her back. He told Adam that Lilith would be commanded to return forthwith, and if she did not, that one hundred of her children would perish every day until she did so.[7]

When the three angels caught up with Lilith above the middle of the Red Sea, where later the Egyptians would miraculously perish, they told her of the words of God and threatened to drown her, but she refused to turn back. She had settled on the desert shore of the same sea in a region populated by lascivious *djinns* and there she gave birth to further demon offspring, the *lilim*, more than a hundred of whom were born each day. Lilith retorted that she could not die (or alternatively, in some versions of the story, she begged to be spared) and declared that she had been created for the purpose of enervating and chastising little children: she had been given power over boys from the moment of their birth until they were eight days old, over girls until the twentieth day. She swore, however, in the name of the Almighty, that whenever and wherever she saw the names or forms of those three angels in a child's room, she would spare that child. For her refusal to go back to Adam she forfeited a hundred of her children every day, and it was said that when she was prevented by the angelic names from stealing a human infant, she would turn in her spiteful fury on her own young and devour or dismember them.

It was thus that the name of Lilith came to be used in Jewish communities throughout the medieval and into the early-modern periods, sometimes along with the names of the three angels on bowls and amulets and scraps of paper, which were designed to protect the owners or wearers from her attentions. She was used as a bogey-woman to frighten children, and in the vulnerable days just after birth, rituals were enacted to keep her far away, spells were written on the walls and doors of the child's room. Even so, Lilith might succeed in entering. If she managed to touch a man-child in his sleep, he would laugh, in which case his parent or guardian should strike his lips with a finger to banish the invisible devil.[8]

The cultural forces that helped to shape the tales of Lilith, Adam and God are obscure and various, but characteristically combine universal psychology – the struggle between man and wife for authority, the anxiety aroused by a woman's potential for harming children or rejecting her nurturing role – with historical factors such as contact with differing sexual customs, concerns over moral, territorial and ethnic boundaries. Linking these themes is an even more primal metaphor, the woman as predatory or scavenging bird, itself based on identification of women with nesting.

As well as her appearance in the Alphabet stories and her subsequent reputation, Lilith is mentioned in the literature of the

Cabbala (the mystical doctrine developed by medieval rabbis) and in more orthodox rabbinical writings. In the former she functions as the female counterpart of Satan, as the tempter of Adam and Eve, as a supernatural harlot and even as the Almighty's own consort while the higher Incarnation of the feminine was in exile; in the Talmud, the book of Jewish religious law, she is briefly described as a long-haired, winged demoness who will seize anyone who sleeps alone in a house. In another tale, Solomon suspected the Queen of Sheba of being Lilith in disguise when he noticed the hairy legs hidden beneath her skirts. The counterfeit queen and her sister Naamah later presented themselves to him in the form of harlots of Jerusalem.

Lilith also plays a part in Christian iconography, where she seems to have become identified with the serpent who tempted Adam and Eve and who appears in many representations – one example can be seen on Michelangelo's Sistine Chapel ceiling – with the upper parts of a human female and the coiling extremities of a great snake.

✶

In the late twentieth century the search for 'fresh' spiritual and magical metaphors and avatars has led to a ransacking of pre-Christian and heretical Christian-era texts. On the basis of her defiance of Adam and of God the Patriarch (even at the cost of her own children), feminists have singled out Lilith, the pre-eminent proto-Vampire, as a powerful and useful heroine. On the basis especially of her insistence on sexual equality, if not dominance, of her identification in some traditions as a handmaiden of Inanna in the selection of young men for ritual sexual congress, and of her later reputation as a succubus, she has also been selected as an icon of magical liberation and power for those who have evolved new theories and practices of the occult.[9]

A modern devotee of Lilith who has erected one of several 'virtual shrines' to her on the Internet tells of her difficulty in formulating a new theology that will recast the ancient demon in a positive light and permit her active worship. For a modern Wiccan (a follower of the neo-pagan white witchcraft cult), she says, the problem is easy to overcome: she or he could just 'plug in Lilith as an aspect of the

Triple Goddess' and use traditional Wiccan rites to worship her. For this Internet writer

> ... Lilith is the goddess of female independence and autonomy, both sexually and in other aspects of life. Lilith bows down to no man or god, not even Yahweh Himself. She is also the goddess of female sexuality for pleasure itself and not merely for reproductive purposes. Unlike the average fertility goddesses, for Lilith the sexual act is not so strongly connected with reproduction.[10]

She grapples with the problem of harnessing Lilith's malign reputation:

> The admiration of ... Lilith is in no way condoning the act of women raping or sexually abusing men. Instead, it is similar to admiring Pan for his unrelenting sexuality, although technically, many of his seductions would be considered rape by today's standards. It is the unrelenting, uncompromising sexuality of Lilith which is being worshipped, not the results on the recipients of said sexuality.

⚴

Black and white magicians have long been interested in Cabbalistic legend in general and the persona of Lilith in particular. A new development is the availability of courses in ritual magic and spells by e-mail, among which appeared an invocation of Lilith. The rite was intended to summon up her spirit and infuse it into the participants. The text contained the following preliminary warnings:

> Lilith is a primal egregore of the dark anima. She is unfettered sexual dominance and power. This invocation should not be attempted by those with little background in ceremonial magic, nor by those who harbor unresolved psychological problems related to sexuality ... If blood is to be drawn, or sexual activities ensure, all precautions pretaining [sic] to the prevention of diseases borne by blood or sexual fluids should properly be observed.[11]

⚴

The instructors recommend a selection of costumes and props for use in the ceremony, including black or purple candles, musk incense, a silver chalice, a black cape, preferably satin, and red wine. It seems that the optional bloodshed is likely, as they add to their list a scourging whip ('cat-o'-nine-tails type') and a sterile scalpel or Exacto (handicraft) knife.

The words of the spell used to call forth Lilith are adapted by the authors from the words purportedly uttered by a spirit conjured up in 1592 by Sir Edward Kelley, known as 'the grand impostor of the world', a friend of the Elizabethan magus Dr John Dee. (Having, with Dee, invented the Enochian magic system, and having famously succeeded in raising a ghost in a churchyard, Kelly renounced necromancy and took up counterfeiting and espionage instead.) This sequence is complemented with words taken from the 'Hymn to Hecate' quoted in Frater's *Secrets of the German Sex Magicians*:

> I am the daughter of Fortitude and ravished every hour from my youth … I am shadowed with the Circle of the Stars, and covered with the morning clouds. My feet are swifter than the winds, and my hands are sweeter than the morning dew … I am deflowered, yet a virgin; I sanctify and am not sanctified. Happy is he that embraceth me: for in the night season I am sweet, and in the day full of pleasure. My company is a harmony of many symbols, and my lips sweeter than health itself. I am a harlot for such as ravish me, and a virgin with such as know me not … make yourselves holy, and put on righteousness. Cast out your old strumpets, and burn their clothes and then I will bring forth children unto you and they shall be the Sons of Comfort in the Age that is to come.[12]

The participants are then required to chant, 'Flesh will she eat, blood will she drink!' while they wait, prostrate, to be overcome by the presence of the goddess. They can indulge in whatever form of frenzy (scourging, orgiastic coupling, etc.) the rite-leader dictates on Lilith's behalf. They end the ceremony by commanding the incarnate spirit to vouchsafe to them a magic Word of Power for their future use in magicking;

Black Moon, Lilith,
Mare of Night,
You cast your litter to the ground,
Speak the name and take to flight,
Utter now the secret sound![13]

✡

Less exotically, Lilith has also been adopted as the name of a Jewish women's quarterly magazine published in the USA. The publication offers in its own words 'American Jewish perceptions on Race, Gender and Class'; specimen articles during 1997 included 'Women and Yiddish', 'Gender and Assimilation in Modern Jewish History' and 'Sexing the Answering Machine'. The old semi-divine Lilith was indeed the Mother of Demons: she was the progenitor of subsequent generations of *lamia*, *larvae*, *empusas*, *striges* and Vampires. And now she is revitalized in the guise of a liberating icon of guiltless femininity, a key player in the neo-pagan and neo-Judaic pantheons.

The same feminine principle, of succubus, stealer of children and flesh-and-blood-consuming demoness produced other mythical beings whose names have figured in literary sources and histories. The *lamia*, a sucker of blood, a stealer of children and a sorceress, appears in Greek and Roman legend. She began as a Libyan queen abandoned by the god Zeus and robbed of her children by his wife, Hera. Afterwards she avenged her loss by stealing the children of others.[14] Other names bestowed on the she-devils include the *empusae* (literally, 'forcers-in', after Empusa, bronze-footed monster and daughter of Hecate, the goddess of sorcery and the underworld), the *mormolyceia* ('terrifying wolves'), and later the *striges* (the plural of *strix*, a night-witch, half crow or owl and half woman) who in turn became the *strigon* of Adriatic folklore, a Vampire who could be male or female.

The underlying concepts that gave rise to all these demonic sisters are clear: a patriarchal culture's fear and loathing of the woman who in the guise of beauty literally or metaphorically seduces the male from righteousness; the personification of the nightmare and night-suffocation; the bugbear whose function is to frighten children into obedience and enforce correct childcare procedures in mothers.

☿

In the Austrian Burgenland, in the very centre of old Europe, a short distance from the borders of modern Hungary and Slovakia, stands the hilltop castle of Lockenhaus, known to the Hungarian families who were its former owners at Léka. Curious present-day tourists, as they are guided nervously around the crypt that lies beneath the fortress, are told of the exploits of the warrior knight, Count Francis Nádasdy, the 'Black Bey of Hungary', whose relatives are buried in that place. But it is not the phantom of the Black Bey, fearsome though he was, who reaches invisibly out of the darkness to clutch at the visitors' hands, but of his wife, a Lilith come to life, the terrible 'Blood Countess', Elisabeth Báthory.

Not far away atop an even more massive peak is the impregnable castle of Forchtenstein, where Elisabeth's maimed victims are said to have been cast down into the 142-metre-deep well after serving as the playthings in her games of torture and blood-bathing. Even now, it is said, the feeble cries of the murdered maidens can sometimes be heard in the caverns under the mountain, mingled with the pleadings of the Turkish prisoners-of-war who slaved for decades to dig the tunnels in the solid rock.

This same feudal sorceress, celebrated in poetry, literature and in the bedtime stories that are used to frighten children throughout Central Europe, haunts other sites in the much-haunted fringes of the old Habsburg lands. Most notably the 'White Lady' is reported to appear at the scene of her own eventual death, among the ruins of her castle at Čachtice, high in the Carpathian mountains of present-day Slovakia. Sometimes, particularly at dusk after one or two glasses of *unicum* or *pálinka*, country people in the wild eastern regions of Hungary, the land of her birth, fancy that they see her cavorting with the other *kis-asszony*, the spirits of young ladies who infest the crossroads and field edges at midsummer and on saints' days and dance away unwary travellers to their deaths.

A most notorious female Vampire, an icon of cruelty cited in text after text, Countess Báthory was a real historical personage who died in captivity in 1614. The legends that have coalesced around Elisabeth depict her as a torturer and murderer of servant girls – between eight and 650 victims are claimed, depending upon sources – who bathed in the blood of these innocents to preserve her own beauty. Strictly speaking the hallmark of the true Vampire is missing: blood-drinking was not alleged in the early accounts, although cannibalism and black magic were, but Báthory has been appropriated as a sadist, dominatrix and lesbian seducer as well as appearing in vampire anthologies as a female counterpart to Vlad Ţepeş, the 'historical Dracula' of Transylvania. As such she has formed the centrepiece for a number of (wildly inaccurate) websites on the Internet.

It is often claimed that Báthory provided one of the sources for Bram Stoker's fictional version of *Dracula*, given that he had certainly read the Reverend Sabine Baring-Gould's work on werewolves, in which she features, and Stoker had dined with the Hungarian scholar and spy Ármin Vambéry, who must have been familiar with her reputation. There is, nevertheless, no reference in Stoker's copious notes to the Hungarian Blood Countess, and if the dead heroine of his posthumously published fragment, *Dracula's Guest*, the Styrian Countess Dolingen, resembles her, it is probably because Stoker had been inspired by an earlier fiction by a fellow-Irishman, the novella *Carmilla* by J. Sheridan le Fanu (see pages 260–2).

Whether there is a Dracula connection or not, the case of Countess Báthory provides a fascinating example of how real political and domestic dramas were reworked and mythicized in succession for an Enlightenment, Victorian and twentieth-century audience. The truth is that the legendary Elisabeth has indeed permeated Vampire literature and Vampire iconography. The first account of her crimes to circulate outside Hungary was published by the Jesuit priest, Father László Túroczi, in 1729. I translated it into English for the first time:

> Elisabeth, washed in that deadly bath, appeared to herself yet more beautiful, under no other influence, no one will doubt, than diabolic mockery.

This first crime, born of her wilfulness, rendered her more courageous and thus thereafter many others were committed. The wicked deeds went on year after year and, you will be astonished to learn, even after the death of her husband, the widow, now advancing in years, was responsible for a sacrilegious shedding of blood ... There are some who believe that her rage led Elisabeth even to eat the bodies of the murdered ones, and she considered no delicacy more delightful. O, delights, obtained by utmost barbarism![15]

Born in 1560, she came from a dynasty of heroes who had ruled Hungary for three hundred years on behalf of its kings, and who reigned in Poland and Transylvania as kings and princes in their own right. Medieval codes of chivalry were a long time dying in Hungary – feudalism was not abolished there until 1848 – and the Countess and her husband Lord Nádasdy exercised, like other aristocrats, the right of life and death over their peasants and servants. Their own power was magnified by their personalities and reputations: the Black Bey was the defender of Christendom against the Turks at a crucial moment in Europe's history, when Islam might once and for all have overrun the West. Poems and pamphlets told of how he danced with the corpses of Turks dangling from his teeth and played bowls with their severed heads.

When Nádasdy died in 1604, Elisabeth took over the vast family estates in defiance of the jealous lords who schemed to dispossess her. She already enjoyed fame as the inheritor of the Báthory glory – her family were renowned for their savage bravery but were rumoured to be possessed. Once her husband was dead, so the stories go, Elisabeth, highly intelligent, cultivated and headstrong, was free to give full rein to her bloodlust and cruelty: moving from one to another of the score of magnificent castles and manors that belonged to her, she indulged with the help of a handful of trusted servants in a campaign of torture and murder directed at the many servant girls and daughters of the lesser nobility who were sent to her courts to better themselves. Rumours of Elisabeth's sinister pastimes and her dabbling in sorcery were rife throughout Hungary; in Vienna it was reported that the monks who lived next to her townhouse there were so incensed at the disturbance from the screams of her victims that they threw their clay drinking-pots at her walls until a deep pile of shards surrounded the residence.

In 1610, against a background of political turbulence (the Turks were still at the borders and there was a danger that Hungary might abandon the Empire and go over to a Báthory-led alliance in the east), George Thurzó, the Habsburg Emperor's vice-regent in Hungary began a secret investigation of the Countess, hearing depositions from almost three hundred witnesses. In her absence the Countess was accused of horrific tortures and the murder of 650 virgins. Just before the New Year celebrations in 1611, Thurzó led a posse of soldiers through the snow-covered forests and along the frozen pathways to the manor-house beneath the castle at Čachtice where he surprised the Countess at dinner. By Thurzó's orders the lady was summarily walled up in her castle; her servant-confidants were dragged away to torture and public execution. Three years later Elisabeth, who had miraculously survived her imprisonment thus far, was found dead at dawn on the floor of her cell. She was the real-life feudal faery queen, the aristocratic sorceress, the wicked stepmother and the medieval *femme fatale*, the last of her line.

The real lady was quickly transformed into a mythical figure, a symbol of feminine evil whose story was embellished down the centuries. Not long after her death the legends of her blood-bathing arose: local people said that she had drained the blood of her victims in order to anoint her own milky-white skin and preserve her beauty for ever. One by one the defenders of Catholicism, Nationalism, Freudianism and Marxism came forward to reinterpret Elisabeth for their own ends; writers of fairy stories, celebrators of the Gothic horror novel, the avant-garde and Hammer Films adopted her as a heroine. Meanwhile her memory lingers, like her ghost, around the scenes of her real or imagined crimes. Strangely it is not the helpless serving-girls in their hundreds who are overheard calling across the hillsides and rustling among the stones of ruined castles and long-overgrown graveyards: it is Bátoričká ('little Báthory'), the Countess herself, who appears in those places.

Only recently has new research revealed another side to the story of the woman nicknamed 'Countess Dracula' in English. Papers unearthed in the previously inaccessible archives of eastern Europe show that a complex conspiracy surrounded her arrest and the show trial at which she was not allowed to present her case. There is no doubt that she was a victim of the political machinations of the Austrians and the greed of the relatives who coveted her lands – and were the 'tortures' really forms of sympathetic magic, healing processes carried out by a gifted and humane white witch? She was certainly a witch or a patron of witches, and the distinction between *maleficium* and folk-healing was ill-defined in those days.[16]

☿

Although our modern perception of the fictional Vampire is distorted by the overwhelming influence of that middle-aged gentleman Count Dracula, when in the eighteenth century the blood-sucker first made the transition from village ghoul to literary protagonist, via Imperial documents and salon gossip, it was again as a *femme fatale*, a lady, that she was cast. Romantic and Gothic poets and novelists took the life-draining quality of their near-contemporary the Slav revenant and projected it on to the classical heroine, or anti-heroine, adapting models from authentic Greek and Roman sources. Goethe revived a succubus figure who would 'suck [the hero's] life-blood from his heart with gusto' in 'Die Braut von Korinth' ('The Bride of Corinth') of 1797, which was later reprised, still decorously, in English in Keats's 'The Lamia' ('swoon'd murmuring of love, and pale with pain') and Coleridge's 'Christabel'.

For the jaded palate of the modern reader Bürger's *Lenore* of 1773 is more pleasingly grisly in its treatment, as is Hoffman's *Aurelia*: '... he felt his hand grasped as if in a vice by fingers cold and stiff as death, and the tall bony form of the Baroness, who was staring at him with eyes evidently deprived of the faculty of sight, seemed to him in its gay many-tinted attire like some bedizened corpse'. Another landmark in the German transition from classical to Gothic was Johan Ludwig Tieck's work, *Wake Not the Dead*, written around 1800:

> ... all that Brunhilda now possessed was a chilled existence, colder than that of the snake ... It was necessary that a magic draught should animate the dull current in her veins, and awaken her to the glow of life and the flame of love; a potion of abomination – one not even to be named without a curse – human blood imbibed whilst yet warm from the veins of youth. This was the hellish drink for which she thirsted...
>
> ... Only during the twilight of the commencing or declining day did she ever walk abroad. But her favourite hour was when the phantom light of the moon bestowed on all objects a shadowy appearance, and a sombre hue. Always too at the crowing of the cock an involuntary shudder was observed to seize her limbs...
>
> ... Whenever she beheld some innocent child whose lovely face denoted the exuberance of infantile health and vigour, she would entice it by soothing words and fond caresses into her most secret apartment, where lulling it to sleep in her arms, she would suck from its bosom the warm, purple tide of life. Nor were youths of either sex safe from her horrid attack. Having first breathed upon her happy victim, who never failed to sink immediately into a lengthened sleep, she would then in a similar manner drain his veins of the vital juice. Thus children, youths, and maidens quickly faded away, as flowers gnawed by the cankering worm: the fullness of their limbs disappeared; a sallow hue succeeded to the rosy freshness of their cheeks; the liquid lustre of the eye was deadened; and their locks became thin and grey, as if already ravaged by the storm of life. The grave swallowed up one after another, or did the miserable victim survive, he became cadaverous and wrinkled even in the morn of existence...[17]

The work powerfully evokes the reversal of the mother-instinct and the helplessness of parents in the face of the loss of their children.

Writing at almost the same time as Tieck, the English author Southey was still drawing inspiration from classical sources, and the melodrama had not yet moved so far towards the grotesque. At midnight Thalaba shelters from a storm by the tomb of his beloved wife, Oneiza:

> And in that hideous light
> Oneiza stood before them. It was She ...
> Her very lineaments, – and such as death
> Had changed them, livid cheeks, and lips of blue;
> But in her eyes there dwelt
> Brightness more terrible
> Than all the loathsomeness of death
> 'Still art thou living, wretch?'
> In hollow tones she cried to Thalaba;
> 'And must I nightly leave my grave
> To tell thee, still in vain,
> God hath abandon'd thee?'

Thalaba's companion, Oneiza's father, commands him to transfix the fiend with a lance, but he cannot bring himself to do so:

> When Moath firm of hearth,
> Perform'd the bidding; through the vampire corpse
> He thrust his lance; it fell
> And howling with the wound,
> Its fiendish tenant fled.
> A sapphire light fell on them,
> and garmented with glory, in their sight
> Oneiza's spirit stood.[18]

Nearly four thousand years later, the echoes of Gilgamesh were still reverberating.

As well as evoking the 'sublime of terror' thrillingly to agitate the sensibilities of the refined reader, these works drew, all to some extent, their genuinely affecting power from a juxtaposition of love and death that was not a mere conceit of fiction. Every family, rich or poor, knew intimately the poignancy of watching a loved one's vitality fade away to nothing. Many must have fantasized hopelessly that in Théophile Gautier's words, 'the blood was again beginning to circulate, under that lifeless pallor, although she remained motionless'.[19]

At the end of the eighteenth century a new cult of 'feeling' allowed men as well as women openly to weep and mourn, obliquely acknowledging their vulnerability to the agents of lifelessness. Despite the appearance of the first masculine Vampires in the literary tradition – Kleist's *Die Marquise von O.* in 1805 featured the Russian expatriate Count F., an undead seducer, and Polidori's Lord Ruthven followed in 1819 – the majority of Vampires, including Kleist's heroine of 1808, the Amazon Penthesilea, were female, and as the years passed the post-Gothic tradition rendered them ever more sexually rapacious and celebrated their malignity – and their male victims' abjection – with greater and greater relish.

Of writers in English it was Poe ('The Angels sob at vermin fangs,/In human gore imbued') who introduced a necrophiliac note in his 'Leonora' and 'Ligeia'; among several Frenchmen to wallow in sinful victimhood, Baudelaire devoted two poems to the supernatural feminine oppressor. The first, 'Le Vampire', a lament by a besotted lover, is relatively restrained, 'Alas! poison and the sword spurned me saying/...Fool! if our efforts were to deliver you from her rule,/your own kisses would revive the corpse of your vampire!', at least by the standards of the second, 'Les Métamorphoses du Vampire', which was banned as soon as it appeared, and its author and publisher prosecuted for obscenity:

When she had sucked all the marrow from my bones,
And when I turned languidly towards her to bestow a loving kiss,
I saw there nothing but a sticky-sided wineskin, full to bursting with pus!
I screwed my two eyes shut in cold terror, and when I looked again?
With the most vivid clarity I saw at my side, not the potent plaything,
Who seemed to have gorged herself with blood,
But, quaking confusedly there, the remnants of a skeleton,
Creaking out the grating cry of a weathercock,

Or of a shop-sign, swinging, buffeted in the wind of a winter night.
At the end of its iron pole.

(The image of the wineskin and its foul contents recalls one of many Balkan versions of the Vampire from folklore; the fiend can appear in the form of a bag brimming with blood, likened by writers to the *gaida*,[20] the Balkan bagpipe.)

Following behind the written celebrations of the female Vampire came a series of paintings, almost a sub-genre in themselves, showing the succubus at work on her prey: the Norwegian Edvard Munch, the Hungarian István Czók and the Frenchman Valère Bernard were the best-known exemplars. In the 1890s Philip Burne-Jones painted her for a British public in a daring canvas showing a beautiful female Vampire astride a male victim; his cousin Rudyard Kipling wrote a poem on the same theme. The painting represented the Vampire as the dark-haired, sultry corrupter of British virtue, the poem conjures up a now-hilarious sense of futile manly decency confounded by the heedless instinctual cruelty of the female of the species – a misogynistic Anglo-Saxon jingle to contrast with Baudelaire's anguished delirium.

A fool there was and he made his prayer
(Even as you and I!)
To a rag and bone and a hank of hair
(We called her the woman who did not care).
But the fool he called her his lady fair
(Even as you and I!)

Oh, the years we waste and the tears we waste
And the work of our head and hand,
Belong to the woman who did not know
(And now we know that she never could know)
And did not understand.

. . .

The fool was stripped to his foolish hide
(Even as you and I!)
Which she might have seen as she threw him aside –
(But it isn't on record the lady tried)
So some of him lived but the most of him died
(Even as you and I!)

And it isn't the shame and it isn't the blame
That stings like a white-hot brand,
It's coming to know that she never knew why
(Seeing at last she could never know why)
And never could understand.[21]

༄

Fortunately for women, at least, it is no longer permissible to cast them as pitiless, instinctive sirens as Kipling did (unless, like the British novelist Martin Amis with his heroine Nicola Six, it is done under cover of irony). For females within the Vampire genre, though, in the later part of the twentieth century their portrayal has descended from the literally sublime to the ridiculous. In the cinema, coinciding with the real signs of female empowerment in the early 1970s, there was a handful of attempts to film a dominant Báthory-like character, but these were invariably skewed by their male directors, producers and distributors towards a voyeuristic celebration of lesbianism. Otherwise, the blood-sucking women in Vampire movies remained as titillating nonentities – accessories in male fantasy – the role that they also played in pulp fiction and cartoons. Only two years before the millennium a movie like *Razorblade Smile*, a British independent production, was widely promoted in Vampire fanzines and at Goth conventions, yet its ambitions extent no further than a repetition of empty visual clichés with routine, cursory nods at leather fetishism, submission/domination and castration fantasies.

A more interesting novelty is the success of the TV series *Buffy, the Vampire Slayer*, a spin-off from a Hollywood teen-pic featuring a high-school cheerleader defending her uncomprehending community from shapeshifting manifestations of ultimate evil. Buffy's antics carry an inspiring message: that adolescents can be morally empowered (even if by magical intervention) and that the unseen terrors that seem to threaten the serenity of family and school life can be overcome. Because her enemies are soulless – in fact, dead already – they provide ideal fodder for spectacular acts of violent retribution; like extraterrestrials, Vampires have replaced the Red Indian and the Nazi as legitimate targets. *Buffy* updates the themes of chastity compromised (in the context of dating rather than courting) and the idea of secret, nefarious conspiracies undermining the wholesome high-school institutions – cheerleading sisterhoods, study-groups, prom-nights. Adults – parents and teachers – are neg-ligent, distracted and uncertain as well as oblivious to the ghouls and demons who lurk every-threateningly on the margins of her world, and there are usually some among her fellow students who will deludedly invite the darkness in.

Ironically, one of the most enduring (even dignified) post-war images of vampiric womanhood is the svelte, imperious Morticia Addams, the demonic counterpart of the 1950s all-American home-maker as incarnated in Charles Addams's drawings, their television and film recreations and in Morticia's TV-vamp epigones, Vampira and Elvira. The most famous comic-book Vampire, the voluptuous Vampirella, who first appeared in 1969, combined the US graphic tradition of the superhero comic strip with the more overtly erotic look of Italian, Spanish and French *bandes dessinées*. Even when revived in the 1990s the series' visual style tended to glossiness and not the more visceral, shocking aesthetics of underground or horror comics, with the result that Vampirella always seems to be hedging her bets; she never resolves the paradox of good or evil. In trying to embody the seductive savagery of vampirism while stuck on the side of 'good' and thus prohibited from actually vampirizing ('A man is a fragile thing. It would be so easy to tear them, drain them of warm, bubbling life … it would be a thrill … but then could I ever live up to my birthright?'[22]) she is ultimately anodyne, merely another pneumatic tease masquerading as a strong woman for the entertainment of hapless males. A new cartoon Vampire girl, Purgatori, was introduced in 1998, but offered only more extravagant graphics. In the revealing words of London Vampyre fan and impresario Louis Ravensfield, 'Purgatori is a tall, slim, long-haired, busty, horned, sexy vampire vixen – hey, sounds like my kinda woman, a "top bit of totty" '[23]

It is ironic that while there are many strong, articulate women among the Goth and Real Vampire communities – at Internet websites, at a recent count, they outnumber the males – the female representations of the Vampire persona that escape into the commercial world are still regressive and one-dimensional. The contradictions involved were again illustrated by the two major gatherings of Vampire fans in the UK in 1997 and 1998; at the first, the *Dracula* centenary convention at Whitby, there were divas performing opera, female rock musicians playing in bands and women giving lectures from the stage; at the Vampyria II event in London the following year the females on display played three roles only: mute handmaiden, supine sacrificial victim and caged go-go dancer.

Several women are engaged, very successfully, in playing with the Vampire persona and orchestrating the Vampire myth, especially in the field of fiction where the best-selling authors Anne Rice and Chelsea Quinn Yarbro rely almost wholly on masculine Vampire protagonists. Poppy Z. Brite's stories, dwelling on fetor, decay and mutation, furnish a neo-Gothic and Goth counterpoint to the bodice-rippers. In the 1980s and 1990s the writers who published popular factual treatments were also predominantly female: Jeanne Youngson, Rosemary Guiley, Norine Dresser, Olga Hoyt, Manuela Dunn Mascetti, Katherine Ramsland and the *Dracula* expert Elizabeth Miller. There is an appreciative rather than coldly analytical quality to all their works: the Vampire, especially in the guise of a suave and fatally dangerous seducer, seems to have appealed particularly to ladies of a certain age.

In avant-garde and underground artistic milieux, women have

avoided the Vampire label, with its taint of exploitation and caricature, but have explored the themes of blood, power and transgression outside the explicit tradition. The French artist Orlan has practised the manipulation of her own body by plastic surgery, even implanting realistic horns on her forehead. The Dutch painter and sculptress Erzsébet Baerveldt, who has adopted the cause and the persona of Countess Elisabeth Báthory, changing her first name to that of her muse and impersonating her in portraits and installations, in her work sees vampirism as a useful metaphor for new ways of considering blood and the body and ritual. Her video-work *Suc* (French for 'sap' or 'juice') shows her sucking and smearing herself with her own blood before a mirror. The short sequence is a complicated mix of introspection, autoeroticism and narcissism, an exploration of the body above, below and through its surfaces. Baerveldt refers scathingly to attempts to apply 'objective' scientific or sociological analyses to those who have considered themselves Vampires. Privately she views vampirism as an authentic condition, which is both a state of mind and a recognition of new, or at least previously unrecognized, biological imperatives – ideas which draw upon traditions of alchemy as well as alternative dietary and genetic theories, and which are close to those held by some of the Real Vampires quoted elsewhere in these pages.

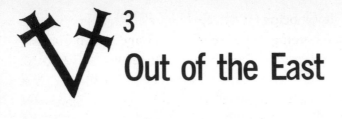

3
Out of the East

With blood his visage was distain'd
Ensanguin'd were his frightful eyes,
Each sign of former life remain'd
Save that all motionless he lies . . .

. . . His jaws cadaverous were besmear'd
With clotted carnage o'er and o'er,
And all his horrid whole appear'd
Distent, and fill'd with human gore!

John Stagg, 'The Vampyre', 1810

It is certainly conceivable that the Vampire forms part of some prehistoric set of universal categories embedded in human psychology, culture and myth, but this cannot be proven. What is certain is that a more or less coherent Eurasian tradition of superstition, in which a proto-Vampire features, was preserved and elaborated by the peoples of central, eastern and south-eastern Europe.

We can trace a sort of evolution of the Vampire from the very earliest written sources – but the word 'evolution' is misleading as it implies a progression from primitive to complex, and it is far from sure that the imagined universes of our far-off ancestors were any less complicated than our own. If we do apply this long perspective, we see the blood-drinker migrate and transmogrify through several distinct phases. Even in the first phase, which takes in terrible gods and the demon haunters of empty spaces, the Vampire is a synthesis rather than a unitary being: it already has elements of the personifications of meteorology; the eaters of sun and moon and the colours of sunsets and storms. It incorporates characteristics of predators and carrion-eaters – vultures, owls, wolves, hyenas – and it is associated intimately with the dead and their abode in cemeteries and desert places.

The commonly accepted path by which beliefs change and cohere begins with cosmological metaphors: the dusk 'eating' the sun, the thunderstorm as the crash of hammer on anvil. These images are then personified more specifically and named, and the disembodied forces of destruction evoked are allowed to take on the forms of living beings – animal, human or a combination of both. At the same time certain human beings, the seers and the wielders of talismans and totems, acquire their special status by claiming to interact with the invisible dimensions and communicate with spirits and deities on the tribe's behalf, propitiating them and annexing their powers by depiction, ritual and, crucially, impersonation. As far as we can tell there were no walls in men's and women's imaginations separating the invisible from the visible, consciousness from trance, mischievous daemon from benevolent, human from animal, but there were, we know, binary conceptions of matter and ether, light and dark, which figured largely in their minds and their fireside stories.

It is interesting to see the latest forms of vampirism in terms of the return of a sort of dualism. With the waning of the influence of orthodox Christianity upon popular culture and upon folk beliefs (witness the upsurge of new-age pantheism, the elevation of angel and faery archetypes over saints), the recognition and, following that, the embracing of the Dark Half has recurred, especially in the USA where there is an actual dualism in the form of born-again devil-baiting Christianity versus a whole set of underground/alternative gestures. In a long perspective we can see the whole history of the Vampire as a submerging and resurfacing of ideas based on dualism, folk-experience and an awareness of the natural world, acting in perpetual opposition to the monist orthodoxies which have served to buttress ruling élites.

And this Vampire tradition – a treasure trove of many different Vampires: the *lamia*, the *strix* or *strigon*, the *vedavec*, the *pijavica*, the *vukodlak* – is essentially a shamanic tradition, perhaps unchanged in its fundamentals from prehistoric times to the early twentieth century when the last stakings of kudlaks in the Balkans were reported. In a strange way we have come full circle since those prehistoric days of the shamanic tricksters who disguised themselves as animal and genii to do battle on our behalf in a parallel spirit world. The human individual is once again treating the inhabitants of the shadow realm not as something unreachable and insubstantial but as entities to impersonate, as magic dramas to enact. The motives are not necessarily the same – today it is wilful individualist transgression, then it was maintaining a privileged status within the group – but in both cases there is the urge to transcendence, the acquisition of power (as if) by magic.

The literature has long accepted that Slavonic cultures above all others nurtured and disseminated the European Vampire myth. Many previous writers have assumed, without necessarily investigating their assumptions, that their origins lie somewhere 'further east', and that they have been mediated somehow by the dualist beliefs that permeated the eastern Mediterranean region from antiquity. The Vampire superstition may be bound up with the practice of burial and its opposition to the cremation practised by other tribes; obviously in a literal-minded interpretation only a corpse put whole into the earth can easily return from the dead in one recognizable piece. This may point back to ethnic rivalries and prejudices in the period before the Slavonic tribes migrated west and south, when they lived in proximity with Turkic and Iranian communities, and Siberian nomads. The Slavs in ancient times, Wiesthaler says, are the only people, among many who knew the Vampire, to elevate it to the status of a semi-deity and even to worship it and sacrifice to it.[1]

Even before their southward penetration of the Balkan peninsula between the fifth and seventh centuries AD the Slav peoples had also come into contact with other eastern, notably Iranian, belief systems, which had left some traces on their languages and quite possibly on their customs, too. Once they had arrived at the Adriatic and Mediterranean, they would have encountered the remnants of the mystery cult of Mithras and the influence of the later Manichaean heresy, both distant offshoots of the Zoroastrian religion of the Ancient Persians. The teachings of Zoroaster, which were disseminated in the seventh century BC, described the unending struggle between Ormazd, the spirit of good and Ahriman, the spirit of evil. Mithras, a version of Ormazd, was the god of light and truth, Mani was the prophet of *mana*, the principle of light and good. All these religions were dualist: they recognized the dual nature of the universe and humanity, giving the forces of Evil, which were identified with darkness, earth, the tomb and corruptible flesh, an equal status with Good, which was identified with Light and the survival of the human soul. In the cosmic and microcosmic struggle, the ultimate prevailing of Good depended upon the liberation of this pure and immaterial soul from the prison of matter and the grave.

In Bulgaria in the tenth century these earlier dualist beliefs, together with elements of Christianity, were synthesized by a sect led by a prophet known as Bogumil ('Beloved of God') and, despite persecution, Bogomilism, as the movement was known, became a potent force throughout south-eastern Europe, and Bogomil missionaries carried their doctrines to the West. (Interestingly, the few vampire tales from medieval England coincided with the activities of Bogomil-inspired Albigensian and Cathar heretics just across the Channel.)

From the little that is known of the Bogomils' ideas it seems that the concept of the omnipresent threat of the Force of Destruction, together with the possession of the corpse and its grave by demons were central tenets. The imagery of light and dark were still prevalent: the evil that stalked a human throughout his or her existence was likened to the shadow; the opposing Force of Creation was symbolized by the sun at dawn and by life-giving air, water and, to a lesser extent, blood.

There was a long dark age for the Slav peoples in eastern and southern Europe, during which their tribes were subjugated, their customs and beliefs were submerged, and scarcely any literature encoded and preserved their ideas. Nevertheless, from the sparse record and from observations made by neighbours, it is clear that strongly dualist concepts of a Good God and a Bad God, of the human body belonging to the devil and its soul to the Good God were prevalent in the early medieval period and remained embedded in the form of the metaphors of light and dark, which suffused Slavonic folk-tales until well into the twentieth century.

It is not surprising that the legend flourished in Orthodox areas, as the Greek Church's doctrines encouraged it (non-putrefaction was a sign either of sanctity or its opposite, heresy, devilishness). Among the words with which the Orthodox Church curses its heretics: 'Your place shall be with the devil and the traitor Judas, and after that do not turn into ashes, but remain as undecayed as stone and iron.'

In tombs of gold and lapis lazuli
Bodies of holy men and women exude
Miraculous oil, odour of violet.

But under heavy loads of trampled clay
Lie bodies of the vampires full of blood;
Their shrouds are bloody and their lips are wet.[2]

✝✝

In pinpointing the actual origin of the being known as the Vampire – something no history has hitherto managed to do – our only real evidence is linguistic. The name *vampir* itself was first recorded in a written source in Serbia in the fifteenth century, but related words such as *upir* are much older, first appearing in the tenth century, around the time that the dualist heresies and other forms of paganism were competing for converts with Orthodox Christianity.

The oldest cognate on record, and perhaps the ancestral term is *Upyr*, used as part of a nickname or epithet *Upyr' Likhyj* ('wicked Vampire') ascribed to a Russian prince in the eleventh century – it appeared in Old Russian chronicles in 1047 and 1059. In Old Polish *upier* and *upior* were the forms, *upterszyca* was a later variant. Another set of words – including Kashubian *vieszczy*, Serbian *vjestica*, Slovene *vestica, vedunec, vedomec, vedarec* are all based on the root *ved-* meaning 'to know', and were originally applied to shamans, wise-folk, wizards or witches but later, like the *volkodlak* (first recorded in Serbia in 1262), were absorbed into the composite Vampire figure.

I am inclined to think that a specific practice, that of naming, then staking and burning real individuals suspected of becoming blood-drinking spectres, is much earlier than these religious rivalries, but no corroborating evidence for this exists. Jan L. Perkowski suggested that the first part of the word might be a reference to the name of a pagan god – the Armenian Vaghan or the Manichaean Bam, but this cannot be proven. He also considered the possibility that it derives from the personal pronoun 'you', which occurs in all Slav tongues with a first element *va-*, but as he himself warns, 'Too many of the *vampir* etymologies are the products of antiquing bolstered by associative logic. Maybe an old manuscript will be found some day and all will become clear. Until then it will remain 90 per cent speculation.'[3]

Slovene and Croatian lexicographers have suggested that the original term would have been *Q-pir*, where the *ǫ-* is a negative prefix and *pir* an archaic Indo-European cognate of Greek *pyr*, 'fire' (hence also an ancestor of English pyre and fire). The meaning would be 'he who was not given to the fire'; this would point to the Slavonic urn burial being differentiated from cremation.[4]

Dr Bruce McClelland of the University of Virginia, who describes himself as a South Slavic demonologist, has researched the origins of the very first Vampires to bear the name. He disagrees vehemently with the burial/cremation hypothesis and is certain that he has discovered the source of the concept and term, Upir (and its later variants, *vampir, lampir, dhampir, vopyr, wupij*, etc.) in early texts referring to pagan sacrifice and feasting: '*Pir* occurs in Old Slavonic (there is textual evidence) with the meaning "feast" or "libation"; some form of *va*, or *va na* could have represented "in", "among" and have evolved into *u-* in Eastern Slavonic (Russian, Polish), *vam-* in

Southern Slavonic (Serbian, Bulgarian), giving the forms *upir* and *vampir* that we know from written sources.'

McClelland underlines that '... mythology about the return of the dead is commonplace, if not universal. But Vampires are specific "incarnations" of such notions, dependent upon an alchemical syncretism between Christianity and certain types of Indo-European paganism.'[5]

> ... the original Vampire was probably an initiate of some sort. This is supported by the initiatory basis of his cousin the *vrkolaka*, [another name for the *volkodlak*, originally a shaman disguised by a wolf-pelt] but also by the *pir* angle, and by his historical connection to the Bulgarian *talasum*, a demon or spirit that guards a space where an animal's blood has been poured or where an animal or human has been immured in the foundation. The *talasum* is also associated with oaths surrounding buried treasure...

The first *upirs*, the forerunners of the Vampires, were notable for carrying out sacrifices, then themselves being ritually punished after death by being dug up and posthumously 'executed'. 'They were, according to this theory, indigenous Thracians in the Balkans who were resistant to Christianization. In Russian texts, however, it was the pagan Slavs who were castigated for indulging in sacrificial feasting. By the eleventh century, whence comes our first written reference, it was not the act of sacrifice *per se* that scandalized the pious, but rather the abandonment – dancing, feasting, drinking – that caused the Christians such consternation.'

'... the Vampire is a scapegoat, but of a special sort: he is dead. Since the original Vampires were probably people who performed sacrifices, actions taken against the corpses of Vampires represent a sort of "sacrificing the sacrificers" ... Destruction of the Vampire restores social order. The scapegoating process meanwhile sanctifies the victim...'

Then as now the Vampire was an outsider, a pariah of some sort who threatened the dominant order: 'He is a pagan, a heretic, a drunk, a person with the wrong values ... But the vengeance wreaked on a corpse, as it turns out, does no harm ...' McClelland points out that the staking and burning of *upirs*, carried out, he thinks, by Christians, although it was dramatic and spectacular, was a much gentler version of the collective violence that earlier societies had practised on living scapegoats.

Whether McClelland is right and the Vampire originated from a specific collision of post-Christian beliefs, or whether the notion was formed during the prehistoric wanderings of the Slavonic and Turkic peoples can probably never be resolved with certainty. This negative conclusion nevertheless takes us further than vampire scholarship has ever gone before.

ѵ

The ancient folk Vampire, in its myriad forms as evoked in thousands upon thousands of spoken tales, made absolutely no impression on the educated classes until a combining of factors accidentally pushed it centre-stage. The so-called Vampire craze or Vampire epidemic that swept Europe, or at least galvanized its salon society in the eighteenth century, was not a new phenomenon at all: what was new was simply that the stories of Vampire revenants were noticed and circulated by the authorities, first in the Habsburg Empire and then in the capitals of Western Europe. It is only recently, though, that the Hungarian historian Gábor Klaniczay has drawn attention to the link between the new Enlightenment fascination with the Vampire and the ending of the centuries-long persecution of that other folk-devil, the witch.

The immediate trigger for the Habsburg Empress Maria-Theresa's legislation against superstition, starting with a ban on measures against the undead, but extended shortly after to encompass witch-persecution, fortune-telling, divination and digging for magic treasures, was the scandal involving a woman named Rosina Polákin, whose body was exhumed, dragged ceremonially through an opening in the wall of the graveyard by members of her family, beheaded and then burned, in order to end her vampiric attacks on her living neighbours. The case, a classic in which a local outcry had prompted the authorities to inspect the marvellously preserved corpse, took place in the village of Hermersdorf on the borders of Silesia and Moravia in 1755.

Let us examine the alleged facts offered as proof of vampirism. Rosina Iolackin [probably Polákin], deceased on 22 December 1754, was disinterred on 19 January 1755 and declared to be a Vampire fit for the fire because she was found intact in her grave. In the wintertime anatomists keep cadavers in the open air for six weeks and even for two months without putrefaction. And it is worth noting that this winter has been especially harsh.

Most of the bodies of the other cadavers unearthed had already decomposed: but it was enough that they were not completely putrefied, so, hurry, into the fire with them! What ignorance is this! Two specialists in sterlization, 'surgeons', who had never seen a dried-up cadaver, who knew nothing of the anatomy of the human body, as they themselves admitted to the commissioners, were the witnesses who were empowered to pass sentence of burning.

It is based on evidence of this sort that this entire history has been concocted, that sacrileges are being committed and that the sanctity of the grave is being violated; disgrace has been visited upon both the dead and their relatives, who can look forward only to more of the same treatment if such abuses do not gradually disappear: the corpses of infants who have died in a state of innocence are thrown to the executioners; men whose lives were above the slightest suspicion have the misfortune to be disinterred, just because an alleged witch has been buried [in the vicinity] . . . Where are the laws that authorize such sentences? It is allowed that they do not exist, but it is asserted baldly that custom requires them. What an abundance of outrages! Such things distress me and render me so furious that I must end my account here before I overstep the bounds of decency.[6]

Official accounts of vampiric activity actually began in Silesia in 1591. The Poles, Czechs and Germans of this region seem to have been particularly convinced that those guilty of 'self-murther' would return to plague the living. The story of one of them, the Shoemaker of Breslau, a suicide who was disinterred and cremated after allegedly haunting, tormenting and sucking the life from his neighbours, was retold for English readers by the Cambridge theologian Henry More in his *Antidote against Atheism*, published in 1653.

... to the astonishment of the Inhabitants of the place, there appears a *Spectrum* in the exact shape and habit of the deceased, and that not only in the night but at midday. Those that were asleep it terrified with horrible visions; those that were waking it would strike, pull, or press, lying heavy upon them like an *Ephialtes* [giant human-headed, serpent-bodied monsters of classical myth]; so that there were perpetual complaints every morning of their last night's rest through the whole town.

... this terrible *Apparition* would sometimes stand by their bedsides, sometimes cast itself upon the midst of their beds, would lie close to them, would miserably suffocate them, and would so strike them and pinch them, that not only blue marks, but plain impressions of his fingers would be upon sundry parts of their bodies in the morning.[7]

After eight months in the ground (significantly during the winter, between September and April) the suicide was disinterred:

When he was digged up, which was in the presence of the Magistracy of the Town, his body was found entire, not at all putrid, no ill smell about him saving the mustiness of the Grave-cloaths, his joints limber and flexible, as in those that are alive, his skin only flaccid, but a more fresh grown in the room of it, the wound of his throat gaping, but no gear of corruption in it; there was also observed a Magical mark in the great toe of his right foot, *viz.* an Excrescency in the form of a Rose.

After being exhibited for six days, he was reburied then dug up again on 7 May when it was observed

that he was grown more sensibly fleshy since his last interment. To be short, they cut off the Head, Arms, and Legs of the Corpse, and opening his Back, took out his Heart, which was as fresh and intire as in a Calf new kill'd. These, together with his Body, they put on a pile of wood, and burnt them to Ashes, which they carefully sweeping together, and putting into a Sack (that none might get them for wicked uses) poured them into the River, after which the *Spectrum* was never seen more.

The shoemaker's housemaid died some time after her master (the cause of death was not recorded), but eight days after her death she, too, returned and her spectre climbed on top of a fellow servant-girl, crushing her so that her eyes swelled up. This female revenant next attacked a child in his cradle, but was repelled by his nurse crossing herself and calling upon the name of Jesus. 'The next night she appeared in the shape of a Hen, which, when one of the maids of her house took to be so indeed, [i.e. mistook for a real hen] and followed her, the Hen grew to an immense bigness, and presently caught the Maid by the throat, and made it swell, so that she could neither eat nor drink of a good while after.'

The maid's ghost continued to slap and molest the townsfolk thereabouts for a month longer, sometimes appearing in her own form, but sometimes as a cat, a dog and a goat, until her body, too, was retrieved and burned. A vampirized person coming back in the form of a bird – here a hen – was not unheard-of, but also hints at an outbreak of hysteria in the servants' quarters.

In 1618 came reports from Bohemia and Moravia, in 1624 from Poland, then Greece, Istria in the northern Adriatic and Turkey in 1702. A notable returnee from the dead, whose notoriety was confined to eastern Europe, was Kaszparek of Lublo, a Hungarian merchant who died shortly after defrauding a Polish customer of his fortune and who reappeared in 1718 in his home town on the border between Hungary and Poland looking just as he had before his funeral. This disreputable vampire-ghost indecently assaulted the maidens working in the fields and tried to lie with his widow in her bed at night. He continued to torment and annoy his neighbours and the authorities were forced to investigate the case and interview purported witnesses. Several fruitless attempts were made to destroy his corpse in spite of his wife's protests, until finally his body was exhumed and burned, after which he was never seen again. In

Hungary the name Kaszparek has served as a nickname for the foolish or mischievous until recently.

The most famous official report of all described steps taken to end the reign of terror of a vampire in the village of Medvedija in Serbia. The somewhat clumsy narrative, under the heading *Visum et Repertum Est* ('As Seen and Reported') was reprinted in London and Paris only a month or so after its appearance in Vienna where it had been lodged with the Imperial office by the Austrian army surgeon, Johann Flückinger (or Fluchinger). It was included in a treatise published in Leipzig on 7 January 1732:

The foregoing unanimously declare that the *hajdúk* named Arnod Paole fell from a hay waggon and broke his neck. During his life this man frequently let it be said that he had been tormented by a Vampyr near Gossowa in Turkish Serbia. It was for that reason that he ate some earth from the Vampire's grave and smeared himself with its blood in order to be rid of the abominable torment. Twenty to thirty days after his death several people complained that the aforesaid Arnod Paole had tormented them, and four were actually killed by him. In order to rid themselves of this evil, at the counsel of their *Hadnack* [standard-bearer] (who had previously been up against such a thing), they exhumed this Arnod Paole forty days after his death and found that he was whole and intact with fresh blood flowing from his eyes, nose, mouth and ears. His shirt, shroud and coffin were blood-soaked. The old nails on his hands and feet had fallen out, and new ones had grown in their place. They could now see that he was really a Vampire. When they followed their custom and drove a stake through his heart, he let out a fierce shriek, and blood gushed forth from him. Then on that very day they cremated him and threw his ashes into the grave. The people also assert that all those who have been killed by Vampires must in turn become the same thing. For that reason the four people mentioned above were treated in a similar manner. Add to this the fact that this Arnod Paole attacked not only people, but also livestock, and he drained their blood. Since people fed on meat from this livestock, several Vampires again appeared among them. In the course of three months seven young and old people passed away, among whom several died without any previous illness in two or at most three days. *Hajduk* Jehovitza reports that his daughter-in-law Stanicka fifteen days earlier went to bed fresh and healthy. At midnight, however, she started from sleep with a frightful shriek, fear and trembling and complained that Milove, son of the *Hajduk*, who had died nine weeks earlier, had choked her, whereupon she experienced severe chest pains and grew worse from hour to hour, until she finally died on the third day.

The report goes on to detail the exhuming and examination of eleven corpses, of which eight were found to be 'in a vampiric state' – that is undecomposed or only partly decomposed. The army surgeon and his four colleagues supervised the disposal of the Vampire's victims: 'We ordered that the heads of all these Vampires be cut off by some travelling gypsies, their bodies be burnt and the ashes scattered on the Morava river, while the bodies that were in a decomposed state were placed back in their coffins.'

The case of Arnod 'Paole' – his real name was probably Pavle -was seized upon because it was set down in detail and came from a credible source: a medical man and an officer in the Imperial Habsburg Army. (Dr Polidori's editor used it to introduce his seminal English Vampire story in 1819: 'We have related this monstrous rodomontade because it seems better adapted to illustrate the subject of the present observations than any other instance we could adduce.') It seems to describe a localized outbreak of superstitious hysteria in a 'primitive' community. Pavle was a Serb, almost certainly of the Orthodox faith, and a war veteran; he was also a *hajdúk*, a member of a mercenary peasant militia, a free brotherhood of semi-brigands who were renowned for their fanatical ferocity. Pavle may well have been traumatized – like hundreds of other former soldiers wandering the fringes of Christian Europe – by his experiences while fighting the Turks on behalf of Austria-Hungary; he certainly believed that while serving in the Turkish zone ('Gossowa' was probably Kosowa in what is now Bulgaria) he had been contaminated by a 'Wampyr' (the report used the Germanized form of the Serb *vampir*) who may itself have been Serb or Turk, as the tradition existed in both societies.

A century and a half later, the atmosphere of a cemetery in the Turkish zone was evoked by the Transylvanian writer Jókai:

> The turbanned graves, with their coffin-like slabs, peer forth, ghastly white, from among the weeping willows. The sound of the approaching footsteps startles away a grey wolf from among the tombs, the sole inhabitant of that desolation. Since the last shower the clouds have dispersed, and here and there the dark-blue sky looks through with its diamond stars.[8]

Pavle had taken steps to cure himself by eating earth from the Vampire's grave and smearing himself with its blood, preventives which were recognized as far away as Poland. One of the women dug up by Flückinger had similarly tried to cure herself by drinking a Vampire's blood, presumably drawn illicitly from one of her dead neighbours.

One feature of the Pavle case, which passed more or less without comment, then and since, is that the principal Vampire has died *five years* before the outcry to which Flückinger responded. It seems that Pavle had introduced a 'Vampire anxiety' into the village, or had compounded an existing anxiety with his frequent announcements that he was tainted. After his death, any cluster of sudden or inexplicable deaths could be put down to him or those infected by him. The 'proof' was either that the victim had complained of nocturnal visits before death, or that they were found intact in the earth after death; such a diagnosis was convincing in the absence of any medical expertise, had all the weight of tradition behind it, and allowed the possibility of a radical do-it-yourself cure.

A normal result of a severe trauma – war, epidemic, the death of a loved one – is a feeling of profound exhaustion, lassitude, even paralysis, which may occur immediately or after some delay. These symptoms are similar to the effects of blood-letting or leeching, leading sufferers to think that they have been the subject of an attack by some unseen parasite. As well as shock and grief, those who suffer a sudden bereavement, or survive an epidemic in which friends and neighbours died, are likely to feel a mixture of guilt and disbelief. In all these circumstances there is another possible after-effect: the search for an external scapegoat, someone or something on to which the intolerable weight of emotions can be offloaded. When doctors and prayers are of no help, the same sort of scapegoat can be summoned up to account for the onset of sickness, too.

Displacement of guilt and grief explains the appearance of the ghost legions made up of former neighbours, which appeared in Hungary in 1600, and also applied to the other case that helped to trigger the eighteenth-century furore.

Peter Plogojevec died in 1725 in Kisilova, also in Austrian-occupied Serbia, and like Arnod Pavle was held responsible for a subsequent epidemic; in this case nine people suddenly fell ill and died ten weeks after Plogojevec. During the twenty-four-hour course of their sickness they described how he had come to them at night and lain on top of them. Plogojevec's wife, who survived, said that her late husband had called on her to take his slippers before leaving for another village. The inhabitants of Kisilova threatened to abandon the village *en masse* if nothing was done about the revenant, so a state representative took an Orthodox priest and supervised the disinterring. They found Plogojevec undecayed and exhibiting what were tantalizingly called *Wilde Zeichen* ('wild signs', sometimes thought to be a euphemism for a post-mortem erection as well as blood around the mouth). This time the authorities stood by as the local 'rabble', in the words of the report, staked and burned the corpse. (Montague Summers gives a more colourful and elaborate account of these events, but the details – the age of the deceased is given as sixty-two – seem to be his own invention.)

The savants of the early Enlightenment period debated the Vampire question in a series of treatises written in France, Germany and Italy. The debate intensified from the 1730s after the widespread publicity surrounding the cases of Pavle and Plogojevec. Some early writers, like Philip Rohr, in his *Dissertatio Historica-Philosophica de Masticatione Mortuorum* ('Historical-Philosophical Dissertation upon the Chewing of the Dead') of 1679, had accepted the widespread belief that the undead gnawed their grave-clothes and devoured their own flesh in their coffins, often making audible chewing noises and grunting like pigs. Although others, notably Michael Ranft in *De Masticatione Mortuorum in Tumulis Liber* ('The Book of the Chewing of the Dead in their Tombs'), published in 1728 in Leipzig, refuted this and put the malignant influences of the deceased down to dreams, the same 'facts' concerning the eating of shrouds were still being expounded in Middle Europe in the late nineteenth century and the sounds issuing from the unquiet dead haunted fevered imaginations for years after the epidemics had subsided: '... those cries are sometimes to be heard in the silence of starless nights ... the groans can be heard three leagues off, borne on the wind from one city to another'.[9]

The most important Italian contribution was Archbishop Giuseppe Davanzati's *Dissertazione sopra i Vampiri*, published in Naples in 1744, which concluded that in spite of the widespread and detailed reports of Vampire activity, these were the *effetto di fantasia* ('effect of the imagination'). He pointed out scathingly that those who were possessed were never persons of quality – 'a scholar, a philosopher, a theologian, a landowner or a bishop' – but always 'base-born plebeians' just as those who believed in the Vampire were 'the half-witted and the ignorant'.

Throughout the debate the French tended to adopt a more resolutely rationalist stance, culminating in Jean-Jacques Rousseau's ambiguous letter in which he pretends that the weight of evidence for the Vampire is overwhelming: 'The juridical proof is most complete. With all this, who believes in Vampires? Shall we all be damned for not having believed? a probable irony or provocation that has repeatedly been taken at face value ever since,[10] and Voltaire's sarcastic dismissal of the superstitions and his transference of the vampire metaphor for the first time to rapacious capitalists: 'We have never heard tell of Vampires in London, or even in Paris. I do admit that there were in both those cities speculators, brokers and businessmen who sucked the blood of the people in broad daylight, but although corrupted, they were not dead. These true bloodsuckers lived not in cemeteries but in the most congenial palaces.'[11]

Additionally Voltaire mocked, rather unfairly, his fellow countryman Dom Augustin Calmet, the Benedictine Abbot of Senones, who had composed one of the most useful and influential compendia of data and ideas on the subject in 1746. Calmet had intended his publication, which received the backing of most of the Catholic establishment, to be the last word on the issue. In it he noted that the instances of Vampire attacks were most frequent in those benighted parts of the continent where nutrition was poor and where plague, hydrophobia (rabies), poisoning and drunkenness were endemic: '... these Vampires are known only to certain countries, as Hungary, Moravia and Silesia, where those maladies are more common, and where the people, being badly fed, are subject to certain disorders occasioned by the climate and the food, and augmented by prejudice, fancy and fright, which are capable of producing or of increasing the most dangerous maladies, as daily experience proves too well'.[12]

In 1904 the English mystic Albert Osborne Eaves came up with a rather different justification for the same geographical bias: 'One reason why these countries ['Hungary and Servia'] are singled out is that their inhabitants have a strain of fourth-race blood in them, and the true Vampire belongs to this race. We ourselves are of the fifth great root-race, and have outgrown these beings of previous evolution.'

The only full commentary by a sceptical eyewitness on the posthumous punishment of a Vampire comes in the travel journal of the aristocratic French botanist, Joseph Pitton de Tournefort. In his *Account of a Journey in the Levant*, published in Paris nine years after his death in 1708, Pitton de Tournefort describes an incident on the Greek island of Mykonos which took place in 1701. The body of a local peasant had been found in the fields, dead of unknown and possibly violent causes. In life the man had had a reputation for being bad-tempered and argumentative, and two days after his burial in the precincts of a chapel, citizens had reported that he had returned from his grave to torment the townsfolk. In spite of the prohibitions on such things by the senior Orthodox clergy and the Turkish occupying power, the leaders of the community waited a prescribed nine days after the burial before digging up the body of the deceased and performing a sort of public post-mortem-cum-exorcism, beginning with an attempt to tear out the heart of the *vrykolakas*. 'The town butcher, fairly elderly and extremely clumsy, commenced by opening the stomach rather than the chest, he searched about for some time in the innards without discovering what he sought, and eventually somebody informed him that it was necessary to cut into the diaphragm. The heart was then torn out to the wonder of the spectators.'

The witness tells how the corpse stank, how incense had to be burned to mask the stench, and how this inflamed the crowd's imagination: they fancied that magical fumes were rising from the body. Onlookers marvelled at the quite fresh red blood in the cadaver, whereas Pitton and his companions could see quite clearly the foul, putrid ichor clinging to the butcher's hands. The account unfolds with the Frenchman and his companions trying diplomatically to allay the people's growing hysteria (by now the whole town was reverberating to alarmed rumours and chants of '*Vrykolakas!*') and remind them that what they were seeing was not out of the ordinary, but all to no avail. The heart of the deceased was ritually burned, but this was not enough to stop his nightly visitations and a short time afterwards Pitton and his party saw from their boat the great funeral pyre on which the remaining parts of the body were being cremated, finally calming the frenzy of the inhabitants, who celebrated by composing songs to mock the devil they had cast out.[13]

At almost the same time as Pitton de Tournefort's experience on Mykonos, the Italian Leo Allatius was publishing, in Cologne, a treatise on Greek folklore, which referred in detail to the *vrykolakas* phenomenon. He testified to the antiquity of the superstition, ascribed it to Orthodox beliefs and told how, on the island of Chios, people would never respond when addressed for the first time, or answer a first knock on their door, believing that the lurking undead were so numerous thereabouts that the chances were that they were being summoned to their doom. Allatius mentioned the likening of the characteristically distended and parchment-skinned *vrykolakas'* corpse to a drum – the name *tympanos* or *tumpaniatos* ('drum-like') becoming a synonym for the vampire in some regions.[14] In 1657 the French Jesuit François Richard mentioned Greek versions of the legends as recorded on the island of Santorini, and Paul Ricaut, the former English consul at Smyrna, confirmed the essential link between the *vrykolakas* and Orthodox beliefs in the non-decay of the excommunicated in a work of 1678.[15]

Travellers were still bringing back colourful anecdotes of stakings and burnings from other Greek-speaking areas, such as Rhodes and Macedonia, in the early years of the twentieth century.

Historians of the Vampire reports writing in English have concentrated on the evidence from Serbia and Greece, and they have done this for linguistic reasons – the recording was done in accessible languages; German, French or Latin. The Slavicist scholar Jan L. Perkowski of the University of Virginia has revealed that there is a much richer collection of hitherto untranslated vampire-lore in the Slav languages, showing the myths spread along a continuum from Macedonia to Russia, while the Hungarian historian Gábor Klaniczay mentions the existence of the same beliefs in Hungary itself and its satellite Transylvania, in western Turkey (where they merged with the witch-figure under the name of *obur*) and beyond Europe to the east in Armenia and the lands of the Caucasus, too, where the Georgian and Circassian peoples had their own vampire legends according to records from the seventeenth century.[16]

Certainly where the Muslim Ottoman Empire and the various ethnic communities of the Balkans overlapped, versions of the Vampire legend were common currency. In the Bosnian hinterland one of the most mysterious populations, the Morlachs, a surviving group of the pre-Slav and pre-Turkish Illyrians who spoke an ancient Latin-based language, were familiar with it. When the Italian scholar priest Alberto Fortis visited the region in the mid-eighteenth century to investigate poetry and folklore, accompanied by a Cambridge professor of modern history, he reported;

When a man dies suspected of becoming a Vampire or Vukodlak, as they call it, they cut his hams, and prick his whole body with pins, pretending that, after this operation, he cannot walk about. There are even instances of Morlacchi who, imagining that they may possibly thirst for children's blood after death, intreat their heirs, and sometimes oblige them to promise, to treat them as Vampires when they die.[17]

The Morlachs, a semi-nomadic people, also lent their services to the Turks as mercenary soldiers of the most terrifying reputation, and would have carried their superstitions to many parts of the Empire.

✝

The Vampire is different from many supernatural entities in that, unlike fairies and devils, it could be and often was identified with real individuals, albeit in many cases dead ones. It was then an interpenetration of the human and magical world, not a human invoker of magical forces like the witch, but an embodiment of malevolence by virtue of being possessed. The causes and symptoms of vampirism varied across the continuum that spanned Slav, Magyar and Romanian beliefs, but those singled out were in some way odd-ities, outsiders, sports of nature, or else had infringed the socio-religious code. The included redheads, the hairless and the excessively hairy, children born with a caul, bastards and suicides. (In some places where Vampire beliefs were endemic, even normally inanimate objects could become possessed: Balkan gypsies warned each other against Vampire pumpkins and Vampire watermelons.)[18]

A Slovak folk-song points up a nice comparison, often made by mothers and daughters in earlier times; the uncontrollable Vampire and the unruly husband:

Oh, mother, mother mine, I'm in such distress,
You wanted to find me a husband, but you gave me instead a *volkodlak*,
He is idle all the day long, indulging only in quarrelling and abuse,
In the tavern, he gorges himself through the night and drinks until morning.[19]

Serbs especially feared the *vukodlak* at Christmas: for them, for the Russians and for most Slav peoples the creature might be both a werewolf and a Vampire simultaneously; only the White Russians, of today's Belarus, and the Kashubians, some of whom emigrated with their beliefs to Canada, preserved the distinction. Both had in common their evil, accursed nature and their insatiable hunger and thirst. Both were predestined by high powers, especially evil spirits, to plague themselves and others. They were conflated in that a sorcerer or a werewolf, along with certain other cursed ones, would turn Vampire after death.

⁂

'The belief in Vampires still flourishes today,' wrote Wiesthaler in 1883, 'it is alive in Poland, in Slavic Kashubia and among the Germans living among Slavs in Western Prussia. The English and the French know it only from books.' At about the same time Miklošić was writing that in Kashubia children born with a caul and teeth and having a red blemish on the body become Vampires, 'as do those who leave this world in a state of anger or rage. They suck out the "life-juices" (not only blood!). The Vampire announces the murder of his relatives by ringing the church bell, dooming anyone who hears it.'[20]

To the Russians the *upyr'* was a wizard who, before death, could be recognized from his lack of a nasal bone (actually a common post-mortem condition: the nose collapses, although the other features of the face and body remain seemingly unchanged) and the lower lip was cleft. Others could become Vampires by being possessed by the devil or simply by a (black) cat walking across their grave. The Ukrainian *mjertovjec* who wandered abroad, rattling his bones, was someone who before death had been cursed by his parents or by the clergy. When the cock crowed for the third time, he disappeared, and might be detected by covering the floor with salt. His body might be found naked, face down, soft and well preserved, although some flesh might have been chewed from the arms and legs and the lips might be bloody. A nail might be hammered into his forehead and/or an ash or hawthorn stake thrust through the chest, upon which a hollow sound would always be heard. His head had to be cut off by a new spade. You had to be careful not to stand on the side towards which the blood gushed out, for this could mean death to anyone it touched. The head was placed between the legs or under the armpit and the grave reconsecrated. Kashubians reburied the body face down and stopped its mouth with earth. Another protective measure in many areas was to keep the Vampire busy in his grave. This could be done by putting money in the tomb, which would both placate and fascinate him, pieces of brick that he must chew on, or poppy seeds, rice, grain, flour, sand or anything else that he must count. Alternatives were a sock, a fishing-net or a garment that he was compelled to unravel a stitch at a time. The danger was that these tricks might enrage the Vampire and provoke him to even worse depredations.

In 1770, during a heavy storm, a living female vampire was burned alive in the Ukraine. There, the vampires were thought to frolic with the dead and commit indecent acts with them, as well as desecrate churches by smearing the altars with blood and smashing the church lamps.[21] In Bohemia and Moravia, before the ordinances of Empress Maria Theresa put a stop to it, panics began when large numbers of citizens complained of asphyxiation or strangulation: the people inspected cemeteries for any sign of the presence of evil, such as scratch-marks and disturbances on the graves, and many Vampires were dragged out of their tombs and summarily burned. In the Bohemian village of Blow in 1337, according to the chronicler Hajek, a shepherd named Myslata was buried, came back to life and began to haunt the neighbourhood, throttling some people and calling out the names of others who invariably died within eight days. After deliberating for some time the villagers decided to dig him up and pierce him with a hawthorn stake. But he mocked them, saying, 'Oh, how you have hurt me now, for you have given me a stick to fight off the dogs with!' And he rose again and his terrible attacks were worse than before. The poor villagers hired two executioners and asked them to dig him up again and bind him – he was as fat as a bull – to a cart by tying him around the waist. He was tied to a stake to be burned, another stake was thrust through his side and blood gushed forth. As they burned him he brayed like a donkey, but most importantly the evil that had been unleashed was thus overcome and the dead man returned no more.[22]

Wiesthaler claimed that more recently, in the nineteenth century, the overwhelming aura of evil attaching to the undead was emphasized less in the Czech and Moravian lands, although people continued to believe that a tear falling on a restless corpse would sear it like fire, that walking on the grave would cause the occupant pain, and that too-tight grave-clothes might cause the dead to grumble and bellow in anger. They were also said to try to talk to their relatives during and after the funeral if they had some last concerns to impart.

For the Czechs, an evil or bewitched woman was resurrected as the night spirit known as the *mura* (*mora* and *mara* elsewhere; the Czechs had a male counterpart, too, the *morous*), which emerges at midnight to terrify the living. The *mura*-soul is laid to rest again by allowing it to strangle the most beautiful cow or horse in the stable.

If the house door is closed, the *mura* – like the Slovene *mora* who also drinks the blood of the living – will come through the keyhole, lie on the chests of adults, drink mother's milk and drain children of their life-force. (In Slovene, the standard expression for having a nightmare is still *mora me tlači* literally 'the *mora* is crushing me'). To free oneself from the grip of this visitation, who causes terrible dreams, one should wiggle the toe on the right foot to start the return to consciousness.[23]

Some authorities believed that the development of a future *mora* or a future *volkoldlak* or *vedomec* could be prevented in babyhood: first put a piece of wood into its mouth and in later life – or death – it will instinctively attack only trees. If the first thing put into its mouth is the mother's breast, it will victimize humans. People with single continuous eyebrows are destined to be *moras*. You can grab a *mora* as it presses upon you and a blacksmith once did this, nailing the creature to the wall. When he awoke and inspected the room, he found his godmother attached to a beam by her clothes. The *mora* is not always a godmother, it may also take the form of a white cat or a huge black fly with a red-striped neck. In the latter case, if you see the fly and think you know whose spirit it contains, you have only to shout out the name and the human form will be standing there before you. Other remedies are a cloth stained with human excrement placed on the sleeper's chest, eating only smoked food, or promising the *mura* bread, in which case it will return in the morning to claim it.[24]

The Vlachs (or Wallachians) believed that a person who was illegitimate and had two illegitimate parents would inevitably become a Vampire, as would someone killed by a Vampire. The *murony*, as they knew the creature, once activated, could change easily into a dog, cat, frog, louse or bug. The Vlachs were so fearful of their dead becoming Vampires that it was common practice in every case of sudden death to a summon a skilled midwife to nail the cadaver's forehead, smear pork-fat on the body and place a sprig of wild-rose thorns next to it in the grave, so that, should the deceased try to rise, his or her grave-clothes would be caught on the thorns. Incense would be burned over neighbouring graves.

Orthodox Romanians referred to the person who had been excommunicated, publicly or secretly, before burial as *drakul* ('devil'). Any movement or disturbance in the earth of the grave would lead to the relatives of the dead demanding that the clergy authorize an exhumation of a *drakul*. The corpse would then be stood against the church all while an exorcism was carried out; if it collapsed, this meant that a more senior priest must be sent for.[25]

The Serbian Vampire will not harm his own wife, although he may come and lie with her, and even have children by her, but these children will have no bones! The Serbs also have the *jedogonja*, a man whose spirit leaves him at night and goes up to the mountains, uproots trees and fights with others of its kind. Whoever wins will ensure a year's fertility to his home village. The *jedogonja* can also sunder rocks and roll them down the mountainside, hence the saying 'jak kao jedogonja', 'as strong as a *jedogonja*'. At the death of such a person, thorns are stuck under his fingernails and the sinews behind his knees are severed with a black-handled knife so that he will not be able to rise again.

Such a creature must be a non-believer or someone over whose dead body a bird flew or another animal stepped and who is now possessed by a demon. He can be glimpsed at night with his shroud over his shoulder in the graveyard or around granaries, especially during the period between Christmas and Ascension. An all-black stallion is taken to the graveyard to step over the grave mounds. He can no more step across the grave of a *vukodlak* than the crows can perch there. The Serbs have an expression '*crven kao vampir*', 'as red as a Vampire', which they often say of drunkards.

Another supernatural tormentor from the same regions, the *vjestica*, is a woman who has a diabolic spirit that emerges from her as she sleeps, in the form of a butterfly (the German *Alp* spirit also takes this shape), a hen or a turkey; she can open the chest of sleeping children and adults, take out and devour the heart, leaving no trace. The victim may die immediately or live on until a time ordained by her.[26]

✝

In the 1880s, in the Pole Czasky's *O Litawskich i Polskich Prawach*, volume II, the author claimed that Vampires still ravaged the countryside there and in Lithuania. In 1826, when he was visiting the town of Slup, Czasky wrote,

A young man had shot himself a few days before and could not be buried as the local people were sure that as a suicide he would be sure to return as a Vampire. Finally he was laid to rest in a distant valley, but return he did, savaging livestock and attacking shepherds. He even assaulted one giant of a man, and this is the report of that struggle as I heard it from the mouth of the winner: 'A cold sweat broke out on my forehead and my hair stood on end, when I saw that he was coming towards me with his arms outstretched as if he wanted to give me a friendly hug. I wanted to scream, but my tongue just rolled in my mouth like a log; I wanted to make the sign of the cross, but my hands would not move. At that moment he came up and seized me round the waist. My dreadful fear brought back my strength and I seized him by the throat and we fought for a long time like two fierce dogs, biting each other in the neck. Then the moon hid behind the clouds, and as we fought on, I could see only his eyes and nothing else. Fortunately the cock began to crow and I looked again to where he had been and he had disappeared.

In the duchy of Cracow the same author witnessed a ritual in which a Vampire was about to be burned. As it lay on the ground, surrounded by villagers, one put a star and a cross woven from poplar on the breast of the corpse and spoke these words: 'Why are you rising from the grave, forgetting the sin committed by Adam and Eve? Do not multiply this sin when you should be concealing it, you damned Vampire!' The person in charge took the ear of the Vampire and muttered words into it for some time, then put a piece of paper on which there were lines from the gospel on the chest of the body and reburied it.[27]

✢

In looking for rationales for the tales of Vampires, *volkodlaks* and other ghouls, we must not forget to consider the simplest common-sense explanations. Members of close-knit families in which several generations cohabited under one roof would have known only too well the feeling of being drained of life by another human: a younger generation slowly sapped of its energy and wealth by elderly relatives, an undernourished mother sucked dry by her voracious baby.

There are other clues to a prosaic explanation for some of the supernatural activity. Reading between the lines recorded by gullible communities or uncomprehending officials, it is clear that a good number of the outrages committed by 'revenants' (monuments defaced, places of worship desecrated, noises in the night, the ringing of church bells and the disturbing of graves) were actually the work of mischievous children or rampaging, probably drunken youths taking advantage of their elders' neuroses. Bulgarian panics resulted, for instance, in terrified village populations huddling together in two or three houses and taking turns to mount guard against marauding *obours*. The peasants burned candles all night, but the presence of the *obours* was demonstrated by their shadows flickering across the interior walls, by howling, shrieking and the uttering of profanities.

In the other empty houses their traces were discovered next morning in the form of blood spat into flour, furniture overturned and cow dung smeared everywhere, even across pictures of the saints.

✣

And if by some mischance we should encounter the Slavonic folk Vampire? The basic means of defence against it are threefold: killing the thing itself, using apotropaics, or charms, against it, or curing oneself if already attacked, but, as several authorities pointed out 'Whoever is infected is probably doomed, as the protections are few and ineffective. Among those are to eat the earth in which the Vampire has rested, to drink or smear yourself with its blood. The most efficacious method is to mix the blood with brandy, then with flour and bake bread with it and eat it.'[28]

4
Istria, Carniola and Styria

'Kind Death, do not delay too long,
You, the key: you, the door; you, the happy pathway,
Which leads us from this place of pain,
To where putrefaction dissolves all chains.'

France Prešeren, *Sonetne Nesreče*, 1834

The village environments of the Alpine provinces of Carniola and Styria as they were under the Habsburgs are still visible in the first photographs taken in farmers' homesteads in the mid nineteenth century, showing a way of life that had continued almost unaltered for centuries. The men wore a national costume of wide-brimmed black hats, decorated waistcoats, white linen shirts, waisted jackets and plain or embroidered breeches tucked into calf-length black boots. The women would wear embroidered headscarves often inside as well as outside the house, with exquisite lacework blouses, laced-together bodices fringed with vividly coloured borders, full black skirts over lace petticoats and drawers – all carefully hand-made – and black-laced ankle-boots bought from the shoemaker in a local town. Inside the long, narrow, low-ceilinged houses – the poorer homes would be shared with the family's livestock – the couple would sit at the kitchen table in the dim winter light of an oil lamp, the wife sewing or preserving fruits, her husband sucking a long-stemmed pipe and fingering a decorated ceramic pitcher of local wine.

These pious, covetous, deeply sentimental and stolid people lived in a reality that was grounded in seasonal routine and legitimized by generations of folk certainties and the religious ordinances passed on by the local Catholic priest. Here, at the northern tip of the lands of the southern Slavs, dominated for centuries by Austria, the priests would be educated local men, sometimes discreetly promoting the survival of their Slavonic national identity and their language, both of which had managed to withstand centuries of 'Germanizing'. But the same priests would sometimes resort to telling magical tales of resurrection and transubstantiation, stories that did not always come with biblical authority, to galvanize the faith of their semi-literate parishioners. Further south, in Dalmatia and the Balkans, especially in the interior, the priests themselves were often barely literate, as superstitious as the members of their flocks, and it is quite possible that they also colluded in spreading stories of attacks by the evil dead to maintain their authority. Obviously this would not find its way into the parish registers, but the Catholic Church in Rome had its suspicions, voiced by Pope Benedict XIV, for example, in his correspondence with local officials during 1766.

In the winter the Slovene farmhouse was barricaded against the months of snow and the world of shadows that lurked outside. In the smoky, warm interior the household swaddled itself against the miasmas and contagions that might sneak in, wedging shut the little windows and stopping the keyhole in the heavy wooden door against them. The midwinter period was always said to be the time when Vampires and assorted other phantasms were at their most active. Not surprisingly, the mortality rate in all age groups, but especially the old and the newborn, would rise dramatically in those months. A Slovene family tree from the 1820s shows four out of six children born to a farming couple dying within the first two years of birth, and three of the deaths occurred in winter.[1]

Even in the long, warm summers life was not idyllic, although the soil of the Alpine foothills is fertile and the air pure. The people who live here have always been beset by the deep melancholy that suffuses the verses of their national poet, Prešeren. Some ascribe this stoical gloom to the 'Slav soul', but they themselves blame it on the claustrophobic life of the valleys, hemmed in by the mountains and the virgin forests and – less obviously, more insidiously – by the frustrations and jealousies of an immobile, inward-looking village society.

Escape from drudgery in the fields or the kitchen would come when the older family members gathered to spin stories from the strands of landscape and memory, interweaving incidents from the interlocking lives of family, friends, neighbours and animals. Later, in sleep, the stuff of the folk-tales would merge into a boundless imaginary universe and a jumbled host of feelings, images and dramas would be given full rein. For many Slovene country people, belief in the immortal soul entailed belief in the individual spirit, an entity that had an independent existence, could leave the body in sleep and could experience and influence events while disembodied. As Nietzsche recognized, 'In the ages of rude primeval culture, man believed that in dreams he was coming to know a *second real world*; here is the source of all metaphysics ... "The dead live on, *because* they appear to the living in dreams": thus man used to reason, throughout thousands of years.'[2]

Carniola and Styria – modern Slovenia and adjoining Istria, now northern Croatia, sleep on, still unnoticed by the outside world. English-speaking folklorists have concentrated their attentions on Romania and Serbia, and more recently Bulgaria, but the Vampire legend is richly represented in the territory between the Alps and the Adriatic. For the first time we can open a window on to an intact folk tradition, which illustrates again how the Vampire is not one creature but a bundle of entities and concepts. Stories and histories never before translated into English show a whole pantheon of turbulent, unruly spirits gambolling in the forests, tormenting the fearful peasant in the cottage, plaguing the townsfolk. Analysis establishes that, beyond their primary purpose of terrifying, the Vampire and its fellow spirits are required to reinforce social values and to absorb a mess of unexamined but real psychosocial pressures.

✝✝

In the 1730s three Englishmen included Carniola in their grand tour of the German provinces. On arrival in the city of Laibach (today the Slovene capital, Ljubljana) they wrote in their travel notes,

> We must not omit Observing here, that our Landlord seems to pay some Regard to what Baron *Valvasor* has related of the *Vampyres*, said to infest some Parts of this Country. These *Vampyres* are supposed to be the Bodies of deceased Persons, animated by evil Spirits, which come out of the Graves, in the night time, suck the Blood of many of the Living, and thereby destroy them. Such a Notion will, probably, be looked upon as fabulous and exploded, by many people in *England*; however, it is not only countenanced by Baron *Valvasor*, and many *Carnioleze* Noblemen, Gentlemen, &c. as we were informed, but likewise actually embraced by some writers of good Authority.

First set down around 1734 and published in volume IV of the *Harleian Miscellany* in 1745, this is the first use of the word 'Vampire' in written English. The Englishmen gave the source of their information as the writings of the Slovene geographer and historian Baron Janez Vajkard Valvasor, who had mentioned Vampire superstitions in his pioneering ethnographic work *Die Ehre des Herzogthums Crain* ('The Treasures of the Duchy of Carniola'). One of several sequences that dealt with belief in bloodsucking spirits referred to the north Adriatic peninsula of Istria, which bordered on both Carniola and Croatia: it is translated and reproduced here for the first time in English:

> The provincial and farming folk of Istria believe very strongly that there are sorcerers and warlocks who drink the blood of children. Such a bloodsucker is known as a *strigon* or a *vedavec* [in some versions rendered as '*vedarec*']. When a *strigon* dies, it is thought that he walks about the village at around midnight. He bangs on doors and rattles the doorknockers, and in the house at which he knocks it is supposed that somebody will die during that time, and if a person in that house dies, the peasants say that a *strigon* devoured him. What is even worse is that credulous peasants

believe that wandering *strigons* crawl up to their wives at night and sleep with them without uttering a word. I am genuinely concerned that it is often the case with widows – especially if young and beautiful – that spirits of flesh truly do sleep with them. Thus it is that they firmly believe that this fearful affliction will not leave them in peace until they pierce its body with a thornwood stake. For this reason this task is undertaken only by the bravest, always after midnight, because they think that before midnight he is not in his grave and he is wandering abroad. They open the grave and push the stake, thick as a fist or a small hand, through his belly, mutilating him horribly. This is when blood gushes forth, the corpse writhing and flexing as if alive and feeling the pain, after which they cover the grave with earth and go their separate ways. This procedure of opening the grave and impaling the dead body with a stake is very common among rural Istrians, that is peasants. Although the authorities, if it becomes known, impose severe penalties since it is contrary to religion, it quite frequently occurs.

Valvasor's editor and assistant, Erasmus Franciscus (the German scholar Erasmus von Finx of Lübeck) appended an anecdote on the same subject, which has often since been referred to but which has not been properly translated into English before. The events described took place in a community then known to German-speakers as Krinck-Markt, now the Croatian hillside village of Kringa 'seventy miles from Laibach in the direction of Mitterburg' (called in Croatian Pazin):

In the year 1672 a most curious series of events occurred. The corpse of a man named Georg (or Giure) Grando was exhumed, accompanied by particular rituals, and the head was chopped off; the purpose being to lay him to rest and to prevent others from being troubled by him ... I will now proceed to unfold my tale in some depth ... Some sixteen years after the aforesaid man had departed this life and had been interred with the usual Christian burial rites, he was seen about the market town of Krinck. Indeed he was first sighted by Father Georgio (a monk belonging to the order of St Paul the First Hermit), who had himself performed the requiem mass and the burial. The aforementioned Father went to visit the widow together with some friends of the deceased. After partaking of supper, when he was taking his leave, the Father saw the deceased sitting behind the door, and he left in a terrified state. Following this, the deceased was often seen at night, walking the streets and alleyways, knocking on front doors. Several people died as a result of this, especially in those houses upon whose doors he knocked. Whichever house he chose to call upon, soon after a death occurred.

He also appeared at his widow's house, and lay with her, and she mightily abhorring this, finally went to the *župan* (mayor) Miho Radetich, to stay with him and to implore him to help her in the matter of her departed husband. As a result, the mayor gathered together several courageous neighbours, gave them something to drink, and asked them to assist him in disposing of this manifestation of evil: for this Georg or Giure Grando had already fed upon many of their neighbours, and in addition had overpowered his widow every night and lain with her.

Thereupon they decided to attack this restless creature of the night and to put an end to his evil acts. They set off, nine of them all, including Mattio Chericatin, Nicolo Macina, Juri Macina, Juira Sorsić, Martino Ildoreičić and Micula Krairaer, with two lanterns and a crucifix, and opened the grave. There they saw the corpse's face completely red in hue, with its mouth open, laughing at them. And with this, these brave vanquishers of ghosts took such fright that they all ran away. This display of behaviour greatly angered the mayor; that nine living persons could not deal with one dead person, but instead behaved like frightened rabbits at the mere sight of him. So he chided them and encouraged them to return with him to the grave, and then attempted to strike a stake made of hawthorn through the belly of the corpse, but each time the stake bounced back and would not pierce it.

At this the mayor, assuming the role of the priest, as it were, held a crucifix up to the face of the deceased and spoke to him thus: 'See here, Strigon!' (this is how the undead are referred to in Istria). 'Here is Jesus Christ, who saved us from damnation and who died for us! And, Strigon, you cannot rest in peace.' And this untimely exorcist or communicator with the dead continued in a similar vein, whereupon tears appeared in the eyes of the spectre.

As the stake would not pierce the body, one of the group, who was called Miccolo Nyena, from Mehrenfels, began at length to chop off the head with an axe. But because he went about it too fearfully and timidly, another who had more stomach for it, namely Stipan Milasich, jumped in and struck off the head. Upon this, the deceased let out a shriek and began to move and turn as if he were still alive, and the grave became filled with blood. After they had finished, the dignified executioners filled in the grave and went home. From this time on the widow and other folk were left in peace.[3]

The writer is at pains to assure us that the story is true: 'You need not doubt the veracity of these events, as I have myself spoken with persons who were present at the time. It is common in Istria and thereabouts to exhume dead people who cannot find eternal rest, but instead roam abroad at night and attack others, and to drive a stake made of briar or hawthorn through the bodies.' He then adopts the tone appropriate for an Enlightenment scholar:

Several years ago in a Venetian village not far from here, as recounted by a certain noble hand, the same occurred and a stake was driven through the heart of the deceased. But if the authorities hear of this, those responsible are severely punished, and indeed rightly so; for it is the devil's work that mocks and blinds people, and moves them to carry out superstitious acts. The words of Francisco Torreblanca are apposite in this context: *Apparitiones & Resurrectiones Mortuorum, quas vobis daemones & magi obtrudunt, non sunt animae; sed spectra & phantasma, etc.* ['The apparitions and returnees from the dead which are, according to you, inflicted upon us by demons and sorcerers are not spirits, but spectres and fantasies, etc.'] Although [Franciscus adds, tempering his rationalism] I would not apply this judgement to all kinds of apparitions.

✝

In those hundreds of little villages scattered across the karst-uplands, among steep meadows and scrub-oak and pineforests, alongside the blue, rocky torrents that rush down from the high pasture and the snow-peaks, by the family hearth and in the tavern, beyond the scrutiny of the distant authorities, even of the local *župan*, the mayor, the stories were exchanged and the dreams recounted. For hundreds of years the coastal strip – Istria and northern Dalmatia – was dominated by Venice, and Italian vied with the dialects of the native Slavonic people. In the foothills of the Julian Alps, further north and west, Slovenes lived side by side with Friulian Italians. Up and down the littoral and inland as far as the German-speaking territories – an area that remained relatively unscarred by the religious conflicts of the north and by the long Turkish wars – there existed an intermeshing, overlapping, subtly changeable web of folk-tales and beliefs. The names given to the supernatural players in these narratives might vary from village to village, but certain elements in common occur in the earliest written records, which date from the Renaissance period, and in the most recent, from the early years of the twentieth century.

Croatia, even more than Slovenia, was a hotbed of Vampire legend. Travelling across Istria today, branching off to visit Kringa, stopping off at Pazin, the difference between the two countries is obvious, both in the relative poverty of this region and in the very different feeling that seems to hang in its air. Istria's Italian overlords used to consider it a backward place, but it had no more sinister reputation until the twentieth century, when the atrocities carried out by the fascist Ustaše militia during the Second World War, the bloody secession from Yugoslavia and the Bosnian war that followed left Croatia with a legacy of bitterness; a surly wariness is visible in many faces. Here it is easy to imagine simmering village feuds, night fears, thoughts of blood.

Fully two centuries later, in the lands celebrated by Valvasor, the German folklorist Hellwald was describing the activities of the *pijavica*, a Vampire (the name means 'drinking-spirit') whose predations were stopped by 'dropping a heavy stone on the head of the restless corpse'. In Istria in the 1880s, in the Krk and the Kastav areas, the Croat writer Milčetić told how battle was again joined against a different night-demon:

The people believe that each clan has one *kudlak* [from *volkodlak*: 'wolf-pelt'] and one *krsnik* ['cross-bearer' and/or 'baptized one']. They are two opposite beings. The *kudlak* plots to do harm to people, and the *krsnik* strives to protect them. They know how to transform themselves into all sorts of animals, most frequently into pigs, oxen or horses. The *kudlak* is usually black, and the *krsnik* white or multicoloured. The *kudlak* attacks men at night, frightening, striking, and even killing them, but the *krsnik* jumps in and they engage in a wild battle. In the end the *krsnik* wins. There are no peasants who do not believe in the *kudlak*. For that reason there are few old people who have not seen one. The *kudlak* most frequently troubles people after its death. If the people suspect that someone who has died is a *kudlak*, they sever the tendons under his knees before they place him in the grave. They think that in this way he will no longer walk at night nor bother anyone. The most recent *kudlaks* in Dubašnica were the Čoporići [family] from the village of Turčić, and that was in 1880.

Milčetić's unnamed witness looks back to an incident during the first half of the nineteenth century: 'The grandfather was a *kudlak* even after his death, and at night he plagued the populace and brought harm to them. To be rid of him the people of Dubašnica exhumed him and at night impaled him with a hawthorn stake...'[4]

The *kudlak* is the same creature as the *volkodlak* of Slovenia and the *vukodlak* of Serbian folklore; they are all incarnations of a Vampire-like entity and from the eighteenth century the terms could be used synonymously with *vampir* itself. The most striking feature of the evil *kudlak* in these stories is its role in a binary relationship with the good spirit-warrior, the *krsnik* (in Slovenia the *kresnik*). This polarity harks back to the light-and-dark conflicts of pagan myth and of the dualist Christian heresies that once held sway in the Balkans (see page 53), but also parallels exactly the behaviour of two other descendants of the prehistoric shamanic tradition, the neighbouring *benandanti* from Friuli in northern Italy and the *táltos* of Hungary, real people who doubled as village shamans, battling in the spirit world at night against rivals and with evil forces to ensure the prosperity of their communities.[5]

The Trieste newspaper *L'Indipendente* in its issue of 14 October 1882 carried a detailed account of actions taken against the *kudlak* (here in the variant spelling *kodlak*):

Yesterday, 13 October, before the court in Trieste appeared the 60-year-old gravedigger Ivan Franković, the son of Anton, from Vokansko in the Voloska region, together with the 59-year-old landowner and regional committee member, Paskal Djačić, son of Andrej, popularly known as Rosić, from Abacija [on the Istrian coast in what is now Croatia] and the 33-year-old servant Anton Benčić, son of Ivan, from Bregev, all three married and the fathers of children. The first-named was defending himself against a presumed crime under article 396 of the penal code, namely that on 17 July last in Abacija he violated the deceased person of Ivan Vrljen by driving five nails into him, one in his mouth and two into each heel. He also cut the veins beneath his knees, before replacing the body in its coffin, face down. The second and third defendants were accused of being accomplices in the said crime. Djačić apparently said to the others that the body of Vrljen had to be mutilated because he was a *kodlak* (in Italian *stregone*), and instructed the other two in the matter. Benčić assisted by providing the necessary tools and explaining how to use them.

In his defence Franković claimed that on that day, as he was digging a grave, he saw two men carrying a coffin into the mortuary. One of them, Benčić, asked him to follow them. Once there Benčić said that the late Vrljen was a *kodlak* who if he were not thwarted might kill the entire population of Abacija, suck out the blood of his [presumably Franković's] children and take them from this world. In order that the whole region not be devastated, nails should be run into the body, for which task Benčić offered to pay a fee of one gold dinar. The other defendants did not deny taking part in the events described but both blamed Franković for what had happened. Another witness named Benčina testified that all across the region there was a deeply-rooted belief in *kodlaki*, and that furthermore, in his opinion, this belief was quite justified because the dead truly did rise from the grave and wander the countryside harming people unless, immediately after preparation for burial, the veins behind their knees were cut. The accused were splendidly defended by the excellent counsels Dr

Janovitz and Dr Cambon. Notwithstanding, at the end of the trial the three were found guilty; the court sentenced the citizen Djačić to three months', Benčić and Franković to two months' imprisonment under the harshest regime.

Prompted by this report, a professor from Pazin named Nemančić wrote to the philologist Dr Jagić pointing out that this was far from being an isolated incident in Istria. 'The priest from Montrilj near Pazin has told me that this is a common practice in the area ... and the person who is deemed to be a *strigun* is often threatened during his lifetime that once he is dead, his body will be treated in the same way. These threats are so naturally accepted that no one would think of taking the matter before the court.'[6]

✧

The middle-European philologists and folklorists of the late nineteenth century tapped into a rich repository of old fables inspired by a belief in the spirit world and by humankind's uneasy coexistence with the natural forces that could at times confound it. A selection of these tales, never before translated, presents the exhibits from a whole gallery of demons, a host of sub-species of blood-suckers and night-spectres.

In Slovenia, as in Istria, the *kresnik* came to be the representative of good in the nightly battles against the forces of evil. His evil counterparts came in various forms and bore many names, but foremost among them were the *vedomec*, the *volkodlak* and the *vampir* itself. The figure of the *kresnik* originally derives from the sun-god in pagan Slav mythology, but he was not always unambiguously good. In early tales he is credited with both positive and negative attributes.

There is an ancient tale about the kidnapping by the *kresnik* of Zora, the daughter of his arch-enemy the Snake Queen. He pays for this deed in the prime of his life by forfeiting his own existence. The brothers of the kidnapped girl find out where their sister is being held and take her home. The *kresnik* pursues them, there is a fight and the younger brother stabs him. The *kresnik* does not, cannot really die, but he lies 'benumbed' (*premrl*) in his grave. At night he rises again and rampages forth in the form of that terrible monster, the Vampire; in this guise he waylays the traveller on his lonely journey; he enters the homes of mortals and sucks the blood of sleeping people. Regurgitated blood, glistening in clots on the earth or among the grass is evidence that Vampire has passed that way. When the sun's rays strike him, he is again immobilized and lies unmoving in the furrows of the field. The *kresnik*'s bewitchment is only temporary (it is the season of sadness and grief for his people); he passes from the realm of light into the kingdom of darkness and thence to light again, and will be condemned to do this as long as creation lasts.[7]

Another malign force deriving from dualist belief, the very ancient monster known as the *mrak* (literally 'dusk' or 'dark') can appear in different incarnations such as a gigantic woman or a man with a face that is decomposing and large and glowing hands. If these terrible arms, they say, are able to grasp someone, then that person is cast into a state where they are neither truly healthy nor truly ill. A *mrak* likes best to harm children, whom he sometimes takes and carries far away from their grieving families. If parents are not watchful, the *mrak* can also harm a child's clothing and this is why garments have to be kept away from the sun. If a child is thus afflicted, and is cast, as they put it into a 'dusky' or twilight state, they use a certain herb with yellow flowers and leaves like rosemary as incense for his or her relief. On Krk, an island in the Adriatic they tell how the awful *mrak* fights the sun, but until today neither he nor his adversary has managed to win the fight. During the day the sun gets the better of his opponent, using flaming arrows to drive the *mrak* into the deepest, darkest gorges, but at night the *mrak* emerges, repels his powerful enemy and pursues the sun with a great net. But every time he is about to close the net over his prey and snuff out the light for ever, the morning star draws near and its diamond light cuts through the net. Despite its reverses, the islanders know that the *mrak* will eventually win the struggle and the earth will be plunged into eternal darkness.

Apart from presenting the familiar figure of the supernatural abductor of children, the *mrak* legends play with the notion of a binary struggle and an end-of-the-world myth in which the sun's light and heat will one day be extinguished. The tales also refer to a gloomy intermediate state between metaphorical night and day, into which bewitched children may fall. By creating a beneficent artificial 'dusk' with the smoke of fragrant incense the poor infant is granted some relief. Much more prosaically, the legends seem to be telling parents to guard their children and keep their clothing safely folded away in drawers and cupboards, not leave the washing out, or abandon clothes where they fall lest they fade.

We can speculate as to whether the fables' cosmic pessimism come from the stereotypical Slavonic melancholy, as Wiesthaler, who collected it, claimed, or are myths like this the source of that melancholy?

Another personification of the negative pole of the *kresnik* is the *volkodlak*, whose power originates in the belief that a man's soul leaves the body during sleep and wanders abroad alone. One of the most common of the malevolent spirits, the feral *volkodlak* was cognate with the werewolf, which occurs in western European folklore and almost certainly reflects a memory of the prehistoric tribal sorcerers whose images can be seen in cave paintings half disguised by the skins of totemic animals. Even before it metamorphosed into a Vampire this Slavonic wolf/man was not a straightforward being; he was sometimes a wolf, sometimes an intermediate animal spirit, sometimes fully human, and shifted constantly back and forth between these states:

In the Gorjanci chain of hills on the Slovene/Crotia border they know the *volkodlak* as a monster in the shape of a dog, only much larger than any normal dog ... he has a medium-length and almost black tail in which is concealed all his magical power [humans born with vestigial tails were among those suspected of turning into Vampires]. At night he roams the forest; during the daytime he sits in deep caves hatching wicked plots against the human race. He howls like a wolf and ranges through the oak-forests like a rabid dog, baying and wailing, and thus frequently misleads the hunter or the farmer. Sometimes he approaches human dwellings to pay a visit to haughty girls, but not in his animal form, rather in the guise of a fine young man!

Volkodlaki, it was said, might be children who have been cursed by their mothers, or maybe children who are born feet first. If the former, they can be redeemed: if people take pity on them and throw them scraps of bread to eat, they become human again. For those born feet first, the only way to prevent their fate is by changing the position of the newborn baby's body at just the right moment. The *volkodlak* sheds his skin at certain times, and again becomes human; however his animal teeth never fall out and he can thus be recognized, although he has a human face. There are, fortunately, not many *volkodlaki*, because most of them die soon after birth and do not grow old.

Again concerning the *volkodlak*, other fables told that such a person is born with a 'garment' [presumably the amniotic sac or caul] on, and unless he is saved he is doomed to become irredeemably evil. He can be protected by having a piece of that garment sewed on to him beneath his shoulder or by giving him a spoon to gnaw on; and when he dies, he must be laid out 'on his teeth', that is face down, or some new coins placed under his tongue. During the holiday season manure must not be left on the fields without being ploughed in, because if it is left there a *volkodlak* will lie under it waiting for the *krstnik* (*kresnik*) with all the switches left behind by other ploughmen in the fields to beat him with. (Here we can see an injunction against neglecting agricultural tasks, particularly at Christmas and New Year when the ploughman become lax and the malicious spirits are at their most troublesome.)

In another, unusually detailed, tale we learn that a beggar came to a Slovene village and enquired in vain at every door if he could be put up for the night. This is why he went to sleep away from the houses in front of the church on the edge of the settlement. At the eleventh hour of the night a *volkodlak* appeared to him and asked him what he was doing in that spot. The beggar told him that he had to find a resting-place there since nobody in the village would give him shelter. Then the *volkodlak* told him to accompany him and the beggar complied. The *volkodlak* picked up three stones from the cemetery by the church and they headed back into the village. When they reached the first house, the *volkodlak* threw one of the stones over the roof and in response a dog barked. The *volkodlak* said, 'This is no good, let's go on.' They reached the second house and the *volkodlak* cast a second stone, but in the yard behind the building a chicken clucked. The *volkodlak* said again, 'This is no good.' They reached a third house, and he hurled the third stone, and no voice was raised. 'This is it,' the *volkodlak* said, and they went into the house together. The two started a fire in the kitchen under the heavy cauldron, which hangs above every hearth; the family had forgotten to unhook it in the evening, which is why the *volkodlak* went into that particular house. The beggar kept feeding the fire with splinters of wood while the *volkodlak* proceeded to the room where the family were sleeping. Soon one could hear groaning and sobbing coming from that room: the *volkodlak* was drinking the master's blood. Shortly after that, the *volkodlak* brought the master's blood from the room, (such blood is called '*prlog* blood'). He threw it into the cauldron to stew. When it was cooked, the *volkodlak* unfastened the cauldron and began to eat, offering the delicacy to the beggar, but the beggar could not even begin to taste it. Urged by his companion, the beggar started to pretend to swallow the blood-dish, but in fact tipped the plate down his shirtfront into his bosom. When the meal was finished, the *volkodlak* said, 'If of this bloody froth lurking here in the ashes, the master were given only as much as would fit beneath a fingernail, he would become quite well again.' Then they dug over the fire and went out into the cold pre-dawn.

On the second morning, while on his way past that same house, the beggar could hear the sound of weeping coming from within. He stepped across the threshold into the hall and asked what the matter was. He was told by the distraught family that the master had suddenly fallen ill and was lying stricken, unable to move. The beggar asked if he might visit the patient. They allowed him to go into the bedchamber, and he gave the master some of the blood-froth that he had secretly retrieved from the ashes under the cauldron and the master miraculously and instantly recovered. Then, so it is said, the *volkodlak* was dug up, and he grinned in his grave and said to the beggar, who stood looking on, 'If I had known you would tell, I would have reduced you to "sun-dust".' They also say that if a *volkodlak* does not find a cauldron suspended over the hearth, he still proceeds to cook without it, but before he lies back into his pit, he disgorges the blood and mixes it with earth.'[8]

Here the *volkodlak* has fully mutated into a Vampire, a blood-drinking revenant, without any remaining wolf characteristics. The themes of this story stress the role of outsiders as both shunned and gifted with special power or insight, and the importance of granting hospitality to strangers. The tale also enforces the need to guard one's home with a dog, or at least a cockerel, and to keep a tidy kitchen at all times lest calamity overtake the household.

Many of the Vampire stories from Slovenia make reference to gobbets of blood scattered by the demon, and the anthologist Jakob Kelemina commented on the dialect words used to describe the phenomenon;

> In Zemono near Notranjska Bistrica this is called '*Prilog* [or *prlog*] blood'. If in the morning people find a piece of red clay wet with dew on a path, they say that this is blood which has been disgorged by the *vedomci*. Having gorged themselves on human blood, the *vedomci* frequently fight one another at night, preferably at some crossroads, and on such occasions they allegedly disgorge the blood they had drunk.[9]

Prilog is usually translated as 'supplement' or 'side-dish' and might have been a term used originally by peasants for a tasty snack or delicacy taken outside meal-times.

Just beyond the light and warmth of the hearth hover numerous other evil entities. In the seventeenth century it was recorded that at certain times, such as Christmas Eve, along the Pivka river a great many spirits appeared whom people called *vedavci*. These malicious phantasms were alleged to suck children's blood so that the children must inevitably pine and die. Fortunately these spirits were opposed by other discarnate beings known as *Šentjanževci* ('St John's spirits'). Many people living at the time of writing had witnessed the fights between them.[10]

The *mora* is a personification of the nightmare, which is the literal translation of its name. Popular imagination also conceived of a closely related demon, the *trotamora*, ('trota' means something like 'parasite') as an exceedingly ugly monster who constantly changes shape. The *trotamora* can appear as a barrel, a worn bedspread, a cow's belly, as a dishevelled old woman with bloodshot eyes and broad feet. People say that this *mora* is an animal spirit and that it can be kept at bay by certain symbols carved into doors or bedsteads.[11]

Slovenes in the Gorica area on the border with Italy generally believe that there is a creature who sucks little children's blood from their chests. However, the name of the fiend to whom such acts are ascribed varies from hamlet to hamlet. They could be the work of the *vedomec* or the *mora* or of another of the voracious night-spirits. The *mora* oppresses/presses a man at night, but it and the *vedomec* can be exposed by the Gorica folk in the following way: they take a container which they fill with urine, seal and hang in the chimney above the fire. As long as the container remains suspended in the chimney over the fire, neither the *vedomec* nor the *mora* can enter the house, or leave it if already inside. If within, neither can escape or indeed 'let its water go', so it must die or reveal itself, although previously invisible. In the mountains, though, people who think that they are frequently afflicted by the *mora* keep a sheaf of straw by the bed and have a cudgel at the ready. At night if they think they are in the grip of a nightmare, they grasp the cudgel and begin to beat the sheaf as if it were the *mora*. In the Vipavska valley houses are protected from the *vedomec* and the *mora* by sticking a knife or a fork into the door, so that the *mora* or *vedomec* is unable to cross the threshold.[12]

In the Bela Krajna region, according to late nineteenth-century accounts, they used to bury stepmothers in a special way. As they were being laid in their coffins, some money, namely a coin of small denomination, (*groschen* or a *kreutzer*) was placed under the tongue.

If this had not been done, it was believed that out of the woman's grave would emerge an infernal succubus, the *vidovina* or *ris*, who would destroy the entire family to its last member. The *ris* was recognized in Eastern Styria, too. Wiesthaler reports that a Mr Stanko Vraz was told by his mother a story about the *ris* so terrifying that his hair stood on end; unfortunately the tale itself has not come down to us.

Vidovina probably comes from the verb 'to see' as in, originally, seer or sorcerer, although the similarity with *vdova*, widow, could be significant. *Ris* means both a lynx – to which an angry woman is proverbially compared in the Slovene language – and a magical circle drawn on the ground at a crossroads, which functions in Slovene magic to summon up spirits like a pentagram in the English occult tradition. There is probably also a connection between this spectral stepmother and the Polish Vampire known as the *sryz*.

A story from Poljane in Gorenska describes the manifestations of another unquiet being:

> When the year turns into autumn, we can see, flickering and dancing along the fringes of the meadows, some bright and unusual lights. These are beings called by the folk hereabouts *vedomci* or *vedunci*. If you do not disturb them they will not harm you, but do not on any account approach them with a light in your hand. Should anyone be foolish enough to do this the *vedomci* will strike and shatter the lantern, then tear the person apart and feast on their blood or in some other way do them great harm. Most of them emerge in the evening when the sky is cloudy: from a distance all that you can see is a multitude of lights rushing to and fro. Every now and again a number of them come together to form a single light, then disperse again.[13]

These dancing lights could be the fireflies, which are numerous and put on spectacular displays in the forest fringes of Slovenia; there are glow-worms, too, lurking in the grass, but both these luminous creatures appear in summer and are usually gone by autumn. If the evening is chill, the fireflies do not emerge, so it is more probable that the *vedomci* might be will-o'-the wisp: the products of marsh gas, or glimpses of the half-hidden campfires of gypsies (if they are not simply hallucinations of the kind that can be provoked by spirits of another sort). Almost identical stories of mysterious lights come from as far away as the French Caribbean, where they are known as *mauvai dife* ('evil fire') and blamed on zombies.[14]

✢

That night I dreamed that I was moving back and forth in front of an old Venetian mirror, and it was a different face I saw in the glass: a dark face (I am fair – greying, actually). In the same dream I was taken up a winding stairway to the rooftops of a street in London's flat suburbia, to see in the distance the sunlit faces of a mountain range.

None of this was surprising. The night before had been Hallowe'en and, on the return journey from a short visit to Venice, much of which had concerned peering from the darkened streets through windows at mirrors and chandeliers, we had stopped to look for the resting-place of a Vampire. The low-slung dazzling autumn sun had been illuminating the Julian Alps and the Karavanke chain as we crossed the Italian border into Slovenia. Dusk turned into night just outside the capital, Ljubljana.

Most Slovene villages in this quiet, prosperous state, which achieved independence in 1991 without the prolonged agonies of the other former Yugoslav republics, are postcard-pretty. Nowhere in the densely forested landscape 'on the sunny side of the Alps', as the tourist brochures have it, is there any of the sense of brooding menace evoked by fairy-tales or Gothic fiction, but there is an illusion of timelessness and an almost unsettling calm. In most of the English countryside the overwhelming impression is of movement: cloud fleets sweep across the streaked sky above the fields, impelled by winds blowing from the Atlantic or from the North Sea. There, birds flock and wheel, cattle and sheep amble, traffic hurries up and down the lanes and highways; little human figures strut and fret every-where. Here it is not like that at all. The air is still, and stillness permeates the countryside. The forests of pine, fir and beech are immobile, the fields are empty. Few birds are to be seen. In the villages there is only fitful movement every now and again when a car door opens or a householder ambles to and from an outbuilding.

As four o'clock in the afternoon became five o'clock in the evening, twilight crept across the countryside, a slow shadow falling. The pale three-quarter moon, at first almost indistinguishable from wispy criss-cross transparent cloud smears, became brighter silver-white. The forested hillside turned from vivid autumn russets and oranges to grey to black, smoke from houses beside the narrow roadway hung in a long, motionless streak along the foot of the hills around Krim, the highest peak in this little range. Below was marshland, now reclaimed as meadows and fields, but still here and there a water-filled ditch; black peaty earth showing through the harvest furrows. In the farmyards strings and heaps of yellow-orange maize-cobs drying, pumpkins, still some lying in their patches and others lined up on concrete, an abundance of firewood bundled and stacked for the coming winter. The smell in the air was a pungent mix of strong cow and pig manure and sweet woodsmoke. Only twenty or so kilometres from the city, the scene was utterly rustic: a few poplars, beeches and oaks, but otherwise just a handful of wayside shrines and houses scattered across the flat ground. The sophisticates in the capital say that the people hereabouts are odd.

There are no road signs that would give travellers their bearings, only the names of the villages one after another. Every other cross-roads has its war memorial to the partisans who fought the Germans (the few memorials to the Fascist White Guard collaborators are hidden away) around which candles are already burning for tomor-row's All Saints commemoration. The sky is pink to the west. And suddenly here is Tomišelj.

A little whitewashed chapel, houses; no shops, no garage, only farms, another church in the lee of the hill. This one seems derelict, its yellow ochre and cream façade is stained and flaking. The votive statues are gone from their alcoves, on each of the twin towers there is an iron clock, with hands showing different times, long stopped;

below the red copper onion dome and weathercocks painted words are barely decipherable – *sub tum praesidium confucimus*. ('We seek refuge beneath thy ramparts'). At the top of a broad flight of stone steps this church was once imposing, on its prominence where it looks across the valley in the direction of the city and the rest of the world. There is a grey stone wall separating the precincts from the forest behind, but no graveyard. The houses round about are, remarkably, old, dilapidated, the wooden hay-frames slightly awry. This is where Žirovec, the man for whom we were searching, had lived and where he should have died.

He is said to have been taken for burial at another place, about five kilometres further along the road that skirts the hills, past two more hamlets, in the little town of Ig. There, there is another, bigger church, square with a single tower and onion dome, but no churchyard either; a hundred years ago the graves were still marked with wooden boards, all now rotted, and the grave mounds have since been ploughed back into the earth. The new cemetery is right outside Tomišelj in the middle of the flat fields. It is quite dark now and the only light is from the candles placed on each of the black marble family tombs, immaculately kept and in neat rows separated by gravel, the whole enclosed by a low wall. The name Žirovec is nowhere to be seen, but in the dim flickering it has become almost impossible to make out the words on the tombstones anyway. We decide to go and come back when it is light.

The journey to Tomišelj was prompted by an anecdote in the 1883 edition of the journal *Ljubljanski Zvon*:

Even now [France Wiesthaler had written] almost the entire region of Ig and all the marshlands are talking about a peasant-farmer called Žirovec who, about fifty years ago, died in Tomišelj, which is a village in the Lubljansko Barje [marshes] near Ig, below the mountain of Krim.

Wiesthaler himself heard the story from several sources, notably a Mr Martin Perutec, a farmer from the marsh village of Černa Vas, and his wife.

This Žirovec was a fairly prosperous and level-headed man, but he turned into a Vampire after his death. He became a *vedomec* as the marsh inhabitants call such a person. People from Tomišelj are buried next to their parish church at Ig, to where Žirovec was also carried. What occurred after his burial? He began to rise from his grave at night and would go to his wife in Tomišelj to spend the night by her in her bed as he did before in life.

There are still old men living who knew Žirovec and kept seeing him, sitting on a stone near his house, putting on just one stocking: whichever way he tried to put it on, either on his right or left foot, the sock would never fit, and that is why Žirovec would always mutter angrily, 'It's the wrong foot!' On one occasion late at night he came to see his neighbours while they were winnowing grain in the barn, and talked to them as if he were alive. However, despite the fact that he did not harm the neighbours, everybody knew the deadly potential of the Vampire and was understandably afraid that he would visit them at night to drain away their life-forces or suck their life-blood from their veins. That is why the priest from Golo and the parish priest from Ig decided to put an end to this *volkodlak*. They dug up his grave and pierced his body, driving a hawthorn stake through his heart, then reburied the transfixed corpse in some other spot and filled up the grave again, all of which was witnessed by a number of people. And indeed, he never did thereafter reappear in Tomišelj to visit his wife, who, the poor woman, it is said eventually went mad with terror and grief. They also say that the *volkodlak*, while his heart was being pierced, cried out, 'Now you have caught me!'. The wife bore a child to the Vampire. Curiously, when the old grave was opened to receive a second body, the hawthorn stake was found to be lying still within it.

By the time of these events the alternative names for the creature, *vedomec* (evidently the local term), *volkodlak* and Vampire, are used indiscriminately. Although they retained their distinct identities in certain places, in the country in general the words had become interchangeable by the mid-nineteenth century.

The reference here to the undead husband sleeping with his wife is not a euphemism for sex, although there is the tantalizing reference (in only one of several versions) to the posthumous child, either a colourful confirmation of Žirovec's power beyond the grave or possibly a suggestion of an illegitimate baby. The detail of the wrong stocking portrays the Vampire as cursed or frustrated, but it may be relevant that in the Ukraine it was said that one could disable the local revenant, the *mjertovjec*, by removing a sock, while Balkan gypsies claimed that a Vampire could be expelled from the community by throwing his sock beyond the village boundary. In Prussia socks would be given to a Vampire to unravel one stitch at a time, thus preventing him from engaging in more dangerous activities.

We can imagine Žirovec's neighbours, having heard that the has returned, working nervously in their barn amid the dust-motes, wheat flour flying in the dim light of an oil-lamp – starting in fear at the strange shapes in the dark recesses, later perhaps telling their friends that they had felt his presence beside them.

The mysterious separation of the stake from the reburied body is a detail, found also in the Ukraine and elsewhere, suggesting that the Vampire has pulled his stake out and is again on the prowl – and that therefore only fire will finally destroy him.

᯼

We returned to Tomišelj in the spring to photograph the church, the fields, the forest in sunlight, and to try again to find some trace of the Vampire, the farmer Žirovec. The way of life and death of which he had been part has now gone for ever; almost no one left alive remembers the old stories any more, and the war and Communism between them did more to erase the troubled, oppressed, poorer past and transform the villages than even the coming of capitalism.

Research over the winter had cast more light on the case, in fact had illuminated everything except the central figure, the revenant himself. The parish records of births and deaths, kept in meticulous detail by the church and the Austro-Hungarian authorities, listed the Žirovec family members whose home had been in the twelfth house on Tomišelj's main street: little Matjaž who lived for only a year and a month before succumbing to a 'recurrent fever' in 1825, Janez who died at eighteen from an inflammation of the lungs, Anton, dead of apoplexy aged twenty-one, and the heir Jožef, the last of the male line, who passed away after a fever in 1849. It was Jožef Žirovec (the name also appears in the German form Scherowz) Senior, the children's father who was remembered by his neighbours as a Vampire. Nowhere is his death recorded, which is something quite remarkable: it was almost unheard-of for villagers to die anywhere but in their own home and even the rare victims of accidents or the suicides who drowned themselves in nearby streams were accorded a neat footnote in the parish archives. Jožef's wife, Magdalena, née Krašovec, died officially not of grief but of 'apoplexy' (a term that might designate a stroke or seizure) in 1838 aged fifty-three. Her husband, referred to as 'father' at the birth of the last child, Matjaž, thereafter as 'the late father', must have died between 1825 and 1832, but where and how we cannot tell. All that can be surmised is that if he had died far away, on a legitimate journey to buy and sell livestock, perhaps, or even, shamefully, on the run from his family, this would be enough to trigger a buzz of comment in the marshlands. Despite the later accounts, no grave was ever officially prepared for Žirovec in Ig, but had the priest, Father Bartolomej Čebašek, wanted to inter someone secretly, he could have done worse than use an unmarked plot beside the little church at Golo, a tiny remote village half hidden among the hills at the end of a steep bumpy track.

Today the church stands illuminated by sunlight in a clearing on its forested hilltop, still in use on Sundays, but usually locked and silent. Back in Tomišelj the Žirovec house is intact but empty, the Vampire and his family quite forgotten.

5
American Myths and Monsters

'How I should like to get my hands on this tail some time,
but it is impossible, the animal is constantly moving about,
the tail is constantly being flung this way and that. The
animal resembles a kangaroo, but not as to the face, which
is flat almost like a human face and small and oval; only
its teeth have any power of expression, whether they are
concealed or bared.'

Franz Kafka, *Dearest Father*

In 1793, in Manchester, Vermont, a spectacular exorcism of a suspected Vampire was carried out before a public audience. A certain Captain Isaac Burton had married three years earlier and his wife had subsequently died of tuberculosis. The Captain took another wife, but this second bride also soon fell ill and seemed likely to succumb to the same sickness. Burton blamed the affliction on the persistent vampiric power of the dead and had his first wife's body exhumed and carefully examined. More than a thousand people gathered to watch as her internal organs were removed and ceremonially burned, but the ritual failed to stop the remorseless progress of the consumption and the Captain and his doctors could only stand by as it drained the life from his new partner. After a few days the second Mrs Burton died in her turn.[1]

So the self-styled Real Vampires who have infested US underground culture since the late 1970s were not the first real or imagined vampiric entities to be recorded on that continent: the native Amerindian tribes of the north, unusually among peoples with a strong shamanistic tradition, do not seem to have foregrounded the blood-drinker or the night-demon in their mythologies. In North American Hispanic and Haitian communities today there is ample evidence for a persisting Vampire legend of a different sort deriving from native sorcery but, curiously, it was among the descendants of white immigrants, probably of Anglo-Celtic stock, that the belief in the power of the dead to drain away the vitality of the living took hold. Montague Summers relayed some later instances of the superstitions in Connecticut.

> During the year 1854 the *Norwich Courier* (USA) reported some remarkable happenings which had taken place at Jewett, a neighbouring town. In 1846–7 a citizen of Griswold, Horace Ray, had died of consumption. Unfortunately, two of his children, young men, developed the same disease and followed him to the grave, the younger and last of these passing away about 1852. It was found that yet a third son was a victim to the same fatal disease, whereupon it was resolved to exhume the bodies of the two brothers and cremate them because the dead were supposed to feed upon the living; and so long as the dead bodies in the grave remained entire the surviving members of the family must continue to furnish vital substance upon which these could feed. Wholly convinced that this was the case, the family and friends of the deceased on 8 June, 1854, proceeded to the burial ground, exhumed the bodies of the deceased brothers and having erected a great pyre, burned them there on the spot.[2]

In 1874 the *Providence Journal* recorded that in the village of Placedale, Rhode Island, a well-known inhabitant, Mr William Rose, himself dug up the body of his own daughter and burned her heart, acting under the belief that she was exhausting the vitality of the remaining members of the family. In the following year Dr Dyer, one of the leader physicians of Chicago, reported a case that came under his own observation: the body of a woman who had died of consumption was taken from the grave and burned, under the belief that she was attracting after her into the grave her surviving relatives.

Among the Irish author Bram Stoker's papers was a cutting from the *New York World* for 2 February 1896 (at that time Stoker had been in the USA supervising his employer, the actor-impresario Sir Henry Irving's tour) reporting scores of exhumations of supposed Vampires in New England. The article summarized 'recent ethnological research' carried out by George R. Stetson in the Rhode Island hamlets of Exeter, Foster, Kingstown and East Greenwich. From Stetson's own report comes the following:

> The region referred to, where agriculture is in a depressed condition and abandoned farms are numerous, is the tramping ground of the book agent, the *chromo* [coloured picture] peddler, the patent-medicine man and the home of the erotic and neurotic modern novel.
>
> Farmhouses deserted and ruinous are frequent, and the once productive lands, neglected and overgrown with scrubby oak, speak forcefully and mournfully of the migration of the youthful farmers from country to town.
>
> ... Naturally, in such isolated conditions, the superstitions of a much lower culture have maintained their place and are likely to keep it and perpetuate it, despite the church, the public school, and the weekly newspaper...
>
> The first visit in this farming community of native-born New Englanders was made to ——, a small seashore village possessing a summer hotel and a few cottages of summer residents not far from Newport – that Mecca of wealth, fashion and nineteenth-century culture. The —— family is among its well-to-do and most intelligent inhabitants. One member of this family had some years since lost children by consumption, and by common report claimed to have saved those surviving by exhumation and cremation of the dead.
>
> In the same village resides Mr ——, an intelligent man, by trade a mason, who is a living witness of the superstition and of the efficacy of the treatment of the dead which it prescribes. He informed me that he had lost two brothers by consumption. Upon the attack of the second brother his father was advised by Mr ——, the head of the family before mentioned, to take up the first body and burn its heart, but the brother attacked

objected to the sacrilege and in consequence subsequently died. When he was attacked by the disease in his turn, ——'-s advice prevailed, and the body of the brother last dead was exhumed, and 'living' blood being found in the heart and in circulation, it was cremated and the sufferer began immediately to mend and stood before me a hale, hearty and vigorous man of fifty years. When questioned as to his understanding of the miraculous influence, he could suggest nothing and did not recognize the superstition even by name. He remembered that the doctors did not believe in its efficacy, but he and many others did. His father saw the brother's body and the arterial blood...

At ——, a small isolated village of scattered houses in a farming population, distant fifteen or twenty miles from Newport and eight or ten from [the painter Gilbert] Stuart's birthplace, there have been made within fifty years a half-dozen or more exhumations. The most recent was made within two years, in the family of ——. The mother and four children had already succumbed to consumption, and the child most recently deceased (within six months) was, in obedience to the superstition, exhumed and the heart burned. Dr ——, who made the autopsy, stated that he found the body in the usual condition after an interment of that length of time. I learned that others of the family have since died, and one is now very low with the dreaded disease. The doctor remarked that he consented to the autopsy only after the pressing solicitation of the surviving children, who were patients of his, the father first objecting, but finally under continued pressure, yielding. Dr —— declares the superstition to be prevalent in all the isolated districts of southern Rhode Island, and that many instances of its survival can be found in the large centres of population. In the village now being considered, known exhumations have been made in five families, and in two adjoining villages in two families ... It does not by any means absolutely follow that this barbarous superstition has a stronger hold in Rhode Island than in any other part of the country.

In neighboring Connecticut, within a few miles of its university town of New Haven, there are rural farming populations, fairly prosperous, of average intelligence, and furnished with churches and schools, which have made themselves notorious by murder, suicides and numerous instances of melancholia and insanity.[3]

This well-attested example of the Vampire phenomenon (although the practitioners had apparently never heard the word itself) among New Englanders is interesting in that its cultural origins are unclear. No chain of evidence links the events of 1793 and thereafter with an earlier tradition that would presumably have been imported by European colonists (the connection between Vampires and wasting diseases is recorded among the Slavs, Hungarians and Germans; some speculate that the same beliefs may have existed in Scotland, for instance), or just possibly borrowed from unrecorded Native American sources. It is also notable that the American belief contains exactly the same elements as other reports of vampiric activity from around the world: the notion of contagion, the fear of the malevolent dead and the scapegoating of ancestors, the central role of blood, the inspection of exhumed suspects and the expunging by post-mortem mutilation and burning.

Hard data supporting the newspaper reports came in 1990 with the excavation of an abandoned family cemetery in Griswold. Archaeologists removed the human remains from the site and carefully examined twenty-nine skeletons. Among them they found the bones of an adult male of around fifty-five, who had been buried in the period between 1800 and 1840 and whose body seemed to have been disturbed and mutilated some time later. The evidence suggests that the man in question, identified only by the initials J.B. on his coffin lid, had suffered from severe tuberculosis or a similar condition, which may have been the cause of his death. When his grave was first reopened, probably to extract his heart and burn it, the body was already little more than a skeleton, so instead the head was removed and the femora arranged in a 'skull and crossbones' configuration on what remained of the chest, presumably in the hope that this would prevent the man from infecting his relatives.[4]

These localized East Coast panics and the Chicago incident from the eighteenth and nineteenth centuries seem to have been the first and last of their particular type in North America, although we cannot be sure that the same superstition was not prevalent, unsuspected by the world at large, in other communities there before and since.

What is particular about these outbreaks is that the specific medical basis for the superstition is made explicit: tuberculosis is the trigger. There are plenty of other conditions, misunderstood and/or incurable, that might have provoked the same response in communities elsewhere and at other times, but this is one of the few instances in which we know for sure what drove otherwise civilized people to exhume and destroy their own kin. There are, nonetheless, a number of lesser-known European cases from different times and places which specify the basis of the panic. Witnessing the ravages of an outbreak of plague (probably pneumonic) in Transylvania in 1709, the Hungarian doctor Samuel Köleséri described the maddened populace digging up dozens of recently buried corpses and either impaling them with poles or beheading them or both, in the conviction that they were responsible for the spread of the disease.[5]

The British anthropologist Mary Edith Durham reported a case from Bosnia in 1906 in which an epidemic of a different kind was the trigger:

> ... there was an outbreak of typhus ... in a village near Vlasenitza. A young man was the first to die. His wife sickened and swore that her husband had returned in the night and sucked her blood, and said "He is a *lampir*!" The neighbours, filled with fear, begged the authorities to permit them to dig up and burn his body. Permission was refused and a panic ensued. The *lampir* was seen and heard by many people and there were fifteen deaths.

She comments:

> It would be interesting to know how many of these died because they believed they must die, owing to the *lampir*. The peasants all through Albania and Macedonia are extraordinarily affected mentally if they believe they must die, and seem to make no effort whatsoever to live ...'[6]

Another Hungarian doctor, György Tállar, is the only man on record to try to treat, over many years, patients from Transylvania and Wallachia who said they were suffering from the effects of vampire attacks. While he cared for them he carefully studied these Romanian and Serbian subjects and came to the conclusion that their convictions were perfectly sincere but their symptoms were caused by nutritional deficiencies in the strict diet ordained by their Orthodox religion. Naturally enough, the effects were most noticeable in the lean midwinter months – exactly when they claimed that vampiric activity was at its height.[7]

ᐁ

More than two hundred years later and several thousand miles to the west, a fresh wave of Vampire activity was just beginning. On Wednesday 15 November 1995, on the outskirts of the city of Caguas, south of the Puerto Rican capital of San Juan, as a Señora Gómez was preparing for bed in the family home which backed on to heavily wooded countryside, she saw, to her horror, an abnormally long, thin arm covered in hair snake through the open bedroom window. The clawed hand at the end of the arm seized a child's teddy-bear from a table-top and tore it instantly to pieces. In her panic Señora Gómez hurled a coffee cup at the thing – she caught a glimpse of a single red eye and a hideous but indistinct face – and screamed for assistance as the arm was withdrawn and the beast made its escape. The police officers, civil-defence officials and members of the local Guardia Municipal, who jointly responded to the emergency call, discovered nothing but a strip of unidentifiable flesh adhering to the window-sill and a smear of viscous slime on the pane.

When Julio González and his wife Julia found their five chickens lying arrayed in a perfect line in their backyard in Vega Baja, also in Puerto Rico – 'as if they were sunbathing,' they said – they examined the birds carefully and found that they were not relaxing but dead, and each had been drained of blood. The couple reported the incident to police and were interviewed by an officer, Pablo Robles. It was in the course of this questioning that they confided that something else had happened in their household at around the same time: their five-year-old daughter Oralis had been marked on the forearm with a tattoo-like impression that read OJO – 10 – OJO. Simultaneously, said her father, her IQ seemed to have increased dramatically and she could now fairly be described as an infant prodigy. The parents were reluctant to press the child about who or what had caused the marks, for fear of distracting her from her studies; the little girl was also reluctant to talk about what had happened to her. News of the family's strange experience spread nevertheless and an alien visitation was suggested. (Coincidentally, the marks left by the aliens contained, repeated, the word *ojo* – Spanish for 'eye' and 'I'm looking' – which is often drawn by children for fun on walls, book covers or on each other's hands, as the shape formed by the letters looks like two eyes and a nose.)

William 'Billy' Nubian was living with his companion Nancy Pontiac in a trailer on North Flanwell Avenue in Tucson, Arizona, in May 1996. One weekend, at around two o'clock in the morning, they were jerked awake by the sound of terrified bleating from Delilah and Mattie, the two goats they kept in a pen outside. Billy rushed out and saw Mattie being attacked by what he described to the *Arizona Daily Star* as a 'large rat-like creature'. In his interview Billy Nubian (the name is perhaps a pseudonym, as Nubians are a breed of goat), still shaken from the incident, was quoted as stating, 'Tha' little pisser had her pinned down in her pen, an' when I came out an' it seen me, it let out this unhuman [*sic*] shriek like some fuckin' banshee or something!' Nancy Pontiac, however, could not corroborate Billy's story: she stated that she had heard the goats' cries and followed Billy out of the trailer only seconds later, but had seen nothing unusual outside. She further described her partner as 'crazy as an elephant in heat'. A few days later, also in Tucson, the Espinoza family placed an emergency call to their local police department saying that their home had been invaded in the early hours by an unknown creature, which mumbled and gestured at them and smelt like a wet dog; the creature had apparently entered the bedroom of the family's seven-year-old-son, had climbed on to his bed and sat briefly on his chest.

All these reports were listed under the same heading, a categorization adopted in the second stage of a prolonged panic that began in the forested central highlands of the island of Puerto Rico in the first months of 1995. At the outset the evidence for some unnatural visitation consisted only of dead sheep and goats with a single puncture mark, usually said to be the width and depth of a finger, in the throat or chest, and drained of blood. In early November a vet tried in vain to save the lives of five nearly bloodless and comatose goats by injecting them with a coagulant, while elsewhere on the island the first footprint or handprint (it indicated six toes, later examples sometimes showed only three) was found after an attack on a herd of steers. Rabbits, hens and ducks began to fall victim to the mysterious predator, too.

From mid-November 1995, the date of the Gómez incident which was one of the first in a mainly urban neighbourhood (wondering locals recalled the activities of the demonic Freddy Krueger in the *Nightmare on Elm Street* movie series), glimpses of the perpetrator started to multiply: by the end of the month at least fifteen residents of the city of Canovanas alone had caught sight of it. Sketches were made and the name chosen for the Vampire-monster, *El Chupacabras*, literally 'The Goat-sucker', echoed around the island of Puerto Rico and reverberated into the international ether.

✝V✝

The reaction to the Chupacabras panic outside the Spanish-speaking communities was reminiscent on a small scale of the mixture of condescension and fascination with which the 'Enlightenment' treated the eighteenth-century Vampire epidemic of eastern Europe. Commentators pointed out, not inaccurately, that all of Latin America was a hotbed of sympathetic magic, was inordinately prone to UFO-mania ('they are generally more accepting of the existence of alien life than many parts of the world are'), and one or two noted in passing that legends of blood-sucking creatures had been recorded there among superstitious 'peasants' (a word that has never been applied to the countryfolk of *North* America, even the inhabitants of Griswold) as far back as anyone can project.

✝V✝

Almost as soon as the first sightings of what local people had initially nicknamed *el canguro* ('the kangaroo') or *el conejo* ('the rabbit') had begun to circulate by word of mouth, the phenomenon was hijacked by special interest groups. The mayor of Canovanas, the Honourable Jose 'Chemo' Soto, who was campaigning for re-election at the time, took to patrolling the outlying districts of the city with a two-hundred-strong volunteer militia dressed in combat fatigues as well as launching weekly expeditions across the forested hills with a goat in a cage as bait, a crucifix and, in conscious emulation of his hero Indiana Jones, a whip. His statements to the press and promises to defend the people against the Chupacabras threat were soon being reported in the Hispanic media in the US and in the *New York Times*. The leading 'UFO-logist' in Puerto Rico, Jorge Martín, supplied a sketch of the beast, based on the first eyewitness accounts, that was published in the populist *El Vocero* newspaper and thereafter posted on the Internet for international consideration. Martín himself, using his own magazine and radio show, sought to discredit some of the other self-styled experts who had rushed to involve themselves, in particular a cult-like group of UFO-researchers named NOVA, whose members declared with confident precision that the Chupacabras was one of a group of twenty aliens that had landed on our planet to conduct experiments with animal and human blood to develop toxic viruses with which they were determined to wipe out humanity. New attempts to depict the Chupacabras were reminiscent of cathedral gargoyles and rumours began to circulate among the Catholic majority that it might be one of the host of pre-apocalyptic demons predicted in the Book of Revelation.

Apart from the interest shown by the print media, first in Puerto Rico itself, then in Mexico and the USA, the hugely influential Miami-based Hispanic talk-show *El Show de Cristina* repeatedly featured news and discussion of El Chupacabras, and its host, Cristina Saralege, declared to the press that she was convinced that the Puerto Rico reports were genuine evidence of an alien presence on the island. A clairvoyant, Brother Carmelo, announced that the Chupacabras were indeed nocturnal, horned extraterrestrial Vampires. He declared that not everyone would be granted the power to capture one of the many representatives of the species that were at large: '... to do so requires the use of a laser beam or a silver bullet'. Carmelo confirmed the speculations that the Chupacabras hid by day in the dense vegetation of the mountain rainforest of El Yunque and in the natural labyrinth of interconnecting caves that lies beneath much of the island.

Once the discussion moved to the Internet, speculation was limitless, much of it devoted to conspiracy theories, especially the claim that secret US government agencies were interfering with the investigations: they were spreading distracting disinformation, which included blaming the outbreaks on giant toads, feral monkeys or vampire bats, or steering reporters towards the more obviously ridiculous personal testimonies rather than giving them access to credible witnesses. Giant vampire bats (which do not occur in Puerto Rico) had initially been suspected by the farmers living in the areas where the first attacks took place and, confusingly, the name 'goatsucker' is correctly applied to a species of bird, the *caprimulgus*, which in fact merely lives among goats and eats only insects or fruit – in Roman times it was thought to suck the milk from nanny-goats' udders, hence the name. As far as science is aware, there is no such thing as a giant vampire bat: the largest South American varieties are small and rarely survive a journey north across the Caribbean. Some 'cryptozoologists' on the other hand have speculated that the terrifying *camazotz* ('snatch-bat') referred to in ancient inscriptions could really have existed and, worse, could conceivably have survived in Central American jungles.[8]

✶✷

By the end of 1995, word was out, the idea of the creature – if not its exact delineation – had implanted itself in the popular consciousness and an exponential panic gathered momentum. Testimonies continued to mount up in Puerto Rico, and then in April 1996 a twenty-one-year-old woman, Juana Tizoc, from the village of Alfonso Calderón in a corn-farming area of Sinaloa state, Mexico, appeared on Televisa, the largest Mexican TV network, to claim that she had been attacked and bitten in the neck by a winged and horned creature. Although police refused to take Ms Tizoc's story seriously, and wits identified the marks as love-bites, her announcement was followed by a spate of reports from all over the north and east of the country. In some areas farmers refused to work at night and parents kept their children at home. A nurse from the suburbs of the capital, Mexico City, was hospitalized with a severed arm and neighbours told journalists that she had been attacked by the Chupacabras, but no more was heard of this case. As the hysteria mounted, the Sinaloa authorities belatedly sent a team of investigators to the site of the Tizoc attack and staked out the area over two successive nights. Just before dawn on both days, roaming packs of dogs launched concerted attacks on the farmyard cattle and were caught in the traps that had been laid, but the news went unnoticed.

Simultaneously, the massacre of sixty-nine domestic animals at Sweetwater, Florida, preceded a wave of reports and sightings in the Latino communities of the southern USA, with isolated incidents claimed as far north as New Jersey, New York City and Cambridge, Massachusetts.

In order to calm public hysteria (manifested in dozens of emergency calls to the authorities every week) the University of Miami, in collaboration with the MetroDade Zoo, carried out public examinations of the bodies of animals identified as victims of the goatsucker. Detective Pat Brickman, who helped co-ordinate the presentation of the findings, spoke to the press as follows:

> We had to conduct these autopsies to say, 'Idiots, these are dog-bites. There are hungry stray dogs out there, and they have to eat, too, so they attack goats and chicken in people's yards.' It happens on every farm and in every rural area in the United States, but when you get people who believe in the Tooth Fairy and the Easter Bunny, they believe everything they see on TV.

The assistant director of the zoo, Ron Magill, expressed a much less robust scepticism. As a part-Cuban Spanish-speaker who finds the existence of UFOs and extraterrestrials credible, he was reluctant to ridicule the fears of the people of Dade County or, for that matter, of nearby Sweetwater, where he inspected the site of a well-publicized attack in early 1996. Nevertheless, he became convinced on the basis of the puncture marks on the victims, footprints and the marks of digging around fences, that the culprit in every case was canine. He also refuted the universal assumption that the animals had been exsanguinated: he found that, although there might be minimal blood around the wounds, in the subjects that he examined the arteries were still full. Many of the owners of livestock and pets had pointed to the fact that carcasses had not been eaten and in some cases had been left lying in rows, but this, too, can be typical of the behaviour of marauding dogs who kill for sport as well as for food, and sometimes pile up their prey like trophies. In 1994, Magill reminded anyone who would listen that fifteen antelopes had been killed in a zoo compound by dog-intruders in exactly the same way.[8]

In Veracruz, Mexico, in the summer of 1996, citizens marched on government offices with placards demonstrating that the authorities take action to protect them from the goatsucker's ravages. For its part the government warned rural farmers that they risked destroying fragile ecosystems when they tried to kill off Chupacabras by lighting fires in caves across the country. At the same time, the first sighting was reported from the former British colony of Belize, where nine-year-olds Tyrel Haylock and Annette Cantún, and Umberto Cantún, aged six, saw the creature stalking their goats and sheep.

Later the scare spread to Baja California, Panama and to Brazil, where a US expatriate claimed to have shot and decapitated a Chupacabras but was unwilling to produce the head as evidence. Puerto Rico and Mexico continued to generate the largest numbers of recorded attacks, with the possible distinction that most of the Puerto Rican reports were linked to visible animal deaths, whereas in Mexico many were based on the malevolent effects of a 'shadow' or unseen presence on a human victim, who was invariably traumatized but rarely physically harmed.

The epidemic seemed to subside in the early months of 1997, but then, on 20 November, fifty farm animals were found dead at Utuado, a town south-west of San Juan, Puerto Rico. The livestock was once again drained of blood, apparently, in all cases by way of inexplicable triangular perforations visible on the bellies of the carcasses.

Physical descriptions of the Puerto Rican monster varied, but not widely, coalescing into a recognizable set of characteristics soon after the first sightings. Michael Negrón, a twenty-five-year college student described it as 'about three or four feet tall with skin like that of a dinosaur. It had bright red eyes the size of hen's eggs, long fangs and multicoloured spikes down its head and back.' Two night fishermen, who were surprised by the beast then chased by it, said it resembled the devil himself and had large ears, luminous oval eyes, which glowed alternately orange and red, claws and wings. It was between four and five feet in height. Other early reports likened the thing to a monkey and a turkey, but all agreed that it was smaller than an adult human and was capable of jumping long distances. A number of those whose property or livestock were attacked also remarked on traces of slime – similar to those left by apparitions in the cult film *Ghostbusters* – and a smell of sulphur at the scene.

A Señora Ada Arroyo, assistant director of a nursing home, suffered a nervous collapse after seeing the Chupacabras. Her testimony was that she heard screams 'similar to those made by a lamb being slaughtered ... I went out to the patio and managed to see a strange hairy figure, grayish in colour, covering its body with a pair of wings. It had a flattened, vulpine face, with enormous red eyes.' But investigators could find no trace of the intruder, or of any animal victims among the herd of cows that were grazing on land adjoining the building.

At first sight the perpetrator of the Latin-American outrages seems to be a uniquely grotesque curiosity, and it would have been easy to invent a more streamlined, unified vision of evil, but the odd, composite nature of the Chupacabras, as well as its comical overtones and its adoption as a mascot, mirrors another chimaera, the mythical *Wolpertinger*, part-duck, part-deer, part-fox, which belongs to Bavaria in southern Germany.

ᐯ

If the memory of the media is wilfully and deliberately short, so often are the memories of communities themselves. As a handful of writers pointed out at the time of the attacks, the Chupacabras was not an original or unique apparition, even in the context of Puerto Rico. In the mid-1970s a similar folk-panic had been generated by the supposed presence of the *Vampiro de Moca* (Moca is a mountain village), that similarly attacked livestock and wild animals and also, it was said, drained them of their blood. Another Puerto Rican blood-sucker of the same period was the amphibious *Garadiablo*, which was reputed to haunt lagoons and marshland. Both these scares died down after an unproven theory was advanced that blamed crocodiles introduced on to the island clandestinely and illegally (by unnamed outsiders).

In the states of Mexico bordering on the southern US the existence of at least two similar beings had been rumoured for years: *La Coruá*, a legendary giant water-serpent, and *El Carbunco*, a winged four-legged animal with a light glowing in the middle of its forehead. The Dominican Republic had experienced a wave of cattle mutilations and blood-draining in 1978; supernatural forces had been blamed, and there had been claimed sightings of an unnamed 'alien' predator, while in both Colombia and Brazil, also during the 1970s, the *Mono Grande* ('Big Monkey'), which was thought to lurk in the inaccessible depths of forests and jungles, emerged from time to time to mutilate goats, mules and cattle. One of its trademarks was the removal of the tongue. Venezuela has long been haunted by *El Coco*, a local version of the peninsular Spanish bogey-man pictured by Goya, a fiend in human rather than animal form who preys on domestic animals and fowl and steals naughty children and drinks their blood, while in 1997 a monster known as the 'tongue-eater', and described as half turkey, half cat, began to prey on cattle in the central Nicaraguan province of Boaca, sucking their blood and, true to its nickname, tearing out their tongues.

Foreign anthropologists offered explanations: 'There are a certain number of these legends of bloodsucking animals in South and Latin America. They are usually analyzed as anti-capitalist, an unconscious means of rebellion by country-people who believe that capitalism is sucking dry the earth and their entire being.'[10]

Foreign ethnographers and folklorists endorsed these rationalizations and drew parallels with the *Loo-garou* from nearby Haiti, a descendant of the French *Loup Garou*, the werewolf, which mutated in the island colony into a blood-sucker alleged to prey upon humans. Like the European werewolves and Vampires it was viewed as shifting between the human, animal and supernatural worlds. The expert consensus is that the *Loo-garou* is the product of a fearfully poorer-than-poor community whose integrity is so precarious that people have come to be mortally afraid of the outside world, even of their nearest neighbours.

The interaction of capitalism and poverty may well be a factor in the persistence of this kind of legend, but something older and deeper animates the *Loo-garoo* and powers the Trinidadian *Soucouyant*, the Ecuadorian *Tin-tin* (both bat-monsters) as well as the Peruvian *Chonchon* (a Vampire identical to the 'flying-head' entities of East Asia).

Any suggestion that such legendary beasts are peculiar to the Hispano-Francophone world or restricted to the ambit of the very poor is misleading: cattle mutation, the draining of animal blood and their attribution to aliens or monsters has repeatedly occurred in the rural USA. There is a long tradition of unidentified predators – Bigfoot, Sasquatch and the Wendigo being the best known – in the wilderness areas of North America, and in the 1970s giant condors had been suspected of invading the Rio Grande valley. More intriguingly, there have been reports since the 1950s of a savage being that resembles both a large rodent and a kangaroo, and possesses glowing blood-red eyes; in the backwoods of the north-east this creature goes under the name of the Jersey Devil.

There was an outbreak of cattle mutilations in the western United States between 1975 and 1978 so severe that state authorities launched their own investigations and the governor of Colorado, where 180 cases were reported during one year, declared it 'one of the greatest outrages in the history of the western cattle industry'. Another estimate put the total number of mutilations at 700 over an

eighteen-month period. What intrigued credulous and more dis-
passionate observers alike was the way in which the cattle seemed to
have been treated after death. The mutilations were concentrated in
unexpected places: tongues were often missing, ears sliced neatly off,
intestines and/or udders and genitalia carefully removed and rectal
areas bored into. Choice cuts of meat were left undisturbed and there
appeared to be no logic to the injuries beyond a sort of virtuoso
display of ferocity. The absence of blood in and around the victims
was a universal feature. Because of the 'illogical' pattern of wounds,
rustlers and marauding meat wholesalers were discounted; deranged
or sexually disturbed individuals were not, but how to explain the
very wide distribution of very similar cases? An ingenious theory was
put forward by a UFO-logist, Dr Thomas E. Bearden, which chal-
lenged what had become a popular assumption: the idea that the
animals had undergone alien abduction and experimentation. Bearden's hypothesis was that UFO activity was not the product of the
physical manifestation of extraterrestrials, but of 'tulpas' or con-
centrations of hostile thoughts that were capable of generating forces
in the real world. The culprits in this case, he said, were the Russians,
whose malevolent impulses were being channelled and directed
against the West to spread a fatally debilitating paranoia. 'The cow,'
Bearden contended, 'is a Western symbol *par excellence*; Western
children nurture on cow's milk. Attacks on livestock should therefore
be regarded as tulpoid phenomena of a sharply symbolic nature.'[11]

There were possible links, too, with other non-Hispanic outbreaks
of animal-maiming and killing. In England in the 1970s the deaths
of sheep and cattle in the south-west were blamed on the so-called
'beast of Exmoor', while in suburban Surrey a puma was said to be
on the loose in 1966 and was spotted periodically for thirty years
afterwards but was never caught (blood-sucking, however, did not
feature in these and other similar scares in UK country districts). The
widespread mutilation of horses has also attracted the attention of
psychiatrists and dramatists, as well as UFO-watchers, and it has
recently become clear that reports of this seemingly bizarre practice
can be traced back throughout human history and across a wide

range of cultures in which the horse has provided a spectacular totemic target for sexual sadists and those who wish merely to void their spite against the natural world or their fellow humans.

✴

Unofficial postings in Internet newsgroups in February 1996 claimed that the NIE, the undercover investigative arm of the Puerto Rico police, had traced the source of the animal mutilations there; that they had been part of sacrificial rituals in the practice of *santería* (the voodoo-like magic tradition that flourishes across the Caribbean and into South America), and that they were specifically attributed to a *santera* (sorceress) from the Dominican Republic, nicknamed 'Yoyi la Santera', and resident in the Hillside district of Rio Pedras.

Frustratingly, there seems to have been no corroboration or follow-up to this report which, even if it was totally spurious, is interesting in two respects: first, the person identified as the origin of the affliction is an outsider, and vampire epidemics, almost wherever they occur, rely on the notion of a threat to the community from an external persecutor. Second, it is surprising that *santería* had not already been suspected, as many of its central rituals involve animal sacrifice and the draining, drinking or sprinkling of blood. In all the areas in which *santería*, voodoo and other similar forms of magic are practised, both the sorcerers and their spirit familiars are also thought to indulge in indiscriminate blood-sucking or drinking. Some experts have sought to trace these still strongly embedded beliefs (entire markets in Mexico openly provide animals for sacrifice and ingredients for spells and potions) to the thirsts of the ancient Aztec and Mayan gods, but the use of blood in shamanistic magic seems to be a universal.

✴

There are various reasons why Puerto Rico could be susceptible to a social scare on the scale of the Chupacabras affair. It is essentially a colony of the USA, despite its Hispanic heritage (it was ceded by Spain to the USA in 1899), and the psychosocial pressures to which this gives rise range from a simple resentment of economic exploitation and the swamping of the native culture to a conviction that the giant observatory at Arecibo, the largest radio and radar telescope in the world, is involved in a US government conspiracy to attract and download alien spacecraft. Other paranoias, reinvigorated by the television series *The X-Files*, refer to the US using the island as a testing site for experiments in chemical warfare or gene manipulation – this theory would suggest that the goat-sucker is a mutation which has escaped from a secret laboratory.

More tangible and demoralizing evidence of an outside threat to the island's way of life is the Aids epidemic, which has hit Puerto Rico hard. The association of a collective fear with notions of blood and contamination is clear, and may link with other sexual anxieties: Dr Neftali Olmo-Terrón, a psychiatrist from San Juan, has suggested that the Chupacabras' attacks on domestic backyards relates to deep fears of penetration from the rear – the symbolism may be political (colonialist exploitation again) or sexual or both at once. The name given to the blood-sucking monster has inevitable sexual resonances for a speaker of Spanish: *chupar*, to suck, is a verb associated naturally enough with oral sex, while *cabra*, which means she-goat, may also refer metaphorically to promiscuous or unclean women, and recalls its male relative, *cabrón*, one of the strongest terms of abuse that can be applied to a man.

On a lighter note, one Puerto Rican expatriate, Carlos Rivas, writing from the campus of Princeton in the USA of his identification with the Chupacabras as a national icon, said not entirely frivolously that Chupi reminded him in his cold exile of an imaginary childhood friend, 'of the monster under the bed to whom I would sneak cookies and other treats when my parents went to sleep'. The Chupacabras breaks through the boundaries of the Americanized consumerist life-style, but stops short at sucking the blood of children or other defenceless human beings. 'He lives the ideal life of the *jíbaro* [the original indigenous people], in harmony with nature and very fond of his animals ... El Chupacabras appeals to that atavistic primitive portion of our psyche that longs for the old days of climbing among trees and hunting for bananas.' (A fellow Puerto Rican student at

Princeton, Hector 'Tito' Armstrong, started the Chupacabras Internet Homepage which reported sightings along with listing examples of the goatsucker's exploitation by advertising and popular culture.)

This may be why the Chupacabras quickly became a folk mascot for Puerto Ricans, on the same lines as the Bavarian *Wolpertinger*, the Scottish Loch Ness monster, Bigfoot or the Irish leprechaun. The craze probably raised the status of the island among the larger, independent Hispano-American states and helped it to assert its distinctiveness from its English-speaking patron. In Mexico and Venezuela satirists quickly applied the Chupacabras nickname to venal politicians, while in the US–Mexican border states fast-food restaurants appropriated it for themselves, and the Texas town of Zapata inaugurated an annual Chupacabras festival. T-shirts with images of the monster were produced all over Central and North America and even by the *Fortean Times* magazines in London. The lyrics of several Hispanic hit records referred to the goatsucker and he (the monster was always assumed to be male) danced and flirted his way through a hugely successful pop video.

Meanwhile, in Puerto Rico, the sworn enemies of the beast refused to be distracted by this wave of frivolity. Three years on, the head of Canovanas Civil Defence, Ismael Aponte, was one of the monster's most resolute opponents and by now an expert on its appearance and behaviour: 'It's described as looking like a kangaroo, but really it is nothing of the sort: it has the snout of a pig and huge slit eyes and pointy ears. Only its feet are like a kangaroo's. But it's fast and strong in a way that a kangaroo isn't. In my personal opinion this was a genetic experiment involving various animals and this was the outcome.' He conjures up a violation of the natural order – committed by foreigners – which recalls H. G. Wells's fantasy, recently filmed, *The Island of Dr Moreau*. He will not be deflected from his mission: 'After so long hunting him, after so many sleepless nights, so many headaches, so much fatigue, if I meet up with him, either he'll get me or I'll get him. This is between the two of us. He might get me, but I won't run away when I get my hands on him!'[12]

✝

In following the trajectory of the Chupacabras-scare from its beginnings in early 1995 to what seemed to be its fading out in 1998, we are presented with a modern case-study of a Vampire legend, albeit one with humorous rather than tragic overtones: no humans have thus far been killed by the monster or made scapegoats (no pun intended) for its attacks. As always, the panic and its underlying causes are not simple, one-dimensional phenomena: they are a synthesis of anxieties and representations, taken up, mediated and elaborated by a variety of agencies who may or may not be conscious of the roles they are playing.

To a sceptical outsider it is fairly easy to dismiss the physical evidence – as medical and veterinary authorities have repeatedly shown: the marks and the state of the bodies produced all point to the normal activity of common predators. Disappointingly, given the imaginative theories, the same argument has been used to dismiss the unusual evidence collected from the US cattle mutilations of the seventies: smaller predators and scavengers alike will concentrate on the softest, tastiest protuberances and orifices rather than gouging for hunks of prime meat. Their teeth can often inflict clean, apparently surgical wounds, and the similarity in attacks across the country only points to species-specific animal behaviour. The absence of blood is just because it has seeped into the earth; sceptics maintain that complete exsanguination is nearly impossible because the arteries would collapse part-way through the process and halt it, leaving some blood trapped in the corpse. It seems that, just as Magill observed at Sweetwater, there is at the root of the 'epidemics', just as with the 'irrefutable' evidence observed on the corpses of the undead in rural Europe, a poor understanding by humans of the workings of the natural world where death is concerned. The ascribing of natural, everyday happenings to dramatic causes has, as well as the many phantom predators lurking in the foliage, another precedent in Latin America in the universal myth (probably originating in Mexico and inspired by Amerindian folktales) of *La Llorona*, the Weeping Woman, a banshee-like ghost, who was invoked to frighten children and explain the uncanny, piteous sounds made by passing creatures in the night.

✢

Most of the (non-Hispanic) practising Vampires interviewed for this book were aware of the Chupacabras side-show in the Vampire carnival but were dismissive: 'I think that it's a backwater superstition and the mutilations that went along with it . . . I don't know. I heard that translated it means 'goatsucker': goats are filthy and they smell a good deal so I could only put it down to another animal or a lunatic.'[13]

'There are enough willing humans around that there is really no need to bring in animals!'[14]

It is important to try to comprehend why and how a whole sequence of communities became caught up in the very real Chupacabras hysteria, and understanding requires empathy. Apart from the more sophisticated theoretical explanations, simple instincts need to be considered: the fear of the wilderness and the dark – felt especially by newly urbanized communities; the desolation experienced by relatively poor households when their home-space is invaded and their precious livestock destroyed; the unconscious yearning for public attention, the longing to participate in a novel and exciting communal experience. Even if it was founded partly on social insecurities, the Chupacabras panic was obviously not based on fear of one's neighbour but, rather, served to increase neighbourly solidarity as people banded together to fight the elusive menace.

Is it, anyway, so surprising that a person brought up within a tradition where Christian miracles are tinged with indigenous magic, an individual living on an island criss-crossed with underground tunnels and caverns, looking up every day at almost inaccessible mountains above which hover aircraft sent by an alien colonizer, a citizen for whom the threat of blood-borne diseases has become a morbid preoccupation, for whom the loss of a goat may mean real hardship, may interpret the subtropical sounds of the night and the carcass in the backyard as something more sinister than the work of dogs? Is it not conceivable (even, perversely, slightly reassuring) that he or she is up against something that all the posturing of local officialdom and all the foreign hardware is powerless against? But why should that something have hind legs like those of a kangaroo? Because if that citizen's fences – the real and symbolic limits of his or her home territory – are being breached, then the intruder must be capable of unprecedented and prodigious leaps.

The New England Vampires seem to represent a relatively short-lived tradition imported wholesale from another continent, whereas the Chupacabras was a home-grown bugbear, straddling the old heritage composed of extended family, church and nation, and a new reality of high-technology and global media.

✣

Among the Native American populations that survived the arrival of the Europeans with their customs more or less intact, there are at least two further and distinct examples of belief in a vampire-like entity. In the lesser pantheon of malignant deities and evil spirits in the Mexican Aztec tradition are found the *ciutateteos* or *ciuapipiltin* (the names signify 'honourable mothers' and 'princesses' respectively). These are Lilith-like creatures of the night who, in common with their European witch-counterparts, gather at cross-roads, hold sabbats and abduct and bewitch children, causing seizures and suffocation and inciting lust in sleeping men. Like Lilith, too, they are associated with the screech-owl and drink the blood of their victims. They are said to be the spirits of women who have died in childbirth. The parallels with the *lamiae* and *striges* of the European classical tradition are so clear as to be astonishing – just as those evil-doers were ruled by Hecate, goddess of sorcery, the underworld and the moon, the *civitateo* serve the female deity Tlazolteotl, who has almost identical attributes. Like the familiar western European witch-stereotype, they sometimes ride broomsticks. Like the early Slav cosmic monsters, one of their tasks is to return the setting sun to the dark underworld at the end of each day. It must be remembered, though, that the only accounts we have of these Mexican beliefs were compiled by Europeans, usually priests, who used their own lexicon and discourse of magic to describe an alien system that was as yet unexamined and hard to interpret.

There is an intriguing parallel to the European post-shamanic roles of *benandanti*, *volkodlak* and *táltos* in another figure from more the recent folklore of Tlaxcala, east of Mexico City. The *tlahuelpuchi* is a shapeshifting Vampire sorceress (there are also rare male examples, but they are said to be less powerful), who is simultaneously an identifiable, although seldom identified, member of the human community.

These entities are able to travel undetected by changing shape after first detaching their bodies from their legs (very like the Filipino Aswang and the Malaysian Penanggalan). They can take the form of a *xopilote* (vulture) or a turkey (one of the forms ascribed to the Puerto Rican Chupacabras), or some other animal, and are indistinguishable from the real thing except for a glowing aura (common to other Central American apparitions). If pursued they can turn into a tiny insect such as a tick (just like the Slavonic *volkodlak*). A typical *tlahuelpuchi* becomes aware at puberty that she has been born into her role: in order to survive she is compelled to drink human blood at least once a month, obtaining it by preying upon young children. Before entering the home of a potential victim, the *tlahuelpuchi* must fly backwards and forwards above the house making the form of a cross. And a metal cross, perhaps in the form of open scissors, can ward them off, as can garlic or onions, mirrors and religious medallions.

The monthly blood-drinking is an echo of the menstrual 'curse' (and may reflect an old and widespread supposition that women will be driven to replace the lost blood by other means). The *tlahuelpuchi* functions as a supernatural explanation for infant deaths, especially when sudden and mysterious, and as an instrument of social control in frightening naughty children and negligent mothers. Both the sorceress's trajectory above her victim's home and the crossed scissors that can thwart her betray the influence of Christian symbolism, while garlic, onions, mirrors are apotropaics in many societies.

Each *tlahuelpuchi* has a defined territory (like the European *kresnik* and *kudlak*), is known to others of its kind and can be recognized by local shamans and *nahuals* (a kind of metamorphosing sorcerer), who leave it alone. Apart from these night-time hunting excursions, the creature lives as a human with its family, who protect it and conceal its terrible secret; if any member of the family should try to kill it, they in turn would have to assume the role. The only way to stop the *tlahuelpuchi*'s predations is to catch it in the act – an almost impossible task.[15]

It is equally impossible to establish precisely how old the beliefs in the *tlahuelpuchi* and *nahual* are, or whether and how far they have been affected by post-conquest European influences. Nevertheless, the existence of these legendary figures among an Amerindian population, together with the many Vampire beings attested in the Caribbean and Pacific, adds weight to the idea of an ancient and universal category in which shapeshifting, blood-drinking and cradle-snatching are the defining features.

What is even more curious from a modern perspective, and has not hitherto been commented on, is the similarity between aspects of the Mexican *tlahuelpuchi* and the North American adolescent Real Vampire of the late 1990s. Both are 'cuckoos in the nest', especially afflicted or gifted members of the tribe, who generally become aware of their condition at puberty; the Real Vampires similarly have a compulsion to feed and are sometimes overwhelmed by their animal nature ('The Beast'), but can generally satisfy themselves with con-senting donors and do not prey on children. Like the *tlahuelpuchi*, they may have a form of pact with other players of semi-supernatural roles such as the fairies, witches, psi-vamps or blood-fetishists who coexist in the same subcultural zone.

✢

The tubercular dead of old New England, the Chupacabras with its lesser-known monster-relatives, the *ciutateteo* and *tlahuelpuchi* provide an array of American Vampires to set against the European varieties. Elsewhere in this book, the blood obsessions of the

Mesoamerican Mayan peoples are also examined. However exotic and alien, even absurd, these manifestations of folk traditions may seem to the Western reader, living in a 'post-belief' society, they all, just like any system of set of ideas which engages the emotions and intelligence of a people, have deep, cultural significance. The same goes for yet another half human, half phantom being from the western hemisphere, an alternative interpretation of the theme of death and resurrection, a creature almost as familiar (and yet as little understood) as the Vampire itself; the zombi.

Before closing the book on the pre-millennial undead in America, it may be enlightening to look briefly at this sinister Haitian compatriot of the *loo-garoo*, and to ask what special cultural conditions provided a stage for it to shamble across. The answer returns us to one of the primary engines of demonic superstition: communal dread and its focuses.

The *zombi* (the word itself, Europeanized as 'zombie', comes from Congolese *zumbi*, meaning both snake-god and good-luck fetish) and zombification form part of the belief system association with voodoo, an officially sanctioned religion related to *santeria* but native to Haiti and a composite of African and Catholic influences. The zombie itself is a dead human being deliberately brought back to life by sorcery. It is not inherently malicious like the Vampire, but is an automaton, a helpless slave, completely subjected to the will of its master. For this reason those who believe in the zombie – most of the rural population of the island – are not afraid of it but of *becoming* it. Local witch-doctors occasionally mount spectacular demonstrations of their powers in which hypnosis, drugs, drums and dance will create a temporary zombie-trance in a chosen victim, but the real process is clandestine, and involves removing the dead subject from a resting place that may be, like many tombs in Haiti, constructed from solid concrete.

From the perspective of comparison, what is significant about the zombie tradition is not whether it is based on any sort of objective truth (the drugs necessary to produce a state of suspended animation are readily available in Haiti, but tests carried out on 'Wilfrid', the only legally recognized zombie of recent years, show him to be an impostor) but how the being relates to the collective imagination. Anthropologists and ethnographers have pointed out that in a people whose whole, terrible past experience and present social dilemmas derive from enslavement, the zombie embodies the greatest communal fear; a dread of being returned to a state of endless, helpless, mute servitude. By the same token, the Vampires of the European past have served to focus their societies' most profound anxieties.

6

Of Burial and Blood

The reek of human blood is laughter to my heart.

Aeschylus, *Oresteia*

The much-debated 'proofs' of the existence of the undead, the tell-tale signs of vampirism as identified on exhumed corpses, are virtually all ascribable to post-mortem changes in cadavers, processes which were imperfectly or mis-understood in the past but which have now been categorized by science.

In seventeenth- and eighteenth-century documents the body of the Vampire is often reported to be a healthy rosy-pink, or even ruddy, in hue, and plump as if well fed. This may arise when bacteria living within the corpse begin to multiply unchecked: chemical changes darkening the blood remaining in the veins may give rise to a marbling effect visible near the skin surface, while in the digestive system in particular, gases are emitted that distend the abdomen and, to a lesser extent, other parts of the body, sometimes leading to the 'human drum' effect referred to in the tales of Greek Vampires from the seventeenth century.

Once circulation ceases, blood settles in the lower parts of the corpse, although not the parts actually resting upon a surface, as the capillaries there are forced shut, causing a strong blush-like effect in those areas, known as hypostasis. This reddening is increased as the bacterial changes in the veins extend to the surface capillaries, and the whole corpse may turn a deep purplish-red. (Later stages of putrefaction will normally turn the skin blue-grey and then black, themselves the frightening 'hues of death' associated in the sagas of the Norse mound-dwellers.)

The eyes and the tongue of a dead body will start to protrude as decay sets in, often resulting in an expression on the face of the departed either of terror or of grinning malevolence. This same bloating can cause a pseudo-erection in a male cadaver and the swelling of the female sex organs. 'Skin-slippage' often occurs as the surface skin of the deceased decays, blisters and falls away from the body. Beneath this outer skin a smooth waxy surface of unblemished skin is revealed, prompting the conviction that the corpse had continued to grow and regenerate after death.

In the nineteenth century some authorities stated that head and body hair would grow on a corpse 'like mosses on the bark of dying trees';[1] they speculated that this was because each hair had its own independent stock of living nutrients. It is a widespread belief even today that the hair, beard and nails of a corpse may continue to grow after death, but this is a fallacy. The seemingly more prominent hair and nails that have been observed are the result of the drying out and shrinkage of the skin and the fingers and toes themselves, while the nails actually just retain their size and shape. Hairs on the limbs and head and face may also seem to extend, but in fact are raised from the skin by the same drying and shrinking process. The receding of the gums similarly causes the teeth to become more prominent.

Whole theses were advanced during the post-Renaissance Vampire scares based on the sounds said to emanate from the graves of the recently dead, and to echo eerily through vaults and empty funeral chapels, sounds that were likened to the snuffling and grunting of pigs, to chewing, to grumbling threats or groans of despair. The reports may owe something to the activities of unseen rats, dogs or carrion, but noises really are emitted by lifeless cadavers, again due to chemical activity producing gases that build up and are then, usually around three weeks after interment, forced from the body through the mouth, nose and rectum. If a body has been properly buried within a vault or deep in the earth such noises may pass unheard, but in the aftermath of an epidemic where numbers of bodies have been hastily buried in shallow graves, or crowded together in improvised pits, it is possible that strange sounds did indeed disturb the nights.

In a few cases, corpses removed from their resting-places have been observed to make sudden movements. This will often have been caused by moving the body, which then settles back into its lifeless posture, but can also result from *rigor mortis*, which first stiffens the corpse into sometimes grotesque positions (even resulting in it seeming to sit upright in its tomb: Max Schreck's 'whole body erection' in Murnau's film *Nosferatu* was not mere expressionist play-acting!), then wearing off, allowing the limbs and head to relax.

Another sign that the deceased had become one of the undead and was feeding upon the living was the presence of blood around the mouth or under the fingernails and evidence of fresh blood in the veins. Although the appearance of blood around the lips and nose is a feature of death from lung inflammation, as in pneumonic plague or consumption (tuberculosis), the dark liquid that escapes from the mouth or nose of the dead individual, or seeps from a post-mortem wound, is often not pure blood at all but a brownish or black watery discharge known as ichor, which may be forced from the orifices by the same internal production of gases during decomposition. This was recognized as long ago as the 1730s when the Marquis d'Argens tried to duplicate this pseudo-blood in his laboratory to discredit the 'evidence' of vampire discoveries that some of his contemporaries were advancing.[2]

Blood normally coagulates after death, as the Victorian serial killer Jack the Ripper complained in a note to police (he claimed to have filled a glass with one victim's blood, hoping to drink it later), but may reliquify. Despite the Ripper's frustration – and his letter may have been a hoax – it is a well-known phenomenon that the blood of those dying a sudden and/or violent death may not coagulate and may remain liquid for long enough to be transfused, or drunk.

As well as signs exhibited after death there are various rare physiological peculiarities that might contribute to a vampire-like appearance in the living. Hypohydrotic ectodermal dysplasia causes the teeth to remain short and stumpy, thus throwing the canines into prominence. Sharp-pointed canines or incisors are common in normal mouths, but if they are not present modern Vampires can and do have fangs created by cosmetic filing and capping. This procedure costs around a thousand US or Australian dollars; in the UK some sympathetic dentists charge only eighty pounds, which will alternatively buy a *de luxe* set of removable prosthetic fangs. Exactly how a Vampire uses its fangs, which, it must be remembered, are only omnipresent in *fictional* representations, to facilitate sucking is one of those banal but essential questions that went unasked for a hundred years, until the author Clive Leatherdale made the mechanical puzzle the subject of a learned paper delivered at the Whitby Dracula Convention in 1997.[3]

Cinema convention has also established that vampires can be destroyed by sunlight, and today's Real Vampires often cite an aversion to sunlight as evidence of their belonging to a different race or species. In the early folklore, this emphasis was absent (again, it comes from fiction: in Professor Christopher Frayling's words, 'Sunlight is Stoker'). Blood-demons *were* the enemy of the life-giving sun, and vampiric activity was usually thought to be limited to the period between midnight and cock-crow, but it was always fire, not light itself, that could destroy a revenant. There are many conditions that may cause a hypersensitivity to sunlight: porphyria (but see below), Sezary's syndrome, Graves's disease and polymorphic light eruption among them. The toothmark punctures on the skin of a Vampire's victim may be caused by any number of inflictions, from attacks by ticks or fleas to the proliferation of sores in conditions such as *pemphigus vulgaris*, a mysterious and potentially fatal illness apparently brought on by extreme anxiety.[4]

In 1985 the incurable, usually hereditary disease porphyria was advanced as a possible key to the symptoms exhibited by living Vampires, and the suggestion immediately caused a sensation. In a paper entitled 'Werewolves and Vampires' presented to the American Association for the Advancement of Science, the Canadian professor of chemistry David Dolphin said that hypersensitivity to light, chronic anaemia and an aversion to garlic were all characteristic of porphyria victims and that such sufferers might resort to drinking fresh blood to alleviate their condition. Dr Dolphin speculated that haem, the deep-red chemical compound in haemoglobin, might reduce the severity of symptoms and that the only way, prior to the invention of hypodermics, for an individual to absorb sufficient quantities would be to drink several pints of fresh blood. Their motivation to do so would presumably have to have been instinctive, much as pregnant women crave substances in which they are deficient, as the condition itself was not recognized until recently. The author Clive Leatherdale added that porphyria could result in the teeth, nails and hair of a carrier glowing in the dark.[5]

Coming as it did with the seeming weight of 'orthodox science' behind it, the porphyria hypothesis was seized on by the press and broadcast media, especially in the USA where it caused considerable distress to many of the country's fifty thousand sufferers, some of whom were treated as pariahs by neighbours fearing vampiric attacks.[6] Fifteen years later the renewed focus on this hereditary disease as it affected the blood relatives of Queen Victoria has confirmed that the symptoms of which sufferers complained bear little resemblance to vampirism, and that a craving for blood was definitely not in evidence. Porphyria is, in fact, a group of associated conditions with differing symptoms and treatments. Haem injections and blood transfusions are given to a very small number of patients, but most experts consider that blood ingested orally would be reduced in the gut and could provide no relief whatsoever. Despite the discrediting of the theory, many popular works on vampirism continue to cite porphyria as a medical basis for vampire outbreaks.

The writer Manuela Dunn-Mascetti asserted in a 1994 publication that congenital syphilis as manifested in children could produce pallor, black-ringed eyes and serrated teeth, not to mention possible deformation of the palate that might mean that only liquids could easily be ingested. Thus she explained the medical basis for some of the characteristic 'wild signs' of the Vampire.[7] In 1998 a similar case was put forward by a Spanish physician, but this time rabies was the culprit. Again, it seems that these otherwise objective analysts are mistaking the symptoms of fictional vampirism – none of which, apart from a predilection for blood-drinking, were shared by the attested undead of Central Europe – for the effects of a real disease.

The question of the luminescence of the Vampire, for example, is more complex than it seems. Since the Norse sagas, mention has been made of 'corpse-lights' coming from burial-places, Greek superstition refers to the graves of restless spirits glowing and in some stories the rural Slavic Vampires were described as white figures, or manifested themselves as dancing lights, but the idea that these are rampaging porphyria sufferers is too far-fetched to entertain.

In looking for a 'scientific' basis for the mythos, perhaps a more fruitful line of enquiry would be a consideration of the chemistry of delusion, of the very real substances or conditions that might lead people to imagine either that they had been attacked and infected by a Vampire, or that they had become one themselves. Some works have examined the possible use of hallucinogens by shamans and witches, but the question of drug-induced fantasy (as opposed to more quotidian effects – see below) has not been raised with reference to the Vampire, except by Johan Christof Harenberg, whose thesis, published in 1739, singled out datura and opium as potential catalysts.[8]

Our ancestors must have had a much more varied experience of narcotic substances than is recorded in surviving sources. We know that ergot poisoning (from mouldy flour) caused spectacular outbreaks of hallucinated frenzy in Europe in medieval and early modern times, and that the amanita and liberty cap mushrooms that grow across Eurasia, as well as cannabis, all substances that might be consumed accidentally or deliberately, can bring on visions and bizarre physical sensations during wakefulness and can transform the quality of dreams for prolonged periods afterwards. To isolate only one strange side-effect of eating liberty caps, there is in many subjects a visual acuity, not entirely an hallucination but an increased awareness of the body that results in seeing everything as suffused with pulsations of red.

If suddenly altered states of consciousness were understood differently than they are today, being ascribed sometimes to possession, enchantment or divine intervention, the more insidious powers of drugs were apparently not understood at all: the English poet Coleridge was addicted for much of his life to opium, but saw his abject state as the result of a purely moral debility rather than a chemical dependency. (The striking parallels between the twentieth-century junkie and the Vampire persona are discussed in Chapter 10: Contagious Ideas.)

Alcohol, the most widely available narcotic, undoubtedly affected the judgement of those who dug up and inspected the dead and those who cowered in their homes in fear of them. Disinterring was a stressful business, carried out by custom at dead of night, and preceded, accompanied and followed in very many cases by a warming, fortifying draught of something strong.

One aspect of the night-demon mythos that definitely related to observable human experience, the oppression by 'pressing ghosts' or *maras*, is a phenomenon that has been common to many previous eras and cultures, but which is no longer so widely reported. The pressure on the chest of the sleeping or dozing victim is said to be accompanied by paralysis, asphyxiation and terror. Since the earliest records of this very real experience it has been personified: in Newfoundland and New England it was given the name 'night-hag', a designation that is still recognized there today. A physiological explanation for this spectacular form of night-terror is that it is caused by an instance of sudden awakening from a deep sleep where the brain becomes conscious but the body remains in a state of suspended animation, it is a more extreme version of the common falling sensation. There may be other even more prosaic keys to the *mara*-attacks: as far as we can tell, our ancestors were prone to eat large quantities of meat or cheese before sleeping. They also used sleeping potions that included laudanum and other opiates, which cause intense drowsiness coupled with a heightening of the imagination. Add to this the delirium brought on by fevers, spiritual malaise, the howling of the wind in the chimney or the stovepipe, rustlings in the wainscot. More simply still, it was the custom in many places right up to the 1950s to sleep under a great weight of bedclothes, sometimes even to bind or swaddle oneself in constricting night-clothes, or to sleep in a space in which oxygen was lacking, perhaps because of a nearby fireplace.

Seemingly normal individuals convinced that they have been assaulted by night visitors, even sexually assaulted in their beds: this syndrome has recently re-created itself with a new set of accom-panying images and implications. Today, especially in the United States, the experience is more than likely to be ascribed to so-called 'alien abductions'. Very frequently the descriptions of the assailants conform to a recognized template of 'extra-terrestrial', categorized by UFOlogists as a 'grey', whose cultural origins are plain for sceptics to see, even if believers do not wish to acknowledge them. The visual attributes of these slit-eyed, hairless, gracile beings from space have been put together from descriptions given by middle-aged adults and are then fed back through the print and broadcast media to other middle-aged adults who duly see them when they undergo an attack. The resemblance between these aliens and space creatures from 1950s science fiction is not coincidence; members of the baby-boom generation will see an E.T.-like creature looming over them in the semi-darkness, just as a medieval victim would be likely to see a devil, a witch or an angel.

The visual impressions of lights, looming shapes, as well as the purely physical sensations – breathlessness, immobility and the rest – that together make up a typical visitation are explainable physio-logically; the different components of the experience have now been located in specific parts of the brain. Furthermore, experiments have been carried out by, among others, Dr Elizabeth Loftus at the Uni-versity of Washington, which show that identical experiences can be implanted artificially in a susceptible subject, who will then utterly believe in the manufactured memory that remains. The data that makes up the night-attack is absorbed while the subject is in a hyp-nagogic or hypnopompic condition (the former defines the state just before sleep, and the latter the state between sleep and waking when dream-like images persist), and is reinforced by the ready-made ideas that have come to characterize a cult of victimhood, ideas once expressed in terms of harassment by evil spirits, now more likely to be couched in terms of a threat of rape or kidnapping by extra-terrestrials.

✴

A very practical question, which vexed both sceptics such as the theologian Augustin Calmet and believers such as Montague Summers, concerned the means by which the undead were able to leave and re-enter their graves: as J. Sheridan le Fanu noted in *Carmilla*, 'How they escape from their graves and return to them for certain hours every day, without displacing the clay or leaving any trace of disturbance in the state of the coffin or the cerements, has always been admitted to be utterly inexplicable.' Calmet had asked similarly pertinent questions in 1746:

> ... the principal difficulty to arrest my judgement ... is, to know how they come out of their graves without any appearance of the earth having been removed, and how they have replaced it as it was; how they appear dressed in their clothes, go and come, and eat. If it is so, why do they return to their graves? Why do they not remain among the living? Why do they suck the blood of their relations? Why do they haunt and fatigue persons who ought to be dear to them, and who have done nothing to offend them?[9]

Montague Summers, steeped in early twentieth-century occultism, theosophy and spiritualism, explained the phenomenon by invoking the notion of 'ectoplasm'. This was the luminous vapour said to be extruded from the bodies of spiritualist mediums while in a state of trance. The material, described by one seance witness as resembling egg-white in water and smelling like semen, usually emanated from the mouth of the medium and could form itself into the physical shapes of the heads or whole bodies of conjured spirits. Although widely believed in from Victorian times until the 1930s, ectoplasm was thereafter discredited – for instance, by photographic evidence produced during the trial of the medium Helen Duncan who was accused of witchcraft in England in 1944. The photographs taken of Duncan clearly show the white streams cascading from her mouth to be sheets of muslin or cheesecloth.

If ectoplasm is ruled out as an explanation for the out-of-tomb manifestations, the sceptics remain unanswered: is the Vampire corporeal, spiritual, present only in the imagination, or does it enjoy some other form of existence? Some European narratives describe the Vampire sitting on top of its grave, others speak of it exiting and re-entering the cemetery, but there are no descriptions anywhere of the exact way in which it enters or leaves its hole in the ground. Similarly, in all the 'true' accounts collected by officialdom there is no instance of a Vampire ever being caught or observed in the act by a credible third party. Its means of travel must therefore be magical, and the tellers of Slav tales sometimes pictured the wandering soul wafted in the form of a blade of grass, a wisp of feather-down or a tiny insect.

As for what it was that animated the corpse in the tomb, most explanations again involved some sort of magical possession, but some, especially at the turn of the eighteenth century, speculated about astral influences or 'vegetative forces' yet to be discovered by science. Others let their imaginations work on what it would be like to find oneself shrouded and placed in an airless coffin under six feet of soil – alive. 'The origin of vampire superstitions must be sought in the ignorance of early races who buried their dead in the earth, for it is singular that the races which cremate their dead have been practically free from Vampire legends. Earth burial has never been free from the possibility of premature interment, and although there is no reason to believe that a man buried alive will not die in his coffin of suffocation, an ignorant peasantry seemed to imagine that he could live, issue forth at night and keep himself alive by sucking the blood of the living.'[10]

The eminent Victorian surgeon, Herbert Mayo, professor of anatomy and Physiology at King's College, London, picked up the theme of premature burial, which had come to the forefront of the nineteenth century's fascination with the morbid (more than twenty books had treated the subject since the turn of the previous century). He made it the centrepiece of a treatise that attempted to rationalize popular superstitions by applying the science of the day. Mayo considered reports of vampire exhumations, in particular the Arnod Pavle case of 1732, and concluded that the documentation was trustworthy: 'It appears to establish beyond question, that where the fear of Vampyrism prevails, and there occur several deaths, in the popular belief connected with it, the bodies, when disinterred weeks after burial, present the appearance of corpses from which life has only recently departed.' He dismisses the possibility of abnormal states due to death from fright, and of supernatural sources of nutrition: 'Let us content ourselves with a notion not so monstrous, but still startling enough: that the bodies, which were found in the so-called Vampyr state, instead of being in a new or mystical condition, were simply alive in the common way or had been so for some time subsequently to their interment that, in short, they were the bodies of persons who had been buried alive, and whose life, where it yet lingered, was finally extinguished through the ignorance and barbarity of those who disinterred them.'[11]

Mayo was forced to seek a rational solution because he accepted that the archive evidence indicated the violation of natural laws. In fact, not one of the characteristics observed in the exhumation reports of the sixteenth to nineteenth centuries cannot be explained away by modern forensic theory, so there is no longer any need to introduce the buried-alive hypothesis. It must not be dismissed out of hand, though, since the living were certainly buried by mistake from time to time: over three millennia during which states of coma and catatonia, even temporary fainting fits, were indistinguishable from death, and at times of social crisis – war and epidemic – when hasty diagnosis and speedy burial were essential, it must have happened time and again. Until the second half of the twentieth century the only sure test for clinical death was the onset of decomposition, and even this was not infallible as, in tropically hot and humid conditions, putrefaction can actually precede death.

Suspended animation and the horrible awakening in the coffin have long fascinated those of a macabre turn of mind. Pliny the Elder wrote of how at least two Roman dignitaries had come back to life just prior to cremation, and fifteen hundred years later Kornmann showed how swoons and 'mute diseases' could mimic death with the examples of the Emperor Zeno and the theologian Duns Scotus.[12]

Folklore did not ignore the notion of trance, but did not seek to incorporate it into a rational framework, as an oddity from Slovenia illustrates;

> In the Notranjska [Inner Carniola] region, Premrl is a fairly common surname, in addition to which the phrases 'Premrl blood' or 'Premol' or 'Premrov blood' are known [and applied to splashes of blood on the earth found the morning after supposed vampire activity] ... *Premrl* means the same as 'benumbed' or 'stiff as if dead', and indeed, a Vampire only lies in its grave 'benumbed', since it leaves the grave to suck the blood of the living.[13]

A hundred or so years ago in Bohemia and Moravia doctors exchanged grim anecdotes concerning women who had died in pregnancy and had given birth to live babies in the tomb. Today there is a handful of news reports every year telling of the dead reviving spontaneously in the mortuary or even at the funeral home, helping the folk terror of live burial to survive as a powerful urban myth. There is, then, proof of recovery on the dissecting table, but there are no stories of anyone (apart, possibly, from one or two yogis and fakirs) surviving days or weeks underground, despite the breathing-tubes and glass coffin-panels installed by some wealthy cadavers-to-be, so that the suggestion that the many resurrected Vampires of the past were all alive in their tombs until they were uncovered and staked, which *never* took place immediately after interment, is risible.

The opening of graves is even easier to account for. It goes without saying that hastily buried plague victims were often disturbed, not only by scavenging half-starved animals but by equally desperate human resurrectionists who would risk disease to take anything of value or use – a pocket-watch, a pair of boots, even a shroud. In Transylvania the undiseased dead were cannibalized on occasion and their flesh sold as food in markets.

Like many 'western' commentators, F. Sharper Knowlton, writing at the turn of the nineteenth century, assumed (quite wrongly) that healthy rationalism had by then put paid to vampire superstitions: 'It is notable that as disbelief in this notion assumed large proportions, owing to the advance of education and refinement, the phenomena disappeared.' But as late as 1872 Professor Perty of Brno in Moravia was explaining vampirism by saying that the buried body is without its soul and needs blood, first its own, then its relatives', but that this blood is converted into an ethereal substance and reconverted only when the soul is reunited with the corpse in its grave.[14] And in the 'east' cases went on being reported well into the new century.

⚊ϒ⚊

The other fixed idea that is a mainstay of vampire lore is that of blood, its spilling and its consumption. A well-known biblical passage underlines the strict taboos surrounding this sacred substance and its use as nourishment;

If any man whomsoever of the house of Israel, and of those come from elsewhere who sojourn among them, eat blood, I shall set my face against his soul, and banish him from among his people. For the life of the flesh is in the blood and I have given it to you, that upon the altar you may make atonement with it for your souls, and the blood may be for an expiation of the soul. Therefore I have said to the children of Israel: no soul of you shall eat blood, nor of the strangers who sojourn among you. Whichever man of the children of Israel, and of the strangers that sojourn among you, if by hunting or by fowling, he take a wild beast or a bird, which is lawful to eat, let him pour out its blood, and cover it with earth, for the life of all flesh is in the blood: therefore I said to the children of Israel: You shall not eat the blood of any flesh at all, because the life of the flesh is in the blood, and whosoever eateth it shall be cut off.[15]

The much later adoption of the doctrine of transubstantiation, the literal substitution of Christ's own blood for sacramental wine that was officially confirmed in the fourteenth century, reinforced and legitimized an age-old identification of the liquid with the sacred essence of life itself and helped to fix the ideas of magical transformations, consumptions and infusions in the popular mind, at first universally, but after the Reformation largely in the Catholic and Orthodox ambit where Vampire beliefs were indeed more prevalent. For many believers, sipping that wine every week of their lives, seeing or hearing of stigmata and the miraculously liquefying blood of saints, a metaphor was a literal and central reality.

The human imagination has always invested blood with special potency, a power in which the physical and the symbolic are intermingled. Many societies considered the menstrual blood of women to exercise a special influence, usually malign. For Europeans in the classical era its proximity could turn milk, blight crops and raise storms,[16] while the Indians of Costa Rica were among those in more recent times who feared that it might contaminate people and kill cattle. According to the Bantus of South Africa, blood from childbirth or, even worse, from a miscarriage had the potential to blight the countryside and the air itself for miles around; the rains would not dare to fall on the spot where it had been spilled. Estonians and Amerindians, like the Jews, allowed the eating of an animal's flesh, but strictly prohibited the drinking of its blood: they thought it contained the beast's spirit, which might enter and possess them.[17]

For centuries blood was used as a charm to ward off evil. In German-speaking regions of Europe, for instance, the blood of executed criminals was collected and, where possible, bottled to be drunk either straight or in brandy: it was supposed to bring luck as well as cure sickness. Handkerchiefs soaked with the blood of King Charles I of England were sold as a cure-all in the streets of London after his decapitation in 1649. Elsewhere, in Turkey, Burma and among the Tartars, for example, royal blood was deemed either too holy or too potent to be spilt, so for monarchs and their relatives other forms of execution were practised, smothering, strangling or 'pressing' being the favourites. Serbs, Pomeranians and Kashubians were among those who believed that the blood of the Vampire itself, if it could be obtained, would protect a potential victim from attacks if it was swallowed or applied to the skin.

The doctrine of sympathies, and other cruder versions of sympathetic magic, used the metaphorical associations of blood with rain, sap, etc., in ceremonies and taboos. In central Australia the Dieri people placated their ancestors and tried to bring an end to drought by bleeding two of their wise men, while in other shamanistic societies it was usually the common people rather than the privileged sorcerer who provided the blood.

In times past there could be a rich ambiguity in attitudes to blood: the sight of it was less familiar than today – women who were constantly pregnant would rarely menstruate, and spilt blood would be quickly hidden – and at the same time more familiar as blood-letting, with leeching, cupping and cauterizing, was one of the commonest therapies from the medieval to the modern periods, practised by all qualified doctors, unqualified itinerant barber-surgeons and by most village folk-healers, too. A bowl brimming with fresh blood would have been a common sight to those who gathered round the sickbed. In the countryside of eastern Europe, particularly in Hungary and Romania, slaughterhouses were uncovered areas, with the blood escaping along open channels; vats of blood from freshly killed cattle were assembled for the making of sauces and soups in ceremonies that had changed little since pre-Christian days. Nomadic and pastoral societies reliant on hunting or rearing livestock had, and still have, in common the habit of drinking blood from living animals, either from necessity for warmth and nourishment in extreme conditions, or in rituals of bonding.

In the English folk calendar 14 March was the day on which blood should be drawn from the right arm, on 11 April the left could be bled and on 2 May either one tapped to guarantee a year free of fever, various types of gout and loss of eyesight. On St Stephen's day, 26 December, it was recommended that horses should be drained of two or three pints of blood from an incision in the gums. In Wales also on Boxing Day and in Scotland on New Year's Day women and children indulged in 'holming', a tradition whereby they would whip themselves or be whipped on the legs with holly branches. Each drop of blood shed represented a year free of sickness.[18]

One of the most frequent focuses of communal dread in central Europe and elsewhere were the reports of water turning to blood, either in the form of bloody rain falling on the land, or of rivers, lakes and puddles suddenly transformed. In Locse, Hungary, in the early seventeenth century peasants collected the dark blood-coloured rainwater in jars and pots; the rain had blistered the skin on contact, later its colour changed to a pale pink 'as the water in which meat is washed'. Fishing lakes turned deep red and a host of fish poked their heads above the surface to stare at the human witnesses of the miracle before dying in their hundreds. Elsewhere the leaves of trees beside lakes and rivers changed from green to red in summer and the water gave off a charnel odour. This sudden staining of rivers, lakes and even seas has a number of different natural causes: the two most common explanations for the appearance of a blood-hue are the multiplying of red algae, caused by unseasonally high temperatures and still water, or the washing down of mineral deposits during flooding or freak storms.

Anyone who witnessed a knife- or sword-fight or who had been caught up in the wars that have ebbed and flowed across Europe since the first millennium would be also familiar with the real thing: Sándor Petöfi, the warrior-poet of nineteenth-century Hungarian nationalism, wrote that history is a river of blood, and an English volunteer in the French religious wars had written that in the last decades of the sixteenth century '... murder is no cruelty ... and [people are] bathing one in another's blood, making it custom to despise religion and justice, or any more sacred bond, either of divine or human constitution'.[19]

The phenomenon of 'bleeding loaves', which is actually caused by a harmless microbe, dates back at least as far as the third century BC when Alexander the Great interpreted it as a propitious sign that his enemies' blood would soon be shed. Later the many reported instances of the 'Bleeding Host' – blood appearing in the bread used for holy communion – were usually blamed on the Jews, who were also commonly suspected of using the blood of Christian children for their own rituals (the so-called 'blood-libel') and were duly put to death by their Gentile neighbours in a whole series of pogroms. The Christians who persecuted the Jews probably did not know that the Romans had accused the early followers of Christ of exactly the same sort of blasphemies – of baking children in dough, for instance, and serving them up to initiates who drank their blood.[20]

⚡

Blood loss will lead quickly to death, and the blood escaping from a wound will steam as the victim's breathing fades. In early societies this association sometimes caused blood to be identified in the human microcosm not with a liquid but with air as the life-giving or life-denying essence. In medieval times it was thought that blood was the physical medium within which the life-spirit – and courage – was contained and carried and was, in Rabelais' phrase, the 'seat of the soul'. Blood sacrifice, as the most visible and spectacular version of human sacrifice, is well known and has been practised on every continent. The Romans re-created earlier Asiatic rites to honour the Mother Goddess Cybele and to mourn the death of her son, the God Attis, which included the Day of Blood, 23 March, each year when hordes of devotees would writhe to the sound of cymbals, horns, pipes and drums, slash themselves and spatter their blood across the altars and sacred trees dedicated to the divine pair. Slightly less ecstatic Hindu and Catholic penitents chastise themselves in a similar fashion today. Much greater quantities of gore were once poured over the altars of the Tibetan and Mongolian Vampire deities, of the Indian Goddess Kali and of Yak-cuc-mo, the Mayan Lord of the West and ruler of the Copan acropolis, the Quetzal-Macaw, the living God of Maize and Blood.

The central mystery of the Mayan religio-social philosophy was the death and rebirth of the Maize God, echoes of which could be seen even in Christian churches after the Spanish conquest; according to this nexus of beliefs, humans were created and formed from maize. The sacred ruler, beyond humanity, death and rebirth, was revered with blood libations during his lifetime, and after his bodily death he was treated as a revered ancestor and again honoured with blood to guarantee that the orderly sequences of nature and society would be maintained and regulated.

Part of the supreme ritual of Mayan kingship was the shedding of royal blood at moments of high drama. One element of sacrifice was the drinking of blood, literally by the king or priest, or symbolically by the god, the earth, the well or river. In another refinement the rulers of the cities could summon the Vision Serpent, the link with their ancestors, into their presence by burning their own blood. Women of their entourage bled themselves by passing cords twined with thorns through their tongues, while the divine lord was required to draw his yet more precious blood by slicing into his genitals with stingray spines, obsidian knives or volcanic glass shards. Once flowing, the blood was dripped on to paper made of bark, which was then burned with incense, and in its smoke the souls of those whose life-essence had been shed would mingle with the soul of the holy pyramid in which the ceremony was taking place.[21]

Victim-blood was also used, and lesser altars scattered across the metropolis were drenched in it, while fragrant wood and sacrificial blood were consumed together in hundreds of burners throughout the city. War was the dominant feature and came to be the *raison d'être* of the Mayan world, but one of the main purposes of war was not the conquest of new territory but the collecting of sacrificial victims for rites that bolstered the terrifying power of the rulers. Élite prisoners from other tribes had precious blood that was of great value in appeasing the supernatural thirsts of the ancestor-ruler gods, so these captives might be kept alive and bled for years.

Finally it appears that the endless sacrifices actually transformed the ecology of the Mayan world and brought it to an end: the wells, canals and rivers became choked with bones and the unending streams of blood polluted the water supply. When the kings failed, brotherhoods of priests took over, revived the system of sacrifices, twenty thousand at a time, and the blood-drenching went on. Never-theless, the society was doomed, the birth-rate dwindled, disease and deformation became rife, and eventually the great cities were abandoned by their starving inhabitants.[22]

The few remaining pagan Mayans still use blood-offerings today, but the blood comes from animals or birds, usually chickens, and the effigies of the gods they placate, tiny dolls made of clay, wood and cloth, are pale shadows of their ancestors' vast and thirsty stone idols.

ᚡ

Dioscorides described how the blood of different species of bird and animal could be used as remedies for specific human ailments, dog's blood against poison, tortoise blood for epilepsy, etc. By implication human blood, even though forbidden, should have some medicinal effect.[23] Marsilio Ficino wrote in the 1560s, seemingly without irony, that the well-known use of children's blood by sorcerers could usefully be emulated by the educated classes: 'Then why might not our elderly, finding themselves all but without hope of survival, suck the blood of a lad? Of a lad, I say, of stalwart forces – healthy, cheerful, well-tempered, having excellent blood . . . Let them suck, then, like a leech . . . This should be done precisely when they are very hungry and thirsty, and at the waxing of the moon.'[24]

In her treatise on bugbears and bogey-men Marina Warner recounts stories of fairy-tale ogres and real-life despots abducting children and drinking their blood. In the days of Louis XV when the rumour spread that the Royal Family was suffering from some dreadful disease, the simultaneous disappearance of some poor children led the Paris mob to run wild. They lynched one man suspected of helping the King to obtain their children's blood as a curative.[25]

In the hundreds of books written about the Vampire the central role that blood plays has been paid surprisingly little attention. Belief in the Vampire suggests a belief in the reality of blood-sucking or blood-drinking, and this in turn suggests that there is some purpose to taking in the blood of a human being by mouth. In Ancient Rome, according to unreliable narratives, noble ladies drank the blood of gladiators as a tonic and it was rumoured that voluptuaries of both sexes took it as an aphrodisiac. In nineteenth-century Europe it is documented that sufferers from anaemia were taken by their families to abattoirs and encouraged to drink the blood fresh from the slaughtered animal carcasses. Butchers and slaughterhouse workers also sometimes drank, and probably still drink, animal blood, either as a supposed restorative tonic for which they would 'acquire a taste', or as a gesture of pride in their work. Recreational blood-drinking is rare, but as I witnessed some people, teenage Vampires among them, become very fond of the astringent taste of steaks eaten raw, still in their bloody juices.

In the twentieth century almost the only discussions of the physiology of human blood-drinking have taken place at websites on the Internet and are frustratingly misleading, with participants adopting blatantly pseudo-scientific or wholly mystical approaches. A strictly factual and final analysis is not so easy to make, since 'respectable' medical authorities have ignored or avoided the whole issue. When they are consulted it becomes clear that scientists cannot pronounce definitively because they have not carried out the necessary tests or participated in the practices themselves – the same problem that also faces anyone looking for an objectively scientific view of drug experiences or 'extreme' sexual experiments.

Earle Hackett stated the orthodox scientist's view of blood more strikingly than usual when he wrote,

> It is valuable stuff. As it flows, bright scarlet, from a wounded body, it is visually more spectacular than splintered bone, burst liver or a mess of brains. But once it has left its owner, its usefulness ends, except in the very special case of transfusion ... For example, as organic fertilizer for plants it has no magical advantage over dead fish or rotten vegetation.[26]

According to doctors and nutrition specialists, if drunk in smallish quantities, blood will be digested and broken down in the gut into its harmless constituents: iron, various minerals and water. (It is not, as sometimes claimed, an emetic, but in most people the consistency or the thought of a large quantity taken all at once might induce vomiting, which would expel the blood itself and also cause the loss of other nutrients.) The nutritional value of a small dose would be minimal; in fact, it would only make a difference in the case of someone for whom no other source of nourishment was available, and it could never provide an adequate diet as its protein quality is insufficient in the absence of the essential amino acid isoleucine.

'You would get as much good from drinking blood as you would from eating black pudding,' says the historian David Pescod Taylor, but this is probably to overstate the case: black pudding is highly nutritious. Those cultures where blood forms part of a traditional diet – the Masai and some Inuits, for example – always ensure an adequate protein level by mixing it with milk or cereal, or preparing it with flour, herbs and spices as a broth like the *pörkölt* blood-goulash enjoyed by Hungarians. The only 'normal' human beings who ingest blood on its own in large volumes are those suffering from bleeding stomach ulcers, who then experience a marked rise in blood-urea concentration. Small quantities of natural chemicals, like adrenaline, or introduced substances such as amphetamine or heroin present in a stranger's blood would not be certain to pass through the stomach wall of the recipient in sufficient quantities to be noticeable; by the same token even the presence of syphilis or HIV in the donor *might* not affect the drinker unless the donor's blood was absorbed directly while still concentrated, through a cut in the recipient's mouth, for instance. Viral hepatitis is thought to pose a higher risk, as is Creutzfeld-Jakob ('mad-cow') disease. There is therefore always a very real danger, and blood-drinking is absolutely not safe in any circumstances.[27]

Practising blood-drinkers are quoted elsewhere in this book rejecting such scientific conclusions and insisting on special properties for human blood, but none of the experts consulted would support their claims, only allowing that unusual states might be produced in the drinker by auto-suggestion, great excitement, or the effects of previous fasting or absorption of other chemicals.

☿

Blood has been used in initiation rites and as a token of bonding and solidarity by brotherhoods and some sisterhoods from school playground gangs to more sinister secret societies, Kenyan Mau Maus and the Haitian Ton-tons Macoutes among them. This sharing of pain, mingling of the symbolic life-essence and mutual breaching of the body's integrity can be exhilarating, and shades into another common form of blood-play, deliberate self-mutilation. In the words of a modern Vampire of nineteen, 'Self-mutilation to me is like smoking a cigarette; you're knowingly damaging your body and you're taking pleasure out of it whether it's release of stress, calming your nerves, all that good stuff ... When people are in emotional distress, they say, "Oh, gimme a cigarette," it brings them some form of emotional relief. It's the same thing as cutting yourself.'[28]

Drinking blood and blood-letting usually differ from self-mutilation: in the former the focus is on the symbolic or actual presence of the blood; in the latter it is on the pain caused or the ritual breaking of the skin. The reasons for blood-letting have been divided by analysts into the following categories; vampiric imitation, curiosity and experimentation, erotic experience, ritual acts in the cause of cult or religious activity, or as a result of delusion.[29] The reasons for self-mutilation by cutting have been characterized, as far as children and adolescents are concerned, as follows: 'The practice is most prevalent among abuse survivors, in gangs or prisons, and among teenagers. Young cutters carve words, pictures and punctures into their skins using Swiss Army knives, paper clips, scissors, tacks or fingernails. They cut to get attention, or to avoid suicide by substituting a physical pain for a nebulous inner pain they can't control, or to acquire a sense of focus.'[30]

This is borne out by Vampires I interviewed for this book, confirmed that slashing the skin could be both a symbolic act and a calming therapy, 'One of the biggest [scars] was when I embraced one of my closest friends. I've got a lot more up on my shoulders [from] adrenaline rushes and bloodlust ... the only thing that would calm down the adrenaline rush was pain.'[31]

For some individuals a desperate need to cut becomes a hobby in later life: 'Nowadays I still cut myself, but I do it for pleasure. I love the way I look when I have twisting lines of blood across my arms, and I love the sensations as the blade caresses its way through my flesh, the ice-cold metal against the warmth of my flesh. Now what was once hatred has become love, in a way.'[32]

Like exponents of most other 'deviant' but not strictly illegal pastimes, such as bondage and rubber-fetishism, some fans of 'blood-play' have abandoned secrecy and set up their own discussion groups and newsletters. Blood-play is also usually distinct from blood-fetishism 'proper', which is a rare fixation in which the drawing or sometimes the donation of blood is the main focus of sexual satisfaction, and from 'Renfield's syndrome', named after the deranged, fly-eating character in the novel *Dracula*, a supposed psychiatric condition said to progress through four distinct phases: the first occurs in childhood when the subject discovers, usually by way of some traumatic incident, that the sight and/or taste of blood is arousing. This is followed by instances of auto-vampirism in which the subject enjoys drinking their own blood, which give way to zoophagia, the drinking of animal blood, and finally the progression to authentic vampirism in which human blood is obtained and imbibed.

Documented cases of the full-blown syndrome are so rare that many authorities deny its separate existence, but I interviewed a number of blood-drinkers who admitted that their fascination had been triggered by an accidental tasting during childhood. Preparing this book brought invitations to drink blood, either by way of communal ritual or supervised self-mutilation: I declined them. Twice, though, a chance to taste the real thing arose by innocent accident. When, while chopping vegetables, a knife gashed a finger, holding it to one's mouth was an automatic response, sucking too. The few millilitres had a milky consistency and a faint, not unpleasant taste of earth, yeast, iron. A few weeks later when a loved one cut her palm, the sight of someone else's sudden vulnerability, the droplets against white skin looked momentarily just as the poets would have it, like rose-petals on snow, a beautiful stigmata on the outstretched hand.

Perhaps the taste was slightly sharper, the consistency a little thicker, but in neither case was there instant euphoria – and the thought of quaffing larger quantities did not appeal. The heightened experience must all be in the attendant circumstances of concentration, expectation, subjection and abasement.

7

Killers and Haemogoblins

*'The cult of evil, however it may differ
in non-essential details in various countries
and at various times, is precisely the same
everywhere, and has at all times been the
same, as it is today.'*

Montague Summers, *The Vampire in Europe*, 1928

Vampire cult boss Wayne Phelps' wild eyes flashed as he slashed the rusty razorblade into his own chest ... then forced a 15-year-old sex slave to feed on his blood. As crazed followers bowed at his feet and clapped with joy, the twisted devil-worshipper brutally thrust his schoolgirl victim's lips deep into the gushing wound in the shape of an inverted crucifix.

Thus began the eye-witness account of a teenage vampire coven's activities as reported in the UK *News of the World* tabloid in November 1996. The group, led by Wayne Phelps, a nineteen-year-old fan of Charles Manson, who called himself by the *nom de guerre* of 'Vandarl the Transylvanian', was a typical example of a Vampire-inspired gang. 'Coven' or more recently 'clan' are the more fashionable designations among those involved in the Vampire subculture, while within a particular group the word 'family' is frequently used; tellingly it echoes the nickname of Manson's murderous band of hippies and confirms that the gang is designed to re-create the strongest bonds of kinship for its members.

The letter that one of Phelps's teenage acolytes sent from a psychiatric unit (she had taken a drug overdose after claiming she was haunted by demons from the afterlife) is revealing of the state of mind of the subordinate coven members:

> Yeah, the Family screwed me up a lot, but I don't blame you guys. I gained so much from being part of it. I learnt what friendship and loyalty was about – and what love was. You were so different, so unique, like our own world. In our own dreams, all searching for the same destiny, it gave me that purpose for living. Now I've none. Please take me back.

Members of the Family were required to sign a death-pact, the wording of which, with minor variations, was as follows:

> I hereby swear by the blood that runs through my immortal veins that for my Family I will be willing to give my life for what I believe in and what is right ... in battle and sacrifice to aid the struggle ... And if I am called for I will go and offer myself for all that is right. I will fight by the side of my brothers and sisters if and when the time comes...[1]

One of Phelps's methods for enticing teenagers into the coven was to show them the film *The Lost Boys*, a seminal portrayal of a vampire clan, which terrorizes a seaside community in the USA, and which, even more than competing titles such as *Interview with the Vampire* or *Near Dark*, has provided an endorsement of – and a blueprint for – the alienated adolescents who band together in imitation of the Vampire lifestyle. For teenagers part of what is on offer is glamorous transgression, for clan-leaders a ready-made means of acquiring charisma and power, almost always exploited ultimately for sexual purposes.

The Phelps case, which unfolded in the seaside town of Weymouth in south-west England, was mirrored in another coastal resort, Virginia Beach, USA, in the same year, by a series of molestations, sexual assaults and rapes culminating in the arrest of Jon C. Bush, a twenty-six-year-old self-proclaimed Vampire who also inducted teenage high-school girls, whether willing or not, into his group of followers by biting them and forcing them to submit to oral sex. Bush haunted shopping malls dressed in black and wearing white makeup, seeking out runaways and girls from troubled families and also using younger male accomplices to lure them into his orbit. Within his thirty-strong group Bush based his dominance on precepts taken from a fantasy role-play game called *Vampire: the Eternal Struggle*. He reserved exclusively to himself the right to initiate new members sexually and demanded absolute obedience from them thereafter. Anyone showing disrespect was made the quarry in a cross-country 'blood-hunt' in which the whole clan took part and once caught was bitten by the others and cast out in perpetuity. As Wayne Phelps went on trial in England, Bush was receiving a sentence of twenty-six years' imprisonment.[2]

The role-playing fantasy games – the most famous being *Vampire: the Masquerade*, the all-time bestselling game first released by White Wolf Inc. in 1991, have been mentioned in the course of many Vampire trials. They are all descendants of Dungeons and Dragons, the quasi-medieval romance mass-marketed from the 1970s, which was itself cited in a 1991 *cause célèbre* in the same Virginia Beach. Shawn Novak, a seventeen-year-old who, his lawyers said, was so lost in the game that he could not distinguish human beings from non-sentient monsters, had killed two younger boys by cutting their throats.

The makers of the games and their fans point out that the rules explicitly forbid players to touch one another and they naturally reject any links with actual blood-drinking or ritual murder, but there is no doubt that underground clans refer to the games, just as they do to horror videos and pulp novels (and, it must be said, serious histories). The elaborate, ready-made fantasies, which can be played in 'table-top' mode or as full-scale 'live action', are used to provide (unlike many real modern families) a model structuring, a strict hierarchy, a set of rules and a pleasingly arcane terminology that lends credibility to escapist story-telling and helps in creating group identity. Crucially, and unlike much electronic entertainment, the games demand participation and interaction with other individuals and allow players to develop their own original characters and plot-lines, perhaps substituting for the creative dressing-up and imagination games 'cowboys and Indians', 'cops and robbers', 'pirates' – which used to be organized spontaneously by younger children in the 1950s. As a practitioner enthuses, 'There is scope for practically any kind of adventure, from blood 'n' guts battles with werewolves to the infiltration of another vampiric enclave, to dealings with the mortal and immortal underworlds, to globe-spanning adventures in an attempt to defeat the plans of an ancient.'[3]

The Internet, of course, also allows the drama scenarios, which are fantastically elaborate but ultimately based on crude, regressive notions such as ethnic wars, 'blood-lines', women being subordinated to 'sires', etc., to be enacted on a virtual stage and a truly global scale.

V

It was broad daylight as the fifteen-year-old schoolgirl took a shortcut through Mowbray Park in Sunderland in the north-east of England one October morning in 1993. As she hurried across the damp grass and fallen leaves, her journey was suddenly and brutally cut shorter by a stranger, a white male with an unwavering, manic stare, who without warning seized her and began to choke her. After nearly a minute the girl lost consciousness. Her attacker beat her with a wooden stake, causing bruises, lacerations and fractures to her cheek and jaw, and inflicting a deep wound in her forehead above one eye, which had already been penetrated by a wooden splinter. As she came to her horrified senses the girl realized that she was being raped and that her assailant was licking the blood from her wounds.

In spite of the ordeal she had undergone, the teenager was able to give police a detailed description of the man who had attacked her, and later the same day they raided a derelict clothing factory where they discovered, in what newspapers later called a 'satanic lair', a twenty-nine-year-old vagrant named Malcolm Foster, whom they arrested for the crime. Under the headline 'The Vampire Rapist' the London *Daily Mail* reported the conclusion of the case, which was heard at the Crown Court in the city of Newcastle upon Tyne at the beginning of 1995. In the intervening year the traumatized victim had been unable to return to her studies and was unwilling to sleep alone; she had received professional counselling twice each week and her injuries were still being treated by surgeons. At the trial of Malcolm Foster police described the circumstances in which he had been arrested and tried to account for his state of mind.

Foster had been living rough since being released from prison two days before the attack took place; he had fashioned a hideaway in the disused factory and had decorated it with 'cabbalistic symbols' and drawings of Nazi storm-troopers. Before ambushing and almost killing his victim he admitted that he had drunk a litre of paint and sniffed the fumes from two litres of glue. Commenting on the lapping up of fresh blood, the police officer in charge of the case, Detective Inspector Joe McClen, told the court that Foster had spent his time in prison consulting horror anthologies (one, *Grisly Trails and Ghostly Tales*, written by a local-radio disc-jockey, included the story of a mysterious tramp who committed acts of vampirism in the Scottish Border counties) and copying out pages of notes on a sixteenth-century countess who had bathed in and drunk the blood of virgins to keep herself young: 'He had a bizarre and morbid fascination with this countess,' the policeman said. Next to the police photograph of Foster – raw-boned and slightly dishevelled, with a wisp of immature moustache on his upper lip and young narrowed eyes – the newspaper reproduced a picture of the 'medieval Transylvanian [sic] killer' – it was, in fact, Countess Elisabeth Báthory, which had been found in the rapist's hideout among the more familiar horror-fan iconography: the pentacle daubed with crow's blood, the symbols of medieval witchcraft and the homemade reminders of neo-pagan Nazi sadism.

Foster was found guilty of rape and wounding with intent, and sentenced to nine years' imprisonment. In phrases that were hack-neyed but sincere for all that, McClen, the police spokesman, paid tribute to the schoolgirl who had suffered so much: 'This lass is by far the bravest young woman I have ever met ... her presence of mind was astonishing ... his wild, staring eyes were something the girl particularly remembered about him, and probably always will . . .'[4]

✝

In 1971 a local newspaper reported that a twenty-year-old farm labourer from the Welsh village of Abergele had killed six sheep, two lambs, four rabbits and one cat to drink their blood. The self-proclaimed Vampire, Alan Dyche, had invited friends to join him while he used blood in sacrificial devotions to the devil. Details of this case were few, but it seems to be an example not of a psychotic or dangerous sociopath (although many murderers do escalate from the killing of animals to humans) but an immature personality indulging curiosity and craving attention.

Another category of Vampire criminal is typified by an ex-convict and former mental patient named Hofmann who stood trial in Nuremberg, Germany, in 1974 accused of an array of blood-related offences. Just over two years earlier, in May 1972, he had surprised a couple sleeping in a car and had shot each in the head, drinking the blood from their wounds. He was also accused of the attempted murder of a morgue attendant, shot while attempting to prevent Hofmann from interfering with cadavers, and of disinterring at least thirty female corpses from fifteen different cemeteries to drink their blood. In a statement to police, Hofmann said he needed to feel a litre of female blood inside him each day. At his trial he was clearly deranged, refusing to speak and staring vacantly, occasionally gesticulating at onlookers in the public gallery. Like the nineteenth-century Sergent Bertrand who raided graveyards in France, the first blood-drinking necrophile to attract public notice (and unlike the grave-robber Victor Ardisson, the so-called 'Vampire of Muy'), Hofmann was probably that rare thing, a genuine 'haematomaniac' (a pseudo-scientific term from Vampire literature denoting 'blood-crazed'), for whom the compulsion was part of a delusionary system rather than a 'mere' sexual imprinting resulting in a fetish.

In 1989 Michael Ireland, a scaffolder from Northampton, England, attempted to suck the blood from the body of a ten-year-old girl, Susan Giles, after incapacitating her with eleven blows from a brick.

Detective Chief Superintendent Arthur Crawley who arrested Ireland for the Giles murder and for the attempted murder of the man's former scoutmaster, Eddie Barth, said that the crazed assailant showed absolutely no remorse for what he had done. Ireland was detained for life.

Voices in the head of Londoner Paul Watts, a hitherto devout and mild-mannered Christian, informed him that his father and brother were Vampires. In 1992 Watts stabbed them both to death with a carving knife. In the same year Georges Castillo, a French chef resident in England, killed Myra Myers by stabbing her thirty-seven times. Castillo claimed that Myers was a Vampire from whom he had to protect his girlfriend. He was acquitted of murder on the grounds of diminished responsibility.

Some real-life Vampires exhibit self consciously bizarre behaviour but may not be classifiable as insane. Their crimes seem to be motivated by uncontrollable fantasies of dominance and a desire for power that is denied them in everyday life. Also in 1974, twenty-four-year-old Walter Locke, an inhabitant of Hamburg, Germany, abducted a stranger, a thirty-year-old electrician named Helmut Max, after felling him with a karate chop delivered from behind in a quiet side-street. Locke dragged or carried his victim back to his candle-lit lodgings and placed him in a silk-lined coffin. When Max regained consciousness he was told by the caped figure that loomed over him that he was in the presence of Dracula himself: Then Locke then struck him hard in the face, collected the blood from the wound in a white enamel bowl and drank it down. According to Max's statements the tall captor then effortlessly hoisted his stocky prisoner from the coffin and began to issue commands. Fearing for his life, Max kissed Locke's feet, pleaded for mercy and swore to serve his master, who then ran with him through the night-time streets to a cemetery where the Vampire, still in full costume, began to perform a 'sinister ritual'. His newly ordained slave escaped and alerted the police who found Locke back in his room, by then asleep in his coffin. They also discovered that neighbours had been aware of the young man's nocturnal regime and the fact that he wished to be known as 'Grand Master' or 'Count Dracula', but medical examinations showed him to be sane and he was sentenced to life imprisonment for kidnapping and grievous bodily harm.[5]

Tracey Avril Wigginton was a tattooed six-foot 270-pound Australian biker; she was also a lesbian, an avowed Vampire and finally, at the age of only twenty-three, a killer. Her victim was Edward Clyde Baldock, a forty-seven-year-old who was stabbed in the neck and back, then slashed across the throat and left in Orleigh Park on the riverside in Brisbane. Whoever had killed Baldock had not only almost severed his head from his body, but had gripped the man's neck, pumped it vigorously and sucked blood from the open wound. What had not been swallowed had drained into the earth beneath the body, which was almost emptied when discovered. As it transpired, the victim could have been anyone, the immediate motive was human sacrifice and the date had been carefully chosen: by the old Julian calendar, 21 October was the date of Hallowe'en. In January 1991 Wigginton pleaded insanity by reason of multiple personality disorder (she was, said doctors, controlled by four different 'entities') and admitted that for many years she had lived on animal blood bought from a nearby slaughterhouse or butchers' shops, shunned sunlight and mirrors and led a strictly nocturnal existence, frequenting gay biker-bars and practising Satanic rituals. Her flatmates, Tracey Waugh, Kim Jervis and Lisa Ptaschinski, confirmed that Wigginton subsisted on blood and testified that she held them all in thrall by the force of her physique, her personality and by special powers, which included telepathy, telekinesis and hypnosis; at the end of their trial in February, Waugh was acquitted, Jervis received eighteen years for manslaughter and Ptaschinski, Wigginton's lover and protégée, who had watched the killing and done nothing to help the victim, a life sentence for murder. Tracey Wigginton was flamboyantly deviant, emotionally and physically unruly and finally uncontrollable, but despite her defence testimony she showed few signs of deep-seated psychiatric illness. She was sentenced to life imprisonment but will be eligible for release in 2006.[6]

ᛉ

In many of the non-fictional works that purport to analyse the forms of vampirism there is a pantheon of famous real-life killers who are cited under the heading of 'psychotic Vampire' or 'Vampire killer'. But however ghastly the perversions and cruelties carried out by Albert Fish, Ed Gein, Ted Bundy, Andrej Chikatilo and Richard Chase were, these men were not in any real sense Vampires. As in nearly all the other cases cited here, the killers' *primary* motivation is never an authentic craving for blood: blood-drinking, if it takes place, is indulged in out of curiosity or as part of a wider repertoire of degradation of the body of the victim, which often includes cannibalism. Nor did any of these monstrous serial killers make reference to vampire legend or explicitly self-identify as Vampires. None the less, two other members of the same grim fraternity do give pause for thought, in that both of them, when trying to explain their mental processes to medical experts, referred to a fascination with blood that, if it was true, indicated a rare and sinister fetish.

After the First World War the psychic malaise that periodically gripped Germany in times of social upheaval produced a clutch of monsters, killers who stalked the moral wasteland of the pre-Weimar years. Karl Denke murdered, dismembered and pickled at least thirty young men in the 1920s, Georg Grossmann slaughtered scores of girls, then sold their flesh as meat, as did Fritz Haarman, who haunted railway stations killing and cannibalizing the runaway youths he picked up there. The enormity of this trio's acts, given that all three went methodically about their business and were not visibly deranged, was overshadowed by the notoriety of the most prolific mass-murderer and blood-drinker yet, the model for Fritz Lang's pariah, *M*, the 'Vampire of Düsseldorf'; an impassive, pale and mild-looking man named Peter Kürten.

Kürten was no sophisticate, no suave Hannibal Lecter, and had little in common with the other modish serial-killers of 1990s fiction – he had grown up in a brutalized family of incestuous borderline simpletons but outwardly he was personable and inconspicuous. He killed for the first time at the age of nine, and the blood-fixation that formed part of a nexus of cruelty, dominance, violation and mutilation arose a couple of years later when he began to combine acts of bestiality with the stabbing of his animal victims, and found the sound and sight of blood to be a powerful erotic trigger. For years Kürten, who systematically committed burglary, arson and acts of petty violence, went in and out of prison unsuspected of the rapes, murders, burnings and maimings in which he also indulged spasmodically. The number of these atrocities increased as he entered middle age, to such an extent that police along the Rhine were convinced that three different killers were at large in the region. Suspects were arrested and even put on trial, but the reign of terror went on: women and girls continued to die of bludgeoning, stabbing, strangulation. Finally, in June 1930, after seventeen years of intermittent mayhem, Kürten was caught, brought before a court and quickly found guilty. He was perfectly rational and willing to give doctors, in particular Dr Karl Berg who subsequently published his notes on the case, an account of his childhood, his adult life and the endless list of perversions that accompanied them. Among the torture, drownings and bludgeonings, he constantly returned to the sexual excitement associated with the spilling and drinking of blood, which he remembered doing on at least nineteen occasions. Awaiting execution by guillotine in Cologne in July 1930, his last expressed wish was to hear the thrilling sound of his own blood as it gushed from his neck.[7]

✝✝

In 1949 when the *Daily Mirror* ran the headline 'Vampire Horror in London SW7', the man they were referring to was John George Haigh, more famous in true-crime anthologies as England's 'Acid-bath Murderer'. From a poor but respectable family who belonged to the puritanical Plymouth Brethren sect, the weaselly Haigh grew up to become a dapper, self-assured fraudster and a would-be playboy, who murdered five respectable, middle-aged acquaintances for money. It was only when he was caught (much to his surprise: he had been sure that the fact that his victims' bodies had disappeared would save him) and put on trial that the stranger aspects of his personality emerged.

Before putting the bodies of his victims into a vat of acid, Haigh said he had indulged in a private ritual: 'I shot her in the back of the head,' he said, of Mrs Durand Deacon. 'Then I fetched a drinking glass and made an incision in the side of the throat and collected a glass of blood, which I drank.' (It was, of course, impossible to verify the claim, as the bodies had been almost completely dissolved.) The expert giving medical and psychiatric evidence for Haigh's defence said, 'I think it pretty likely that he tasted it ... [but] from a medical point of view it was not important, for the reason that the question of blood runs through all his phantasies from childhood like a motif.' The prosecution and the judge gave defence witnesses short shrift, and it was true that Haigh's boasts of drinking his victims' blood and his own urine were hard to reconcile with his calculating methods of killing and careful concealment of his crimes. So the evidence of vampirism, put forward as a suggestion of insanity, was brushed aside, the forensic data that the prosecution had managed to amass made a guilty verdict certain and the judge placed the traditional black cap on his head before pronouncing sentence of death.

But perhaps there was more, after all, to the blood-obsession than the judge and jury credited, or perhaps in his last days Haigh's own lies invaded his subconscious and his sleep: just before his execution, and only briefly, he lost his air of unconcern and, alone in his cell, began writing down the details of the blood-drenched nightmares he was experiencing. Night-terrors, remorse or whatever it was did not completely snuff out Haigh's jaunty manner. In his last week he volunteered to make the hangman's job easier by rehearsing his own death on the gallows, but his offer was briskly refused. On Monday 10 August 1949, at the prescribed time of nine o'clock in the morning he was hanged by the neck until dead and buried in an unmarked grave behind the prison walls.[8]

There are three principal folk-devils who have fascinated the entertainment media at the millennium: the Alien, the Serial Killer and the Vampire. Aside from one very practical function that these share –

each provides a villain who is itself a legitimate target for the extreme violence that audiences relish – they also reflect, in a distorted mirror, a similar set of desires and fears, peculiar to our collective identity. The Alien, who replays ancient fears of intrusion, subordination, abduction (all, incidentally, attributes of the Vampire, as we have seen) is not necessarily a projection of recognizable human traits. The other two are.

The last years of the twentieth century have been marked by a fascination with the Serial Killer, a being who has acquired an aura of glamour and a resonant label (replacing the older, vaguer' mass-murderer') in the same way as the fictional Vampire. As they are represented in popular culture, the two personae have much in common – in fact, several important features are identical. They carry the cultural weight of other avatars – Nietzsche's *übermensch*, operating 'beyond good and evil', and the 'Outsider' figure, familiar from post-war existentialism – but more significantly they represent the Western individualist taken to the furthest extreme, the ultimate consumer, unfettered by old-fashioned restraints (family, religion, deference) and playing off society's own weaknesses and moral contradictions. The language of Vampire role-play and fiction incorporates this heartlessly post-modern concept by referring to the lone predator as 'culling' the common 'herd' of humans.

֎

In societies outside Europe and the USA, the traditional haunts of Vampire and Serial Killer, the combining of blood-drinking and murder is also surprisingly common. The same private impulses seen in largely Anglo-Saxon societies combine there with slightly different sets of cultural imperatives to produce alternative but recognizable patterns of behaviour, which are encountered in many different settings.

In a case that, although bizarre, is not unique, a young female villager in southern Sumatra killed five husbands in succession to feed her desire for fresh blood. Bahya Lenpeng would use tea laced with a sedative to drug each husband on their wedding night before opening a vein and drinking the sleeping man's blood. She continued to tap her victims for weeks after the nuptials until the blood-loss led to death. In 1975 the twenty-five-year-old Lenpeng's sixth intended victim, a police officer, was suspicious of his bride and only pretended to drink the tea she offered. When he realized what she was trying to do to him, he overpowered her and dragged her by the hair to the nearest holding cell. Somehow, Lenpeng, who was charged with manslaughter, escaped a prison term and was publicly forgiven by the husband who survived.

In places where ancestral folk traditions, ethnic rivalries or magic-religious rites are still strongly embedded, 'vampiric' crimes nearly always bear some relation to those beliefs and involve a ritual as well as personal element. A Chinese folk tradition has it that foxes are able to shapeshift into beautiful fairy women who operate like the European succubus in draining the energies of male victims by vampiric sexual attacks carried out while they sleep. In modern China the fox-fairy has not yet been banished by dialectical materialism: in August 1992 Zhang Zhike, a peasant from Anhui province, killed his new bride Lu Zhihua after a sorcerer convinced him that Lu was a fox-fairy spirit. Lu was a dutiful wife and, more unusually in that region, a devout Christian, who had become alarmed at her husband's state of mind – his obsessive superstitions and fantasies included the conviction that he could become a new emperor of China. The conclusion to Zhang's trial was not reported, but the standard fate of murderers in China, whether sane or demented, is a bullet in the back of the head, paid for by the condemned criminal's family.

In April 1993 Alfred John of Adamwa state in eastern Nigeria admitted to the murders of two hundred individuals whose blood he claimed to have sucked from their lifeless corpses. When arrested in the state capital, Yola, John was dressed as a woman, a disguise he assumed when luring his victims to the banks of the river Benue where they were killed and vampirized. No mere cross-dresser, John claimed that he was a female water deity, and that other water spirits helped him to overpower mortals and carry out his blood sacrifices.

In 1979 police in Bangalore, India, arrested the sixty-eight-year-old sadhu (a homeless holy man in the Hindu tradition) Laxman Singh Giri, on suspicion of murdering three children and assaulting numerous others. The children's deaths had taken place over the preceding three years, each on the night of a full moon near the burial ground at Srirampuram where the sadhu lived. When the authorities set up a covert surveillance of local cemeteries, Giri and three others were surprised and taken into custody. Giri remained silent under interrogation, but his accomplices, two men and one woman, confessed that they had been made responsible for luring away children who had been preselected by Giri, offering them sweets, then cutting their throats and draining their blood into a bottle. The sadhu supervised rituals in which the blood was offered as a sacrifice to the goddess Kali in order to achieve power and immortality. Following a solar eclipse on 16 February 1980, the imprisoned holy man confided to his female disciple that he had lost his spiritual power; he then ceased to eat or sleep and died on 5 March of the same year.[9]

$$\psi$$

Folk culture in the West is no different in essence from that of the developing countries, but its dominant iconography now tends to come via the electronic media rather than direct from story-telling and religious sermons. It is, above all, in Middle America; not so much a geographical location – the Midwest, the Sunbelt South, the empty northern forests – but an unfilled space in the collective imagination in which the vampire legend has come to reside. It is from the tensions and frustrations endemic in small-town and suburban America that the monster draws its power. The mother of a convicted teenage Vampire puts it more memorably: 'The big city's come to the little town and people had better wake up. It's Mom's little angel and hell's brewing underneath.' Here, far away, psychically even if not physically, from the worldly metropolis where, as another teenage clan-member ruefully imagined, 'even the presidents of big corporations can be Gothic', the delinquencies, misdemeanours and occasional murders linked to Vampire subculture have begun to reproduce familiar patterns.

In March 1998 four teenage boys claiming to be Vampires went on a vandalism spree in the middle-class Dallas suburb of Lake Highlands. The boys, named as Lucas Charles Simms, seventeen, Brandon Lee Ramsey, eighteen, Charles Randal Kinnard, nineteen, and an unnamed fifteen-year-old juvenile, were observed by investigators as they gathered to survey the scene of their worst outrage, the burning of a local Lutheran church. After smoking marijuana and ritually drinking one another's blood from scratches on their arms, the four slashed car tyres, splashed corrosive fluid over car bodywork, spray-painted 'Satanic graffiti', obscenities and racist slogans on fences and house-walls and smashed windows in the neighbourhood. The churchs' pastor, Carol Spencer, was quoted as saying, 'My sadness is not for us. It is for those people who do not know the joy of life.'[10]

The boys had aimed their attack at the most visible symbols of adult consumerism and conformity, the car and the church, and used as their canvas the fences and walls of the neighbourhood – a practical choice, but with added symbolic significance: the white picket fence as the sign of suburban territoriality, the enclosing and excluding walls marking out the nuclear family compound.[11]

ᛉ

Sixteen-year-old high-school student Michael Devine, described as a computer-loving homebody and a conscientious young man, went missing at the end of September 1991 in the little Pennsylvanian town of Parkesburg. Sixteen days later his body, the torso almost entirely eaten away by decomposition and the ravages of animals and insects, was discovered near the railroad tracks in the adjoining hamlet of Pomeroy. The cause of death appeared to be multiple stab-wounds to the back and neck.

A telephone tip-off and an anonymous note led police to Chad Franciscus, another teenager who, despite being a straight-A student, had gained a reputation among his 'Gothic' friends as an unpredictable rebel, a Satanist and a habitual sniffer of paint-thinner. Franciscus had also told them that he was a living Vampire. While still high from the effects of solvent and marijuana he had boasted to a former girlfriend that he had killed someone, and at around the same time he took a male friend with him to show him the location in which he said a body was hidden. Franciscus seems to have been a combination of two familiar but distinct types: the solitary psychopath/sociopath and the would-be charismatic leader. His crime was carried out in secret and for his benefit alone, but before and afterwards he went to peers for approval and to enlist them as accessories. Although the point was not pursued at the trial, it seems likely that Franciscus was part of a loosely organized group of Vampire fans, who flirted with occult ideas then disavowed him when he went too far.

In the event Franciscus was the only suspect; his statements to the police and behaviour during investigation suggested an unnatural detachment and indifference. In his room they discovered an occult altar on which were a Latin incantation, herbs, candlesticks, antique goblets and a kitchen knife with a nine-inch blade, customized to resemble a medieval dagger. Elsewhere he had concealed books on Satanism and witchcraft as well as copies of the role-playing game Dungeons and Dragons, anarchist publications, a copy of Bram Stoker's *Dracula* and photographs of graveyards and tombstones.

Although he denied the crime to police, when Franciscus admitted the killing to his friend, he said that he had lain in wait for any suitable stranger to pass before cutting his victim's throat; he was surprised by how easy it had been and how elated he had felt. To a fellow detainee he explained after his arrest that his aim had been to take a life, to experience the power that this would bring him and thereby dedicate himself to the Dark Side; despite his repeated claim to be a Vampire there was no evidence that he had collected or drunk Devine's blood. Two years after his trial, Franciscus was sentenced to life imprisonment without the possibility of parole.[12]

An American domestic tragedy was reported by NBC TV's *Dateline* on 24 November 1997 as a Vampire-related multiple homicide. The suspect was John Feeney, a high-school teacher from Springfield, Missouri, whose family were murdered (the wife and one baby bludgeoned to death, another child strangled) while Feeney was away from home attending a conference. Although no clear motive was advanced for the crime, the prosecution asserted that the husband had been a player of fantasy role-playing games since the 1970s and that police had found the rule-book for *Vampire: the Masquerade* in his home. Paint had been daubed at the scene of the killings, including the word 'bit' and some initials that might have been 'MV', which the prosecution alleged stood for 'Master Vampire', although this is not a designation used in that particular game. John Feeney admitted that he was in charge of his school's role-play gamers' club and stored their equipment at his home, but denied playing the Vampire game, just as he denied the murders. Someone, Feeney or an outsider, had run amok, perhaps indeed under the influence of Vampire fantasies (as well as adolescents a significant minority of over-thirties take part in the role-plays, too), but the link was not established beyond all doubt. At the time of writing the truth of the case had not been resolved, but what was notable was the way in which police and press now fastened on to the Vampire connection as evidence of a new sub-category of violent crime.

ᛉ

One of the most notorious acts of violence associated with the activities of Vampire gangs took place in Florida on 25 November 1996. The full story has not been told in print before, although the Internet is awash with related press extracts and discussions, especially on Vampire websites. The affair deserves closer attention as it brings together and into focus all the elements common to these cases as well as the ambiguities that remain unexamined in the terse, often sensationalist press reports.

A middle-aged couple, Richard Wendorf and Naoma Ruth Queen Wendorf, were discovered beaten to death in their home in the rural township of Eustis, thirty or so miles north-west of the city of Orlando. Early reports stated that the injuries to the couple showed that each had been bludgeoned by more than one assailant and the letter 'V' surrounded by circular imprints had been burned into Richard Wendorf's body, but these details were missing in later accounts. The family car, a red three-year-old Ford Explorer, was missing and so was the couple's daughter, fifteen-year-old Heather. Although the police were firstly and naturally concerned for Heather's safety, their questioning of neighbours and schoolfriends persuaded them that the girl was probably more a suspect than a victim. For about seven months previously she had been behaving strangely by the standards of rural Florida: she had dyed her hair purple, taken to dressing only in black and told her few friends that she had communed with spirits after a ritual involving the drinking of blood. She had become convinced that she herself had been a demon in a past life. It was known that she had been in contact with sixteen-year-old Roderick Ferrell, who lived with his mother in Murray, Kentucky, but had attended high school in Eustis, where he and Heather Wendorf had been considered, fellow-pupils said, 'as outcasts'.

After a manhunt lasting only a few days, Heather Wendorf, together with Rod Ferrell, Howard Scott Anderson, seventeen, Dana L. Cooper, twenty, and Charity Kessee, seventeen, were arrested at a motel in Baton Rouge, Louisiana, after a tip-off from Kessee's mother. As they were hustled into custody, the youngsters were subdued except for Ferrell, who, looking manic, even elated, poked out his tongue at the surrounding press and television cameras.

The part of Kentucky in which Murray is located is known as 'the buckle on the Bible-belt', a region where there is one church for every three hundred citizens. The small town of Murray itself is a teetotal community of thirteen thousand and is home to the National Boy Scout Museum, a college famous for its basketball team and, if the publicity for 'Circus Skate' is to be believed, the biggest indoor roller-skating rink in the USA. It is also, according to a former friend of those accused of the Wendorf murders, 'this *papier-mâché* town, this piss-hole Bible-bangin' Sodom-and-Gomorrah-infested shitbox of a Bible belt, consisting of Murray, Kentucky, and Paris, Tennessee...'[13]

Roderick Justin Ferrell was just eighteen when he was given the death sentence for the double murder. He had been brought up by his mother, Sondra Gibson, not herself a role model in the eyes of the Christian right; she had enthusiastically joined in Vampire games with her son and his friends, had been going out with a tattooist who adopted the role-playing name 'Kile' (apparently denoting 'one who had crossed over into Vampiredom') and had been charged with a misdemeanour herself after trying to persuade a fourteen-year-old boy to have sex with her by writing to him that he could thereby become her 'sire' and she his Vampire 'consort' for eternity.

For some time Ms Gibson and her son had been estranged from the boy's father, although Rick Ferrell, once and briefly Sondra's high-school sweetheart, was traced and summoned to testify at the trial. During the proceedings Ferrell senior avoided eye-contact with Rod, whom he referred to as 'the child'. After his day in court, he disappeared again.

In person Rod Ferrell makes a conscious effort – on the whole a successful effort – to be soft-spoken, precise and articulate. He looks slightly distant, puzzled: 'My greatest wish would be to go back to the year 1992, before I became engrossed in the darker side of life . . . [to] where I could just be a child again.' It was in 1992 that Rod Ferrell met his former mentor Stephen Murphy, whose vampire-name is 'Jaden' and who after the trial reflected: 'I thought he was wise enough, mature enough not to do something like this. The darker side of the soul – everyone has it. He let it envelop him instead of pushing it away.'

They met as high-school seniors, aged fifteen. At that time Jaden was the undisputed leader of a group of teenage Vampires who gathered in a woodland hideout, called by them the Vampire Hotel, but later dubbed by the press the den of 'the Haemogoblins', where they drank beer, smoked marijuana, enjoyed the usual role-play masquerades and developed and embellished their own versions. Jaden was the senior 'sire' and vetted and usually initiated the prospective cult members.

'I never really had a father anyway,' Ferrell recalls, 'so I looked to Jaden more as a father-figure. I was with Jaden and the Jaden Family for a few months. He had inducted me into the vampiric way of life; he had taught me the true ways of it, separating the myths and legends from the reality.' At the appropriate moment Jaden took Rod to Old Salem cemetery, to a certain tree where, he told him, all the other 'chosen' ones had been 'made' by their 'sires'. Jaden took out his blade. Each made three slits on his arm and drank from each other's wounds. Then they sat together in quiet meditation in the graveyard for several hours.

Membership of the group demanded total loyalty and putting the Family first in all circumstances. The members did not try to hide their lifestyle and became notorious: dressed in black, with black-painted fingernails and dyed hair, they flaunted their difference and stood out defiantly among the jocks, rednecks and regular citizens. The teenage Vampires despised and feared the social environment in which they were trapped. Even today Ferrell says, 'I believe Murray itself *is* evil . . . there was so much cultic activity there then, I think it comes from within every citizen within Murray, kind of like a Stephen King novel. It's supposed to portray harmony, and trust, and peaceful existence, when in fact beneath the skin it's this raging demon who gets his rocks off by doing all sorts of blasphemous things.'

Jaden concurs: 'A lot of people look at us as being inherently evil when it's *them*. We live in a society of separation, where they don't want to understand and therefore they fear it, and what they fear they hate, and what they hate they try to destroy.'

The first signs that Ferrell was going to go further than his companions' self-scarring and blood-sharing came when, walking with Jaden in a trailerpark, feeling angry and troubled, he smashed a kitten against a tree and killed it. At a local animal sanctuary in October 1996 a number of puppies were taken from their enclosures, tortured, mutilated, torn apart and stamped into the grass. The local police voiced suspicions that the animals' blood had been used to pour over participants in some sort of ceremony, although how they knew this is not clear. No one was charged, but then as now Ferrell was the chief suspect, although he still denies involvement.

Later Rod Ferrell and Stephen Murphy fell out and Rod was banished by Jaden's gang, cast out by outcasts, but Ferrell made new friends and, exploiting his brooding outsider's charisma, began to 'cross over' his own younger disciples, fifteen-year-old Michael Shafer and others. These impressionable teenagers saw Ferrell as their 'vampiric father'; they knew, they later said, that he would 'go all the way' for them, and they were in a sense right: 'I had decided to take the darker path, the evil path. I found that more exciting, and I was willing to go the distance to see what that side held.'

The group ranged around, resentfully and listlessly, played their music and shared their blood while they plotted to escape from the town once and for all. During this period Heather Wendorf and Rod had been phoning each other regularly and it was planned that she would join them when they set off on their ultimate exodus. According to his statements, he issued Heather with an ultimatum, demanding she leave her real family for his; in response, she asked him to come to Florida, twelve hours' drive away, specifically to kill her parents (the others claimed in their evidence that they had not planned to murder anyone). At that time the intense feelings generated within the group acted as a narcotic on all of them, but Ferrell was using drugs heavily, too: 'I was out of control – acid, marijuana, PCP ['angel-dust, a disorienting animal tranquillizer], crank [speed, probably in the form of methedrine] and heroin.'

On 25 November 1996 Heather Wendorf met her Vampire family outside the home of her natural family, a detached house set back from a quiet side-road in Eustis. Rod, who had taken LSD, and Scott went towards the building while the girls, Heather, Charity and Dana, sat in the car. The boys circled the house peering through all the windows to locate the two adults inside. Mrs Wendorf was in the shower; her husband was lying on the couch in the family-room. The intruders went through the garage, picking up a crowbar, then continued through a washroom and past the father, who was watching television. As Richard Wendorf rose from the couch in surprise, Ferrell struck him on the head, knocking him to the floor, and then, when he would not stop breathing, beat him and stabbed him in the chest with the crowbar. Ferrell then went to search for the keys to the Wendorfs' car and as he did so Mrs Wendorf came from the kitchen carrying a cup of coffee. As soon as she saw Ferrell, according to his account, she lunged at him and he knocked her to the ground, striking the back of her head with the crowbar. When he described the sequence of events during the killings in a taped interview with detectives Ferrell's tone was simultaneously animated, defiant and precise.

As he announced his sentencing decision after a guilty verdict had been returned on Ferrell, the judge paraphrased an earlier statement the gang-leader had allegedly made just after he was arrested: 'When I killed those people I felt a rush. I felt like a god. But I guess if I was a god, I wouldn't be here today now, would I?'

Scott Anderson was given a life sentence without parole, Dana Cooper received seventeen years' imprisonment, Charity Kessee ten years. Heather Wendorf went free, despite protests from Ferrell that she was as much to blame as any of them. On Death Row, nearly three years after the murders, Rod Ferrell says that if it had not been the Wendorfs it would inevitably have been someone else, 'maybe many others'. He still talks in a matter-of-fact way about 'moments of truth in everyone's life, when you have to decide whether to kill or not'. The self-dramatizing and bravado sit uneasily with the thoughtful, repentant tone of his other observations.[14]

ᛈ

When their lease ran out on their shared apartment, the remaining members of Jaden's original Family left behind Murray, Kentucky, and its 'hunting, beer-drinking, rodeo-riding, truck-driving rednecks', and headed for Los Angeles, pleased at their Internet notoriety and their status as associates of Rod Ferrell. Their experiences in Murray had been a way-stage, a rite of passage, but as they quit the town they reaffirmed their dedication to the Vampire cause and the coven ideal: 'What you get here is a family, people to take care of you, people to care. People who will listen to you when you have problems, people [whose shoulders] you can put your head on when you want to cry.'[15]

ᛈ

Reviewing the many crimes linked to vampirism of one sort or another throws up some significant conclusions. First, the drinking of blood – the most terrifying compulsion claimed for the vampire – is virtually never the direct motive for the crime in question: blood-drinking is usually either absent from the evidence, or present in the form of a bonding ritual performed by the perpetrators of the crimes. The element of vampirism that most cases have in common is the notion that initiation, either by some taboo act or by dedication within a group, can bestow membership of an 'immortal' élite and the chance to exercise undeserved power over others. The crimes carried out by teenage Vampire families highlight something else: the societal basis for the phenomenon that comes into play where – even though 'traditional values' are proclaimed – additional structures, value-systems and relationships have broken down. Interviewed for a British TV documentary, a Murray citizen summed up the dualism of small-town America: 'If you didn't have a battle between Good and Evil, you wouldn't have Christianity.' Seen from this perspective the champions of the right and the born-again exist in a binary relation to the Vampires; it is almost as if they have called their enemies into being.

A psychologist who has investigated the US Vampire underground says, 'My feeling is that society at large – mainstream culture – is really a very self-deceived entity in the sense that we really promote vampiric values. We worship people in power and fall on our knees before people who *take* from us. We give in to co-dependent relationships and want to stay with someone who has power even if they're defeating us. And yet we pretend that what we're really all about is family values and good and charity.'[16]

From his death cell, Roderick Ferrell again reflects on the act of murder, 'I really don't understand it myself. There's really no reason. There never was.'

8
Subspecies

'**T**here is one big problem for all the vampire wannabes, though: they want to be the vampires of fiction, foppish but alluring, not the vampires of legend. They cannot trace their "immortal souls" back to Vlad Dracula or any other regal figure, because they believe in a creature invented by novelists and filmmakers. And no amount of blood drinking can change that.' So wrote *Bizarre* magazine in May 1997 in a feature on the – for Britain, at least – recent upsurge in interest in contemporary Real Vampires.

On the Internet, meanwhile, the 'wannabes' had posted their apologia:

By removing the remaining negative traits of the Vampire, bloodlust and the animated-corpse theory, we have an extremely sensual, sexual, aristocratic, magically and physically powerful being. If one learns to emulate the powers of the Vampire while keeping strongly in mind the intrinsic elegance and 'Aristocracy of the Blood' that has developed within the archetype over the years, we now have the ingredients for a magical personality/persona known as the Vampyre.[1]

If an Internet surfer enters 'Vampires' in their search engine, they will instantly get a selection of several hundred sites to visit, many of which offer further onward links. The total number of Vampire-related websites is impossible to calculate (many are 'copycat' sites that plagiarize other richer sources of information, some are moribund, some are better defined as borderline-Goth, movie-fan or sex-oriented sites, others come and go), but at the beginning of 1999 probably ran into the thousands. The few 'authoritative' locations have a special importance, offering as they do definitions and histories of the Vampire and guides to vampiric procedures and protocol:

> I am using the term 'Real Vampire' to refer to people who appear to be living, organic, human beings, but whose essential nature is so different from that of ordinary humans that Real Vampires are, on the most fundamental level, non-human. Real Vampires are born into human families and utilize human (or humanoid) bodies, but their non-material 'bodies' or energy-forms are of a distinctly different type.[2]

There are discussion groups and message boards hosted by Vampires or sympathizers and there are even a handful of organizations offering to initiate and instruct neophytes, such as the Temple of the Vampire based in Lacey, Washington, part of whose published Vampire Creed runs as follows:

> I worship my ego and I worship my life, for I am the only God that is. I am proud that I am a predatory animal and I honor my animal instincts.
> ... I acknowledge the Powers of darkness to be hidden natural laws through which I work my magic. I know that my beliefs in Ritual are fantasy but the magic is real, and I respect and acknowledge the results of my magic.
> ... I am a Vampire.
> Bow down before me.[3]

A member of a rival temple described the willed transformation that the true Vampire undergoes:

In order to be fulfilled, a Vampire must first strip himself of 'mortal conscious programming' to reveal and begin to act according to one's true inheritance as a ruler. Mortal conscious programming is not a joke or a concept that we have created, it is a truth of the mass manipulation of society through public education, media, government, religion, and other avenues. Society wants a subdued and silent creature that will not object to certain things, and the Vampire must first strip away influence from his/her surroundings and upbringing. A Vampire will in time exist as a current which will affect the outside world much more than the outside world will affect it. In order to be fulfilled a Vampire must act, face danger, face tasks, conquer them, and embrace the chaos that is the nature of terrestrial life.[4]

Although they are numerous, the Internet Vampires are only a small minority of those captivated by the macabre and eldritch. In her short story, 'Isolating Madison', the British writer Nicola Barker offers a less radical statement of allegiance:

'I am a Goth, and Goth is a belief system which goes way beyond accident or appearance ... For me, Goth encapsulates both a way of life and a general philosophy,' she continued, emphatically but with a twinkle. 'I dress mainly in black. I collect Victoriana. I wear too much makeup. I am cynical and dissolute. I am feminine. I am ghostly. I eschew modernity. I am dark. I have great nails.'[5]

The Goth subculture exists quite distinctly from Vampire fandom or true vampiric practices, although it shares much of the iconography of those two tendencies and some of the sensibility that pervades them. A small number of Goths may imagine themselves Vampires and indulge in blood-drinking, may even participate in the blood fetishism or sex magic which also overlaps with the Vampire matrix. More importantly, many of those who self-identify as Vampires have been inspired by the Goth movement to take its dark fantasies to their logical conclusions.

Goth evolved in the UK at the very end of the 1970s and coalesced at first in 1981 around a small and temporary Soho club, the Batcave, which attracted those former devotees of punk who had concentrated on one element in that movement's image-repertoire: the iconography of the horror movie and the fairy-tale of terror. The proto-Goth stance with its funereal musical accompaniment had been pioneered by punk groups the Damned and Siouxsie and the Banshees, the latter becoming the first figurehead band of the new musical genre.

The Goth movement established itself like all tribal youth cultures by focusing on one (albeit complex) aspect of the adolescent personality, giving it expression and exalting it. That same identification with one enduring psychological trait ensured that Goth would be exported (especially into the USA and Northern Europe) and survive into the 1990s after its novelty and commercial significance had waned, flourishing amid a welter of competing and overlapping subgenres in a do-it-yourself underground linked by specialist shops, fanzines, clubs and the Internet, blending with related musical styles such as Death-metal, Darkwave, Ambient Ethereal.

Goth's essence was its melding of three poses, flippantly summed up by one US devotee as 'the Tortured Artist/Intellectual, the Vampire and the Punk', with their signature attitudes, 'pretension, death and angst'.[6] Put more sensitively, the movement played upon the notions of brooding introspection, melancholy – and other values: nostalgia, old-fashioned vanity – that had been sidelined by the preceding youth fads and completely negated both by the extrovert tribalism of the nineties powered by unthinking hedonism, and by the 'Slacker' or 'Generation X' tendency in the US, whose keynote was apathy. (Significantly, though, some American Vampires do see their activities as an extreme version of the Generation X stereotype of bored, disillusioned youth: it is they who categorize themselves ruefully as 'Generation Dead'.)

The British media lost interest in the Goth movement in the later 1980s when it was overtaken by those more fashionable hedonist tendencies – Rave, Techno, Hip-hop, Jungle – but in Middle America 'Gothic', as it was called, imprinted itself as a radically alternative look, and this was reflected back at a popular audience by Hollywood through a spate of fairly mainstream 'Victorian-Gothic' movies – *Edward Scissorhands*, *The Nightmare Before Christmas*, *The Crow* and *Interview with the Vampire* among them. Like all selfconscious poses Gothic invited mockery and – to a very limited extent – indulged in self-mockery, too:

Little wolfskin boots
And clove cigarettes
An erotic funeral
For which she's dressed
Her perfume smells like
Burning leaves
Every day is Hallowe'en
... Loving you was like loving the dead.'

As they evolved, the prevailingly antique-plus-punk Goth fashions absorbed influences from the biker, heavy metal and industrial looks, adding these to the lingering memory of glam rock and the dressing-up cult of the foppish new romantics, who had occupied the Batcave in an earlier incarnation. In the words of one social commentator, 'At least from an outsider's perspective, compared to most post-punk subcultures the Goths/Gothics seemed remarkably coherent as a group – linked for ever in the tender comradeship of the undead, finding sustenance in the poignancy of their fate.'[8]

In 1999, in a remarkable example of subcultures' ability – like the Vampire – to adapt and mutate, a 'New Goth' movement began in London, re-energized by a process of 'crossover' whereby quite distinct street styles are suddenly synthesized, resulting in vigorous new hybrids. In this case Goth appropriated avant-garde latex and rubber fashions from the fetish scene together with vastly improved technology from dance-floor and rave clubs; lingering doubts about sharing its venues with Vampire enthusiasts were put aside and the enlarged movement was once again in vogue.

Most of the Real Vampires under the age of forty acknowledged the Goth influence:

> In my early teenage years I started to get into the newly emerging Goth scene. I remember the first time I went to a Goth club. Man, was I blown away! I could feel the energy coming from the dance-floor and all those beautiful Goths dancing. For the first time in my life the cravings weren't so bad. (I believe that Goth clubs generate a lot of negative *chi*, and I was absorbing some of that energy.) I was moved by all the feelings of emotions from the dancers and I knew this was where I belonged. (All my life I've always been empathic, and I prefer the good kinds of negative energy like the type produced by Goth clubs or cemeteries than the ones produced by anger and hatred) I started to meet people my age who understood what it was like to be different. I was accepted.[9]

> Growing up in Florida and being fair-skinned, I had already put myself apart from my 'peers'. I was also interested in Victorian fashion and the restraint and repression of that era. I wore a lot of black. So being [illegible], not interested in going to the beach, and listening to 'different music'; Bach and Siouxsie [and the Banshees], I fell into the out crowd. These were kids that wore a lot of black, read a lot and were into the whole vampire, 'creature-of-the-night' thing. If you go out only at night and wear a lot of black, blister up in the sun and feel 'different' at fourteen, you have a tendency to relate to something and it was the Gothic tendency.[10]

> It wasn't difficult for me to get into Gothic and then take it further, because since I can remember my parents were already dressing in black and purple with silk scarves and mystical pendants and this kind of stuff. They were witchy, I guess in their way from the hippie days . . .[11]

As in all subcultures, fine distinctions are emphasized: 'I'm not a Goth and don't dress in the "expected" mode of dress. I like Doc Martens, black jeans, black T-shirt and a semi-Mohawk [Mohican hairstyle] and spikes. I'm more of a heavy metal vamp.'[12]

꙳Ꝟ꙳

For a number of those interviewed for this book even the Goth scene was too gregarious, too intimidating, or involved too high a risk of exposure. These Vampires, who mostly shunned bars and clubs indeed any face-to-face encounters that had not been carefully planned – recalled the near-impossibility of making contact with like-minded individuals before the advent of the Internet. Nowadays specialist message boards on the Internet – usually coded so that 'Vampyres' (lifestylers and club-goers) are distinguished from 'Vam-pires' ('Real' blood-drinkers) and Psi-Vamps – function in the same way as personal ads and lonely-hearts columns in the conventional world. Their catchment is not confined by national boundaries, although the great majority of postings come from North America.

Many ads are brisk and to the point:

M: I was raised to have a Vampire companion. Now it is time for me to find one. E-mail me and we can exchange blood.

A: (16, female) in search of victims ... blood donors (males preferred, females accepted) in Northern/Central California ...

V: Will you be my prey tonight? I love to bite and scratch. Please write, especially if you're in the L.A. area.

R: I am looking for others like me. I have no time for fakes or role players. Only true blood-drinkers need reply.

A posting from a psi-vamp is typical of that category:

T: I am a Psychic Vampire and I completely accept what I am. I am very strong-minded and like others to be the same way, as I get bored if I can gain control over people, which I can most of the time. I need large amounts of energy to feel good and have no control over it so have given up trying. I would like to hear from anyone who finds themselves in this situation.

A number of messages take the form of grandiose proclamations:

R: And those whom commeth [sic] in falseties [sic] need not reply for I pity you and shake my head in discust [sic] at your poor attempt and your stupitidy [sic] and am no longer amused ... and truelly [sic] you know not what you play with ... and manny [sic] shall commeth [sic] after me ... But I shall stand and rise above them ... for I hast [sic] come for thou...

There are many *cris de coeur* from the isolated...

S.A.: I am looking for a dark angel to talk to and possibly exchange blood. I am having absolutely no luck finding any other Vampires at all where I'm at...

... often poignant...

W.N.: I am alone, roaming and wondering if there is anyone like me out there ... Please someone, explain why I feel the way I do ... I have an idea what is happening to me, but something is missing ... I can't do it alone, will anyone help me? ... I hate being alone, so call me...

Other messages range from the slightly arch...

I am 23 – female. As for how old my soul is, well, never ask a lady her true age. I look 23, and that's good enough ... I usually do not search out my own kind, we tend to step on each other's toes. However, I am lethargic [sic] of mortals who cannot believe no matter what they witness.

... to the matter-of-fact...

I am a sensual person with an interest in light BDSM [bondage and discipline sado-masochism], much more interested in the D&S [dominance and submission], with me as a sub ... I seek a male Vampire...

Just as with sex sites the system allows the advertisers to make contact on-line without exposure to danger, explore one another's fantasies and then, in due course, perhaps to meet face to face in RL

The end of a 16th-century Bohemian Vampire

Varney the Vampire *in flagrante*

The Church at Golo; supposed resting place of žirovec, the Slovene Vampire

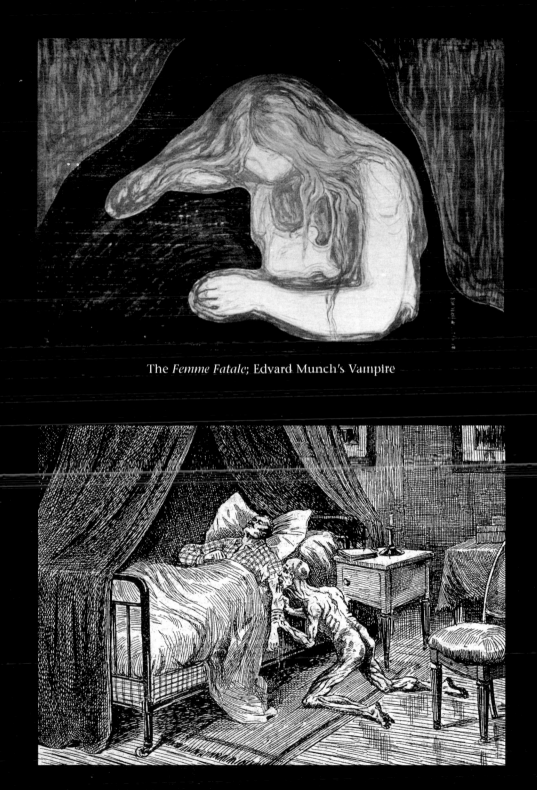

The *Femme Fatale*; Edvard Munch's Vampire

A Vampire and his victim – engraving by unknown artist from 1910

Klaus Kinski in character in 1988

The night-school student and her mentor in Ferrara's *Addiction*

(real life) or, as it is also known in computer jargon, 'meat-world.'

✛

In North America there is a fluctuating number of clubs catering to the Vampyre or Vampire communities. In the USA they are concentrated in New York, (the Bank, Downtime, Click-and-Drag, the Limelight, the Realm, the Batcave), New Jersey and Philadelphia on the East Coast, and Los Angeles on the West (most prominently the Fang Club in Beverly Hills), but almost every large city has at least one. At the time of writing Toronto has several, including the Sanctuary Vampire Sex Bar. Australia has a few, most in Sydney, and in Europe there are well-known clubs in Holland, Germany, Scandinavia and Poland. In the UK the clubs tend to be less opulent and more temporary meeting places, often hired rooms in pubs and cheap hotels where Dracula fans, Goths and Vampyres can come together weekly or monthly.

In all these places, but especially in New York City, the hedonistic club culture overlaps with a more seriously dedicated underground network based on prostitution, sado-masochism, sexual role-playing, fetishism and their variants. The so-called sex industry in New York is highly organized and lucrative, and within it the Vampire image is currently fashionable. As Christine, a New York dominatrix explained in 1997, 'You can get a lot of money for blood-play. It's the next taboo. Once some guys have lived out their fantasies in a commercial dungeon, they want to up the odds. Need to. And this is one of the ways to make it extra-forbidden. They are literally giving you their life-force ... I only do this with clients I've been seeing for a long time. Sometimes I just spit it out after I've cut them and sucked, and make them lick it up. Some women I know do stuff with their menstrual blood, making the guys suck their tampons...'[13]

Nearly all the Real Vampires interviewed by this writer were dismissive of club culture. As a member of the Temple Azagthoth put it, 'I care very little for the excitable and fashion-oriented "vampire club scene" of today, as it has little or nothing to do with actual vampirism. These are the people who accept some part of the legend of the vampire, while dismissing other parts. They may be hip, alert, and dynamic – however, many of them are also undisciplined, scared, and weak. A true vampire is a creature that commands dominance. This dominance comes from mastery and control over their own physical flesh and blood, thus mastery over others.'[14]

Some saw the 'transgressive' underground as a symptom of cultural change: 'The Marquis de Sade, he was considered a very sick, very evil degenerate at one point: they have *clubs* for that kind of stuff now!'

The atmosphere inside the North American clubs is typically restrained, even sedate by European standards: there is none of the open drug-use or abandoned, ecstatic mass-bonding that characterizes rave and jungle venues in London, and no frantic stage-diving and beer-throwing as seen at Doomcore and Death-metal gatherings such as the Vampyria event. Smaller venues resemble singles bars in which knots of costumed figures stand around nursing cocktails, beers, conversing furtively against the thundering backdrop of Gothic rock, a few nodding in time, fewer still dancing listlessly.

ᛉ

One estimate gives the number of practising Real Vampires in the USA as fifteen thousand, another 'around eight hundred'. The *Village Voice* sex survey *Red Light*, to which Susan Walsh contributed, identified 'no more than a few thousand ... predominantly white, middle class and in their early 20s' in New York City alone. A decade or so older, and of uncertain class affinities, Jerico DiAngelo is a performance artist who lives in a blacked-out basement apartment in the New York suburb of Queens. He regularly removes the sarcophagus from his living room for use as a prop in on-stage erotic rituals, which may include simulated sex with a vampiress or drinking his own blood, often both. When pressed he estimated a total of 'at least a couple of thousand bloodists in the tri-state area'.[15] A fifty-three-year-old female blood-drinker from Brooklyn who goes under the name of Neecha the Night Creature told the New York *Daily News* in 1998 that her own networking service for Vampires had more than nine thousand subscribers across the US.[16]

Among the many claimants to the label of contemporary 'Vampire', it is possible to distinguish several different categories, although these are not mutually exclusive. The largest group of all consists of the horror buffs: fans of the macabre and fictional Vampire fantasies who may go beyond mere passive enjoyment of movies, comic-books and novels to celebrate their hobby by dressing up, joining collectors' clubs, attending conventions and taking part in role-play games in person or via the Internet. These enthusiasts, particularly in their role-playing guise, are generally despised by members of other more radical groupings, and dismissed in the jargon of the Web as RPG-ers (role-play gamers) or LARPS (live-action role-players). Commenting on the Vampire underground in Austin, Texas, Marc Savlov of the *Austin Chronicle* wrote, 'Some of them share blood, but the vast majority spend their days holding down mundane computer-tech jobs, endlessly rescreening *The Crow*, and working on the personas of their *Vampire: the Masquerade* roles. There's a geek quotient here, to be sure...'[17]

A second large section is made up of devotees of 'Vampire chic', club-goers, the more resolute Death-metal and Goth music fans. Even within this category there is a scale of fanaticism ranging from a flirtation with images that may be seasonal – a surfer in summer, a Goth in winter – to a decades-long identification with the melancholy and the morbid. Both the foregoing groups usually prefer to be known as 'Vampyres', the antique spelling distinguishing them from those who use the 'Vampire' spelling or 'Real Vampire' label and are likely to indulge in more extreme practices.

The extremists, the Real Vampires, often place themselves and their fellows in further sub-categories, but some claim an underlying unity ... 'I have found that the only thing in common among all Vampires is the Hunger. What one craves is not always the same, though. I know some who hunger for blood, some hunger for emotion, others for life energy, directly bypassing blood as a vehicle for it. That hunger defines what a Vampire is. Without it, you are not one of us.'

The relatively recent appearance of a hardcore of Real Vampires seems to have begun in San Francisco and Los Angeles in the mid-1960s where the idea of consciously emulating Vampire practices and lifestyle was taken up by a small number of adult sophisticates, many of whom were already dabbling in the occult. The charlatan Anton La Vey helped to crystallize this tendency with the foundation of his Temple of Satan in 1966 and the publication of his Satanic Bible in 1969; when the Temple was disbanded in 1975, former members set up splinter-groups, some of which have survived.

At the turn of the millennium, La Vey's influence is still felt, as is that of the British magician Aleister Crowley, but younger Vampires are wary of old-style black magic: 'The occult doesn't interest me in the least so you might have to ask another interviewee. I can say that I am aware of the importance of blood in a lot of occult rituals. I steer clear of that sort as I have found that they are usually mentally unbalanced and that is not the sort of person that you share important information with.'

It is more common to find self-styled Vampires advancing a home-made combination of 'neo-pagan' ideas with an admixture of some elements of hermetic and alchemical tradition, almost always sup-plemented by reference to Ayurvedic notions such as 'pranic energy' and often to Chinese Taoist and folk beliefs in *chi* energy, lines of cosmic force, yin–yang balances, etc.

Sometimes sharing in the hermetic and black-magic rituals of the occultists are Vampires whose motivation is primarily sexual, whether professionally, as in the case of the dominatrices, prostitutes and pornographers, who use blood games as part of their repertoire of arousal, or amateurish, as in the case of lovers for whom the mutual shedding of blood becomes an essential token or element of foreplay. These practitioners of forbidden pleasures tend for obvious reasons to operate clandestinely and are often reluctant to share their secrets.

Social Vampires, aged between fifteen and twenty-five, may be organized into so-called 'clans', otherwise gangs, or may only com-municate and congregate 'virtually' with the aid of Internet sites and chat-rooms. These individuals are convinced either that they are members of a Vampire species, or that by joining together they can mobilize vampiric forces; blood-drinking – in widely varying quantities – is practised by most of them. Clans are usually locally organized 'extended families', often democratically among co-evals at a particular high school, for instance. They also frequently form themselves around or are recruited by one charismatic individual.

There is an undefined number of solitary individuals of all ages, but primarily adolescents, who ascribe their 'difference' from others to the fact that they are Vampires, either from birth or by virtue of having been 'turned' by another living Vampire. They claim a distinct set of symptoms in common: an aversion to light, acute sensitivity of skin, nocturnal tendencies, and almost all suffer, they say, from a real craving for blood, and usually only human blood will do.

Any attempt to create a typology of Vampires is flawed by the obvious fact that the categories blend into one another and that any one Real Vampire may exhibit attributes of several categories to varying degrees. For many adolescents it seems that a vampire identity is substituting for a subcultural identity that is no longer generally available to them. The solidarity and ready-made imagery of the hippie movement, heavy metal, punk and its offspring, Goth, have each passed away, leaving only the extrovert, materialist, conformist cults of dance-floor, techno, hip-hop, easy listening and the rest. Punk in particular met the needs, indeed created itself around the persona, of the sensitive, alienated adolescent wishing to glamorize angry inadequacy with a pose of violent – but really only symbolic – deviance. The devil-imp look, the scratched scar-tattoos, the autistic, convulsive gestures, the borrowed iconography of sado-masochism, Nazism and the horror movie were all enlisted in the cause of elevating the loser to the status of doomed saint. As an alternative stereotype for the outcast to adopt, the Vampire suits in every way.

༝

The Vampires who agreed to be interviewed for this book were asked to describe themselves and explain how they became aware of their unusual nature:

What can I tell you? What would you like to know? Age unknown. Can't give you answers to what I don't know. I just seem to have always been. I can't remember a beginning. Nationality???? Pale skin, silver/grey eyes, pale blond hair. You figure it out. The doctors always told my pseudo-parents that I had a rare blood deficiency. I just liked the way it tasted.[18]

The only British Vampire so far to have achieved some public notoriety, Lydia (also known as Cynarra), offered a detailed account of her life:

In 1995 and 6 I was featured in all the national press and some TV shows. I am now almost thirty years old and was born a vampire. My true nature did not start to develop seriously until I was about eleven. I had always had an interest in the darker things and grew up watching the Addams Family, Hammer Horror, etc. By the time I was 13 I was unable to tolerate sunlight directly on to my skin – if I did, my skin would blister and weep so I was diagnosed by my doctor as being photosensitive. I developed a need for blood then, too, and would eat any raw meat I found in my parents' fridge and conned school friends into 'donating' to me by telling them that it was the only way they could join my club. I survived from then on on my own blood (which didn't do much to help the craving, being only a form of recycling), and the meats that my mother would buy for our cat.

I left school and had my first relationship. I told the person I was with of my true nature and they freaked out so I didn't succeed in drinking from them. I had now added raw black pudding to my list of fixes. During the following years my skin and eyes became more intolerant of light. I was then working as a secretary and had to wear dark glasses whenever I worked on the computer (as I do now) and cover any exposed areas of my skin with total sunblock whenever I had to go outside. My skin became paler and paler and more translucent and the colour began fading from my eyes. At 22, I met the partner that I have been with ever since ... I didn't actually tell her of my nature (because of the bad reactions from past partners) but dropped a few subtle hints. She actually asked me if I needed blood one day and willingly gave it to me.

In 1995 I became unable to work, due to the effect daylight was having
on my skin, eyes, memory and energy level, and saw a specialist who told
me that I have a reversed body clock and should live nocturnally. This was
fine for me as I would have had to try and avoid any exposure to light
from then on anyway. I bought some contact lenses to try and save what
little colour I had left in my eyes and started obtaining cow's blood regularly
from a local butcher, as I would only drink from my partner when she
offered and I felt she had the strength to give it. I can also drain people in
close proximity to me 'psychically', which happens subconsciously for me,
when I am particularly drained and 'victims' of this have told me that they
can feel the energy being sucked out through their arms if they are in
contact with my body. I cannot tolerate garlic, the smell of it will send me
into convulsions and my metabolic rate is very slow.

Its pretty hard to know what else to say ... I class vampirism as more of
an affliction than a gift and wouldn't wish this existence on anyone...[19]

The symptoms Lydia describes are similar to those claimed by
other contemporary Vampires, pointing to a condition of extreme
sensitivity; it is worth noting that they do not accord with the few
details we have of the Vampire revenants reported from eastern
Europe, who seemed to be ruddy (although some were glowing white)
and robust. The aversion to garlic is a standard feature of the cinematic
and literary Vampire, but was only rarely mentioned in historical
sources.

Another female Vampire from Britain, aged only sixteen at the time
of writing, refers to Vampires as members of a subspecies or mutation:

I am a born Vampire [as opposed to 'made', in the current terminology].
According to the laws of genetics, this means that both my mother and
my father must carry the vampirism gene, but also the human gene
(I must therefore have homozygous [two identical, therefore dominant]
vampirism genes). Neither my parents, nor my sister are Vampires, and I
have never met anyone else who claims to be a Vampire. It is very difficult
to find someone who tells the world they do not exist![20]

Maria's theory and her confident presentation of it were paralleled by several others, including the American 'TM':

> I have known that I was a Vampire since I was about 12 years of age. Someone told me that I should study my family tree, and to focus on the eighth generations in particular. That is how I found out . . . No, my parents are not Vampires. My mother knows about it: it is from her side of the family after all. I believe my father is catching on.[21]

Maria again:

> Only two close friends know what I am, but that is no substitute for the complete understanding another Vampire could give me. My family try to love me, but never could if they knew, and I try to understand them and love them in return, but without understanding their emotions it seems kind of hopeless. I have always known that Vampires existed: even though I had no evidence, something in my head told me they had to. Even before I knew that I was one, I would spend hours searching through bookshops and magazine racks hoping to catch a glimpse of the word 'Vampire'. For some reason I needed to see it, and was drawn to it as if it were my name. At the age of about 12 or 13 I began to feel depressed. I have always suffered from severe insomnia, and that didn't help matters. I would sit in the dark staring out of the window for hours every night, and tell myself I was stupid to feel like this when I had no reason to. One day it grew so bad that I sliced one of my wrists with a pair of kitchen scissors. I began to suck the wound (I assume to ease the pain, I can't think why else I would do it). Almost immediately I felt better. It was amazing. For the next few weeks I felt more uplifted than I ever had before. When the depression returned a few months later I slit my wrist again (I can't remember if it was the same one, since the scar had healed). Again I drank a small amount of blood, and recovered quickly. I still had not made the connection, however, and did not know that I was a Vampire.

The emotions and sensations recounted here can all be rationalized as part of the emotional turmoil of adolescence, an extreme manifestation of the common (but usually transient) feeling of being a 'foundling' or 'alien' in the midst of an uncomprehending family. The therapeutic effect of physical pain upon emotional distress is seen as a unique revelation, and the symbolic act of sucking becomes doubly soothing.

For Maria, as for most of those interviewed, the Internet was a catalyst, though not at first a comfort:

> The first time I had access to the Internet, I immediately entered 'Vampire' into the search engine. For the following few months I was fooled into believing a group of LARP gamers, and though their claims were not wild, they convinced me that I was human, and they were not. When I finally realized that these people had spend the entirety of our correspondence in fantasy I felt more betrayed then I can put into words. They had no idea how much their ignorance had hurt me. However disappointing my experiences had been, I now knew how to spot a LARP web page and could filter through the results of my 'Vampire' searches. The first Real Vampire site I found was entitled 'So you want to be a Vampire'. It was small, but listed a number of Vampire characteristics, all of which I recognized as my own. Further research produced similar results, and about half a year later, I knew for certain that I am a Vampire.

•

During an exchange of e-mails over about three months I suggested to Maria that her problems might be susceptible to other explanations and gentler remedies – new-age healing or eastern philosophies, for instance – but her conviction that she was a Vampire remained firm.

Older and more experienced Vampires had become equally certain of their identities. Their stories, of which the following are typical, conformed to certain patterns:

> How and when did I realize I was what I am? It was a gradual process – total acceptance about three years ago. I always knew I was 'weird' and not like most others – just figured it was me. I finally gave into the blood a few years ago. It took a lot of insanity to get through that one. Back and forth arguing with myself whether I was nuts or not. How is it different from

being as others? Finding the vampire websites has been a help. To find that there are others like me out there. Not so lonely.[22]

I guess I was the weird kid that was in every school. I couldn't relate to the other children, so my early childhood was filled with pain and loneliness (plus my homelife sucked real bad). I felt deep down inside that I was a Vampire. I understood what I was, but I didn't know *why* I was the way I was. There was something still missing.[23]

I'm female, 28, I have an IQ of 167, I sleep on the average about five and a half hours a night, I design websites and I am an artist, I smoke but I don't drink hard alcohol, I do like stout on occasion, I work out but I do have a real diagnosed disease that keeps me out of the sun [Graves disease: it makes heat unbearable].[24]

I view it as a condition that I was born with. Probably much the same as diabetes or something. It's not something you can change except learn to live with it.[25]

I am not quite sure how I became what I am today. I have only theories. My mother was a witch, did all sorts of spells when I was very young, then something scared her terribly. She refused to go back to it. Ever since we have had a black shadow-like creature with us. Mostly me. Perhaps this has something to do with it. Perhaps I was destined to this fate. Perhaps I was born this way and it awoke the older I got. All I know is that I look like I am between 14 and 16 years old, but I left that age long ago.[26]

How does one come to realize the fact of what they are? There are several theories on this, some say that one has to be 'made' and others say that it is a genetic default. I personally feel that some people are born with a certain genetic makeup that allows tendencies towards certain activities to come into play. I also feel that events that occur in life sometimes bring these tendencies to the surface. My own personal experience was that I was always interested in the dark underbelly of reality and this brought me into contact with a different type of person than one would normally meet on the street. I feel that realization for me was a slow evolutionary process that is still evolving and moving me forward. I don't think that there was any defining moment that made me wake up one day and say, 'I van to drink yer blhad!'[27]

... I know several [other Vampires], we are all good friends. I have a male friend who is, and he and I are like brothers. There are several females, all of who are either really good friends, or have been lovers at one point and time in my life [28]

I don't really know where to begin. I was thirteen when I first found out I was a Vampire. I'm 23 now. Really I want to just be accepted for what I am, not laughed at or made to feel uncomfortable. Other than that I just want what everyone wants. To be financially stable, have a family someday. I sing in a band, I write books myself, mostly fictional. And I do a lot of drawing. What else would you like to know? Just ask I'll be happy to tell you.[29]

I hate the sun, I hate the heat and I live where it gets 105 in the summer. Ack! I burn extremely easy – from several layers out. My eyes are extremely sensitive as well. I am lethargic during the day and perk up during the night, etc. I have noticed that these tendencies have gotten more intense now that my lifemate and I are drinking more and letting the Vampire out.

Although they are a minority, there are older, usually more sophisticated participants on the fringes of the Vampire scene, some who practise blood-drinking, some who observe and study:

Regarding myself ... in this incarnation I have not yet reached my fiftieth year. I am an artist, musician, and scholar. I have made a modest study of Theosophy, which has granted me a wider appreciation of the universe and its myriad wonders. Vampirism, mythology and folklore have always held great interest for me. It is a pleasure to be able to exchange views and information with you.[30]

✝✝

A US correspondent passionately summed up the 'us and them' conflict, which animated many of his fellow American Vampires:

> Things are getting bad out there. The freedoms that I enjoyed when I was a teenager are being destroyed by the corporate/media/government/religious fundamentalist powers that control our country. I guess one of the benefits of being a 31-year-old Vampire is that I am immune to all the bullshit propaganda aimed at today's youth. I rebel against my generation's (and the baby-boomer generation, which has all the power) attempt to wage war on the youth of America.[31]

This overwhelming sense of 'ideological' alienation, based on a generation gap or a threat from a right-wing complex of oppressive institutions, was confined to Vampires from the USA. Although European and Australians sometimes complained of localized frustrations such as parental indifference or police harassment, for them the 1960s notion of a 'straight' versus an 'alternative' society seemed to have receded. Poppy Z. Brite, the cult author of novels and short stories that blend club-culture, the rural American Gothic and taboos involving sex and blood, asserts: 'The Christian Right always needs scapegoats, and the rise of Aids since the mid-eighties has made a convenient scapegoat of anyone whose sexuality encompasses more than breeding in the missionary position.'[32]

The Right, or some version of it, is fighting back, and there are scores of Internet sites dedicated to combating the ungodly and unpatriotic. Most erect a front that suggests the presence of a powerful organization, but could as easily be a single individual or a small group of friends; nevertheless, cults beget cults. One such is the American Psychological Evaluation Corporation, with its slogan 'APEC knows'. At its website is an exposé of blood cults written by one S. A. V. Chamma of its 'Cult and Conspiracy Investigation Division', which claims that APEC has infiltrated and exposed groups of blood addicts in Boston, Atlanta and Los Angeles, and ends with a call to stamp out this menace to society with its 'potential for mass addictive behavior' before it spreads beyond the current active membership, put very precisely at 7,500. The Corporation asserts that 'all blood cults ... require periodic sacrificial murder of victims by exsanguination', but admits that to date no member of the cult groups to which it refers has been indicted for any criminal act.

APEC also presents a profile of the typical blood-drinker similar to those found at other websites and in the writings of press investigators like the Texan Jeff Guin. The typical 'bloodist' is male, Caucasian, aged twenty-eight, of above-average intelligence, with at least two years of college education and an income (in 1998) of above $50,000 per annum.[33] (This accords roughly with my findings, but describes only one category of Vampire, the 'adult sophisticate'. A much larger group is made up of adolescents and another set, of unknown number, consists of the older occultists and new-agers.)

Most of the Vampires who contributed to this book were courteous, even gentle. Only occasionally did they display bravado or aggression, although these are common on message-boards and in on-line discussions:

I am not the sad little Vampire figure we see in most movies: I am the dark and evil one ... I drink blood, have fangs. A little over a year ago a friend of mine got into trouble with the gang 'bloods' and I beat them half to death, alone and without any weapons ... I live in California and have recently become single ... By the way, I'd like nothing better than killing and feeding on any RPGers who contact me.[34]

A Vampire designated only as 'F' wrote, 'I think you will agree that it is better to communicate this way [via e-mail]; I don't imagine you would really wish to come face to face with an indiscriminate killer?' There was a brief follow-up correspondence during which F was evasive about his or her remark; communication was then abruptly terminated.

In the course of researching on-line I received a number of terse, anonymous warnings followed up with any further messages: 'Do you realise the very real dangers that you are in in seeking to make contact with us?' and, 'Do not tamper with secrets that, as a mortal, do not concern you.'

Correspondents and interviewees had heard rumours of vampire-related violence, but always at second-hand: 'There are stories about people who get into the Vampire lifestyle and do some sick things. They are not necessarily Vampires, but they use it because they want to be able to get close to people and maim them, rape them, whatever. I've heard that people have been killed and, you know, it's been covered up or the bodies have never been found, but I don't have the details, of course.'

Real Vampires talk in terms of 'vamping out', which refers to a strong impulse to behave 'vampirically' or give in to one's Vampire-self. At a far more intense level is the attack of primal desperation known as 'The Beast'. Maria, the teenage English Vampire, describes the condition:

It had now been about six weeks since I last fed – an unusually long time – but my body was coping surprisingly well. I was lying in bed, listening to murmurs from the next room ... the transformation was just as severe coming into the Beast as coming out of it. I felt a strength unimaginable to my usual self. I was alert to everything around me ... I didn't want any other living creature to encroach on my personal space. I felt powerful and had a rage burning inside me like no other I have experienced. It is the only time in my life when I have felt capable of extreme violence. I could have killed with my bare hands. If anyone had had the misfortune to have entered, they would not have survived ... There was so much passion in the emotions that I felt that I cannot find the words to describe them. They were raw, untamable, animal instincts.[35]

Of course, it could be argued that once a condition is defined susceptible individuals will begin to experience it. Judging by her tone the instance described here was real and authentically frightening for the young woman who underwent it, and it may be significant that it took place during a hypnagogic phase (see pages 137–8).

Several Vampires suggested that, while they posed no threat themselves, they were in danger from the activities of 'Vampire Slayers' or 'Vampire Killers'.

> Did you know that there is an actual fad for being a Vampire Slayer? This is dangerous stuff, due to this TV show [*Buffy the Vampire Slayer*], there are people who think that by hunting down a vampire and killing it, they will become the smart handsome/beautiful hero that they are so desperate to be. This is why showing your identity is a danger. If it ever comes to the attention of the police you are in a nut-house the next day, no questions asked ... that is yet another reason to be careful who you take from.[36]

There has as yet been no report of the actual (as opposed to 'virtual') killing of a Vampire by a 'Vampire-Slayer', but these latter do exist, in their own imaginations, in some bars and fraternity houses and, naturally and primarily, on the Internet where they 'out' Real Vampires by publishing their true identities, telephone numbers and addresses and persecute them by 'flaming' (bombarding with electronic hate-mail) and 'spamming' (jamming their e-mail facilities with redundant data). Rumours that gangs of young Nazi-sympathizers are planning to incorporate 'Vampire-hunting' into their activities should not be discounted, especially after atrocities such as the Columbine High School massacre carried out by just such a group near Denver Colorado in April 1999.

ᚠ

The present generation of Real Vampires do not seem to be suffering from any recognizable medical or biological condition, despite their desire to do so, but they could be said to be part of a distinct psychosocial syndrome, a condition that is, to a large extent, culture specific. There are interesting precedents for quasi-medical conditions that are, in fact, culturally determined, and there are also social panics, which are clearly linked to and limited by the beliefs of certain communities. An example of these would be so-called 'Multiple Personality Disorder', whereby patients discover a host of separate personalities or 'alters' within themselves, usually while undergoing hypnosis, which also reveals suppressed memories of childhood abuse (25 per cent also recover memories of devil-worship, ritual murder, cannibalism, etc.). The curious features of MPD, which was first publicized in the USA in 1973, were that the number of cases discovered increased exponentially over twenty years from fifty to 20,000, coinciding with feminist groups and the media promoting its importance, and that before the early 1990s no cases at all had been reported from outside the USA. Once North American analysts embarked on lecture tours overseas, isolated cases began to show up. While believers in the syndrome will naturally claim that real cases were previously going undiscovered, sceptics think that there is virtually no hard evidence for either the abuse or the reality of the alters, and that the condition is actually spread by publicity.[37]

There are obvious parallels here with 'neo-vampirism', another rare and mysterious condition that may be fabricated from personal and social circumstances, mediated by the imagination working under the influence of a spectacular and efficient promotion. 'Vampire' is a memorable and familiar label, which, in the cases of the subjects interviewed here, is now being applied to an identifiable set of ideas and experiences shared by real people. Instead of dismissing the Vampires' convictions as deluded, wrong-headed, childish or perverse (all of which they may be, depending on one's viewpoint), it makes more sense to ask why the label has been appropriated at this time and by these particular, seemingly sincere individuals. Linguists say that a new term comes into being or an existing one is transferred from a different context when a 'lexical gap', a concept or thing that is as yet indescribable, becomes apparent in a language. The gap in this case is a void that occurred when certain expressions and the ideas they encoded fell out of favour a hundred or so years ago. It was once perfectly acceptable to talk of 'sensitives' and of 'neurasthenics' and 'naturals', of mild 'melancholia' and 'accidie', but our societies no longer have time for the conditions they describe, just as words like 'enchantment', 'bewitchment' and 'possession' now sound quaintly antiquated.

9
Generation Dead

'*But how much tape do you have with you?*' *asked the vampire, turning now so the boy could see his profile.* '*Enough for the story of a life?*'

Anne Rice, *Interview with the Vampire*, 1976

Once I had made contact with members of the Vampire community from the US, Canada, Australia and the UK, I interviewed them face to face, or more often, given their desire for anonymity and the distances involved, by telephone and e-mail over a period of between a couple of weeks and a year. Roughly the same set of questions was put to each interviewee, but in conversational mode, not as a questionnaire, with the order and form of the questions varying according to previous responses. A large number of Vampires were willing to take part, but I had to be ruthless in easing out of the process those who were simply looking for an opportunity to fantasize, or a means of self-publicity, or were obviously joking. What remained, once repetitions, irrelevances and suchlike had been removed, were the reactions of around three dozen individuals. (Even this approximation has to be made with caution as individuals can log on to the Internet under several different names and remain undetected providing they are using several different e-mail addresses.) Many responses were very similar, probably because respondents were taking their cues from the same fictional or online sources, so in many cases one Vampire's observation stands for several others.

Blood-drinking seems to be the main defining characteristic that

sets Real Vampires apart from all others, so those who admitted to
using blood were asked the obvious questions: whether it was necessary, how it was obtained and what sensations it provoked in the
drinker.

Of the precise effects of drinking blood, accounts differ. The New
York dominatrix Goddess Rosemary bases her view on long familiarity: 'It has a narcotic effect, it really does. It's very, very odd, very
strange, and it does it immediately and it does not take a lot. But it's
true. The best way to experience it if you don't want to drink a
person's blood is to take a very, very raw steak . . . you know how you
feel after you eat a very, very raw steak and you get the feeling like
you're a little drunk – light-headedness – that's it, it's the same thing.
It's like the chemical (is it phenylalanine?) that's in turkey; when
people eat turkey at Thanksgiving or Christmas, they get all happy
because of the drug in the blood. It doesn't seem to work which your
own, I don't know why that is. I think that the other person fills with
adrenaline when you are doing it, and when you take it you get a
chemical reaction, something like that. And even if it's your own
adrenaline reaction, it's triggered by the blood. The minute you put
your tongue on it, it reacts like that. The quantity doesn't matter,
you can just put your tongue on it, not even a drop, will do it; on the
tip of your tongue or under your tongue where the veins are so it
goes straight into your bloodstream, like homeopathic remedies.'[1]

A more typical Vampire, an anonymous Canadian female in her
thirties, emphasizes the indiscriminate craving or 'hunger' that many
others cited:

Blood *is* important to me. I drink almost nightly. I feel very sick if I do not.
I get it from anywhere. I think you might be shocked (but perhaps not) to
learn that most vampires will deliberately *work* in a field that they can
have easy access to blood. Some are nurses, and I know of one doctor as
well. But this, as you can well imagine, is kept *very* quiet. I like the taste of
blood. Even a simple small taste to fill my mouth is sometimes all that I
require – I can not imagine draining a whole cow, or person, for that

matter, although I have seen that too. I prefer human blood, that of animals is un-tasty, but sometimes I have drunk it.[2]

Another Canadian, also female:

I have traveled out of my area and sometimes out of Canada if I am to do any harm to a person. You'd be surprised to know how many 'little guys in Goth bars' will willingly let you draw blood and lick at it. Being a *very* good-looking lady, I have not had anyone refuse me yet in 15 years! I have a great feel for people, and seem to know whom I can persuade to go along with me.

In Toronto a flamboyant member of the Vampire underground, Rachel, the Marchioness, states,

It seems to be a real primal urge for me, and when you're cutting someone and when you see that scarlet line start, I start salivating. It's like built-in. Maybe it's going back to a primitive part of us, that maybe the rest of the world is ignoring. The need to feed [on] blood ... It's a release and when you see the blood it relaxes you. You get a euphoria from it, it makes you feel better.

Blood is a big thing for us and I was lucky enough to find a lineage of people who drink blood and call themselves vampires, which I am now part of. I guess I'm a modern-day vampire ... with a very old soul.[3]

Other members of the Toronto group say they think of blood-sharing as 'an ancient rite enabling the transfer of spiritual energy from one person to another'. The process involves slicing open the chest 'just a shallow surface slit' and dripping a few drops of blood into a small silver or pewter goblet from which it can be drunk.

'Ferris', a twenty-eight-year-old American female Vampire describes the 'taking';

It's pretty involved; there isn't a lot of poetry to it. Simply put, you find a willing donor and go about your business. I guess that since it is a daily part of life it isn't a big deal to me – but then it *is* a big deal.

Is it essential? I think so. I don't know that I would die without it but then I haven't gone without it too long. I do think that from my discussions with others that it varies from person to person. I can go about a month absolute max, but I've only done that once and it was to test myself. I won't do that again if I can help it. (*Big smile*) I do think that for some people that it is symbolic but that is the fetish crowd. Good people to have around, as they kind of want the same thing that you want. Does it have paregoric value? I think that you said *hallucinogenic*? I do think that has some validity to it as I have experienced this up to a point. I have not had anything so vivid as, say, LSD, but that kind of thing in its full power isn't available any more anyways. You can feel someone's heartbeat in your mouth and in your throat, it's a fantastic feeling. So I would have to say *yes* to the essential and partial to the hallucinogenic. How much is needed? It depends on how long it's been. Sometimes it's roughly about a cupful as I have a tendency to keep pulling. Never less than six tablespoons or six mouthfuls. If it runs dry or starts to seal up, the wound isn't deep enough and I usually go over it again with a razor and drop it down a little deeper. Scars are a small problem. I don't scar easily but some people have a tendency to welt up. This is usually solved by putting vitamin E oil on the wound the next day and for the next month after.

Ferris describes some experiences that may have been formative in instilling the 'hunger':

There are a few moments that I feel brought this to the surface. When I was six I bit the thumb of a neighbor boy that was teasing me, I drew a good deal of blood as I had hit the bone and when I came into the house my mother freaked out because I wouldn't let her clean his blood off my face. I waited until it was dry, picked off the flakes and kept them in a box for years. I still have no idea why I would do that. After that I had a generally happy, typical childhood and didn't think about it again until I was 15 or 16. I had a group of friends that I hung out with regularly and one night the group of us had gone to this pub and one of the guys – let's call him Tim – had started to draw on his arm with a razor, very lightly so that only small beads welled up on his skin. After a while we all did it with contests on who could do the most detail. I had an incredible crush on Tim as he was a superior artist, so he and I went outside for a walk. He asked if he could take the blood off my arm, I thought he was going to wipe it off. We sat on a bench and he started to lick it off. I was kind of disgusted, but only because I was afraid someone would see. Guilty pleasures ... He started to pull at it – when I say pull, I mean suck very hard to *pull* out every last available drop – I passed out. Maybe I was so shocked, maybe it was because it opened a floodgate of sensations that I couldn't deal with. Tim and I never hooked up, I left town shortly afterwards. I do think about him on occasion but not often.

I moved to another town in Florida, and a year or so later a friend visited from Colorado with a friend of his. This friend of a friend, Patrick, showed up on my doorstep with a bag in hand a month later. He stayed, we stayed together for two years. He started it in full swing. I don't remember the circumstances but he came out of the bathroom one night with this cut in his arm – crook of his elbow – and says, 'Take it.' I was thrilled but not sure what this meant. Once a week for the next two years we took from each other. Rarely during, before or after sex but the times that we did it was truly amazing. Like riding a motorcycle at night on a deserted road in September. Cold but comforting. We parted ways and it was amicable.

After that I went out and found willing participants that I could take from for a year at a time. I just realized this and it's really funny, I knew about six blood-drinkers from the same tiny town on the west coast of Florida. We are all in different parts of the country and our paths crossed briefly in different states and with several year-long intervals. I did not take from all of these people from this town, we just knew each other through similar circumstance. That's about how it goes or at least how it went with me. I have not looked back, really.[4]

The Vampires all emphasized that those who donate blood to them always do so willingly, even if subtle persuasion might be necessary:

I don't take advantage of fools or halfwits. I will not take from those that are unwilling or that seem mentally unbalanced – funny that *I* should say that. It really has to be consent only, otherwise I would be in jail. As far as getting people to give it up ... I do not really tell them the whole truth about who I am and what I want to begin with, as too many people would prefer to hear a lie ...

Aids is something that I worry about, so I prefer to take from someone that I have been involved with for a while. A few people I know keep one person as backup: I haven't found a backup in this town as I like to spend a lot of time with a person first.

An equally common response was 'You're desperate. You get lucky. You're not going to wait to ask questions. It's like unprotected sex – everyone's doing it, whatever they tell you.'

The Real Role of Blood? Hmmm. Well, honestly, it's because I love everything about it. It's warm and slick and tastes better than anything you have ever had. The metallic taste that you hear about so much isn't really noticeable and it really is the best stuff. I think it does a good deal for me. As I am an artist I really enjoy the sharp focus and the intensity of colours that come about after drinking, though I couldn't even believe that I had to wear sunglasses for the next few days after drinking. A really odd feeling.

I haven't really tried to go without it for a long period, maybe five months. Maybe it's been eight years since I started actually drinking ... I was positive about who I was by 16 but didn't start till I was 20. I hate attention – getting put in the spotlight is the worst thing that can happen as it makes one very noticed so I steer clear of being obvious. I stay away from kiddos that wear plastic fangs to clubs as this is a dead giveaway for a kid that causes a lot of trouble. I don't have fangs. I have long incisors but I use a small razor blade. Since the Anne Rice books became popular it's been a good idea not to be obvious. I live in Texas now, near the border of Mexico. It's nice to be in a much larger state. When I drink I just feel much better on the whole. I never get sick. That's really nice. I like the whole aspect of it, though it does get tiresome looking for the next.

Habitués of the New York Vampire club scene were, on the whole, blasé: 'It's just something you do, like getting pierced, getting a tattoo – except you can keep on doing it. It's no big thing'; 'The thing last year [1997] was branding – you know, getting a motif burned into your skin as a skin decoration. That's a whole lot more painful than a little blood-play'; 'I think all those who say it has some magic effect are just blowing smoke. Drinking blood or cutting is a visual thing. You can see the intensity of the colour on the skin, and I guess it's really an aesthetic experience.'[5]

A British Death-metal fan speaks for a number of others: 'Most people I know have done it [drawing and/or drinking blood], but most of them only did it once or maybe twice. It's curiosity and after that there's not a lot of point, is there?'[6]

ᛦ

In looking for an 'authorized version' of modern Vampire doctrines, neophytes usually consult one of the Internet websites that set out their authors' personal creeds. One such is written by Inanna Arthen, also known as Vyrdolak, who has been sharing her changing per-ceptions of the Real Vampire community for several years now in the form of a series of commonly asked questions followed by her answers. She explains the taking of blood as *prana*, a term for the vital principle taken into Western mysticism from yoga and the Jain religion:

Do Real Vampires drink blood?

Many Real Vampires do not drink blood. They all should, but some will never be able to overcome deeply ingrained social conditioning. Blood is the most concentrated material source of life force or pranic energy. Real Vampires are not astral entities. They have physical bodies. Although many Real Vampires become extremely adept at absorbing pranic energy from their living environment, the craving for a more substantial source of energy remains. Some Real Vampires become vegetarians in order to max-imize the pranic energy content of their diet. Only Real Vampires can directly utilize the pranic energy content of blood. They are highly tolerant of human blood and can drink it without becoming sick . . .[7]

Maria, the British teenager, voices another view held by several of those interviewed:

Feeding is an awkward thing to talk about, but since it is for the purpose of educating others, I'll drop my guard for a while. I have a theory which contradicts the Arthenian 'pranic energy theory'. I think that as blood is exposed to the air, a chemical reaction occurs between two or more of the elements present. The gas involved cannot be oxygen or carbon dioxide, since these come into contact with the blood inside the body. The compound created by this reaction is what stops our craving, at least temporarily. A craving is usually depression, insomnia, lethargy and head-aches, leading to, in severe abstinence from feeding, memory loss and dizziness. The reaction occurs during the short time when the blood is exposed to the air. If it is exposed for too long, this compound denatures, which is why Vampires cannot feed on scabs [urgh!].

I feed about once every six weeks. The cravings begin two or three weeks later, and for the next three or four weeks I just live with it. If I were to give in earlier, I am afraid that I would become overly reliant on blood. I have heard of quite a few Vampires who feed once or twice a week. I have only ever fed on two people's blood: my own and a friend's. I have to say I prefer mine as it's thicker. The friend's was a bit weak. I only need two or three drops for the blood to have an effect, and have not yet had the courage to cut deep enough to know if a larger amount would put off the cravings for longer.

Cynarra, British, female and thirty years old: 'I had some fangs made when I was 21 but haven't actually used them to obtain blood . . . this is done with a scalpel blade. Without my doses of blood I become so weak that I can hardly speak.'

Even though there are professing Vampires who do not drink blood, some form of the *idea* of blood always plays a crucial part in their beliefs. According to a British devotee of magic, 'Blood has a really powerful symbolic and magical effect in occult rituals, and it always has had, ever since it was used in sacrifices. And human blood has always been more powerful than animal. The role it plays depends on the ritual; sometimes it's a sacrifice, so it's poured over something – a stone, a figure, a parchment, sometimes it's drunk like communion wine.'

A US follower of occult or, as he would have it, 'mystical' vampirism pronounces:

In vampirism, we believe literally that the blood is the life. This is true on a physical level, yet also holding a more important truth within our entire realm of being, not just our denser physical matter. We see the truth of the existence of this spiritual blood essence just by mere observation of the importance of blood in various cults, such as Judeo-Christianity. In rural areas of the United States especially, there are many hymns that mention blood in phrases such as 'power in the blood, power in the soul', 'cleansing blood of the lamb', 'Oh – the blood of Jesus', and many many others. We see clearly that Christianity is obviously based upon the redeeming qualities of the blood of Jesus of Nazareth. This is a mystical truth, one that is perhaps better understood within Roman Catholicism than [Protestant] Christianity. One thing is for certain, they are not just speaking of a purely physical blood substance. There is a primary practice ... of consuming blood essence in its astral form. This is accomplished through awareness and bringing into conscious functioning parts of the self that exist largely as unconscious actions within the minds of humanity.[8]

Other Vampires commented:

I believe it varies from Vampire to Vampire, but I can cope for up to two months without feeding. I have not fed since Easter Sunday [about seven weeks]. As I am still maturing I probably have not experienced the Thirst to its full extent, and will, in later life, probably have to feed more often. When I do not feed I suffer from severe depression and insomnia, as well as headaches and, though only recently, memory loss.

You could say that Vampires do not physically require blood in order to survive. We could probably live without it. The only danger may be of the Thirst becoming so intense that we would kill ourselves. It would not be the thirst which would kill me, it would be the fact that my mind couldn't cope.

When I do feed, I drink only very small quantities – a few drops at a time. The blood has no psychedelic or drug-like effects. It is more like a medicine. Just those few drops can completely transform the way I feel. For about a week afterwards I feel happy, I feel at ease, and I can fall asleep almost as soon as I climb into bed.

In the experience of a male 'clan'-leader,

You need a small stream of blood so as to ingest 'a few ounces'. My blood tastes real metallic, like sticking a spoon in your mouth. Everyone's blood is different: the taste, it's all about how your life is, how much stress you've got in you at that moment, for instance.[9]

A common response to questions about blood was 'You will only understand if you try it.' Apart from that, there was no overall consensus on any of the blood-related issues – the amount necessary, the physical or psychological effects, the underlying rationale for drinking or even how it tastes.

✝V✝

Given the important part played by sexuality in the incubus-succubus myth and in the makeup of the fictional Vampire, it was surprising that many of those interviewed were coy about discussing sex. A number repeated the widespread assumption that 'Vampires are impotent' (never, it seems frigid). Several of the female Vampires, who were reluctant to dwell on the subject, later casually mentioned their preference for female partners. For a large minority the sexual component, whether hetero-, homo- or bi-, was vitally important.

'Azriel' is twenty-five and lives in a small inner-city apartment, which she keeps in permanent semi-darkness. The most prominent item of furniture in the room is a desktop computer, which she has nicknamed 'Ossuary' (a medieval receptacle for the unsorted bones of the dead) and with which she edits a Goth fanzine, one of many with the title *Dark Angel*. Azriel believes wholeheartedly in two of the modern manifestations of the Vampire: the psychic or psi-vamp and the sexual Vampire. 'Sexual vampirism is like fucking someone's brains out and getting high on that energy. I bite people when I'm having sex. For me it's mutual. If I bite someone and they get off on it, I get high on that. I get high out of giving them pleasure. At the same time they are in your power. I could go just a bit further and break their skin or really hurt them – and they know it. There's an element of fear there. An element of control. They are feeding off that. It's like a power trip.'

She can theorize beyond the sex-play, touching on that most potent of taboos that links vampirism with the junkie lifestyle. 'Whether you hit up, use drugs through a needle, or have sex, you're dealing with penetration; all of it is about getting high, about penetrative pleasure.'[10]

Sade is a twenty-one-year-old musician who drinks his partner's blood during sex. 'It's very erotic and one of the main attractions of it, I suppose, is that it's almost like pure fantasy. I've always liked Vampires and the imagery, the movies, the books. I always thought it would be great to be one. I like the elegance of them. It started off by just biting the neck of someone during sex. I just wanted to take it a step further. I can't think of one thing that triggered it. It was with this partner I had been seeing for 12 months. We were just caught up in the whole sexual energy. I fed from the wrists, just from cuts.' He is aware of the dangers of using razors or cutting the neck. 'Generally the safest place to feed is from the arm. You've got to be careful, though, because the whole passion takes over, but half of the fun is the spontaneity. By the time you have gone through all the precautions, it won't be as exciting any more ... I'm so carried away I have no idea how much blood I swallow, but if you have too much you feel sick.'[11]

Goddess Rosemary is one of several dominatrices in New York City who specialize in vampire sex; although she has been 'outed' in the *Village Voice* newspaper and in *Red Light*, a guide to the New York sexual underground, as providing S&M services combined with blood-drinking, she maintains that she has been caricatured and that her blood games are actually grounded in something more subtle: 'To me it's very romantic and all about romance. To me vampirism is like the walk up the steps to the bedroom, because once you get to the bedroom everyone knows what happens in there, but to me it's like the romance of going up the bedroom steps again and again; because that's the most exciting part of romance, and to recreate it again and again, that's how I look at vampirism. It's like making that particular moment linger. Vampirism is very much like foreplay; whether or not you have sex after, it doesn't matter, but it's that expanded somehow; it's like you take that moment and open it up. So many of these things are "gore", and that's not what it's about at all. A lot of the people who are involved in it are just plain angry, angry at themselves, they are doing it for self-mutilation purposes, there's too much S&M involvement in it – it's fine to do S&M, but this is somehow different. They haven't the foggiest what they are doing. It's a mess of emotions, it's almost just to be a brat – yes, to be *brattish*. I see a lot of ugliness in it when it can be beautiful. You can add the macabre for the theatrics, but not make that the whole.'[12]

Observations offered by other Vampires range from the considered:

I am not particularly familiar with the intimate details of sex-magic; however, I have found that most Vampires with whom I have spoken claim bisexuality. Upon reflection, this would ensure the Vampire's ability to procure his or her sustenance regardless of the donor's gender. It has been reported that whilst energy may be garnered from either sex with equal facility, the female essence reputedly vibrates at a higher frequency, and is apparently sweeter, lighter, hotter, and more potent.

to the somewhat offhand:

Vampires have a strong sexual attraction for 'normal' people, and vice versa, but it's nothing to do with the blood thing.

... the relationship between two Vampires is very volatile, so I personally have never met a vampire couple that lasted very long.

Vampirism is all about sex and power, and those things are fundamental and you can't separate them.

Sex Games? Well, that's not an issue for *me* but maybe it figures in the lives of others. Sex Games are from the realm of the fetish crowd and I have nothing against them but I don't let that figure in my drinking habits ... these people are good to know, though, as they are willing to allow someone to cut on them.

There is a very small number of self-declared blood-fetishists who claim that to imbibe or in some cases to donate blood is an overriding sexual compulsion. These blood-drinkers or blood-givers do not necessarily adopt any of the other attributes of the Vampire and often deliberately reject the black clothes and Victorian paraphernalia associated with the Goth subculture. Says Aaron, a bookstore owner aged thirty-eight, 'Having it done to you is an indescribable kick. You can feel the blood being sucked out, it's a kind of reverse ejaculation. There's a pain there, sometimes great pain, sometimes nothing, but that's only a small part of the point; that just makes it more interesting. It's not ritualistic or anything like that, it's just addictive, it's about giving up one's energy to someone else. It's a very extreme kind of intimacy.'

Generally, not surprisingly, the younger Vampires were more reticent about their sexuality, reinforcing the theory that for some, especially adolescent boys, vampiric encounters function as a mimicry of sexual intimacy without the risk of failure and ridicule.

⚡V̇

As well as complaining of heightened sensitivities, which render them vulnerable and uncomfortable, many contemporary Vampires lay claim to special powers, some spectacular, some banal. The testimony of David S. an assistant professor in his mid-thirties from the US covers a range of these:

... Well, I can only speak of the changes I noticed in myself since I realized what I am, as well as the things I've seen others of my kind do that is [sic] not considered 'normal'.

The first is the heightening of the senses. I can see in almost pitch blackness, I can hear up and down the normal human range – for a ten-year-old! I can smell things before those around me can, and my eyesight has gone from 20/60 to 20/30 or so in the last few years. I have always had a deaf spot in my hearing right at normal human speech, but ever since my awakening I have had an easier time hearing speech.

The second power I have noticed is the ability to not be noticed when I don't want to be. Not just sneaking up on people, but sitting there in plain sight and have people sitting in front of me be startled when I finally speak.

Third would be the ability to command weaker wills. Anyone of weak will will simply do what is told. I tend to do this to almost anyone around me. It's not that I have an especially strong will, at least in my own opinion, but if I tell someone to do something simple, it is usually obeyed before the person even thinks about it.

Fourth, and related to this ability to command would be presence of power. Most around me, until they get to know me, will feel comfortable following my lead. I am not a natural leader, and am quite uncomfortable in that position, but when I take charge of a situation, people will follow.

Health. I've become healthier than I have ever been. I was a sickly child, and in the years since I awoke, I've been sick only once ... and that was when all the other vampires I know got sick as well.

There are other powers I've seen ... Weather control. Let me tell you, pink lightning clashes with purple. I have only seen this done once, but wind control I have seen on multiple occasions.

Strength. Though I feel that in times of need I will not lack the strength to accomplish almost any task, I have not personally been able to go beyond reasonable human limitations. This is not true for everyone. Adrenaline notwithstanding, I have seen others of my kind lift heavy machinery without thinking. Usually they realize what they've done half-way through the operation, and quickly drop the quarter-ton stove they just levered up...[13]

Some felt that their sensitivity empowered them;

I have been gifted. I have the ability to look into and communicate with others' minds. Telepathy. I am also a romantic; there is an attraction that I can create to get any female that I desire.'

The female Vampire, Ferris, reported,

I have had increased sensitivity after taking and it is very strange to think that you are seeing the world for the first time. I have noticed that I do need extra dark sunglasses and I can see in the dark. It isn't like true sight, it's more like infrared but everything had a white glow to it, so in a pitch dark house it seems like the house is full of moonlight. That's nice, no more banged up knees.

Felicity:

My senses were heightened extremely. I could hear things I couldn't hear before; it happened to *all* of my senses ... it's not easy for me to get sick or get hurt. For example, say you hit an average person, they'd get a bruise, right? Well, I don't get bruises or cut. I can feel pain and, yes, I can die, but my skin is a lot more tolerant to such things as punches, falling, cuts, etc.

Flying? Well, I wish I could do it ... although I suppose I *can* fly. What flies with me is my astral body; it flies to the astral plane.

Others see their sensory acuity as more of a trial. Maria:

At the moment I am sleeping for about two or three hours every night. Another thing which has only occurred recently are [sic] heightened senses.

For the past week my senses of smell and hearing have been excellent. I can smell what a person has been eating from a few metres away, and to be honest it makes me feel quite sick. A few days ago I was woken up at 5 a.m. by the sound of a corner of a poster falling off my sister's wall. It sounded like a loud ripping noise right beside me, but my sister's bedroom is only down the hallway!

I hear what others are thinking ... I can hear their thoughts. Sometimes it drives me mad.[14]

ᔦᐠ

Taking their identities from a two-hundred-year-old concept from the history of pseudo-science or parapsychology are the psychological or psychic Vampires, once known less flatteringly as 'psychic sponges', who practise either deliberately or unwittingly a parasitism on the energy or will of others. In her work Psychic Self Defence, published in 1930, Dion Fortune (the author's real name was Violet Mary Firth) dealt with attacks by psychic Vampires. The book helped to synthesize the view developed during the nineteenth century that the psi-vamp is either a disembodied and mindlessly parasitic 'astral entity', or alternatively a projection of the will of a personality inhabiting the human or spirit world. In both cases the effects on victims will consist of a sudden, radical, otherwise inexplicable draining of energy.[15]

One of the current Internet guides further subdivides the psi-category: '... some examples include psychic Vampires who "feed" during sex, those who "feed" on large crowds, those who draw energy from the natural world and visit parks or wilderness when "hungry" and those who "feed" by finding people in highly energized states and either calming or further provoking them'.[16]

A British psi-vamp, 'Sonja', reminisces:

I can't remember when I didn't have strange perceptions of things; knowing what others were thinking or feeling, knowing when things were going to happen ... being aware of potential danger or mishaps, and always the dreams that contained images of the future or of those who had died. In an unhappy and sometimes frightening childhood it was often less painful to simply shut down and block everybody out so that I didn't experience such things. As a young teenager things got worse. I began to have night-mares of being attacked in the night by evil beings that hovered over me and held me prisoner by means of intense fear followed by overwhelming despair. I would feel a weight pressing on my chest and felt as if I was suffocating. For a long time I could only wait for it to go away, but eventually I learned to interrupt the attacks and make them stop, and finally to repel the attacker immediately.

In addition to this I felt empty and 'hungry' all the time. I craved something desperately that I didn't know how to get or even what it was I needed. I began to manipulate people to get strong emotional responses ... it didn't matter what emotion. I was easily overwhelmed by other people's emotions too ... if I was with happy people I felt almost giddy, with sad people I was deeply depressed, and with agitated people I was filled with rage. I absorbed their emotions unconsciously and became that emotion. A loner by nature, I generally stayed away from others (and they from me as I wasn't at all a pleasant person to be near), but when I got hungry I would become desperate to be around other people. If I didn't get my emotional feeding I would become cranky, lethargic, and suicidally depressed...[17]

Another psi-vamp describes an awakening in late adolescence, followed by a sort of acceptance of the condition:

I did extensive research on the subject then, but the majority of what I found was very negative. I began to see myself as an evil creature. I isolated myself in order to protect others. I starved myself because it was unethical to feed. In short, I underwent a massive identity crisis. Only one thing gave me hope and it took a long time for me to be able to grasp that hope. One author mentioned that some psi-vamps can become 'evolved' to a point that they no longer exhibit such negative traits that characterize most psi-vamps. I found mentors for myself. A self-proclaimed psionics teacher, a blood-drinker, and two practitioners of the magical arts. They taught me to embrace and to control my abilities. They taught me to see myself as more of a genetic anomaly than a demon. I delved deeply into the occult and eastern philosophy, emerging with a philosophy all my own that enables me to survive in a world that I don't really fit into.

An occult-oriented observer of the North American Vampire scene known as Grand Vzier has himself made a study of psychic Vampires. He was willing to contribute some anecdotal evidence to this study:

One interesting event which I am able to share occurred between 'Moira' and 'John'. Moira is a young lady in her mid-thirties; she is a registered nurse, has worked as a phlebotomist, and partakes both of blood and psychic energy. John is a professional in his mid-forties who relies solely upon energy.

Although they had never met one another personally, Moira and John had established a strong rapport via computer and telephone. More often than not, John would draw energy from Moira, as having it withdrawn proved uncomfortable to him, manifesting as a dull ache in the chest, followed by headaches and exhaustion. On this particular occasion, the energy flowed both ways, forming a closed-circuit. Both experienced a feeling of heat, accelerated heart-rate, rapid breathing, a slight roaring in the ears, and a tingling sensation, as if the air about them were electrified. John elevated the exchange to the point of climax, wherein he felt as though there were a solid barrier present between them. With a firm push, this wall shattered, falling downward like shards of glass, with a comparable noise. Revealed with its passing was an endless void, devoid of all light, and numbingly cold. At this point, John panicked, and immediately withdrew. Moira felt as though an elastic cord had snapped. Although Moira thought little of the incident, John continued to feel unsettled, and was aware of an uncomfortable pulling sensation at the solar plexus. Too, he experienced a loss of vital energy, and found it increasingly difficult to keep himself warm as his strength continued to wane...[18]

There are a few Vampires who operate in both the blood-drinking and psychic modes: 'I get a rush and a thrill and ultimate satisfaction by feeding on others' psychic energy. I do this because it is not socially acceptable to feed off of people physically. But that [the physical] is the best there is.'[19]

Like a number of exclusive blood-drinkers, 'Ferris' is dismissive of the notion of the psi-vamp:

Yes, there are people who exist off other people's emotions but they usually aren't aware of it and can be helped through a good therapist. (I'm being facetious, I thought that was a funny question.) I think of them more as Personality Vampires . . . Everyone knows that one guy or girl who will say yes to every position that you take, this person has a tendency to agree with everything that you say until someone else comes in and has more 'clout' — the new person seems to know more about the subject – and suddenly your very agreeable little friend is agreeing with everything that this new person has to say even if they had just said the opposite! These misguided gits can be very amusing.

Another Internet site notes that

Under certain circumstances, ordinary humans may become so exhausted, emotionally needy or imbalanced that they begin to draw energy from those close to them, leaving their lovers, housemates or friends feeling drained and ill. This is a temporary and correctable condition, and it would be unconstructive and cruel to label such people 'psychic vampires', no matter how difficult they might be to deal with. They are people who need help.

'Grand Vzier' took a very different line, more in keeping with Dion Fortune's insights:

I am inclined to believe that the psi-vamp, for one reason or another, is possessed of a flawed or damaged aura. It is impossible for him to maintain a constant, balanced level of 'lifeforce'; thus, he must procure this essence via an external source. He is unable to recoup this energy whilst asleep, as one would normally replenish oneself. On occasion, he may consciously or unconsciously seek such nourishment in astral form. Should this occur, he will feel refreshed and energized upon awakening. The donor may recall having 'dreamt' of this person, or, if he is aware of the psi-vamp's nature, acknowledge the visitation.

I have found that energy fluctuations are responsible for sudden alterations in mood. If the psi-vamp's energy level is extremely low, he may experience depression, chronic fatigue, lethargy, headaches, irritability, and/or a general feeling of malaise; conversely, a surplus of energy may lend itself toward manic behavior, giddiness, a feeling of invincibility, and a devil-may-care attitude toward even the most dire situation.

Psi-vamps are neither supernatural nor possessed of evil spirits. Whilst I believe that it may be possible for an incorporeal entity to affix itself to an individual, it is my opinion that the talents manifested by the psychic Vampire are intrinsic to his being. These innate skills may include clairvoyance, clairaudience, clairsentience, precognition, and the ability to heal, amongst others. I have found empathy to be a common trait; in fact, it is usually the first ability to manifest, and quite likely the most powerful.

I have often wondered if the term 'Vampire' is entirely accurate. Whereas the psychic Vampire does, indeed, require energy from an external source, the term 'energy manipulator' may be more apt. When effecting a healing, for example, energy is gathered and directed to the afflicted area. This enables the ailing person to utilize their own energy to heal themselves, with the guidance of the healer.'

In many ways the psi-vamp is an easier concept for the sceptic to accept than the blood-drinker, and sinister 'energy-drainers' appear in a number of 'drawing-room horror' stories of the early twentieth century. From one such, *Aylmer Vance and the Vampire*, comes a rationalization by the stock narrator-figure:

'I suppose', I replied cautiously, 'that there is such a thing as vampirism even in these days of advanced civilisation? I can understand the evil influence that a very old person may have upon a young one if they happen to be in constant intercourse – the worn-out tissue sapping healthy vitality for their own support. And there are certain people – I could think of several myself – who seem to depress one and undermine one's energies, quite unconsciously, of course, but one feels somehow that vitality has passed from oneself to them.'

But his suspension of disbelief does not prepare him for the terrible events that follow.[20]

☥

The Vampires were asked how they thought the Real Vampire underground of today, to which they all belong, relates, if at all, to the historically documented Vampires (rather than the fictional creations) of the past. This question perplexed many of the interviewees. Nearly all of them seemed to have read or heard something about the blood-drinkers of the ancient world and the Slavonic Vampires of the eighteenth century, but most found it difficult to confirm plausibly or deny any connections.

I don't relate at all. I do think that there *might* have been some grain of truth to some of the legends, but I feel that most of that has been lost in the retelling of such stories, and perhaps embellished to make it more interesting to the listeners so I don't think much of most of it.

I don't feel any affinity with a shambling European peasant just risen from the grave ... if that's what you mean.

Hmmm. There are many signals that point to the existence of vampires or vampirism since the advent of civilization ... The American Indian and other primitive cultures have drunk the blood of their kill thinking that it will transfer the qualities of that particular animal into their body/spirit. The Bible says, 'The blood is the life, and you shall not eat the life.' Does that mean the same as 'thou shalt not kill', or something else? I don't know but I do know that we are *abominations of God* – that's what the Church will tell you.

Seems that people have always had a love-hate relationship with blood, the raising of the dead and the blood giving life. We raise the dead now in hospitals, a person goes flatline and we jolt him/her back to life and we give transfusions to save lives, so what's new?

Much of what has come down to us is heavily influenced by ignorance, and with a heavy Christian influence. Who knows what was reality? Anyone who couldn't stand the sun either adapted or was burned or hanged as a witch. Just owning a Bible in the Dark Ages was punishable by death [sic]. Knowledge was dangerous and meant death – even most of the monks couldn't read, they just memorized the verses.

This identification with a persecuted minority was echoed by others:

I think we've always been around, but it's only now that we can come into the open and communicate with each other.

You have to look very carefully, and read between the lines in old books and stories – the word 'Vampire' isn't necessarily used, but the concept is there if you can find it.

One male Vampire of a mystical bent offered an interesting perspective on the 'shambling European peasant' revenant:

In times before this century or basically when people were superstitious, believing in God and also believing in us [Vampires], my race travelled the earth and would make new converts and obviously new converts needed guidance and understanding of themselves to maintain the balance, because in the conversion from mortal to immortal – and this is going very deep – the seed of life itself changes and humanity changes to demonic. It was important for the individual to be shown by way of the intellect how to understand the changes that had taken place so the demonic side didn't take over completely. And if it did, you had a being who functioned without intellect, a mindless thing who would then follow an animal's life, feeding on the nearest things he knew. There was no cunning, not even the worry of being followed to their graves, and no worry if they particularly preyed on family and friends and therefore were recognized.

An associate of Rod Ferrell, the eighteen-year-old sentenced to death for the 'Florida Vampire Murders', summed up the views of many of the younger devotees of the culture. 'We really have no clue, you know, where actual vampirism started, but we know for a fact that archaeologists and scientists can *prove* that the myths of Vampires goes [*sic*] all the way back to the beginning of time.'

In other words, Vampires have a reassuringly long pedigree, even if its details and chronology do not much matter.

ᛉ

A corollary was the suggestion that it was the *fictional* persona – from books, movies and games – that had created the new breed of Vampire. Predictably, this polite probe drew heated replies.

> I don't relate to the historical Vampire as I am not being hunted down all the time and I certainly don't relate to the Media Vampire as it is a crock [of shit]. I can't fly. I don't care for the attention that the Media Vampire receives. I want to stay 'in the shadows' as this is how I am able to continue on.

It was put to older Vampires that the new generation had been seduced by a showbiz parody of vampirism and that they were largely unaware of the older traditions of sex-magic and occult or psychic exploration.

> I concur with the above assessment: these individuals have become quite enamoured of the cinema and such authors as Anne Rice, who paint a romantic portrait of fantastic beings who are superior to 'normal' humans. In actuality, vampires are practically indistinguishable from those around them. There are the occasional instances of photosensitivity and pale skin, to be certain, and perhaps even unusually pointed teeth; but the portrayal of the tall, excessively emaciated bloodsucker with cavernous eyes and gnashing fangs is myth.[20]

I would agree most strongly. While Rice details the fantasy life of fictional

Vampires, including the intense pain and centuries of feelings – the current wannabe vamps only see the glamour. Being a Vampire is a pain in the tail most of the time. The upside is increased psychic stuff, increased senses, increased psychic empathy with others – up and down, healing quick from wounds and illness. Downside – the craving for blood, especially down in these days of Aids and hepatitis.

As the occultist Emperor Norduk sees it,

... the imagery of fiction and movies is often – in fact almost always – taken from symbols in mythology and manipulated according to the writer/screen writer's own artistic perception. In short, before there was 'Dracula' there were documented vampiric creatures, such as the Ekimmu, who drew blood from mortals through use of what was called 'an evil wind gust', within Ancient Sumeria. The Sumerian vampire begat later versions of the vampire, not the other way around. It is the utmost folly for people to try to interpret vampirism, which is ancient, deriving as it does from Sumeria and then Babylon, through the use of modern metaphysical research, and especially through modern pop-culture values. Real vampirism begat fictional vampirism as a way to obscure the tradition from prying eyes, not the other way around.

In Inanna Arthen's view,

The books of Anne Rice have encouraged sympathy with a vampire subculture that has its own history, one in which human beings are little more than walking snacks. Vampires are even romanticized by some as 'culling' the human population of criminals and other undesirables – a pretty dangerous model to adopt.[21]

Several, however, found that media-led expectations made their own lives more difficult:

Can you imagine how annoying it gets to have 17/18-year-olds throwing themselves at you? 'Turn me', 'Make me', 'Take me', 'Be my mentor', 'Be my friend', 'Be my mother'. It's all out of Anne Rice books that these people get their ideas. I cannot fly, I cannot will you to give me all your money and then forget it ever happened. I mean, really, it's laughable the things that people believe![22]

✝✝

Until the late twentieth century a fundamental characteristic of all Vampires was that they were perceived as *evil*. Whatever name they bore, whichever form they took, they were predators whose over-riding compulsion was to harm the living. It seemed important to ask today's Vampires whether they, too, saw themselves as essentially diabolic. Responses to this question tended to be flippant, sometimes evasive, nearly always relying on the notion that concepts of good and evil are outdated.

Hmmm. I would have to say that I am not evil. I deny it and I think that religion is bunk. I feel that the Catholic Church took Dracula and Varney the Vampire all the way to the bank. Because as you know we all are *living outside of the laws of God* and that is the ultimate sin.

It is true that we are predators, but the Good/Evil question -I call it the *big* question – is anything but simplistic. Ask most people about good and evil and they will struggle with their religious faith every time. Yes, we are Parasites but so is everything else. I think that it all depends on how you view it. Can 'Good' exist without 'Evil'? Would you know 'Good' if you only knew 'Evil'? Can there be darkness without light? Blah Blah Blah...

I do believe that the energy *we* feel is at a higher level and can probably be channelled into magickal work more easily. There is no 'black,' or 'white' magick. Magick is energy, it's what you do with it that makes it negative or positive.

Yes. We most certainly are parasites and predators. Period, end of story. Could it be that most people would prefer not to be regarded as a parasite and therefore will not implicate themselves by responding to such a question? There are many ways to avoid causing damage and if these measures are taken one can become less parasite, more predator. Is a tiger an evil entity for eating other animals? It's in his nature to do so.

I admire predators in a way, but this would be a very chaotic world if there were more human predators so there is a balance in how it's working out. Do we have more predators now [in the twentieth century] or did they just hide themselves better before?

It turns out that I do have a simplistic answer for you. Yes.

A Vampire is by nature a predator. A Vampire subsists upon the blood, this blood is drawn through an occult technique into the Vampire. The Vampire, as a creature of the abyss and the blood, circulates this within his/her nature causing development and alchemical change – actual vampirism is not that far removed from the alchemical path as taught within Britain's notorious Satanist group, the Order of the Nine Angles. True Vampires are not 'evil', because when vampirism came to light, it was during a time which predated the popular Western concepts of 'good' and 'evil'. A Vampire is a creature of balance: we enjoy our love, we enjoy the hunt, we enjoy our progress, etc. Yet at the same time, we are not operating from a human perspective . . . we cannot try to bring the Vampire down to being a human creature full of human fears, weakness, and worries. This is simply not what a Vampire is.

It is important once again to mention that the Vampire is not the polar opposite of 'good' on a cosmic scale. This is just not the case. One cannot understand Hinduism by reading a book on Wicca, and in the same way one cannot understand Vampirism in a real and meaningful manner by stuffing it into the split dichotomy of good and evil. Vampires do, and can, prosper in successful – and even exceptional – enterprises within normal human society. A Vampire is the true wolf in sheep's clothing.

V

As a final provocation the Vampires were asked, given the number of references to solitude and alienation that appear in the small ads and the Internet discussions, was it not in fact *loneliness* that was the true common characteristic of the modern Vampire?

Some rejected the idea:

> I can see why some people feel lonely. I'm not lonely, I don't allow myself to be separate from the rest, singling yourself out for inspection is not a good idea. The whole emphasis is on blending in. Or it should be.

> There is a *ton* more to it than that. I'm tired of books making us/me look like a bunch of shoegazing [introspective] wishy-washy twits. I am sorry to see that so many books that seem to be research-based make a lot of us out to be morons. This isn't the case. The very few Vampires that I have met have been very intelligent, good people that are willing to take the high ground rather than the debased freaked-out kid that drinks blood 'because he is of the devil, blah blah blah, that's terrible!'. I don't want to hurt anyone. I take pains not to do so. This is just who I am, I'm happy with it and would like to continue to be so. People are lonely because the nature of this life – as the media would have them believe – is to be turned out into the night, with no friends, feared by everyone. That just isn't the case. I think that you will find that the people saying this are eighteen, unhappy and dysfunctional. I'm just tired of it, it's stupid and insulting.[23]

Nonetheless, more than half the interviewees either hinted at or openly admitted their acute sense of isolation:

> If all the horror, the pain, and the loneliness of my life were to pool together in one great lake of blackness, its depths would still be more inviting than those which I have been drowning in today. I long so dearly to let go, and sink into the darkness, where there is no hate, no hurt, and where nothing matters.

> I would dearly love, just for one day, to be a normal human, so that maybe I could understand the emotions which I seem to spend my life trying to imitate. But, becoming a human for the rest of my life, I don't think I

would be comfortable with. I have almost come to need the Thirst. I'm not sure if I can explain it so that you can understand. I think I would feel I was leaving the real me behind. My 'soul' or 'essence' is that of a Vampire and I wouldn't want to destroy that part of me.

I long to have a companion who has been turned, so that he or she knows both sides of the story and can maybe act as my link to humanity. Someone who could explain human emotions to me. To be able to do this, you would have to have experienced both worlds.

I was a quiet little girl. Shy, I suppose. I felt lonely a lot, and different. As I grew older, I blamed it on the fact I had a learning disability or learning difference. But there was something else to it, I had no idea what it was. I used to cry a lot about this.[24]

I am coming out of the coffin ... I am a vampire. I am lonely, depressed, heartbroken, and mad as hell.[25]

I do not entertain visitors except on rare occasions, and I have no physical need of people in my life. I am very lonely, but at the same time disgusted by what I see in the world. My opinion is that man has become pampered, dilute in his passions. There are no true heroes, no adventurers or explorers. I feel that a great deal of man's courage has been lost to luxury, technology – an irony, as I type this to you on a computer – and complacence.[26]

Not surprisingly, loneliness was most often admitted to by so-called 'wannabe' Vampires, many of them teenagers, whose main aim was seeking companionship by way of the Internet ads and chat-rooms:

I am a 17 [year-old] white female from the endless bounds [sic] of Canada ... I seek the unseekable and wander desperately lost and alone. I yearn for companionship and search for the unbelievable and majestic.

The British sixteen-year-old Maria confessed,

I have never loved anyone ... I have never loved my parents, neither my family nor friends, and until recently I thought I was incapable of feeling love for anyone. I just thought it was a strange, foreign emotion that I would never feel or understand. But I have made a new friend via the Internet who is also a Vampire ... she is the first person I have ever known who seems truly able to understand what I am feeling ... I have come to the conclusion that I can love, but only as a Vampire.

10
Contagious Ideas

'The supernatural is born of language, it is both its consequence and its proof: not only do the devil and vampires exist only in words, but language alone enables us to conceive what is always absent: the supernatural.'

Tzvetan Todorov, *The Fantastic: A Structural Approach to a Literary Genre*, 1970

... with a strange howling cry that was enough to wake terror in every breast, the figure seized the long tresses of her hair, and twining them round his bony hands he led her to the bed ... the bed-clothes fell in a heap by the side of the bed – she was dragged by her long silken hair completely onto it again. Her beautifully rounded limbs quivered with the agony of her soul. The glassy, horrible eyes of the figure ran over that angelic form with a hideous satisfaction – horrible profanation. He drags her head to the bed's edge. He forces it back by the long hair still entwined in his grasp. With a plunge he seizes her neck in his fang-like teeth – a gush of blood, and a hideous sucking noise follows. The girl has swooned and the vampyre is at his hideous repast![1]

It is Victorian England, the victim is female, her assailant is male, aristocratic – and British. The transformation of the blood-fiend from female, Continental and originally rustic and plebeian was complete by the time *Varney the Vampyre* began his 800-page fictional reign of terror, but the anonymous author of Varney's serialized adventures (it was probably an industrious hack named J. M. Rymer) was not the first to assemble this new composite, which had been introduced to an English readership under a more distinguished name some fifty years earlier.

It is still something of a mystery that a far from polished novella by an unknown writer was to trigger a Vampire mania across Europe and establish that new identity for the Vampire – masculine, well-born, seductive – that has endured until the present day. The work was entitled *The Vampyre* and the real author was a young Englishman of Italian descent, Dr John William Polidori. Clearly, Polidori's master-stroke was to bring together two of the most potent icons of his time, then invest their narrative with his own troubled, driven personality. The two key ingredients were the literary Vampire, until then likely to be represented as a female predator, and the most irresistibly notorious leading man in fiction and in reality: George Gordon, Lord Byron. If Polidori thought that renaming his anti-hero 'Lord Ruthven' would in any way distance him and his work from Byron's long shadow, his publishers thought otherwise and when the slim book was published in 1819, first in London and then within weeks in Paris, it was under the Right Honourable Lord Byron's name, guaranteeing it bestseller status and prompting Goethe to assert that here was that author's greatest work.

Of course Polidori had stolen the inspiration for his story from a conceit of Byron's uttered three years earlier in the Villa Diodati above Lake Geneva in Switzerland. Byron, Shelley and their entourage had amused themselves over several evenings in June by composing ghost stories, among which were a first version of *Frankenstein* confected by the nineteen-year-old Mary Shelley. Byron's contribution was the germ of a story about a charismatic individual named Darvell who made a pact of secrecy with a friend while they travelled together. When the friend realizes that Darvell is a Vampire, now back in England, he cannot expose him without breaking his vow. This echo of his own relationship with Byron, in which Polidori could recast himself both as the hero's confidant and his nemesis, formed the eventual plot of *The Vampyre*.

The bumptious young prodigy (he had been the youngest ever graduate in medicine at Edinburgh), and son of an Italian immigrant,

Polidori had been engaged to accompany Byron on his European travels as the great man's amanuensis and personal physician. In the latter capacity he was responsible for providing a steady supply of laudanum and ether to supplement the wines and brandies that his patron also ingested constantly. Apart from a fee of five hundred pounds, the attraction for Polidori was that proximity to the great poet might inspire his own literary efforts. Not long after they left England, it became clear to Byron that Polidori was going to be an irritating and less than robust companion; relations between the two men began to sour and Byron's treatment of Polidori after that veered between casual condescension and cruel contempt.

In September 1816 John Polidori had been dismissed from Byron's employ and returned, disenchanted and embittered, to England where he turned his impressions, plus Byron's fragment, into a story, probably under the influence of *Glenarvon*, Lady Caroline Lamb's *roman à clef* in which the barely disguised Byronic hero/villain '. . . left a name to all succeeding times,/Link'd with one virtue and a thousand crimes.'

When asked whether he had written the Polidori piece, Byron affected amused disdain. 'If the book is clever it would be base to deprive the real writer – whoever he may be – of his honours; – and if stupid – I desire the responsibility of nobody's dullness but my own.'[2] But still he protested, 'I have a personal dislike to Vampires, and the little acquaintance I have with them would by no means induce me to reveal their secrets.'[3] He could hardly deny all knowledge of the undead, as evidenced by lines he had written in 1813:

But first on earth as Vampyre sent,
Thy corpse shall from its tomb be rent,
Then ghastly haunt thy native place,
And suck the blood of all thy race . . .[4]

While Byron's reputation utterly eclipsed the poor doctor's then and now, it is a nice irony that whereas there are millions who have since become familiar with one or other of the descendants of

Polidori's Vampire, and thousands who have even read *The Vampyre* itself, Byron is for most people only that, a magnificent reputation. He was one of those individuals whose manners and appetites might qualify them in today's terminology as a 'psi-vamp'. Polidori describes his mesmeric effect:

> Those who felt this sensation of awe, could not explain whence it arose: some attributed it to the dead gray eye, which fixing upon the object's face, did not seem to penetrate, and at one glance to pierce through to the inward workings of the heart; but fell upon the cheek with a leaden ray that weighed upon the skin it could not pass...
>
> In spite of the deadly hue of his face, which never gained a warmer tint, either from the blush of modesty, or from the strong emotion of passion, though its form and outline were beautiful, many of the female hunters after notoriety attempted to win his attentions, and gain at least, some marks of what they might term affection: Lady Mercer, who had been the mockery of every monster shewn in drawing-rooms since her marriage, threw herself in his way, and did all but put on the dress of a mountebank, to attract his notice...

Even allowing for the uncritical adulation greeting a supposed fragment of Byron's, the sustained Vampire frenzy that followed publication of *The Vampyre* is hard to credit. Perhaps Polidori, unknowingly, had 'legitimated' the vampire for mass consumption by making him male. In a patriarchal, highly stratified and outwardly conservative society, a woman, let alone a Vampire-woman, could never be the object of a public fascination bordering on obsession. He had also transferred the Vampire for the first time to prose (in English at least, Kleist had introduced a Russian Vampire-count in 1805), opening up a market for novelizations – one of the only things that Byron could not do was write novels – and had inspired in Paris the first of many dramatizations for the popular stage.[5]

To its English readership this Vampire was for the first time not 'foreign', but a product of Scotland, even though a cosmopolitan figure. To a Continental audience, though, Lord Ruthven/Byron was the personification of ideas from 'outside' that entranced and repelled in equal measure. He was the rapacious, rich despoiler of their daughters and wives, the exploiter of the poor and the colonized, the embodiment of *permissible* deviance and decadence, the representative of a society whose self-satisfaction was the envy of the world. In the end, Lord Ruthven appears to modern eyes as a *moral* menace, a potential cause of social scandal; the other, grander themes of love, sex and violent death are merely sketched and the characters are not engaging, the brief tale unaffecting. In an essential sense Ruthven was not even 'Byronic': he was magnificently dangerous, but he was untroubled by tragic self-awareness. The public always hoped, in vain as it turned out, that Byron would one day publish his confessions and bought *The Vampyre* hoping that this was what they had been waiting for. Readers' willing imaginations no doubt supplied this missing element of the iconic personality.

As for Polidori himself, he was another of those tragi-comic figures (like Stenbock, Lugosi, even Summers) who came to be caught up in the baleful slipstream whirling behind the mythos as it gathered momentum. Despite his early promise he was handicapped by his foreign ancestry, his lack of a title or influential friends and his irritating manner. After a few more years of frustration, the young doctor died in mysterious circumstances after swallowing poison.

✝

It has been suggested that there was a shameful, even overt sexual element in the short-lived collaboration between Polidori and Byron with its hypnotic and exploitative master-to-servant bias. There is absolutely no evidence for this in either man's journals, but once beyond the attentions of English drawing-room society Byron was promiscuously bisexual, had experimented with many strange vices. In his private journals Polidori stated that many of the events in his life were too extraordinary to be confessed. In one passage he wrote that he had to be discreet for the sake of the living, for the dead, and 'those who must be both'. Was this simply phrasemaking by a disappointed fantasist, or did the words hide some enduring secret?

During one of his escapades, perhaps in Polidori's company, perhaps in Greece, had Byron confessed to him that he thought himself *vampirized*?[6]

⁘

The other literary landmark, Bram Stoker's *Dracula*, has been comprehensively done to death by the critics and will no doubt continue to be dissected and deconstructed for some time to come as will the author's personality. Some writers have seen an echo of the Byron/Polidori tension in Stoker's slavish devotion to Henry Irving and it has become popular to portray the writer-factotum either as a closet homosexual or as a duplicitous, syphilitic frequenter of prostitutes. Much more affecting than the image of a sinister Stoker, though, is the almost certainly true version – of a self-effacing, part-time if prolific writer, committed full-time to hard work, family and the maintenance of propriety. His well-known statement on the corrupting effect of sex upon literature and morals in general has been interpreted by some as ironic, but this is not in the nature of the man. As the cultural historian Christopher Frayling points out, 'He tried to present himself as a very serious pillar of the establishment. There isn't a single photo of Bram Stoker smiling ... but there's something going on underneath. There's something about Bram Stoker that doesn't quite fit. None of the biographies have cracked him ... They are the eyes of a frightened man.'[7] Indeed, the recent rediscovery at Trinity College, Dublin, of Stoker's first full-length story, *The Primrose Path*, shows that twenty years before *Dracula* he was rehearsing a Puritan fear, a dread of demon contamination: the main character, a theatre carpenter, is tortured by visions of evil brought on by alcohol.[8]

With *Dracula*, Stoker consolidated the achievement of Polidori in turning the Vampire into an anti-hero that suited the times, this time as much for the baggage the Vampire carried with him as for the Count himself – a theatrical Beelzebub, he was also the antique threat from the East, the bad father, a parody of the Judeo-Christian deity and the Victorian paterfamilias. The single anti-hero has to be contained by a whole team of heroes, representing British integrity, American pluck and European sagacity, and their attendants: had Stoker not excised another half-dozen or so characters, his narrative would probably have foundered, like a lifeboat overloaded with escapees. Whatever its hidden significances, its hints of social and sexual unease, it is clear that at a surface level *Dracula* was, for Stoker and its first readership, little more than a proto-thriller, a yarn whose originality lay in the way it married the Vampire, the great icon of the Gothic tradition with those other pop genres, the ghost, the detective and the adventure story, spiced with passages of travelogue and the deployment of the latest technical gadgetry.

With all its painstaking research and assemblage, the novel took Stoker years to write (the original idea had come from a nightmare that Stoker had in 1890 in which he was preyed upon by three Vampire women; coincidentally, *Frankenstein* and *Dr Jekyll and Mr Hyde* were also conceived in dreams). Its style was nothing like the allusive, feverish poetry of earlier literary works on the same theme, yet it was markedly different from the 'penny dreadfuls', *Varney* among them, which relied on predictable melodramatics for their effects. It was brisk and journalistic; a fiction that looked like reportage mixed up with extracts from the journals and letters of decent if mediocre people (a novelty borrowed from Wilkie Collin's mystery-novel bestseller *The Moonstone*). This was also to be part of its success: the British reading public was never going to embrace the sort of decadence espoused by Baudelaire, Gautier and especially Huysmans, whose *Là-Bas* still has the power to shock. England's appetite for ghost and horror stories, like its unique predilection for whimsy and its exaltation of childhood, was something more decorous, even if it was also a displacement of Puritan repression. Stoker's novel represents the *defeat* of the grotesque and the triumph of bourgeois morality; quite different from the subversive engagements with the uncanny indulged in by aesthetes, voluptuaries and neurasthenics. (One critic has convincingly contrasted the rapidity and energy of the Romantic tradition – to which, by this theory, both Stoker's novel and Murnau's later film of it belong – and the 'sterile inertia' of the Decadent and *Fin-de-siècle*.)[9]

In *Dracula* good triumphs and evil is destroyed, and this may be another simple reason for its success. In many of the preceding fictions, as for Stoker's Parisian contemporaries, it is the Vampire who is triumphant. In Polidori's tale there is no comfortable resolution: the narrator is confounded, the innocent are defiled and the demonic Ruthven escapes, as does Varney the Vampire, who is resurrected over and over to suck again until he stages his own resolution by jumping into the crater of Mount Vesuvius.

✴

On Celluloid there have been literally hundreds of creaking duplications featuring one or another version of that 'cardboard booby' (a phrase coined by Ian Fleming for 007, another saturnine pop-hero), the shadowless, reflection-free, caped, fanged, garlic-and-crucifix-fearing, daylight-shunning cliché, the Vampire. Most of these films, even those usually singled out as milestones in the genre, do not merit the kind of analysis wasted upon them; those that are worth examining as part of the whole evolution of the Vampire and our reactions to it, are the handful that have been quirky, innovative, even perhaps profound, or so bad as to be memorable.

One of the first movies ever made, Georges Meliès' *Le Manoir du Diable*, dating from 1896, had as its subject the appearance of a vampire bat. There is a handful of films which have disappeared and because of this have acquired mythical status; there are one or two others that have been forgotten or neglected, unjustly. The lost include what may be only the second Vampire film ever, the Swedish production, *Vampyr – En Kvinnas Slav* from 1912, and the first full-length attempt to film Stoker's novel, the Hungarian *Drakula*, made in Berlin in 1920 by Károly Lajthay. There are unconfirmed rumours of an even earlier version completed in Russia at the beginning of 1920, about which nothing more is known. Somewhere there may be a print of *Drakula Istanbul'da*, the legendary Turkish production from 1953, directed by Mehmet Muhtar, but it has not been seen for years.

The first full-length filmic treatment of the Vampire that has survived is the 1922 German production, *Nosferatu, Eine Symphonie des Grauens*, directed by Friedrich Wilhelm Murnau and starring Max Schreck as 'Count Orlok'. The makers of the movie changed the names of the principal characters in order to pirate the plot of Bram Stoker's novel and named the film itself after the 'plague-bearer' mentioned in Emily Gérard's writings on Transylvania. Murnau's Vampire physically recalls Struwwelpeter, the wild child and the anguished grotesques in the Weimar paintings of Georg Grosz and Otto Dix. Max Schreck plays him as a mockery of nature, part rodent, part bat, part reptilian or insectoid, part human. He – or rather it – is a frighteningly abstracted presence whose sole *raison d'être*, like the Vampires of the past, is negation. He has no time for petty sensuality: his instincts are to taint and destroy. Count Orlok 'finishes by being a monster without either psychology or individuality, he becomes an archetype, a symbol: he is the proto-vampire, the origin of all evil'.[10] The film is pervaded by unease and a presentiment of social infection. Its acting style, and to some extent its scenery, is within the Expressionist tradition that also produced *Der Golem* and *Das Kabinett des Doktor Caligari*, two other aesthetically stunning visions of a Europe sleepwalking into a holocaust. *Nosferatu*'s moral is that a world in a state of grace is vulnerable to cold atavistic savagery and that only self-sacrifice – in a twist entirely absent in the novel the heroine deliberately gives her own life to destroy the monster – can redeem it. Like *Caligari*, but more subtly, Murnau's film is a masterpiece of *chiaroscuro*. It is light that triumphs: the monster is transfixed and annihilated by the rays of the sun, in what more than one critic has seen as a metaphor for the cinema itself.[11]

It is a huge irony that *Nosferatu*, the film that in some ways transcended Stoker's novel and which indisputably reanimated it, was chased off the screen by his widow's litigation. Legally, of course, she was within her rights, as the German court found when it decreed that all copies of the film should be destroyed. Aesthetically, cinematically, it was a near-disaster. Luckily one or two prints survived to set against the anodyne mainstream *Dracula*s churned out in later years.

A handful of other early films, non-anodyne, pre-mainstream, drew on a sensibility formed by cold, melancholy Nordic myths, and the middle European *unheimliche*: film versions of the Viennese *Schauer-romane*, Fritz Lang's *Lilith und Ly*, and deservedly the best known, the Dane Carl Theodor Dreyer's *Vampyr*, released in 1932, which hauntingly combined an amateur cast, minimal dialogue and fluid, indistinct half-tone images (some scenes were shot through gauze) to create the 'daydream on the screen' (inspired partly by Le Fanu's *Carmilla*) that the director intended.

ᚡ

Before Anne Rice the face of the American Vampire as imprinted on the popular imagination was the face of Béla Blasko, alias Arisztid Ölt. By the time this Hungarian refugee arrived, at the age of thirty-nine, in America, he had changed his stage name again and had adopted that of his birthplace, the village of Lúgos, and so begat the star whose name should by rights be pronounced 'BAY-la LOO-goshee'. Lugosi, a foreigner, an undifferentiated *European*, urbane, hypnotic and sinister, although a ham, symbolized the threats from unfathomable Bolsheviks and Fascists: he was chosen to play Count Dracula in Universal Studios' hit of 1931. Poor Lugosi's character was one-dimensional, stodgy from the beginning and he was saddled with it throughout the rest of an increasingly sad career. By 1940 and *The Devil and the Bat* he was mired in self-parody and finished his days hopelessly addicted to morphine, propped up in sideshow displays, still imprisoned in the opera-cape and tuxedo in which he was buried, at his own insistence, in 1956.

The Magyar actor actually brought a little bit of Hungary to Hollywood, itself a place that was deliberately and wilfully ignorant of the rest of the planet, even though many of its founders were refugees from the Vampire's homelands. Lugosi began as a fine stage actor but he never fully mastered English: his accent remained pleasingly heavy and he memorized his lines phonetically, sometimes without under-standing them at all. This may have actually helped his onstage and onscreen persona by investing it with an eerie inappropriateness, but the result, coupled with his ponderous, ceremonial movements, more than anything conjures up a Budapest *maître d'* or an ageing cabaret hypnotist. The best that can be said for Universal's Vampire is that he is 'the icon that is emblematic but always immobile and emptied of meaning: the Vampire rendered myth, a token for cinephiles and fetishists, a mere object of consumption without authentic life'.[12]

When Tod Browning made *Dracula* for Universal, using the author-ized stage play as performed in London and New York rather than the novel as a starting-point, he was hampered in that Hollywood had no tradition of horror, only of melodrama, and by the interference of producers who insisted that anything truly disturbing be excised from the script. Although Browning was potentially a director of genius, as the later *Freaks* showed, although the first half of *Dracula* has atmospheric moments, and although the movie has retained its popularity with film buffs and Vampire enthusiasts, the exercise just commodified and hobbled the fictional Vampire for the US mass market, a process Anne Rice's novels would repeat forty-five years later.

V

The first attempt at the Vampire in the British cinema was, ominously, *Old Mother Riley Meets the Vampire*, a parochial music-hall joke of 1952 (and another step on Lugosi's downward path), but a little later Britain reasserted a dominance that had been lost after Stoker. Terence Fisher's first Dracula movie made for Hammer Films in 1958 was the forerunner of a whole series of Technicolor B-movies by that studio, some of which are now held up by connoisseurs of Celluloid kitsch as masterpieces. What most of these horror films had were straight-forward, consistent plots and even stronger, more coherent if slightly mannered performances from a stable of actors trained for character parts in the British theatre. Two of the greatest exponents of this style were the distinguished Christopher Lee, who came to personify the

Count for a post-war generation, and the earnest, debonair Peter Cushing, who here played van Helsing. In the double-act their relationships seem reminiscent sometimes of the British wartime combat-myth: the brisk, dignified struggle of a righteous and reluctant hero against a well-matched but fatally flawed enemy.

What prevented any of the Hammer movies from becoming 'art' was their deliberate targeting of an undemanding mainstream audience and their literal, even humdrum take on fantastic, exotic themes. In a way their tone is like that of Bram Stoker's novel: they are adventure stories of good versus evil, with a dash of half-explicit sexual and social references. As the times changed there was more visible blood, and 'cleavage' gave way to 'toplessness'; there were always histrionics.

Such films are inevitably, to some extent, a mirror of their times, and in this first British attempt at Dracula it is easy from a modern viewpoint to see the vampirization as a metaphor for adultery and promiscuity and the 'awakening' of the female victims as the quivers of the sexual liberation that was waiting to happen to post-war Britain. In this way, it can be seen as a mock-serious counterpart to the bedroom farces that were popular at the same time and employed some of the same support casts. But the 'horror' in Hammer is a camp complicity with the audience: it is never truly horrible and it never really subverts. The terrible themes are always ultimately manageable.

Hammer horror was exportable and the 'new' British Vampire conjured up for foreign audiences, just as Lord Ruthven had, the lingering romance of an outdated feudal-aristocratic social order in which the constant threat from outside, from the irrational and the horrible, seemed deliciously appropriate.

Meanwhile the domestic European cinema was using the same icon for a series of mainly plotless, sub-surrealist pieces of low-budget cinematic erotica. Forty or fifty years on these movies have often been overrated by B-movie fans, but the work of Jean Rollin, Mario Bava and Dario Argenta was always visually interesting at least. The same Continental tradition highlighted the female blood-sucker inspired by Countess Báthory: Jorge Grau's *Ceremonia*

Sangrienta, Harry Kümel's *Le Rouge aux Levres* and, above all, Walerian Borowczyk's *Contes Immoraux*, (like his demented vampiric version of Stevenson, *Dr Jekyll et les Femmes*) have all aged better than their tamer English-language contemporaries.

✢

The most famous screen Draculas can be seen as typical of their cultures: Lugosi, although a genuine middle European, was set up as an American idea of a villain; the sort of ageing roué whom parents and fiancés suspected might prey upon female graduates on a tour of European capitals. Christopher Lee was the British vision of Continental perfidy, whose character never strayed far from a home-grown gentleman-gone-wrong, his dangerous instincts barely held in check by a veneer of stern superiority. The actors who conveyed the authentic horror at the heart of the older Europe, the scuttle across Peter Kürten's killing fields from mass murder to genocide, were Murnau's leading man, Max Schreck (his surname means 'terror') and the manic, unstable, gargantuan Klaus Kinski.

Kinski's autobiography is shot through with unconscious images of vampirism, which reach a climax when he agrees to play the leading role in the remake of *Nosferatu* for his old adversary, the director Werner Herzog. When a personification of the Id meets a personification of the Ego, and both are psychic Vampires in their way, the result is a powerful chemistry: Klaus Kinski, the unreconstructed Id, is confronted by the arch manipulator and obsessive, Werner Herzog, the Ego. Kinski's description of his director eerily recalls the reports of exhumations two hundred years earlier:

> ... even if he were unconscious he would keep talking. Even if his vocal cords were sliced through, he'd keep talking like a ventriloquist. Even if his throat were cut and his head were chopped off, speech balloons would still dangle from his mouth like gases emitted by internal decay ... he's high as a kite on himself for no visible reason, and he's enthralled by his own daring, he tolerantly closes his eyes to the spawn of his megalomania, which he mistakes for genius.

This phase in Kinski's frenetic, tortured existence coincides with his losing access to his young son. Distraught, he haunts the streets of Paris:

I usually walk everywhere – if possible, only at twilight or at night. I can't stand people gaping at me and discovering the lethal torment in my face, which kills and kills and kills and kills. I can't hide it from anyone. I can't stifle the shriek that rages in my face. Everything in me shrieks, shrieks, shrieks! ... I race along the quais. I keep turned away from the pedestrians and vehicles ... they stare at me. A monster. An Elephant Man. Too disfigured not to be discovered. It is *my shriek* that dashes through the streets, not belonging anywhere.[13]

Ѵ

As a young child Kinski had been scrabbling for food in the ruins of post-war Berlin not long after the boy Roman Polanski had fled the horrors of the Warsaw ghetto. In 1967 Polanski, another mesmeric figure with 'something of the night' about him, made one of the only effective spoofs of the Vampire movie genre, *Dance of the Vampires*, which starred the director as a clumsy *ingénu* and his wife, Sharon Tate, as a beautiful victim. In spite of its slapstick and teasing, the film has an underlying edginess that does not come only from the shadow of the Manson Family and the rumours of black magic that cling to it in retrospect. It may be Polanski's pervading certainty that we are ultimately doomed and innately either stupid or bad that stops the film from being funny or it may be the *Simplicissimus*-like Middle-European knockabout. It did, however, effectively subvert the over-familiar conventions and make it increasingly difficult for subsequent films to avoid an ironical or self-aware approach.

An impressive piece of kitsch was *Blood for Dracula*, released in 1974 as a product of the Andy Warhol stable, ostensibly directed by Paul Morrissey, but actually completed by the Italian Antonio Margheritti. It starred Udo Kier, physically a cross between Schreck and Lugosi, and was notable, like Ferrara's later *Addiction*, for its literal look at the reality of blood-drinking: at one moment Kier vomits uncontrollably on screen after mistakenly swallowing the blood of a non-virgin.

One film that has been hailed as a significant step in the serial reinvention of the fictional Vampire is John Badham's 1979 version of *Dracula*, which starred Sir Laurence Olivier, Kate Nelligan, the ubiquitous Donald Pleasence and a Broadway leading man, Frank Langella playing the main part as a sort of elderly John Travolta – the actor, incidentally, for whom *Interview with the Vampire* was originally optioned. Historians of film point out that the movie reasserts Dracula as a romantic figure, an attractive seducer and the representative of a dying past, fighting for its existence against modern materialism. Langella has been hailed by American critics *d'un certain age* as the sexiest and best of the screen Vampires, but from a jaded European perspective the bouffant hair, the white blouse slashed to the waist is redolent of a half-hearted and uncertain seventies camp.

†ぴ

Among the thousands of forgettable Dracula spin-offs filmed in English have been *Blackula*, *Deafula* (the dialogue is signed), *Spermula*, *Gayracula*, *Dragula* and *Rockula*, while beyond the ambit of Hollywood and the European art/erotic movie a B-and Z-film industry has flourished, dedicated to producing macabre and spectacular entertainment for domestic audiences in the so-called developing world. An enormous proportion of this vast horror, action and sexploitation output – more than fifty Vampire films were made over three decades in Mexico alone – makes use of the Vampire theme in one way or another. Sometimes the movies borrow the Euro-American Vampire, as in Japan, where the character has symbolized a colonization or infiltration by foreign evil, and very often they make use of one of the Vampire-like creatures from local folklore which seem to exist in almost every culture.

Some of the first films to be made in the Philippines were Vampire movies, drawing on the islands' versions of ancient pan-Pacific legends. Jose Nepomuceno made the silent *Ang Manananggal* in 1927, and the first talkie was *Ang Aswang*; the former featured bloodsucking sorceresses and the latter a night spirit who sucks blood through a long hollow proboscis. In Thailand, Indonesia and Malaysia the local version of this flying she-Vampire is the *penanggalan*, featured in many B-movies, such as the 1981 *Leak*, whose publicity poster summarizes its plot: 'The true story of an AUSTRALIA girl who learn the mystic of LEAK BALI (Bali). The tremendous mysticism of LEAK, Bali is always feared the people of Bali ever and ever.'[14]

The *penanggalan* is a distant echo of the European *lilith*, *lamia* or *strix*, a female night-predator inspired by scavenging birds, a witch who in her south-east Asian formulation can detach her head while sleeping and fly off with her innards trailing behind her to devour the flesh of corpses and suck the blood of the newborn. Other demons and wonders recovered by film-makers from local myth include the Brazilian *jaracaca* snake-vampire, the *vetala*, *pisacha*, *masan* and *rakshasa*, all blood-drinking entities from India, and for a Hong Kong series that combined Vampire attacks and martial arts, the revival of an old Chinese Taoist tradition of resurrected hopping corpses.

These films, to generalize about a vast variety, are not restricted by the norms of the 'Western' genres: they may combine hardcore sex and unthinkably explicit violence with accomplished visual atmospherics, laughably poor production values with startlingly expressionistic performances by actors. Novelties abound: in the first and once banned Argentinian Vampire movie, *Sangre de Vírgenes* ('The Blood of Virgins'), bats are replaced by seagulls dyed red, a rising mist for the Turkish version of *Dracula* was provided by the crew and extras furiously puffing cigarette smoke across the set. (Europeans also improvise: for Werner Herzog's remake of *Nosferatu* the director had eleven thousand laboratory rats painted grey.) In Japan, the Philippines and elsewhere, the movies have a symbiotic relationship with pulp comics from whom they borrow characters and storylines and to whom they donate the same.

☥

In film, the French took the post-war lead in matters of the *outré* and *recherché*, just as they had in the literature of the previous century, and as early as 1960 Roger Vadim, another potential psi-vamp, Svengali and *roué*, directed the first sexually explicit film version of *Carmilla*, entitled *Et Mourir de Plaisir* ('And To Die of Pleasure'), starring Annette Vadim and Elsa Martinelli. Nevertheless the modern Vampire, whether fictional or real, is essentially an American construct. Following on from Bela Lugosi's impersonation of Count Dracula for Hollywood in 1931, the Vampire icon was commodified and replicated throughout popular culture, becoming implanted in the common imagination just like Santa Claus or Mickey Mouse, but still retaining a more complex identity than those two unidimensional beings. As with Polidori and Stoker in the previous century, the most successful vehicles for the enduring myth were not the most original or the most profound, but those that matched the needs of the time. The milestones in the Americanization of the legend can be located in 1966, in 1976 and in 1987.

Nineteen sixty-six was the year in which the television series *Dark Shadows* was first broadcast. The show was revivified in 1967 when the central character of Barnabas Collins the Vampire became established, and it ran until 1971, with the programmes later being syndicated as reruns. The importance of this hugely popular series (fanzines and fan clubs were still thriving thirty years later) cannot be over-emphasized: it placed the vampire figure firmly in a recognizable American setting – the Maine town of Collinsport – hinted at the frustrations and longings of real Middle Americans and, more importantly, it introduced a sympathetic leading man with whom the baby-boomers and their children would identify for a generation afterwards. A sense of parody helped to distance the horror elements – the human characters in the show seemed blissfully unaware that their town was plagued by monsters and supernatural events, and the Vampire was played by the Canadian actor Jonathan Frid, under rather-too-heavy makeup, as a tragic, reluctant and courtly anti-hero.

By 1976 the figure of the Vampire was everywhere: in film, television, in advertising, even in children's books ('I know you'll think this is ridiculous, but I think all the teachers are turning into Vampires'[15]) and on greetings cards. It was only in book form that there was no mass-market vehicle catering for everyday tastes and sensibilities, for those in whom *Dark Shadows* had awakened a yearning for mystery, glamour and tragedy in an accessible package. Adult Vampire fiction had become mired in the tackiest pulp, ghettoized in the minority genres of comic-book horror, fantasy and sci-fi, or semi-pornography. And it was a sometime writer of pornography, Anne Rice, who filled the space in the readers' expectation with novels that celebrated very American notions of transgression and amorality but dressed these up with mock-European mystique. Rice's writing in *Interview with the Vampire*, the first of her Vampire chronicles is nothing like as bad as her detractors have made out; the book tapped a vein of yearning in a certain public – many of her most ardent fans had never read a full-length novel before – and it eventually became a worldwide bestseller.

Rice's books sanctify – and this is the appropriate word – weakness, sensuality, compulsive self-indulgence. They are not daring, or transforming, they merely offer an escape from the day-to-day to a world of clichéd glamour. The blood-drinking is not a metaphor for sex, it is an excuse for an unreal dream of passion without sex. More viscerally, they represent graphically the American obsession with *sucking*, the oral infantilism of the couch potato.

It was when she adapted her work for a filmed version directed by the Irishman, Neil Jordan, that the 'semi-florid, declamatory dialogue' and the callow nastiness of the theme of vampirized children (unsettling, too, from a mother who had lost her own young daughter to a wasting illness) were exposed under harsher lights. Exquisitely miscast, the two all-American stars of *Interview with the Vampire*, Tom Cruise and Brad Pitt, posed like hairdressers' models clumsily acting the fop; the more spirited if still quite un-sinister Antonio Banderas was relegated to a vaudeville turn. As one critic sneered, 'As both a book and a movie, *Interview with a Vampire* is laboriously pseudo-clever in a shallow, adolescent male[!] sort of way. It's like one of those graphic novel comic-books that give Superman or Batman "real" feelings.'[16]

Despite the carping of snobs, Anne Rice's productions have continued to sell in their millions, and she herself has become a celebrity, presiding over book signings attended by thousands and the annual 'Gathering of the Coven Ball', her own version of a Vampire *mardi gras* in her hometown of New Orleans. The merchandizing of her characters covers a line of perfumes, a wine and a restaurant inspired by the Vampire Lestat, and her tips on makeup and dress.

✝

A new generation of Vampire movies, all North American, have since the 1980s moved the Vampire firmly into the landscapes of Modern America, alongside the yuppie, the geek, the trailerpark and the shopping mall. Neil Jordan's *Interview with the Vampire* only partly does this: the interviewer is a figure from the recognizable present, but everything else is, just as in Polanski's *Dance of the Vampires*, Herzog's *Nosferatu* (both firmly part of a European tradition), redolent of the antique. It was probably George A. Romero's half forgotten *Martin*, made back in 1976, that pushed the Vampire past the stereotype of counts, playboys and adult decadence into urban America (Pittsburgh, in this case) and the domain of adolescents. The movie is nothing profound (Romero once said, 'Just because I'm showing somebody being disembowelled doesn't mean that I have to get heavy and put a message behind it') but raises some interesting contrasts between immigrants and 'natives', old-world values versus new, the generation gap. It never manages to make the crucial differences between the old legends and the new compulsions of the young cohere; a tension that was still vexing American Vampires more than twenty-five years later.

In 1987 two movies were released in the USA that are still referred to as seminal influences by fans and would-be Real Vampires alike; they were Joel Schumacher's *The Lost Boys* and Kathleen Bigelow's Vampire road-movie *Near Dark*. Schumacher's motives in updating the myth, and the seriousness with which he undertook it, were summed up in an interview in which he said, 'Vampires bring up a lot of stuff. In the Victorian period, when people lived such repressed lives, a lot of sexual fantasies were lived out through these stories. But I don't think our movie deals with any of those things at all. I think it just says: 'Hey! There are still Vampires, they just dress better!' The movie made the link once and for all between vampire clans and youth gang culture, dressing the adolescent Vampires in an all-purpose transgressor's uniform blended from hippie, punk, biker and heavy-metal influences. In the year following its release *The Lost Boys* was alleged to have influenced the suicide of one fourteen-year-old girl living in the southern Bible-belt who hoped to be quickly resurrected as a Vampire and lead her schoolfriends to a better life, and the murder in Sauk Rapids-St Cloud, Minnesota of a thirty-year-old homeless man by three youths who beat and stabbed their victim before licking his blood from their fingers.[17] The movie is still hailed by fans as an inspiration. As one incantation on the Internet put it in 1999, 'The Lost Boys sleep all day, party all night, never grow old, never die. It's fun to be a Vampire.'[18]

The Lost Boys was a major step in equating the Vampire clan with the adolescent gang and associating both with the haunted nights of provincial small towns. Two later contributions, Abel Ferrara's *The Addiction* and John Carpenter's *Vampires*, present vampirism as part of daylight and the everyday, the first in New York academia and street-life, the second in brightly lit open spaces and on the road.

Abel Ferrara, the lapsed Catholic bad-boy who began his career with *The Driller Killer*, which is still banned in the UK, touched casually, perhaps even accidentally, upon a key link in the long interlacing of Vampire references. The Vampire as metaphor transfers easily to the Junkie ('the Vampire is a kind of addict, hemmed in, needing to return to his home-earth in the coffin. He is touching and vulnerable,' says Christopher Frayling) but particularly to the urban heroin addicts of New York and Paris in the 1970s and 1980s, whose lifestyle had evolved into a self-dramatizing, black-clad subculture, feeding on and into music and fashion.

Committed heroin users (the special attributes of heroin itself, by far the most powerful of all opiates, set them apart from users of other narcotics) share a remarkable number of the defining features of the Vampire, from the superficial – pallor, hollow eyes with pinpoint pupils, a lack of interest in food and sex – to the essential: the Junkie is acutely fixated on the overriding compulsion to feed the habit and to do this he or she will turn predator, preying on the 'straight' world, which is seen as grey, lustreless and undifferentiated. The Junkie is a member of a classless, sexless, timeless élite, who has access to ecstasies undreamed-of by other mortals, but the ostracized outsider Junkie is victim as well as oppressor. He or she is a victor in the struggle for ultimate self-gratification, but a victim to helpless dependency and to exclusion. The Junkie is detached, inert, nocturnal, in daily contact with penetration and blood, intimate with coma and inevitably acquainted with death. The Junkie's body bears the familiar stigmata of red pinpricks on white skin. To the wondering unaddicted onlooker, the Junkie is one of the walking dead and a literal *nosferatu*, a carrier of contagion. When the ultimate contagion, Aids, is added to the matrix of blood/euphoria/death, the resemblance between the Junkie and the Vampire becomes uncanny.

Little had been made of these parallels until Abel Ferrara's 1995 movie, *The Addiction*, whose script contains a couple of lines that could be the literate Junkie's maxim: 'Dependency is a marvellous thing. It does more for the soul than any formulation of doctoral material.' At street level in New York City where the film is set, the Vampire subculture and the Junkie lifestyle may indeed overlap: many contemporary Vampires are recreational drug-users, some Vampires have been or become addicted to hard drugs, but drugs are not an integral part of Vampire paraphernalia and long-term users tend not to gravitate into the Vampire scene as, *in extremis* and *de profundis*, they have no need of its additional trappings.

Ferrara is no stranger to drug-culture, and travels within his native city and around the international circuit with an entourage nicknamed by the press 'The Walking Dead'. His movie is in grainy documentary black-and-white and its action moves between the sidewalks, the college seminars, the libraries, the hospitals of New York in a resolutely realist journey towards its climax a feeding-renzy by the coldly matter-of fact Vampires by whom the dowdy victim-heroine has been infected. The film's literal-mindedness its relentlessly black mockery of earnest students, night-school philosophy, its evocation of a noisy, crowded but empty city, set it apart from the usual genre-horror and from the grandiose disappointments of *auteurs* like Coppola. It is as peremptory and unresolved as Polidori's novella, but has the same timeliness and is oddly memorable for being, like very few other movies, horrible.

The Addiction was the best known of a set of three commercially unsuccessful, resolutely independent Vampire films made within a year of one another and each drawing on the livid lowlife backdrops of the run-down Victorian East Village (where Real Vampires gather still and where Susan Walsh was at that moment beginning her explorations). The other movies, like Ferrara's, made by native New Yorkers steeped in the City's sensibilities, were *Habit*, directed by and starring Larry Fessenden, and *Nadja*, directed by Michael Almereyda.

Fessenden's self financed minimum-budget venture, begun in film school, was originally to be called *The Addiction*, then *The Hunger*. Its cinematography benefits from the fact that the location crew could not afford lights and portrays, in grimy, muted shades, the gradual breakdown of an aimless drink-sodden writer, falling victim to a Vampire lover who may or may not be an alcoholic hallucination.

Nadja gave the same impression of being a Manhattan Vampire's home movie, but took the conceit to its extreme by intercutting clumsily filmed black and white footage (microphones are in shot, dialogue is archly minimalist) with Pixelvision sequences shot with a Fisher-Price toy camera.

All three films brought together the theme of vampirism and the spirit of the time, a culture of the disaffected young caricatured as 'Slackers' and 'Generation X' and an ambience labelled 'grunge', but their central concerns were different. *The Addiction*'s main character, the NYU philosophy student 'Kathleen Conklin', is a mouthpiece for the Catholic scriptwriter and lapsed-Catholic director's confused blend of nihilism and metaphysics: 'We are not evil because we do evil. We do evil because we are evil', 'Existence is the search for relief from our habit, and our habit is the only relief we can find', and, more bafflingly, 'Medicine is just an extended metaphor for omnipotence.'

Abel Ferrara holds his scriptwriter entirely responsible for the philosophizing; 'It's Nicky St John, he studied that stuff back when it wasn't the thing to be doing.' On reconsidering *The Addiction* five years later, he thought it stood up fairly well, 'There's some things in there I'd like to have back', but brusquely rejected any thought that he had the authentic Vampire underground in mind when he made it. 'I was coming from completely the other direction. I'm not much interested in anyone who actually says, "I'm a Vampire." '[19]

Fessenden's story, as the eventual title suggests, is also about dependencies, '. . . the things we go along with [that] end up being the instruments of our demise', and about degeneration, 'Whatever decline you want to talk about,' the director states, 'cultural or personal, comes about in little steps – little jabs . . . that all add up.'

In *Nadja* the tone is satirical: the plotless action takes place in singles bars, casual bisexuality, incest and dysfunctional families – the Draculas and the van Helsings. The film also plays with the idea of blood contagions and one of the spurious cures proposed for Aids at that time (an extract of shark embryo) features in the film as an antidote for the Vampire's bite.

At the end of the 1990s Stephen Norrington's *Blade* and John Carpenter's *Vampires* confirmed that the cinematic Vampire was going to ride out the millennium, although both movies were rightly criticized for bringing nothing fresh to the genre. Any influence that movies might have on real people's behaviour was under threat in any case from the effects of that new multi-media phenomenon already referred to: the computerized or live-action role-play game.

༦

Alongside the Vampire 'canon' – the body of Vampire-related novels, short stories, poems and plays, even movies now deemed worthy of serious study – has grown up a wealth of critical theorizing. The Vampire is, as one critic comments, 'one of those protean figures whose metaphorical charge is polysemic, and who, consequently, has attracted interpretation representing different critical perspectives'. This, while true, rather understates the case. The Vampire's susceptibility to analysis has attracted disciples of almost every conceivable abstraction and ideology: Jungians, ethnographers, anthropologists, folklorists, feminists, Marxists, post-colonialists, formalists, structuralists and post-structuralists, Lacanians, Foucauldians have all participated. From the early attempts to fit the bloodsucker into just one tradition, say Freudianism, things have progressed to the point where the post-modern critic has at her or his disposal a whole battery of perspectives from which to interpret the undead object of scrutiny or, to be more exact and to use a key item of critical terminology, its *representations*. Such interpretations can be tortuous. In one, chosen at random (it was sent to me by mistake), we read:

> ... in Dracula, we have vampires who are both succubus (Dracula's women, principally) and incubus (Dracula himself). So Harker, a male, and Lucy and Mina, females, have the wet dreams, while Dracula, who ostensibly practises the male role of penetration, receives the 'vital fluid', which is blood, but which also might be semen. When Mina drinks blood from Dracula's breast, Stoker compares the act to that of a kitten drinking milk. Consequently, blood now suggests lactation, reaffirming the bisexual nature of vampirism. While Dracula seems to prefer women, he attacks men as well...[20]

In its search for meaning, modern criticism retreats from ultimate resolution through an endless regression of alternative 'readings' – Derrida's famous *différance* or 'deferring'. Dracula is male, is female, is bisexual; blood is semen, is milk, is blood ... In the same essay comes the following:

> ... the young saviors are desperate to pull Lucy back from Dracula's influence by transfusing her. She exhausts four strong young men, which makes it obvious, in the blood/sperm equivalency, that they are terribly eager to inseminate her collectively, thereby affirming their endogamic control against the exogamic vampire. The image also suggests symbolic gang-rape. The pursuit of the vampire and the blood that the saviors eagerly volunteer to pump into Lucy Westenra go beyond male bonding,

suggesting a locker room homoeroticism that has caught the eye of various commentators.[21]

The rationalist riposte that Bram Stoker worked in ignorance of 'exogamy', 'endogamy' and of the verbal formulations, if not the realities of 'gang rape', 'male bonding' and 'locker-room homo-eroticism', can be brushed aside; the author was not conscious of what he was implying, the concepts are universals. But the use of the word 'obvious' is provocative, and the analyst is surely trying to have his cake and eat it, too. In trying to save Lucy's life by the only means open to them, the male heroes of the novel are symbolically raping her, cementing their collective manhood, indulging in a homoerotic thrill as well as reasserting sexual exclusivity within the tribe (endogamy) against the sexual threat from the outsider (Dracula, the exogamist) thereby moving towards an Oedipal killing of the bad father, all at once.

Without in any way denying that there are undertones of sexual uncertainty and emotional repression in Stoker's writing (perhaps reflections of imperial and social malaise, too – why not?), an alternative reading of this particular scene is that, as in many other passages, Stoker – the innocent, old-fashioned male – is actually celebrating the new technology of his day, here the exciting technique of blood transfusion, long since understood but only then beginning to be practised. Elsewhere in the text other innovations, the portable typewriter, the phonograph, the telegraph, the camera help the action along, as do those mainstays of industrial civilization, the railway and the repeating rifle; there may also be a nod to the recent revival of that ancient custom, cremation.

There is no doubt that Vampire fiction permitted strait-laced Victorians a lightly disguised depiction of sex – witness the violation scene that opens the proto-soap opera *Varney, the Vampyre*; only the site of penetration is displaced above the waist. And there are scenes in Dracula which, it is true, cry out for a knowingly modern reassessment. One favourite is Mina Harker's recollection of her encounter with the Count in her bedroom:

... he pulled open his shirt, and with his long sharp nails opened a vein in his breast. When the blood began to spurt out, he took my hands in one of his, holding them tight, and with the other seized my neck and pressed my mouth to the wound, so that either I must suffocate or swallow some of the – Oh, my God, my God! what have I done?

The tell-tale sequence of actions, plus Mina's inability to name the liquid that she was swallowing, is a glaringly obvious suggestion of forced fellatio ... or is it? Again, an 'innocent' surface reading might presume that a Victorian bourgeois like Stoker, unlike a libertine aristocrat or denizen of the streets, might possibly not be familiar with fellatio, enforced or otherwise. It might point out that Mina had named the liquid once as blood, but subsequently was struck dumb by the realization that she may have become contaminated and put her companions' lives at risk. A curious footnote is that this gory vignette not only mimics oral sex, but provides a textbook description of how blood is actually drunk by Real Vampires today: the breast and lower arms, not the neck, being the preferred sites for scratching and lapping.

⚡

In line with his fervid belief in man's essential 'blood being', a hectoring D. H. Lawrence seized upon the Vampire as metaphor: 'In spiritual love, the contact is purely nervous. The nerves in the lovers are set vibrating in unison like two instruments. The pitch can rise higher and higher. But carry this too far, and the nerves begin to break, to bleed, as it were, and a form of death sets in ... To *know* a living thing is to kill it ... For this reason, the desirous consciousness, the *spirit*, is a vampire.' For Lawrence, then, we are all potential Vampires; for the French author Michel Tournier, in a work of a dryer, more cerebral flavour, *Le Vol du Vampire*, the reader and the critic are seen as 'vampirizers' of the text.

A great many other writers have abstracted the Vampire, taking as their starting-points the notions of the Uncanny (Freud), the Sublime (Edmund Burke) or the Fantastic (Todorov). These attempt to ascribe the power of the Vampire in fiction to psychological absolutes, and the manipulation of universal human responses. The Vampire is seen, for instance, as an 'excess', a surplus to the orthodox psychosocial order and one that cannot be reconciled despite continuous attempts by fictional characters who bear witness to it, thus creating the primal anxiety that is the dynamic of the Gothic novel.[22]

Whether the unfamiliar, the terrible 'thing' is labelled as a manifestation of the sublime, the uncanny or the fantastic, one insight is significant above others, and it concerns the relationship of the Vampire with the dawning of 'modernity', as it occurred in the so-called Age of Enlightenment. Foucault and others asserted that the Enlightenment, in order to establish itself and render itself coherent as a new intellectual order, had to identify and stigmatize its opposite; in other words, Reason had to define Unreason to itself in order to banish it. The old superstitions had to be exposed, ridiculed and legislated away. In this new cultural climate, unfolding across Europe in the course of the eighteenth century, the Vampire plays two key roles, one political, one literary. While the documented cases of 'real' Vampire- stakings and -burnings perfectly illustrated the follies with which humanists and sceptics sought to do away, the primeval, irrational was fighting to re-enter the culture by way of modish fiction.

While it came to dominate the intellectual discourse of western Europe, the Enlightenment never overcame the tendency in the Catholic tradition, and to a lesser extent in the Eastern Orthodox, of *depicting* the forces of darkness and ungodliness in all their grotesque and fascinating spectacle to chastise, mock and disempower them. This contrasts with the Protestant – at least Anglican – determination to deny and banish images of superstition and evil, an eviction of the marvellous that created a dissatisfaction, then a new yearning for enchantment, ironically ensuring that the monsters survived.

⊻

One drawback to all the abstractions and theorizings, just as with attempts to explain the Vampire by scientific rationalism, is that the

'Vampire', which is taken as the object of scrutiny, is a sort of vaguely imagined stereotype. It generally does not conform in any meaningful way with actual representations or contextualized instances of the Vampire's presence. It occurs in the form not of a 'thing' but of a space, which can be filled by manifestations of the grotesque; lovingly foregrounding the monstrous and thus setting up a challenge to the rule of conventional morality, the fixity of authorized meanings.[23]

'In the unconscious mind blood is commonly an equivalent for semen,' wrote the Freudian Ernest Jones in *On the Nightmare* in 1931. But was it? Is it? It is only now, at the end of the twentieth century, that the reality of subcultures has brought the metaphors together, so that the slang code 'liquid protein' is used by male homosexuals for semen and by Real Vampires for the blood they drink. What is indisputable is the connection in the imagination between Vampires, blood and contagion. The type of contagion might vary according to the time: in the late nineteenth century syphilis, racial pollution, or degeneration under the influence of alcohol – with their frightening corollaries, the decline in the master-race's birth-rate and the collapse of established hierarchies; in the twentieth, Aids, drug addiction, hereditary and newly resistant diseases, still the menace to a healthy society from more primal, morally or physically deficient outsiders.

✝

It does not take a theorist to point up the links between vampirism and other manifestations of human desire:

> 'Bite me! Bite me!'
> I bit her. I sunk my lips into her so deep I could feel the blood spurt into my mouth.
> It was running down her neck when I carried her upstairs.

This was James M. Cain, the pulp thriller author, writing in 1934. Three decades on, Georges Bataille described a breach of etiquette;

> I pierced her thigh through her clothes with the point of a fork without a

moment's hesitation ... her naked thigh pleased me: one of the points of the fork, sharper than the other, had torn her skin and blood was seeping out but it was only a scratch of no importance. I threw myself at her and there was no time to prevent me from pressing my lips to her thigh in order to suck the tiny quantity of blood running from it...[24]

Just as the symbolism of blood lends force to the Vampire myth, so is the sexual component suggested by the sequence of insatiable desire, possession, penetration, consummation and lassitude. There is also the poignant, potentially sexual opposition of innocence and animal malignancy. In discussing the first stirrings of the Vampire craze in the seventeenth century, the historian Gábor Klaniczay has observed that,

Leaving aside more ancient examples [*lamiae*, *striges*, succubi, etc.], it is possible to detect the prehistory of the sexual Vampire in the erotic fantasies of the previous century. The symbolic, skeletal (but apparently male) figure of Death made his appearance as the Middle Ages waned: he was increasingly frequently contrasted with the most extreme expression of secular beauty, that of the young woman. By the beginning of the sixteenth century the confrontation implicit in this contrast had developed into a morbid sexual picture. In the paintings of Hans Baldung Grien, Death embraces and seduces attractive naked ladies; he bites their throats very much in the fashion of the later literary Vampires.[25]

In modern pulp romance the nineteenth-century cosmopolitan, the Vampire as glamorous and seductive *flâneur*, predominates. The Vampire is subversively the answer to a woman's real desires, masked by Victorian proprieties. He is superhuman and sub-human, but never restrained by the merely human conventions that govern the bourgeois male. 'He will sup, indulge in symbolic cunnilingus, where others will only dominate and impregnate. Feasting at the secret cicatrix ...'[26] Underground fiction, rock-music lyrics, Internet poems still delight in mixing the same metaphors: the wound or gash, the rose and the vulva.

The screen Countess Dracula, the Polish actress Ingrid Pitt, sums up the enduring sex appeal of the movie Vampire in more accessible language: 'He's outside, scratching at the window. When you are lying there, lonely, you think, Anybody, anybody, just come in and see me!' And defines a woman's preference: 'Not Murnau's filthy creature with his talons and his halitosis . . . but gorgeous Christopher Lee coming slowly towards you across the carpet, with this incredible voice saying, "I am here. You have called, my dear, and I am here." They just throw back the covers and seem to say, "Have me! Have me!" And he does.'[27]

We can evaluate the sexual identity of the Vampire from more than one perspective. A common-sense observation would be that the archetype of the Vampire established in the nineteenth century is usually represented as a tall, distinguished, saturnine, commanding older male. This being is invariably invested with an overwhelming and irresistible, yet forbidden power to seduce and to defile, and thereby to spread contagion. He is also an agent of betrayal: the kiss becomes the bite. Thus surely adds up to a female incest fantasy: the personification of the bad father, adored but corrupting. In a society where the broken home and the absent, if not abusive, father has become commonplace, this would be a most relevant imaginative construct.

One school of modern criticism, which to some might seem obscure or merely provocative but which brings some interesting insights to bear on Vampire fiction and Vampire sex, is the so-called 'queer criticism'. Not surprisingly, this approach focuses on the Vampire as transgressor, but is a little more subtle in seeing the being not simply as an outsider, the 'Other', symbolizing the irruption of the primal and the repressed into an ordered conventional existence, but as the catalyst that actually brings about a collapse of normal values and of our acceptance of them. In this reading the Vampire thoroughly subverts the order of existence itself, whereby 'alive' is good and 'dead' is bad. Even superficially it is possible to see clear relevance to the three (for us) most important manifestations of the Vampire. The Slavonic folk-Vampire substituted a dream world of the night in which the dead could punish the living but in which, equally, poor, barely literate countryfolk wielded powers unimagined by kings, roaming the world, battling the forces of evil and ensuring fertility and prosperity. In the case of the fictional nineteenth-century Vampire, the fatal seducer and all his pale, real-life imitation Lotharios, the 'blood-sucker' is the catalyst who releases perilous desires in women, and sometimes in men. Equally importantly, and deserving more emphasis than it has received, is the real point of the Vampire's sexuality: the sex of the victim and the mechanics of the sexual performance do not matter, only the Vampire's irresistibility and the act of consumption count.

Whether we follow the queer criticism into its furthest ramifications, there are several examples of nineteenth-century Vampire literature which, even at a shallow sub-surface level, reveal the presence of 'queerness', of sexual inversion. Of course lesbianism was known to exist, even if, as is often claimed, Queen Victoria's ignorance prevented it from being criminalized in Britain. The intensely paternalist societies of western Europe (it is often pointed out that Vampire stories of the period are over-stuffed with male authority figures struggling to reassert the *status quo*) meant that love between women was rarely articulated publicly, let alone by women themselves, and yet one of the justifiably most famous vampire tales is suffused with Sapphic eroticism – and it was written by a man. The author was Joseph Sheridan Le Fanu, whom we have met before, another outwardly respectable middle-aged Irishman. His novella *Carmilla* describes the relationship between a young and innocent noblewoman, Laura, and the mysterious Countess Carmilla Karnstein. A modern reader can only luxuriate in the delicious ambiguity of Laura's surrender to the older woman:

> I experienced a strange tumultuous excitement that was pleasurable, ever and anon, mingled with a vague sense of fear and disgust . . . I was conscious of a love growing into adoration, and also of abhorrence.

and wonder at the author's intentions and his Victorian readers' responses:

... my strange and beautiful companion would take my hand and hold it with a fond pressure, renewed again and again; blushing softly, gazing in my face with languid and burning eyes, and breathing so fast that her dress rose and fell with the tumultuous respiration. It was like the ardour of a lover; it embarrassed me; it was hateful and yet overpowering; and with gloating eyes she drew me to her, and her hot lips travelled along my cheek in kisses...

The story teasingly replays conventions common to both romance and pornography:

... was there here a disguise and a romance? I had read in old story books of such things. What if a boyish lover had found his way into the house, and sought to prosecute his suit in masquerade...?

These are the most effective sections of the narrative: the few action sequences, in which a Vampire is trapped and the inert Carmilla is staked and beheaded are, apart from the dramatic arrival of Carmilla's coach at Laura's *Schloss*, flat in comparison. In the conclusion to the novella Le Fanu, still speaking with Laura's voice, seeks to rationalize away the earlier excesses: 'The vampire is prone to be fascinated with an engrossing vehemence, resembling the passion of love, by particular persons.'

While for some readers aspects of male homosexuality are traceable in Polidori's novella and Stoker's novel, they are unmistakable, even flagrant, as presented in another, little-known Victorian curiosity. *A True Story of a Vampire*, by Count Stenbock, written in 1894, three years before *Dracula*, begins, 'Vampire stories are generally located in Styria: mine is also. Styria is by no means the romantic kind of place described by those who have certainly never been there. It is a flat, uninteresting country, only celebrated for its turkeys, its capons, and the stupidity of its inhabitants.' The short tale is a sort of facetious counterpoint to *Carmilla*, wherein Styria is described as rapturously beautiful; Stenbock's female narrator, Carmela (!), also lives in a castle with only a handful of domestics, including a Belgian governess. In

Carmilla, Laura's governess is Swiss. Again, the doctor is summoned from Graz. If the Styrian landscape is here uninspiring, the contours of Gabriel, Carmela's brother, are described in ecstatic terms: 'the grace of that lovely mouth, shaped verily *"en arc d'amour"* ... lips that seemed to exhale the very breath of life. Then that beautiful, lithe, living, elastic form!'

The mysterious visitor to the household, Count Vardalek, soon exercises a predatory and amatory hold over the young boy, an unnatural, if not pederastic bond that would be unmistakable even to an unsophisticated reader, but not, of course, to the narrator or her father:

> Vardalek always returned looking much older, wan and weary. Gabriel would rush to meet him, and kiss him on the mouth. Then he gave a slight shiver: and after a little while began to look quite young again.

Vardalek's behaviour towards the beautiful mesmerized faun, Gabriel, is that of a lover:

> 'My darling, I would fain spare thee; but thy life is my life, and I must live.'
> 'O Gabriel, my beloved! my life, yes, *life*...'
> Vardalek bent down and kissed him on the lips.

In a final, bathetic scene Carmela, now grown old, is living in expatriate gentility in Westbourne Park (an appropriate location for a queenly retirement), where she keeps an animal shelter in memory of her poor 'gazelle-like' brother's uncanny affinity with nature.

The eccentric Count Stenbock was another of the tragi-comic personalities associated with the history of Vampires. Eric Magnus Andreas Stanislaus von Stenbock, Comte de Borges, Baron of Tarpa (Estonia), was closely related to the Swedish Royal Family but preferred to be known to his circle in London as Harry Stenbock. As well as 'The True Story of a Vampire', included in a collection entitled *Studies of Death*, he also produced some rather self-conscious literary conceits: macabre and romantic poems and short stories including

The Other Side, Myrtle, Rue and Cypress and *Love, Sleep and Dreams*. Stenbock, who habitually attended social events with a live snake wound round his neck or a toad upon his shoulder was an exquisite, a decadent and a founding member of the Idiot's Club, an association to celebrate the persona of the Fool, formed by and for 'London's only true Bohemians'.[28]

The club was associated with the better-known Rhymer's Club, with whom it shared members such as Oscar Wilde, Robert Louis Stevenson, James McNeill Whistler, Arthur Symons, Ernest Dowson and W. B. Yeats, and also with the occult Hermetic Order of the Golden Dawn. All these groupings of dilettante decadents owed much to the more committed depravity that had been practised in Paris since the 1840s by the Symbolists and the Club des Haschischins.

Stenbock, like his fellow club members, was a seeker after altered states of consciousness by way of black coffee, wine, hashish and opium, and it was certainly under the influence of some of these that in 1895, in the company of some friends, he proposed a Toast to Death; as the glasses were raised he fell backwards into a fireplace and was consumed by flames at the age of thirty-five.

⚥

The Vampire has permeated American popular culture to such an extent that at the turn-of-millennium its repeated use as a social metaphor is taken for granted. Two prominent and not untypical examples are a publication by Daniel and Barbara Rhodes – a novelist of the occult and a psychiatric nurse – entitled *Vampires: A Guide to People Who Suck the Life Out of You*, and Barbara E. Hort's *Unholy Hungers*, subtitled *Encountering the Psychic Vampire in Ourselves and Others*. The Rhodeses' work describes three sub-types of emotional Vampire, 'their habitats, modus [*sic*] operandi, choicest victims, the signatures that inevitably give them away, the antidotes to the strike and the means of warding them off altogether'. Touted as an attack on the culture of victimhood, the book boldly places blame where it is due: 'on the suckers and drainers of that small font of emotional energy we carry into the world each day'.[29]

Unholy Hungers uses the Jungian notion of archetype and constructs models from literature and popular culture, interspersed with case studies, of categories of predator and victim. Such books closely resemble the spiritual self-help guides produced by Albert Osborne Eaves and Dion Fortune seventy years before, but are responding to a different environment. They try to find metaphors and meaning in the common cultural stock to make sense of a fragmented, unanchored reality which, in the US at least, with its still-strong traditions of fundamentalism and patriotism cannot be assimilated: 'Behaviors that qualify as hypocritical vampirism include doing favors for someone whom we have secretly wronged, donating resources to groups we otherwise disdain, patronizing subordinates whom we secretly exploit . . .'

☙

The old-hat, instantly recognizable theatrical Vampire has become so ubiquitous, appearing on, or as a free gift in breakfast cereals, chocolate bars, in educational TV programmes and children's language primers, that its meaning has been all but bled away. The commercial appropriation of the Vampire is keeping pace with the creature's mutations, though, as a TV and cinema commercial for Ray-Ban sunglasses from 1998 evidences.[30] The clip shows a group of hip, healthy, cheerful and fit black-clad twentysomethings sitting, simultaneously posing and relaxing, on a flight of steps under a subtropical sun. When a companion joins them, they notice nonchalantly that he is the only one not wearing his Ray-Bans: as he takes his place the sunlight blasts him to a cinder and a wisp of smoke. The grins on the faces of the others reveal neat, pearly-white fangs. Chic, certainly, but in spirit not so very far evolved from Herman Cohen's ludicrous Vampire bobby-soxer in the first on-screen collision of the youth/Vampire bandwagons, *Blood of Dracula*, made in 1956.

Conclusions

'You can't kill what's dead. Eternity's a long time. Get used to it.'

Abel Ferrara/Nicholas St John, *The Addiction*, 1995

The Devil, a Biography by Peter Stanton has as its – unintended – subtext the revelation that in the Judeo-Christian cultures we have never really been able to come to terms with the Evil One because we have not worked out how fully to imagine him. Whether as a trickster, as a grandiose villain or as an invisible force, he is always somewhere on the margins of realization, never completely focused. In some ways we have used the Vampire as a more accessible Satan, a universal bugbear, but one whom we can locate, play with, even impersonate, and crucially that we can, as a last resort, 'pin down' and thereby destroy.

Any cold-blooded analysis can reduce the marvellous quickly to banality or absurdity, but there is no denying the convulsive fervour of the act of vampirism if, for a moment, we imagine it as a literal truth – an attack in the night by a reanimated dead thing, powered by some vastly inhuman and unearthly impulse; the transfixing, the inexorable draining, the thought of irreversible contagion, of being *absorbed*...

Fighting back, staking the dead family member or neighbour, mimics the trapping and killing of the devil; it enacts the vengeance of the powerless who cannot ever hope to triumph in the world outside the cemetery. Posing as one of the undead at the end of the twentieth century is in some ways similar: those without power are symbolically defying their imagined enemies – fellow students, parents, officialdom, the military-industrial complex.

We have never managed to make the devil meaningful: it is the Vampire who has represented and represents for us what we fear and try to repress, the Vampire who is always scratching at our window. Historically, humanity has passed through four phases of anxiety, prompted in turn by natural forces and human frailty, by neighbours and death; by a desire to confront the macabre and the twin taboos of *eros* and *thanatos*, then, on the brink of the third millennium, by a fragmentation of social values and the dissolution of personal identity. Each of these anxieties has mobilized a different version of the Vampire as its embodiment and focus.

Since the Enlightenment chased away the sacred and the spiritual, the scratching at the window has become more and more insistent. By coincidence our need for new magic has peaked just at the time when technology can make shamans of us all. The Vampire has been locked in an eternal struggle to be admitted, to become alive again. Society's fear has been that if we admit the Other it will consume us. Sophisticated capitalism neutralizes the demon by annexing it, commercializing it, reduplicating it *ad absurdam*. But this only dilutes the Other temporarily, as Derrida remarked, it does not make it go away. A more modern response is to embrace the Vampire and appropriate it for ourselves, incorporate it, enjoy it.

The existence of hundreds if not thousands of blood-drinking Real Vampires, the appearance of movies – *The Lost Boys*, *The Addiction*, John Carpenter's *Vampires* – in which the demon is no longer an antique but completely integrated into everyday life, advertisements like the Ray-Ban commercial, shown worldwide, which takes the link between hip youth and vampirism for granted, all these are evidence of the beast's tenacity. The inescapable truth is that Vampires are emerging from fiction and folklore into everyday life. The thing that is emerging is still something profoundly ambivalent: as it always has been, the Vampire is both a sad pariah and the supreme parasitical predator.

The Vampire is not reducible to a single meaning, even if its most common representation – red eyes, chalky face, pointed smile – is one of the most immediately graspable images anywhere. There seems to be no limit at all to the forms it can adopt and the impulses it can incorporate at different times in different places: the ancient, the Slavonic, the literary and the modern Vampire each served a clear social or cultural purpose. At the millennium we can see it as a metaphor for the unfettered ego that is central to consumerism, or as a necessary response to what consumer specialists and futurologists call our 'yearning for re-enchantment', but in years to come its label may be stuck upon something with quite different and unimagined connotations.

⚥

When vampirism is just an adjunct to sex or partying it is of no particular significance outside itself. At first sight the same would apply to the elaborate role-playing indulged in by Vampire masqueraders, but this is a hint of something more, opening up the possibilities of a creative identity-shifting, the construction of multiple selves. Even if we sneer at the *Rocky Horror* tastelessness of most of this gaming, once participants go beyond ready-made stereotypes to develop original personas, they enter the wonderfully limitless domain of opportunity that virtuality and the Internet also offer. Perhaps it will become commonplace to re-create ourselves as mythical creatures, as elves, giants, satyrs, mermaids, and perhaps these new selves will start to function in the everyday. Where transgressors go, art and cosmetic surgery follow, and ideas fermenting inside youth sub-cultures – the unacknowledged social laboratories of the last fifty years – have a habit of appearing in the mainstream after a decent interval.

An interesting question for the guardians of orthodoxy is, how can we possibly oppose the Vampire without holy water and crucifix? More importantly, without faith? The question for the Vampires themselves, just as for anyone who takes 'transgression' as their *raison d'être* is one that millennial pop culture does not seem to ask itself.

What exactly are 'transgressors' subverting and what future is there for such a stance in a world in which the notion of the avant-garde has become meaningless – where all the boundaries can routinely be crossed without risking anything more than a momentary bleat of disapproval? In the entertainment industry the Vampire has become a sort of reflex action: it is dusted down and re-exhibited, but no one expects it to change – indeed, its familiarity is comforting – no one is frightened any more.

Despite the self-promoting fantasies of cult-busters and vampire-hunters, we need not be afraid of the Vampire. At least, outsiders have little to fear from the young sensitives and their sub-species, or from the fan-clubs and neo-Goths, or even from the consenting-adult sharers of blood and their private rituals. Psychotics and sociopaths can batten on to the Vampire subculture, just as with any other movement or cult, but their numbers are insignificant. Vampire clans may sometimes erupt into vandalism or even violence, but for the moment they pose far less of a threat to private safety and public order than street-gangs, survivalists, spouse-beaters, child-abusers . . .

The Vampire's opposite would seem to be the Angel: snowy white to its soot-black, equipped with creamy dove-wings rather than its rustling, creaking bat-membranes, sporting a halo instead of fangs. But the Angel is a one-dimensional, depthless being, an inane personification of a bland, indefinable goodness. If we are looking for a meaningful counterpart to the arch-predator, a better choice might be the Buddhist saint, the Bodhisattva. This being, like the Vampire, can be simultaneously both human and superhuman. Unlike the supremely selfish Vampire, whose aim is permanent gratification, its *raison d'être* is selflessness: even after managing to overcome the desire that is at the root of all human suffering, the Bodhisattva postpones its own entry into Nirvana to help the myriad creatures who are left behind, still enmeshed in the material struggle. We can choose which creature we wish to identify with; but if we look around us carefully, there are plenty of instances of vampirism to be seen. Few Angels and few Bodhisattvas.

In deciding where you stand, heed the words of the Temple of the Vampire:

> Mortal life is swift and short. You have this one chance to join us as a member of the Religion of the Rulers, a Vampire, an immortal master of the earth, or be lost to the winds of time.
>
> ... The choice is yours.

Acknowledgements

Thanks must go first of all to the many Real Vampires, anonymous or pseudonymous, who were willing to talk about themselves and their kind. With the exception of a couple of veiled threats and a few cryptic rebuffs, all their communications were friendly and courteous, even from those who found it painful or difficult to share their secrets. Especial gratitude is due to F. V., Ferris, Felicity, Cynarra, Sonya, Dana and Hunter, Maria, Robert, Raven, Flame, Morla, Omega, David S. and to Sanguinarius.

Sincere thanks to the Vampire experts, Katherine Ramsland, Father at Sabretooth, Grand Vzier, Emperor Norduk of the Temple Azagthoth, and for kind permission to quote the thoughts of Vincent Alexander Verthaine and Inanna Arthen, a.k.a. Vyrdolak. Attempts were made to contact Eve Kochel and Astirch Leasre to thank them, but without success.

For information on Lilith, I am particularly grateful to Alan Humm and his erudite website dedicated to that dark deity, and to Renee Rosen, the keeper of her shrine.

Among scholars who supplied invaluable insights and corrected false assumptions were Professor Christopher Frayling, the authority on the nineteenth-century literary Vampire, and the eminent philosophers and critics, Slavoj Žižek and Mladen Dolar. Those from King's College, London, who contributed important data included Dr Peter Emery and his colleagues in the Department of Nutrition. It was a privilege to draw on the expertise of Professor Jan L. Perkowski, the eminent Slavicist from the University of Virginia whose comments expanded upon his exhaustive and fascinating study, *The Darkling*, and Dr Bruce McClelland of the same institution who was willing to discuss his original and exciting theories of Vampire origins and the etymology of the word itself in advance of the publication of his thesis. A debt of gratitude is also due to the historians Professors Gábor Klaniczay and Gábor Várkonyi of Eötvös Lorand University, Budapest.

Very generous help from the broadcast and print media came from Paul Sieveking, editor of the *Fortean Times*, from Alex Finer and Alice Earle of John Brown Publishing, from journalist Tim Fennell, who kindly shared information collected by him in Australia, from Emma Pinder for Anglia Television who kindly gave permission to quote from their documentary *Kentucky Teenage Vampires* and from *Bizarre* and *HQ* magazines.

My thanks to Abel Ferrara for permission to quote from his movie *The Addiction*.

Thanks also to the Vampyre enthusiasts of the Whitby Dracula Society, especially Vanda, also to the London Vampire Group, and to Dark Delicacies store in Burbank, California.

To Goddess Rosemary go thanks, and to Katharine Gates of Heck Editions, Henry Boxer, Erzsébet Baerveldt; to Araceli Uriarte, Kat Smith, Jennifer Hor and Ingrid Pitt, Lyn Webster-Wilde, Cristina Nogueira, Mateja Gajgar and Roman Vučajnk.

Gratitude is due to the staff of the British Library, the library of King's College London, the Bodleian Library, Oxford, the National and University Library in Ljubljana, to Glyn Watson for the invaluable book-searches and to Nigel Gearing for helping in exploring the archives. Other institutions that provided unique access to historical materials were the Ethnographic Museum of Slovenia and the Archdiocesan Archives at Ljubljana where Sister Fani Žnidaršič provided generous guidance.

The project would not have been possible without the support of Julian Alexander, of Lucas Alexander Whitley, of Seán Magee at Gollancz, Humphrey Price and Hazel Orme.

For help with translations thanks go to M. M. as always, and to Pál Ritóok, L'uba Vávrová, Irmgard Wanner and Geraldine Horan. All translations are the author's responsibility and are by me unless otherwise indicated.

Lastly, I would like to offer appreciation to the shades of Montague Summers, John Polidori, Harry Stenbock – and to Susan Walsh, wherever she may be – in the hope that they would approve.

Note: The author and publishers have made every attempt to credit and acknowledge all sources of information and copyright-holders. The provenance of some material, particularly that included on more than one Internet website, or at defunct sites, can be difficult to establish with complete accuracy: if notified, any errors or omissions will be rectified in future editions.

Notes

Bibliographical details of the principal works mentioned in these Notes will be found in the Bibliography (pages 282–288).

Introduction

1 Bram Stoker, *Dracula*.
2 Jorge Luis Borges, *The Book of Imaginary Beings*.
3 Montague Summers, *The Vampire – His Kith and Kin*.
4 D. J. Enright (ed.), *The Oxford Book of the Supernatural*.
5 Kathy Brewis, 'Bloodsuckers', *Sunday Times* magazine, October 1998.

1: Children of the Night

1 Walter Map, *De Nugis Curialium* ('Courtiers' Trifles').
2 William of Newburgh, *Historia Anglicana 1196*.
3 H. R. Ellis-Davidson, *The Road to Hel*.
4 Mark S. Harris *et al*, 'The Walking Dead: Draugr and Aptrganger in Old Norse Literature' at Greg Lindahl's Internet homepage.
5 Frederick Klaeber (ed.), *Beowulf and the Fight at Finnsburg*.
6 C. J. Billson, *County Folklore: Leicestershire and Rutland*.
7 Ludwig Pauli, *Keltischer Volksglaube*, cited in Paul Barber, *Vampires, Burial and Death*.
8 K. M. Briggs, *The Anatomy of Puck*.
9 Antony D. Hippisley Coxe, *Haunted Britain*.
10 Ibid.
11 Stoker, *Dracula*.
12 Le Comte de Lautréamont [Isidore Ducasse], *Les Chants de Maldoror*.
13 Joris Karl [Charles Marie Georges] Huysmans, *Lá-Bas*.
14 *Bande-moi les yeux*
   j'aime la nuit
   mon coeur est noir

   Pousse-moi dans la nuit
   tout est noir
   je souffre

Le monde sent le mort
les oiseaux volent les yeux crevés
tu es sombre comme un ciel noir

Tu es belle comme la peur
tu es folle comme une morte

Georges Bataille, 'Archangélique', Paris, 1962.

15 *Von deinen schönen Wangen*
den frischen Purpur saugen
Alsdenn wirst du erschrecken
Wenn ich dich werde kussen
Und als ein Vampir kussen:
Wann du dann recht erzitterst
Und matt in meine Arme
Gleich eine Totden sinkest
Alsdenn will ich dich fragen
Sind meine Lehren besser
Als deine guten Mutter?

Heinrich August Ossenfelder, 'Der Vampir'.
16 Emily Laszowska de Gérard, 'Transylvanian Superstitions'.
17 The largest South American bat of all, with a possible one-metre wingspan, is a pseudo-vampire, *Vampyrum spectrum*, a carnivore that does not subsist on blood alone.
18 Oscar Wilde, *Requiescat*.
19 Dennis Wheatley, *The Devil and All his Works*.
20 A. Osborne Eaves, *Modern Vampirism: Its Dangers and How to Avoid Them*.
21 *Bizarre* magazine, May, 1997.
22 Tony Allen-Mills, 'Baring the Truth', *Sunday Times*, 11 August 1996.
23 Andy Beckett, 'Missing, Presumed Undead', *Independent on Sunday*, 1 September 1996.
24 Interviews with the author, January 1997.
25 Marc Savlov, review of Larry Fessenden's *Habit*, *Austin Chronicle*, 2 March 1998. (The movie was completed in 1996.)
26 *Weekly World News*, Lantana, Florida, 2 December 1980, quoted in Jan Perkowski, *The Darkling*.

2: Femmes Fatales

1 James Malcolm Rymer, *Varney, the Vampyre*.
2 Ancient Assyrian incantation against the Ekimmu, from R. Campbell Thompson, *Devils and Evil Spirits of Babylonia*, retranslated by the author.
3 Phoenician/Canaanite inscriptions on a protective plaque discovered in Hadattu, now Arslan Tash in Northern Syria, quoted at Alan Humm's website, 'Overview of Lilith', http://ccat.sas.upenn.edu/humm/Topics/Lilith
4 Samuel N. Kramer, 'Gilgamesh and the Huluppu Tree: A Reconstructed Sumerian Text'.

5 Isaiah 34: 14.
6 Steinschneider, *Alphabetum Siracidis*.
7 Robert Graves and Raphael Patai, *Hebrew Myths: The Book of Genesis*.
8 Alan Humm, *op. cit.*
9 The revivers of Lilith have also been influenced by the fact that Carl Gustav Jung chose her to symbolize one aspect of the *anima*, the 'dark feminine', in his system of archetypes.
10 Renee Rosen, 'The Goddess with No Tradition: My Theaology [*sic*] of Lilith'; the Lilith Shrine www, quoted by kind permission.
11 Joseph Max. 555 and Lilith Darkechilde. 777, Ritual Magick via e-mail: 'The Invocation of Lilith – A Rite of Dark Sexuality'.
12 If this sequence is indeed the work of the mountebank Kelley, it is further proof that the gift of rhetoric was bestowed even on the unworthy in the Elizabethan age.
13 Max and Darkechilde, *op. cit.*
14 Versions of the legend are mentioned in Horace, *Ars Poetica*, Apuleius, *Metamorphoses*, Aristophanes, *The Wasps*.
15 László Turóczi, *Ungaria Suis cum Regibus Compendio Data*.
16 Tony Thorne, *Countess Dracula*.
17 Johan Ludwig Tieck, (attributed) *Wake not the Dead*.
18 Robert Southey, *Thalaba the Destroyer*.
19 The reanimating lady is Clarimonde in *La Morte Amoureuse*.
20 The *gaida* reference comes from a remark by Dr Bruce McClelland.
21 Rudyard Kipling, *The Vampire*.
22 *Vampirella*, © Harris Publications Inc.
23 *The Chronicles: The official Fanzine for the London Vampyre Group*, issue 5, 1997.

3: Out of the East

1 Franc Miklošić, 'Upiri' in *Lexikon Palaeoslovanski*.
2 W. B. Yeats, 'Oil and Blood', 1929.
3 Professor Jan L. Perkowski in correspondence with the author, January 1999.
4 Marko Snoj, *Slovenski etimološki slovar*.
5 Dr Bruce McClelland in correspondence with the author, January 1999.
6 Gerard van Swieten, in a letter to Empress Maria Theresa, 1755.
7 Henry More, *An Antidote against Atheism*.
8 Maurus Jókai, 'Midst the Wild Carpathians.
9 De Lautréamont, *Maldoror*.
10 Jean-Jacques Rousseau, *Lettre à M. Christophe de Beaumont, Archevêque de Paris*.
11 Voltaire [François-Marie Arouet], *Dictionnaire Philosophique*.
12 Dom Augustin Calmet, *Traité sur les Apparitions des Anges, des Démons et des Esprits, et sur les Revenants et Vampires de Hongrie, de Bohème, de Moravie, et de Silésie*.
13 Joseph Pitton de Tournefort, *Relation d'un Voyage du Levant*.
14 Leo Allatius (Leone Allacci) *De Graecorum hodie quorundam opiniatibus*.

15 Paul Ricaut, *The Present State of the Greek and Armenian Churches, Anno Christi 1678.*

16 Evliya Celebi, *Seyahatname*, vol. 7, Devlet Matbasi, Istanbul, 1928; mentioned in Gabór Klaniczay, *The Uses of Supernatural Power.*

17 A. Fortis, *Travels into Dalmatia.*

18 F. Wiesthaler, 'Volkodlak in vampir'.

19 *Mamka moje, mamka, nevol'a je taká,*
   Chcelas mi dat' muža, dalas vlkodlaka,
   Celý deň nerobí, len dudle, haruší,
   Cez noc v krčme, žerie, ráno mňa tantuší.

   Janez Trdina, 'Ljubljanski Zvon II', Ljubljana, 1882.

20 Franc Miklošić, *Die Fremdtworter in den Slawischen Sprachen.*

21 *Kviti z cizich luhu*, vol. III, 1852; cited by Wiesthaler, *op. cit.*

22 Valvasor quotes Hajek, who had probably obtained the story from Neplach's *Latin Chronicle* for the years 1355–62.

23 Franc Miklošić, *op. cit.*, and Lili Potpara, in conversation with the author, March 1999.

24 Dr J. V. Grohmann, *Aberglauben und Gebräuche aus Böhmen und Mähren I.*

25 'Erinnerungen aus Slavonien', *Vaterländische Blätter*, Vienna, March 1816.

26 Vuk, entries for 'Jedogonja' and 'Vjestica', *Srbski Rječnik.*

27 O. F. Karl, *Gdanszky Pravlic.*

28 J. J. Hanuš, 'Die Vampyre' and W. Mannhardt, 'Ueber Vampyrismus' in *Wolfs Zeitschrift für Deutsche Mythologie und Sittenkunde IV.*

4: Istria, Carniola and Styria

1 Etnografški Muzej, Ljubljana.

2 Friedrich Nietzsche, *Human, All Too Human.*

3 Janez Vajkard Valvasor, *Die Ehre des Herzogthums Crain*, trans: Geraldine Horan and the author.

4 I. Milčetić, 'Vjera u osobita bića', *Sbornik za narodni život i običaje južnih slavena*, quoted in J. Perkowski, *The Darkling: A Treatise on Slavic Vampirism.*

5 Carlo Ginzburg, *I Benandanti. Stregoneria e culti agrari tra Cinquecento e Seicento*, and Gábor Klaniczay.

6 Jagić, *Archiv für Slawonische Philologie.*

7 Jakob Kelemina, *Bajke in Pripovedke Slovenskega Ljudstva.*

8 Wiesthaler, *op. cit.*

9 Kelemina, *op. cit.*

10 Valvasor, *op. cit.*

11 *Novica*, issue no. 5, Ljubljana, 1865.

12 S. Rutar, *Zgodovina Tolminskega.*

13 *Kres, II*, Maribor, 1877.

14 Lafcadio Hearn, *The Country of the Comers-back.*

5: American Myths and Monsters

1 Bob Tamarkin, *Rumour Has It*.
2 M. Summers, *The Vampire: His Kith and Kin*.
3 G. Stetson, 'The Animistic Vampire in New England', *American Anthropology IX*, 1898.
4 Paul S. Sledzik and Nicholas Bellantoni, 'Bioarcheological and Biocultural Evidence for the New England Vampire Folk Belief'.
5 Gyula Magyari-Kossa, *Magyar orvosi emlékek*, cited in Gabór Klaniczay.
6 Mary Durham, 'Of Magic, Witches and Vampires in the Balkans'.
7 Georg (György) Tállar, *Visum repertum anatomico-chirurgicum von den sogennanten Vampier, oder Moroi in der Wallachei, Siebenbürgen und Banat, welche eine eigens dahin abgeordnete Untersuchungskomission der löbl K.K.*, quoted in Gabór Klaniczay.
8 Andrew D. Gable, 'Two Possible Cryptids from Precolumbian Mesoamerica'.
9 *St Petersburg Times*, Florida, 1996.
10 Professor Richard Grinker, George Washington University, quoted in the *San Juan (Puerto Rico) Star*, 6 May 1996.
11 Quoted in Ian Blake, 'Slaughter by Starlight'.
12 *Fortean TV*, produced by John Godfrey for Rapido Television, broadcast on Channel 4, 1998.
13 Ferris, in e-mail correspondence with the author, April 1998.
14 Morla, in conversation with the author, June 1998.
15 Hugo G. Nutini and John M. Roberts, *Bloodsucking Witchcraft: an Epistemological Study of Anthropomorphic Supernaturalism in Rural Tlaxcala*.

6: Of Burial and Blood

1 Wiesthaler, *op. cit.*
2 M. le Marquis D'Argens, *Lettres Juives*, Paris, 1738.
3 The paper was presented at the Dracula centenary celebrations in Whitby, UK, in May 1997; its content will form part of a forthcoming publication by Dr Leatherdale.
4 *Bizarre* magazine, May 1997, reporting the theories of cemetery historian David Pescod-Taylor and forensic biologist Mark Benecke. See also Paul Barber, *Vampires, Burial, and Death*.
5 Clive Leatherdale, *Dracula: the Novel and the Legend*.
6 A detailed account of the scare is given in Norine Dresser, *American Vampires*.
7 Manuela Dunn-Mascetti, *Vampire*.
8 Johan Christof Harenberg, *Von Vampyren*.
9 Calmet, *op. cit.*
10 T. Sharper Knowlton, *The Origins of Popular Superstitions*, date 'around the turn of the century', quoted in Leonard R. N. Ashley, *The Complete Book of Vampires*.
11 Herbert Mayo, *On the Truths contained in Popular Superstitions*.
12 Kornmannus, *De Miraculis Mortuorum, Opus novum et admirandum in X partes distributum, in quo mirabilia Dei miracula et exempla mortuorum et U. et N. collecta habentur*.

13 Wiesthaler, *op. cit.*
14 Maksimilian Perty, *O mističnih přikaznih človeské naravé*, 2nd ed., Brno, 1872.
15 Leviticus 17: 10–14.
16 The superstition was reported by Pliny.
17 Sir James Fraser, *The Golden Bough*.
18 Quentin Cooper and Paul Sullivan, *Maypoles, Martyrs and Mayhem*.
19 Quoted in J. W. Thompson, *The Wars of Religion in France*.
20 Minucius Felix, quoted in Norman Cohn, *Europe's Inner Demons*.
21 These and other details were recorded in the BBC2 documentary *Mayan Blood Rituals*, broadcast in summer 1998.
22 Early Copan Acropolis Project, University of Pennsylvania Museum.
23 *The Greek Herbal of Dioscorides*.
24 Marsilio Ficino, *Della Religione Christiana Insieme con due libri medesimo del mantenere la sanita e prolungare la vita per le persone letterate*, quoted in Marina Warner, *No Go the Bogeyman*.
25 Marina Warner, *No Go the Bogeyman*.
26 Earle Hackett, *Blood the Paramount Humour*.
27 Some information supplied by the general practitioner Dr Thomas Hall and the nutritionist Dr Peter Emery of King's College, London, in conversation with the author, November 1998, and February 1999.
28 Extracts from the TV documentary, *Kentucky Teenage Vampires* courtesy Anglia Television Ltd.
29 http://www.xmission.com/ ~ gothics/subculture/blood-drink.html
30 'Sex in the USA part 1: Scar Lovers', *Spin* magazine, no date.
31 *Kentucky Teenage Vampires*, Anglia Television, *op. cit.*
32 Fiona Corealis, 'The Bleeding Ribbon Bloodplay Awareness Campaign, www.geocities.com/SoHo/Cafe/1260/blood.html

7: Killers and Haemogoblins

1 *News of the World*, November 1996.
2 'Vampire Sex Slaves in Virginia', in *Startling Detective* magazine, July 1997.
3 Derek Johnston, 'Dicing with Death', *Bloodstone*, September 1998.
4 'Vampire Rapist', *Daily Mail*, 9 February 1995.
5 Case-histories are adapted from reports in the *Fortean Times* by kind permission of the editor.
6 'Lesbian Vampire Killer', *True Police Cases* magazine, October 1996.
7 Margaret Wagner, *The Monster of Düsseldorf*; Dr Karl Berg, *Der Sadist*.
8 Reports from the *Daily Mirror*, *Evening Standard* and *Daily Express* for March and August 1949.
9 Steve Moore (ed.), *The Fortean Times Book of Strange Deaths*.
10 *Dallas Morning News*, 5 March 1998.
11 Compare the reports from eighteenth and nineteenth-century Bulgaria and elsewhere of 'Vampires' vandalizing buildings and desecrating churches.
12 Steven Barry, 'The Night Vampires and Satan invaded Smalltown USA', *Detective Files*, March 1996.

13 *Kentucky Teenage Vampires*, Anglia Television, *op. cit.*
14 Ibid.
15 The account of the Wendorf case is compiled from agency reports, including information from Fox News Network, Associated Press, and the *Washington Post*, the *Orlando Sentinel*, the *Lubbock Avalanche-Journal*.
16 Marc Savlov, interview with Katherine Ramsland, *Austin Chronicle*, 2 November 1998.

8: Subspecies

1 Eve Kochel, *The Net Vampyric: Essence of the Vampire*.
2 Inanna Arthen, 'Questions about Real Vampires', quoted by permission of the author.
3 The Temple of the Vampire Internet Homepage: mail address: PO Box 3582, Lacey, WA 98509, USA.
4 Emperor Norduk of the Temple of Azagthoth, in a communication to the author, May 1998.
5 Nicola Barker, 'Isolating Madison', *Independent on Sunday*, 12 July 1998.
6 Anonymous, *Stereotypes*,
   http://www.xmission.com/~gothics/subculture/archetype.html
7 Type O Negative, *Black no. 1 (Little Miss Scare-All)*.
8 Ted Polhemus, *Street Style*, London, 1993.
9 Alexander Verthaine, quoted by permission.
10 Ferris, *op. cit.*
11 Spectre, in conversation with the author, November 1998.
12 Dana, in e-mail correspondence with the author, July 1998.
13 Seth Dickson, 'Vampires Uncloaked', *Bizarre*, 1997.
14 Emperor Norduk, in e-mail correspondence with the author.
15 Frank Bruni, 'Count Dracula never Had His Own Cable TV', *New York Times*, 10 August 1996.
16 Article by Linda Yglesias, *Daily News*, 27 October 1998.
17 Marc Savlov, 'Theatre des Vampires', *Austin Chronicle*, 2 November 1998.
18 Flame, in an e-mail to the author, March 1998.
19 Lydia/Cynarra, in correspondence with the author, May 1998.
20 Maria, in a correspondence by e-mail with the author, during 1998.
21 TM, in e-mail correspondence with the author, May 1998.
22 Dana, *op. cit.*
23 Alexander Verthaine, *op. cit.*
24 Ferris, *op. cit.*
25 Robert, in e-mail correspondence with the author, August 1998.
26 Astirch Leasre, at her website.
27 Fog V, in e-mail correspondence with the author, May 1998.
28 TM, in e-mail correspondence with the author, April 1998.
29 Raven, in e-mail correspondence with the author, February 1998.
30 Grand Vzier, in e-mail correspondence with the author, during 1998.
31 Alexander Verthaine, at his website, quoted by permission.

32 Quoted in *Ex Cathedra 5*, November 1995.
33 APEC, www.fright.com/vmoon
34 Small-ad at Sanguinarius's Vampire web-page, January 1999.
35 Maria, in an e-mail of October 1998.
36 Fog V, *op. cit.*
37 Article by Elaine Showalter in the *Observer Review*, 14 June 1998.

9: Generation Dead

1 Goddess Rosemary, in conversation with the author, May 1998.
2 In conversation with the author, June 1998.
3 Marchioness Rachel interviewed for *Fortean TV*, produced by John Godfrey for Rapido Television, broadcast on Channel 4, 1998.
4 Ferris, *op. cit.*
5 This, and the preceding comments, occurred in conversations with the author in February 1998.
6 In conversation with the author, September 1998.
7 Inanna Arthen, *Questions about Real Vampires* http://www.netlplus.com/users/vyrdolak/question.htm, quoted by kind permission of the author.
8 Emperor Norduk, *op. cit.*
9 'Jaden', quoted in *Kentucky Teenage Vampires*, courtesy Anglia Television Ltd.
10 Recorded by Tim Fennell in Australia in 1995 for *HQ* magazine, reproduced here by kind permission of the author.
11 Tim Fennell, *op. cit.*
12 In conversation with the author, March 1998.
13 David S. in e-mail correspondence with the author, August 1998.
14 Astirch Leasre, *op. cit.*
15 Dion Fortune, *Psychic Self Defence*, London, 1930.
16 Sonja in e-mail correspondence with the author, April 1998.
17 Grand Vzier, *op. cit.*
18 Astirch Leasre, *op. cit.*
19 Alice and Claude Askew, *Aylmer Vance and the Vampire*, quoted in D. J. Enright (ed.), *The Oxford Book of the Supernatural*.
20 Grand Vzier, *op. cit.*
21 http://www.netlplus.com/users/vyrdolak/question.htm#what
22 Fog V, *op. cit.*
23 Ferris, *op. cit.*
24 Caldoria in e-mail correspondence with the author, September 1998.
25 Astirch Leasre, *op. cit.*
26 Matilte, in e-mail correspondence with the author, March 1998.

10: Contagious Ideas

1 Anonymous (probably James Malcolm Rymer), *Varney, The Vampyre; or, The Feast*

of Blood, 1874; the entire text can be found on the Internet at http://www.comclin.net/humphrey/varney/text/varny001.txt

2 Phyllis Grosskurth, *Byron, the Flawed Angel*.

3 Byron's letter to the editor of *Galignani's Messenger*, 27 April 1819.

4 Lord Byron, *The Giaour*, 1813.

5 In England, too, there was a spate of derivative stage melodramas including William Thomas Moncrieff's *The Vampire*, 1829; James Robinson Planche's *The Vampire, or the Bride of the Isles*, 1830, and George Blink's *The Vampire Bride, or The Tenant of the Tomb*, 1840.

6 The idea has been mooted by the British vampire author Tom Holland.

7 Professor Frayling's comments are taken from conversations with the author and from the BBC Radio Scotland feature *The Usual Suspects*, broadcast on 23 December 1997.

8 Bram Stoker, *The Primrose Path*.

9 Mario Praz, *Romantic Agony*.

10 Roberto Cueto and Carlos Diaz, *Dracula, de Transilvania a Hollywood*.

11 One among several is Carlos Losilla, 'Nosferatu, el Vampiro, de F. W. Murnau', *Dirigido* 256, Barcelona, April 1997.

12 Cueto and Diaz, *op. cit.*

13 Klaus Kinski, *Kinski Uncut*, trans: Joachim Neugröschel

14 Pete Tombs, *Mondo Macabro*.

15 Virginia Ironside, *Vampire Master of Burlap Hall*.

16 Steve Warrick, 'Vein Man', *Modern Review*, December–January 1994–5.

17 Norine Dresser, *American Vampires*.

18 pendragon.ml.org/vampire/vampfilm.htm

19 Abel Ferrara, in conversation with the author, 31 March 1999.

20 Michael Kline, 'The Vampire as Pathogen: Bram Stoker's *Dracula* and Francis Ford Coppola's *Bram Stoker's Dracula*.

21 Ibid.

22 The Slovene Lacanian philosophers Mladen Dolar and Slavoj Žižek have both written on the Vampire, Žižek claiming that in its primal status outside the constraining human sphere it is more alive than we are.

23 For a comprehensive review of theories of the Vampire, see Ken Gelder, *Reading the Vampire*.

24 Georges Bataille, *Le Bleu du Ciel*, quoted in Ornella Volta and Valeria Riva, *The Vampire, an Anthology*.

25 Gabór Klaniczay, *op. cit.*

26 Adele Olivia Gladwell, 'The Erogenous Disease' in *Blood and Roses*.

27 BBC Radio Scotland, *The Usual Suspects*, *op. cit.*

28 The Idiot's Club, or a version of it, is periodically revived. In 1998 it had its own Internet site.

29 Barbara E. Hort, *Unholy Hungers, Encountering the Psychic Vampire in Ourselves and Others*.

30 The ad was made by the New York branch of the Delaney Fletcher agency.

Bibliography

Allatius, Leo (Leone Allacci), *De Graecorum hodie quorundam opiniatibus*, Cologne, 1645

Ashley, Leonard R. N., *The Complete Book of Vampires*, New York, 1998

Askew, Alice and Claude, *Aylmer Vance and the Vampire*, 1914

Barber, Paul, *Vampires, Burial and Death, Folklore and Reality*, New Haven and London, 1988

Bataille, Georges, *Les Larmes d'Éros*, Paris, 1961

Berg, Dr Karl, *Der Sadist*, Acorn Books, 1938

Billson, C. J., *County Folklore: Leicestershire and Rutland*, London, 1895

Blake, Ian, 'Slaughter by Starlight', in *Rapid Eye*, vol. 2, London, 1975

Borges, Jorge Luis, *The Book of Imaginary Beings*, London, 1970

Briggs, K. M., *The Anatomy of Puck*, London, 1959

Byron, George Gordon, Lord, *The Giaour*, London, 1813

Calmet, Dom Augustin, *Traité sur les Apparitions des Anges, des Démons et des Esprits, et sur les Revenants et Vampires de Hongrie, de Bohème, de Moravie, et de Silésie*, Paris, 1746

Chapman, Paul M., *Birth of a Legend: Count Dracula, Bram Stoker and Whitby*, Huddersfield, 1997

Cohn, Norman, *Europe's Inner Demons*, London, 1975

Cooper, Quentin and Paul Sullivan, *Maypoles, Martyrs and Mayhem*, London, 1994

Cueto, Roberto and Carlos Diaz, *Dracula, de Transilvania a Hollywood*, Madrid, 1997

D'Argens, M. le Marquis, *Lettres Juives*, Paris, 1738

Davanzati, Gioseppe, *Dissertazione sopra i Vampiri*, Naples, 1789

Derrida, Jacques, *The Gift of Death*, 1996

Dioscorides, *The Greek Herbal of Dioscorides*, trans. John Goodyer, London, 1655

Dresser, Norine, *American Vampires*, New York, 1989

Dunn-Mascetti, Manuela, *Vampire*, London, 1994

Durham, Mary, 'Of Magic, Witches and Vampires in the Balkans', in *Man*, XXIII, 1923

Ellis-Davidson, H. R., *The Road to Hel*, Cambridge, 1943

Enright, D. J. (ed.), *The Oxford Book of the Supernatural*, Oxford, 1994

Ficino, Marsilio, *Della Religione Christiana Insieme con due libri medesimo del mantenere la sanita e prolungare la vita per le persone letterate*, Florence, 1568

Fortis, Alberto, *Travels into Dalmatia*, London, 1778

Fortune, Dion, *Psychic Self Defence*, London, 1930

Frayling, Christopher, *Vampyres – Lord Byron to Count Dracula*, London, 1991

Frazer, Sir James, *The Golden Bough*, London, 1925

Gable, Andrew D., 'Two Possible Cryptids from Precolumbian Mesoamerica' [n.d.]

Gautier, Théophile, *La Morte Amoureuse*, Paris, 1836

Gelder, Ken, *Reading the Vampire*, London, 1994

Ginzburg, Carlo, *I Benandanti Stregoneria e culti agrari tra Cinquecento e Seicento*, Turin, 1966

Gladwell, Adele Olivia, 'The Erogenous Disease' in *Blood and Roses*, London, 1992

Graves, Robert and Raphael Patai, *Hebrew Myths: The Book of Genesis*, Garden City, 1964

Grohmann, Dr J. V., *Aberglauben und Gebräuche aus Böhmen und Mähren* I, 18–

Grosskurth, Phyllis, *Byron, the Flawed Angel*, London, 1997

Guiley, Rosemary Ellen, *Vampires Among Us*, New York, 1991

Hackett, Earle, *Blood, the Paramount Humour*, Adelaide, 1973

Hanuš, J. J., 'Die Vampyre' in *Wolf Zeitschrift fur Deutsche Mythologie und Sittenkunde IV*, Göttingen, 1859

Hardy, Phil (ed.), *Horror, The Aurum Film Encyclopaedia 3*, London, 1985

Harenberg, Johan Christof, *Von Vampyren*, Leipzig, 1739

Hearn, Lafcadio, *The Country of the Comers-back*, 1889

Hippisley Coxe, Antony D., *Haunted Britain*, London, 1975

Hort, Barbara E., *Unholy Hungers, Encountering the Psychic Vampire in Ourselves and Others*, New York, 1997

Hoyt, Olga, *Lust for Blood*, New York, 1984

Huysmans, Joris Karl [Charles Marie Georges], *Là-Bas*, Paris, 1891

Ironside, Virginia, *Vampire Master of Burlap Hall*, London, 1987

Jagić, *Archiv fur Slawonische Philologie*, Zagreb, 1882–3

Jókai, Maurus, *Midst the Wild Carpathians*, trans. R. N. Bain, London, 1894

Karl, O. F., *Gdanszky Pravlic*, Danzig, 1844

Kelemina, Jakob, *Bajke in Pripovedke Slovenskega Ljudstva*, Celje, 1930

Kinski, Klaus, *Kinski Uncut*, trans. Joachim Neugröschel, Bloomsbury, London, 1997

Kipling, Rudyard, *The Vampire*, 1897

Klaeber, Frederick (ed.), *Beowulf and the Fight at Finnsburg*, 3rd edn., Lexington, 1950

Klaniczay, Gábor, *The Uses of Supernatural Power*, Princeton, 1990

Kline, Michael, 'The Vampire as Pathogen: Bram Stoker's *Dracula* and Francis Ford Coppola's *Bram Stoker's Dracula*' in *Philological Papers*, vols 42–3, West Virginia University, 1997

Kornmannus, *De Miraculis Mortuorum, Opus novum et admirandum in X partes distributum, in quo mirabilia Dei miracula et exempla mortuorum et U. et N. collecta habentur*, Frankfurt, 1610

Kramer, Samuel N., 'Gilgamesh and the Huluppu Tree: A Reconstructed Sumerian Text' in *Assyriological Studies of the Oriental Institute of the University of Chicago*, Chicago, 1938

Laszowska de Gérard, Emily, 'Transylvanian Superstitions', in *XIX Century*, London, 1885

de Lautréamont, Le Comte [Isidore Ducasse], *Les Chants de Maldoror*, Paris, 1868

Leatherdale, Clive, *Dracula: the Novel and the Legend*, Wellingborough, 1985

Le Fanu, Joseph Sheridan, 'Carmilla' in *Dark Blue* magazine, London, 1872

Losilla, Carlos 'Nosferatu, el Vampiro, de F. W. Murnau', in *Dirigido 256*, Barcelona, April 1997

Magyari-Kossa, Gyula, *Magyar orvosi emlékek*, Vol. IV, Budapest, 1930

Mannhardt, W., 'Ueber Vampyrismus' in *Wolf Zeitschrift für Deutsche Mythologie und Sittenkunde IV*, Göttingen, 1859

Map, Walter, *De Nugis Curialium* (Courtiers' Trifles), trans. Frederick Tupper and Marbury Bladen Ogle, London, 1924

Marigny, Jean, *Vampires: The World of the Undead*, London, 1995

Mayo, Herbert, *On the Truths contained in Popular Superstitions*, London, 1851

Milčetić, I., 'Vjera u osobita bića', in *Sbornik za narodni život i običaje južnih slavena*, Zagreb, 1896

Miklošić, Franc, *Die Fremdtworter in den slawischen Sprachen*, Vienna, 1879

Lexikon Palaeoslovanski, Vienna, 1888

Moore, Steve (ed.), *The Fortean Times Book of Strange Deaths*, London, 1994

More, Henry, *An Antidote against Atheism: or, An Appeal to the Natural Faculties of the Mind of Man, whether there be a God*, Cambridge, 1653

Nietzsche, Friedrich, *Human, All-Too-Human*, 1878

Nutini, Hugo G. and John M. Roberts, *Bloodsucking Witchcraft: an Epistemological Study of Anthropomorphic Supernaturalism in Rural Tlaxcala*, 1993

Osborne Eaves, A., *Modern Vampirism: Its Dangers and How to Avoid Them*, Harrogate, 1904

Ossenfelder, Heinrich August, *Der Vampir*, Leipzig, 1748

Page, Carol, *Bloodlust*, New York, 1991

Pauli, Ludwig, *Keltischer Volksglaube*, Munich, 1975

Perkowski, J., *The Darkling: A Treatise on Slavic Vampirism*, Columbus, Ohio, 1989

Perty, Maksimilian, *O mističnih přikaznih človeské naravě*, 2nd edn., Brno, 1872

Pitton de Tournefort, Joseph, *Relation d'un Voyage du Levant*, Paris, 1717

Polhemus, Ted, *Street Style*, London, 1993

Praz, Mario, *Romantic Agony*, Oxford, 1970

Ranft, Michael, *De Masticatione Mortuorum in Tumulis Liber*, Leipzig, 1728

Ricaut, Paul, *The Present State of the Greek and Armenian Churches, Anno Christi 1678*, London, 1679

Rice, Anne, *Interview with the Vampire*, New York, 1976

Rousseau, Jean-Jacques, *Lettre à M. Christophe de Beaumont, Archévèque de Paris*, Paris, 1763

Rutar, S., *Zgodovina Tolminskega*, Tolmin, 1869

Rymer, James Malcolm, *Varney, the Vampyre; or, The Feast of Blood*, London, 1874

Sharper Knowlton, T., *The Origins of Popular Superstitions*, New York (n.d.)

Sledzik, Paul S. and Nicholas Bellantoni, 'Bioarcheological and Bio-cultural Evidence for the New England Vampire Folk Belief', in *American Journal of Physical Anthropology*, no. 94, New York, 1994

Snoj, Marko, *Slovenski etimološki slovar*, Ljubljana, 1997

Southey, Robert, *Thalaba the Destroyer*, London, 1801

Stanford, Peter, *The Devil: A Biography*, London, 1996

Steinschneider (ed.), *Alphabetum Siracidis*, Berlin, 1858

Stetson, G., 'The Animistic Vampire in New England', in *American Anthropology IX*, 1898

Stoker, Bram, *Dracula*, London, 1897

The Primrose Path, Desert Island Books, London, 1999

Summers, Montague, *The Vampire – His Kith and Kin*, London, 1928
   The Vampire in Europe, London, 1929

Tállar, Georg (György), *Visum repertum anatomico-chirurgicum von den sogennanten Vampier, oder Moroi in der Wallachei, Siebenbürgen und Banat, welche eine eigens dahin abgeordnete Untersuchungskomission der löbl K.K. Administration in Jahre 1756*, Vienna and Leipzig, 1784
Tamarkin, Bob, *Rumour Has It*, New York, 1993
Thompson, J. W., *The Wars of Religion in France*, London, 1957
Thompson, R. Campbell, *Devils and Evil Spirits of Babylonia*, London, 1903
Thorne, Tony, *Countess Dracula: The Life and Times of the Blood Countess Elisabeth Báthory*, London, 1997
Tieck, Johan Ludwig (attrib.) *Wake not the Dead*, *c.* 1800
Tombs, Pete, *Mondo Macabro*, London, 1997
Turóczi, László, *Ungaria Suis cum Regibus Compendio Data*, Tyrnava, 1744

Valvasor, Johann Weichardt (Janez Vajkard), *Die Ehre des Herzogthums Crain*, Laibach, 1689
Volta, Ornella and Valeria Riva, *The Vampire, an Anthology*, London, 1963
Voltaire [Francois-Marie Arouet], *Dictionnaire Philosophique*, Paris, 1764
Vuk, *Srbski Rječnik*, Belgrade, 1880

Wagner, Margaret, *The Monster of Düsseldorf*, 1932
Warner, Marina, *No Go the Bogeyman*, London, 1998
Wheatley, Dennis, *The Devil and All His Works*, London, 1971
Wiesthaler, F., 'Volkodlak in vampir', in *Lubljanski Zvon*, Laibach, 1883
William of Newburgh, *Historia Anglicana* (1196), ed. H. C. Hamilton, London, 1896

Zoftius, Johann Heinrich, *Dissertatio de Uampiris Seruiensibus*, Halle, 1733

Index